THE TROUBADOUR

HISTORICAL NOVEL

by

STAMATIS M. KAMBANIS

ISBN: 978-1-7751022-0-5

This is a work of fiction; characters, names, locales and events in this book are shaped by the writer's imagination.

Published by Michael Moon Publishing 2018
Cover by Michael Moon

Contents

ACKNOWLEDGEMENTS

I am very grateful to my son Michael for encouraging me to write this novel and his extensive editing of the text and the rewriting of all the book's songs. I am also grateful for his work with the book's layout, the cover design, pictures and publishing.

I thank my son Nicholas for the initial typing of the text.

Thank you to Ann-Marie Boudreaux, Marilyn Gang and Richard Geer for their grammatical expertise and corrections.

DEDICATED

TO MY TROUBADOUR SONS

MICHAEL AND NICHOLAS

The Kambanis family crest.

Introduction

Though this story is ultimately the work of my father's imagination it is firmly rooted in historical facts. All the events and characters in this book are historical. The general moods and styles of the times are also historical. What Stamatis has done is research history to the point where he began to see connections and personalities come through the mists of time and speak to him. These personalities and relationships are not entirely made up but were suggested to his imagination by little facts and stories of history until they came alive in his mind as characters. They lived and died in times that were extreme and therefore almost unbelievable, which makes for a great story, true to life and filled with suffering. Though these were fairy tale times there could be no fairy tale happy endings. For this was how history played out.

Stamatis has always been fascinated by history and has learned as much as he could about every era his attention was drawn to. As a child his uncle was a well-respected historian who hoped Stamatis would follow in his footsteps and so he mentored him. Though Stamatis ultimately took a different path, history always fascinated him and he continued learning all he could. Throughout my life I have been blessed with my father's vast knowledge of history and incredible memory of its details. I've often said to my friends proudly, "Ask him about any time and place in history and he'll tell you all about it." It's not just the details he shares but also an underlying understanding of how everything is connected and how it all comes together to help form the present.

This story takes place in the land of Occitania, which was also known as Languedoc and incorporated the regions of Toulouse and Provance as well as some areas of northern Italy and Spain. The area was defined by its own culture and language, which lasted from approximately 900 to 1300. This area, now known as Southern France, by the 12th Century had become a very creative, tolerant, free and colourful culture from which the troubadours were born.

This time had always fascinated my Father but it really began to come alive after he began tracing the origins of a crest found on our family's old tower house on the island of Andros in Greece. The crest was unmistakably heraldic in nature but found on a Greek island. This mystery intrigued him and through learning the details of the area's history and tracing the family name down through time by gathering information from rare books, such as the accounts of a Jesuit monk named P. Sauger, the details slowly came together and led him to find our distant ancestor Peire Cardinal de Campagnac. In the process of uncovering how and why a family from Southern France ended up on a Greek Island this amazing story was revealed.

I remember the day I first heard this story. I was helping my father put together some furniture and being a monotonous task I asked him to tell me a story from history, as I often have in the past. This time, though, he told me a story that was so personal it shook me to the core. What shook me was that a year before I had a dreamlike experience where I saw myself in this same time and place experiencing a lot of the same details he was sharing. At the time of the dream I had felt such deep emotion about it in a way I had never felt before. This experience had felt so real that I literally cried on and off for days. I had never heard about my father's story or even knew about our ancestry so when I did hear him share the story I was in shock. It was exactly like the dream that left me feeling so much. Life is truly mysterious with history echoing and repeating in patterns that go beyond the facts. Though this book's framework is based on solid historical fact it is not pure history but an intuitive, empathic and imaginative walk through history based also in this primal ancestral connection that we trust will give the reader an intimate feel for this unique time and place.

The songs of this book, like the rest of the story, began as historical fragments. Many were developed from remaining songs written by the Troubadours whose characters appear in the book. With history preserving very little of these songs on top of the translations from Occitanian to French to English plus all of my father's additions filling in the missing gaps, they became quite unruly and no longer felt like songs. I found while editing the book that, as a musician, I could not feel or sing them. The lines all had different meters and no rhyme. When I researched the music of the period I found that the Troubadour's music was filled with a wonderful rhythm and rhyme that was very innovative and far ahead of its time. So I reworked these songs keeping the meaning and words yet moulding them back into something poetic and musical that I hope captures the spirit of the original songs for modern times.

Not everything in this book can be considered history but we feel it gives a good feeling using as much solid details of the time as possible. All the dates, major events and main characters are in fact historical. Every character was built and elaborated upon what we know of them from historical accounts and helps weave a feeling for this time and place. As you read there is no need to memorize or keep track of all these characters though, as the story makes there roles clear in each place they appear. The major events and dates of the story are also all historical and again their backdrop helps paint as true a picture of these colourful times as possible. The story is a birds eye view of about 80 years of history taking in many momentous events through the eyes of these people and how we feel they may have thought and felt from the little we know about them. The fictional details are used to weave the story but not elaborated on too much in order to leave as much as possible to the imagination of the reader.

The pictures in the book have been collected from around the Internet. Many are miniatures and decorations from manuscripts of the time. Some are paintings from a few centuries later. We have tried to give as much credit as we could find. If any was left out in error please forgive us and feel free to let us know and we will add any due credits.

Michael Moon May 27 2018

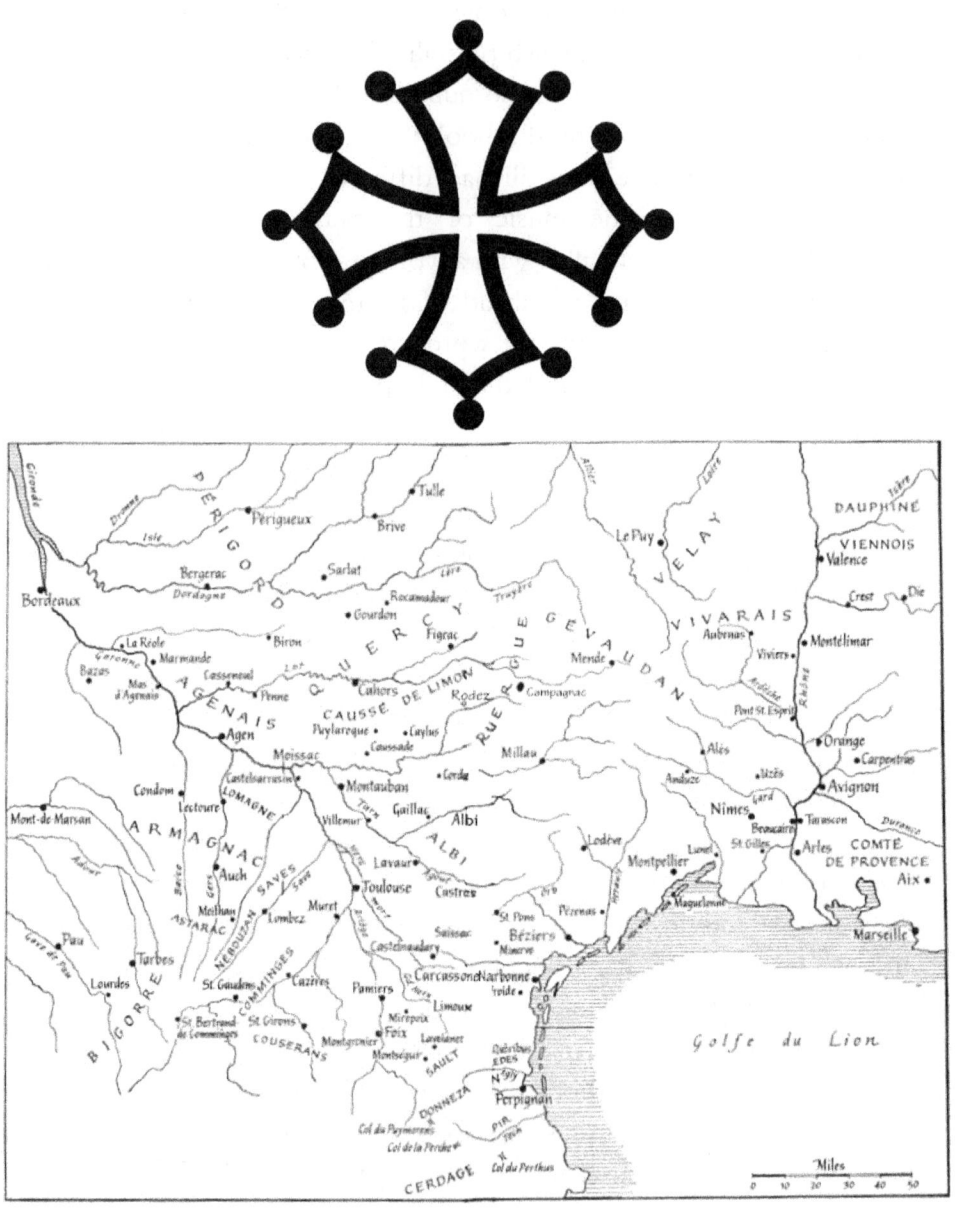

Occitania 13th Century

CHAPTER 1

THE CANON

n August 15th 1200 in the majestic cathedral of Saint Marie Le Puy-en-Velay a grand celebration was taking place for the holy Mother of God. The cathedral was radiating with great pomp and ceremony for this was a special holy day, dedicated to the feminine aspect of God. The interior of the cathedral was bathed in a delicate multi-coloured light, which filtered through the stained-glass windows as if the angels themselves were floating above. This mystical light mingled with the glorious sounds of musical instruments and the heavenly voices of cantors singing hymns to Marie the Mother of Jesus. One cantor in particular stood out for the enchantment that his rich and melodious voice was spreading throughout the entire congregation. He was a tall and slender young man robed in black cloth. He had very handsome features, was clean-shaven and well groomed and his long bronze hair was shining in the heavenly light. His hazel eyes sparkled with deep passion as his voice rose to the high vaults of the cathedral, touching the hearts of all present.

This important feast day had brought to the cathedral of Puy-en-Velay a number of very exalted personages from the lands of Occitania and beyond. First and foremost, at the front and resplendent in silk, stood Raymond VI the Count of Toulouse, and next to him the tall martial figure of Boniface Marquis de Montferrat. Around them were proudly arranged the knights and troubadours of their retinues, as both magnates were well known to be gallant warriors and patrons of troubadours. The hosts, the elderly count and the Archbishop of Puy-en-Velay were sitting on their thrones by the Altar. Next to them gathered the ecclesiastical figures of Peter of Castelnau and Arnauld-Amaury, together on a mission from Pope Innocent III. Both were Cistercians, trained to handle complex issues of dogma and to impose the will of the Catholic Church upon the people.

At a certain point the Count of Toulouse turned toward his attendant, troubadour Raimon de Miraval and asked in a whispering voice. "Who is this priestly young man who sings so well?"

"He is Peire Cardinal de Campagnac, indeed a remarkable young man, trained as a canon and a scholar but he also seems to know the art of poetry and music like an accomplished troubadour. I was also told that he possesses the skills of a true knight. His father is the Lord of Campagnac, who owes allegiance to the Count of Rodez who in turn owes allegiance to you sir."

"It seems to me that this gifted young man is wasted as a canon, a career as black as the cloth he is wearing. Surely, I must talk to him, hopefully to persuade him to join my court, for his skills are otherworldly."

Raimon de Miraval quietly promised the count that he would approach Peire for a meeting. In the meantime, the festive mass had come to an end and the congregation was slowly streaming out of the cathedral. The nobility and the Church dignitaries mounted their horses and their carriages and moved toward the majestic castle of the Count of Le Puy-en-Velay.

The Count of Toulouse rode side by side with Boniface, the Marquis de Montferrat, and they started talking to each other pleasantly. "What are you up to at this time, my dear Boniface? Aren't you tired of adventures?"

"I never tire of adventures Raymond. What is the meaning of life without them? This time, I think a crusade is brewing in the deep mind of the Church and I am ready to take the cross whenever it is proclaimed."

"A crusade to the holy land again, I guess. To rescue our fellow Christians and liberate Jerusalem from the Saracens."

"Do not make fun of such things Raymond. Sometimes your frivolous spirit comes close to blasphemy."

"For heaven's sake, Boniface! You sound like those self-righteous clerics who continue to pester me back at home with their piously hypocritical admonitions and threats for everything I say and do! Meanwhile I am trying to enjoy life and protect the freedom for my subjects to do the same. As you know, my grandfather, Raymond IV, was the leader of the First Crusade that secured Jerusalem for Christianity. His descendants followed his example by abandoning their beautiful domain to its own devices with the catastrophic consequences I have inherited. I have a lot of problems at home and most of them derive from power seeking clerics such as Peter of Castelnau and Arnauld-Amaury, who are here today, and many others like the cistercian Peter of Vaux-de-Cernay. You can understand I am not so keen to take the cross to liberate the holy land for the Church while this very same Church is threatening me at home."

"I know what you are saying, Raymond, and perhaps you are right in essence, but politically you are wrong to make them see you as their enemy because they are powerful and you must respect that fact. The Kings of France, from Charlemagne onward to this day came forward as the champions of the Church and this wise policy consolidated and augmented their power and pre-eminence among the European Monarchs. Contrarily the Emperors of Germany and the Kings of England did not fare as well because from time to time they would fight with the Pope and his Prelates. As for myself I have chosen to be an obedient son of the holy Church and I will take the cross when I am commanded."

"Good for you, Boniface, but allow me to differ with you because I can not stomach the way the Church is manipulating everybody to do their bidding and consolidate their power. It is hypocritical and has nothing whatsoever to do with God. I have my own relationship with God and if I bend my ways in order to please these power-hungry demons I will lose my soul and become someone else, a stranger that I cannot live with. I was born and brought up in the beautiful land of Occitania and I love its language and way of life and hate anyone and anything that threatens to change it. I love the women, the songs, the laughter, the sports, the jokes, the pleasant conversation, even the interminable fights and skirmishes in this pleasant land where we even kill each other with joy. I hate the humourless clerical bastards who threaten to put an end to our glorious and gallant way of life."

"You have made your point, Raymond, and I share your feelings and your point of view in most respects. Do not forget I am part of the Occitanian culture too." As they were talking they were entering the inner court of the castle. They found themselves inside a magnificent spacious hall together with many other noteworthy people who were also invited to attend the secular part of this special feast. At the furthest end of the hall on a dais were the thrones of the Archbishop and of the Count and upon them the corresponding personages were seated. Lower seats were arranged to the left and right and on them were seated various ecclesiastical and secular dignitaries. The Count of Toulouse and the Marquis de Montferrat sat next to the Count of Le Puy-en-Velay. Those of lower rank sat or stood below and in front of the dais around tables that were being covered with roasted meats and copious amounts of wine. Between the dignitaries and the rest of the guests, famous troubadours and their jongleurs performed their exquisite arts of song, music and dance.

Raimon de Miraval offered a love song to a mysterious lady, who was probably married to a jealous husband. His passion poured out of him, intense and true, and everybody applauded with great appreciation with the exception of the Cistercians who displayed their disapproval with sour faces.

Raimbaut de Vaqueiras, the famous troubadour and personal friend of Montferrat, sang the adventures of his patron when he rescued a beautiful lady from an unworthy and cruel adversary for the sake of love. This song made a strong impression on everyone even on the Cistercians. Finally, the Archbishop urged his canon Peire de

Campagnac to sing a sirventes lamenting the plight of Christians in the holy land and a call for a crusade. Peire sang beautifully with the accompaniment of his vielle, bringing tears to the eyes of his audience. Both Raymond of Toulouse and Montferrat were moved to stand up and congratulate Peire.

Later on, Raimon de Miraval approached Peire discreetly and told him that the Count wanted to talk to him privately. Peire followed him eagerly to the private chamber of Raymond, wondering why he was being asked to see the Count. Raymond looked at Peire with piercing interest and said, "I must congratulate you again for your performance as a cantor in the cathedral and as a troubadour of crusading sirventes in the palace. This amazes me because I understand that you are not just any cleric but a canon of the cathedral and also a nobleman since you are to succeed your father in the lordship of Campagnac. As you probably know, Campagnac, Rodez, Milau and other such holdings of Rouergue and elsewhere, were given to members of my family long ago. So I could even consider you my kinsman."

"It's a great honour for me that you are my liege, lord and kinsman and that you have requested my audience. I declare before you that I am a devoted admirer of you due to your free spirit, your gallantry, your magnanimity and your tolerance of other peoples' beliefs and differing ways of life. To me you represent the true spirit of our dazzling country full of singing rivers and green pastures, embraced by proud mountains and hills, home of glorious cities and castles, surrounded by rich orchards and vineyards. I am very lucky to live in a country such as this and to have a Lord such as you. You rule like the mistral that sometimes caresses and sometimes blows fiercely across this land of Toulousain, Agenais, Bigorre, Rouergue and Provence. In this paradise on earth, love and song reign supreme. This is the land of my soul and you are the lord of this land."

"Peire Cardinal de Campagnac, obviously you are wasted as a canon even with a very promising future in the gray world of the Church. You are a born poet and a gifted musician, a true troubadour! I ask you to join my court, in order to enjoy the pleasures of this beautiful world that you have just so poetically described. With me you will have the opportunity to use your wonderful skills and to further develop them towards excellence. You will be encouraged to use your musical skills for your own enjoyment as well as for the enjoyment of many others, including myself, who will truly appreciate the beauty of your art. You, just now, have praised me for attributes that your Church brethren consider abhorrent or even devilish. How can you reconcile the deep yearnings of your soul with the contrary mentalities and policies of the Catholic Church?"

"My lord, I am deeply moved and flattered with your offer to join your Court. I am very tempted and could even do so gladly. There are many issues in my life that I cannot reconcile with the black cloth I am wearing as a canon. For some time now I have been brooding over the idea of abandoning my career in the Church. During my training and then while exercising my function as a canon, I was confronted with sanctimonious and self-righteous attitudes, cruel intolerance and dogmatic inflexibility, blatantly contravening the message of love given by Jesus Christ himself. Some of what I see around me in the Church reminds me of the hypocrisy of the Pharisees and I have become deeply disappointed with the Church establishment. I could never abandon the true essence of Christianity though, which is solidly rooted inside of me. I have been feeling that I can no longer remain a cleric and certainly not a canon when I detest many of my colleagues and some of my superiors, such as the visiting Peter of Castelnau and Arnauld-Amaury, who are now here and lurking around us. At the same time, I have quietly longed to be able to live my life as a poet and a troubadour, to sing out the beauty of this world and express my protest and disagreement against those who advocate ugliness and intolerance. I would like to also explain, my Lord, why I joined the Church in the first place. Certainly, I am entitled to the lordship of Campagnac after my father's passing but according to the custom of Occitania my brother is also entitled to his share of Campagnac. In the domain of the King of France the first-born inherits everything and the principalities remain intact, but down here in the South we are divided and subdivided until the principalities become fragmented into insignificant portions and eventually into nothingness. I am sure that you are aware of this problem, as it constitutes a major weakness in our paradise. By joining the Church I helped my brother to keep the principality intact and in any case I was inclined scholarly and took the only way open to me that would help me to develop my skills of learning and scholarship. My mother is the sister of the Archbishop of Le Puy-en-Velay of the family Cardinal and so I became his protégé' and acquired the name Cardinal as well. By the way, the Archbishop is one of the few people in the Church that I respect and love and so it will not be easy for me to tell him that I am leaving the Church for it will surely hurt him deeply. I hope you understand me, my Lord."

"This is certainly a very tricky path to follow but you must do it sooner or later and better sooner than later. Perhaps you can tell him that you will be prepared to atone by going on a crusade as soon as it is proclaimed. My friend Montferrat is itching to lead one and you could join his retinue of troubadours such as Raimbaut de Vaqueiras. I am sure that will help you part company with your uncle, the Archbishop, pleasantly and on good terms. In the meantime, until the crusade happens, come join my court in Toulouse. I can tell your uncle that you can be useful to me also as an adviser in my effort to handle the heretics in my domain. By that I mean the Cathars or the Dualists or whatever our hardheaded Cistercian clerics call them. Personally, I never had any problem with them because they are as gentle as lambs and they do not bother me at all. They carry on their private lives and religious practices without disturbing anyone and they pay their taxes unfailingly. To tell you the truth I do not understand their religion and I do not care to understand it. The majority of my subjects like them and they find them to be good and respectful people. However, the clergy make an uncalled for fuss about them because they perceive them as a threat to the Catholic Church, which is itself gradually growing to be a threat to my power and me! I am becoming extremely worried about all of this! But enough, I am getting carried away; there is still so much to enjoy in this beautiful land. Now what do you think of my idea?"

"My Lord, your idea about the crusade could certainly convince my uncle to let me go but your idea to use me in your supposed debates with the Cathars could cause problems for you. It would certainly cause him to send Cistercian clerics, trained to combat and persecute heretics. I am sure that you would not like their interference."

"Peire, you are driving straight to the source of my problems which is the dark side of the Church. Anyway, talk to your uncle and let us hope for the best."

The next day Peire talked to his uncle the Archbishop, using all of his diplomacy and skills of persuasion. The Archbishop was at first very upset that this gifted young man, his protégé, would not take advantage of a God given career in the Church but would throw himself into the uncertainties of a secular life. The desire Peire expressed to take the cross eventually convinced him of his deep Christian faith and piety and he released him with regret, saying. "Go my son but you are abandoning the spiritual glory of the Church for the vanity of this world."

Peter of Castelnau, when he heard that the young Canon had abandoned the Church in order to follow Raymond of Toulouse, expressed his disgust and anger to Arnauld-Amaury in these words. "The Arch devil himself disguised as Raymond of Toulouse seduced a member of the Church into the slippery and sinful ways of the songs of damnation and debauchery leading straight to the mouth of Hell."

Arnauld-Amaury, gaunt and dry as a burnt-out tree cracked a sinister grin, laughingly saying,

"It will be soon when the Count and his friends will burn together with their accursed land of sin. All they think beautiful will melt with blood and fire and turn to smouldering ashes."

Even the choleric Peter of Castelnau shivered hearing this outpouring of hatred.

Peire Cardinal

CHAPTER 2

ON THE WAY TO TOULOUSE

aymond and his large retinue of knights, sergeants, troubadours and jongleurs left Le Puy-en-Velay and headed south towards Toulouse. The absence of clerics was embarrassingly noticeable and certainly reported on by his jaundiced critics. Raymond VI was a lukewarm Catholic and rather uncaring of religion in general. The clerics were annoying to him to say the least. His total lack of diplomacy made his dislike for them manifestly obvious and they reciprocated with cold hatred. This mutual dislike and distrust rendered any kind of negotiations between him and the Church authorities an extremely difficult proposition. Unfortunately for Raymond, in his extensive domains west and east of the Rhone River both secular and ecclesiastical authorities headed all of his cities. These two very different authorities were constantly squabbling and fighting with each other for control and without constant and continuous negotiations strife and chaos would take over his lands. Raymond knew all this, but in most cases, he avoided coming to terms with it, as he much preferred escaping into the more pleasant company of troubadours and beautiful ladies.

In the back of his mind he was considering employing Peire de Campagnac to carry out some of these negotiations for him and with this in mind he called Peire to ride with him for a while.

Peire was now dressed as a knight with a tan jerkin and breeches, wearing a sword at his side and a vielle on his back. He felt more like himself. Like a caged bird set free. The Church was a safe haven for a spiritual and creative man like himself but never felt quite right. He had learned a lot and developed his voice but longed for adventure, freedom and love. He had always heard songs in his head he could not sing in the confines of a church. He had more recently been dreaming of a beautiful woman who could share the deepest longings of his soul. These seemed like impossible dreams, but now as he rode free he began to realize that his impossible dreams were quickly becoming real. As he cast off his black church robes one last time a weight had lifted off with them. He now felt like a new man, full of hope, vision and passion, riding in the company of Count Raymond VI of Toulouse!

Count Raymond's voice interrupted Peire's reverie "I am glad to see you dressed smartly as a knight and a troubadour rather than a whispering shadow gliding along the melancholy corridors of churches and monasteries. I am eagerly waiting to hear you sing your songs in my great hall in Toulouse. Your religious training may even turn out to be quite useful in confronting the multitude of Bishops, Archbishops and monastics, who pollute my domain. There are unending disputes concerning power and property between the secular and the Church nobility. The Pope always stands by his prelates with legalistic arguments and threats of excommunication. After every dispute my power and authority are irreversibly eroded. They constantly interfere with my people and with the way I am running my state and personal affairs. They are buzzing around me like wasps and flies taking the joy of life out of me. I need help from anywhere I can get it and I believe your skills could be of great help. Would you be willing to help me? To help our land?"

Peire felt a deep compassion for the plight of this kind Prince and with warm spontaneity said, "My liege, I will try to help you to face this insidious predicament with all my heart but I do not know if I can. It is like trying to cut through a spider's web as thick as the distance between Toulouse and Rome. I know the way the Church works and I see your predicament to be even more threatening than you even realize! Sir, if I can presume to give you advice, I would urge you to try and make friends with some of them and exploit the differences they inevitably have between themselves. Unfortunately, they consider me a renegade and I will not be effective as your representative but I can advise you or your representatives the best way I know how."

"I appreciate your understanding and your advice but I still think that in some cases you could be effective as my representative. You certainly exaggerate that they would consider you a renegade, for you know very well you are not. Just to change the subject I would like to inform you that I am planning to stop in your father's principality, Campagnac on our way, and am hoping for a warm welcome."

"My Liege, my family and I will be honoured to have you stay with us. Yet my father will be terribly upset to learn that I just abandoned a promising career in the Church for the vanity of this world and my brother will be worried lest I claim my share of the inheritance. As for my mother I'm sure she will be inconsolable, but in time I hope they will all learn to live with the situation of my new status. By the way my Lord, are you also planning to visit Rodez and Millau? They are certainly more important than Campagnac."

"No, I do not have such plans at this time, as these towns are the seats of Bishops whom I dislike intensely. After Campagnac I intend to go straight to Albi, then to Lavaur and from there to Toulouse, my loving home. Of course, I will stop briefly in Rodez to meet with my vassal the Count and hopefully collect some taxes due to me. The Count of Millau will have to come and meet me at Campagnac, rather than me going out of my way to visit his town.

For three days Raymond and his jovial retinue rode through the rough mountainous territory outside of his domain and jurisdiction. Through the friendly towns of Velay, Vivarais and Gevaudan they trod, skirting the forbidding mountains of Velay, of Margaride and Abrac. In the craggy uplands and wild forests of the Causse de Sauveterre, they managed to find time for some good hunting, which was a pleasant respite on the long rough ride.

Peire was not used to riding for such a long period of time after the ascetic, yet comfortable life he had led in the Church. As exhausted and sore as he was, he felt elated and totally alive. He took in several deep breaths smelling the fresh mountain air and marvelled at this pure feeling of freedom!

Riding through these beautiful mountains felt like a dream come true, which brought back many childhood memories and dreams. Even the tedious town of Mende felt joyous to him, though Raymond and his entourage seemed to be tiring a bit. At long last they reached Rouergue and finally entered the more familiar domains of Count Raymond VI."

As they were getting close to Peire's home of Campagnac, Peire blurted out "I am really hoping, my Lord, that Campagnac will not be as tedious as Mende or even more so to you, as it is a smaller town. At least I hope that you will appreciate the countryside around it, which as far as I am concerned is paradise on earth."

"Not at all my dear Peire, Campagnac is a most beautiful place. I remember it overlooks the sparkling blue meandering Aveyron River to the south and to the north it is gently shadowed by the dark green fastness of Aubrac Mountain." "Yes" said Peire excitedly, "Its lush meadows and pastures are interspersed with the orchards and vineyards which surround the town and its humble but strong and prominent castle. South of the Aveyron River, the banks gradually rise to meet the high plateau of the Causse de Severac, which is a wilderness of grey rocks jutting out of bushes. The canopy of grassland there explodes with flowers of many colours and shades. Abundant wild life and game roam freely in this verdant land, at least until hit by a hunter's arrow! It is an excellent hunting ground, one shared with the lords of Rodez, Campagnac and Severac to the east. There are often disputes though between these lords that are never quite settled, so bloody skirmishes, single combats and negotiations unfortunately often take the place of a good hunt. My father is the lord of Campagnac and is the lowest in rank between the 3 Lords but not necessarily the weakest, as can be seen by his impregnable castle."

The castle rose before them as they approached Campagnac. Built on high ground at the edge of the town with a trapezoid shape formed by four towers and its keep inside. It did look imposing. Two towers rising close together protecting the gate and the other two in the back further apart. The four towers connected strong outside walls with the highest tower being the keep, which also connected to the other four towers with equally strong inner walls. The eight walls were thick enough to contain allures, inner corridors and rooms, altogether forming causeways protected by battlements. Each of the inner walls with a gate permitting access from one inner court to the next created a carefully designed maze, which could become a death trap to any unfriendly visitor, even if he managed to enter. At the front of the gate was Peire's family crest carved into the stone. Two garlands of lilies left and right embracing two battling figures at the top, with two towers or phallic shapes below. At the bottom on a sun-like surface the words "Paradge Campagnac" were written. The Campagnac's were an offshoot of the Counts of Toulouse but the origin of the crest had remained a mystery.

Raymond VI and his company were welcomed by Gaucelm de Campagnac and his son Bertrand at the gate of the castle. Peire embraced his father and his brother and in a few words informed them of his new status and asked them to discuss it later on when they would be in the presence of his mother Bieiris. Raymond praised Peire for his talents and for his decision to join his court and that put their worries at ease and turned their disappointment into a guarded relief.

Two jovial days passed with rejoicing and songs in the castle's spacious hall and with hunting in the Causse de Severac. The Count of Millau did come to pay his respects and his taxes to Raymond, which was a bit of relief and added to Raymond's happiness.

When the Campagnacs finally met privately many explanations were given and even Bieiris was convinced that Peire did the right thing for himself and for the whole family. To be a troubadour was an honourable and glamorous vocation. The two brothers promised to each other that they would stick together and that they would always be faithful to the house of Toulouse.

Peire composed a song to celebrate this unique moment of harmony between people suspended in the glorious and smiling nature around them. His voice filled every corner, corridor and vault of the intricate castle with benevolent vibrations attracting wispy, loving emanations of the spirit world. Raimon de Miraval joined in a tenso countering all this optimism and goodness with the lurking doubts and uneasiness unfolding from the depths of envy and hostility of evil. The good and evil battled each other for a while with verse and sound until peace and harmony prevailed at last. The Count listened to the tenso in a pensive mood because he knew very well that his happy disposition in life was increasingly threatened by the dark and insidious designs of certain powerful quarters of the Church. He often had a feeling that he lived on borrowed time.

Indeed, the time had come to bid farewell to Campagnac and this special few days. The next morning, under the first rays of the sun, the cavalcade galloped away towards Rodez, along the meandering Aveyron River.

At the gates of Rodez they were met by the municipal authorities and the Count himself, surrounded by his knights. There were reports of discord between those present and the Bishop who did not deign to appear and pay his respects to the Count of Toulouse, the suzerain of Rodez. The reason was that the Bishop had commenced persecutions toward the Cathars, against the wishes of the secular authorities. There were also disputes concerning the city revenues and that was a much more serious issue for Raymond VI who arbitrated in favour of the secular authorities extracting for himself his share. He also ordered the cessation of the persecutions and declared that the unfortunate victims were under his protection. Thus, he earned the respect of the nobility and burghers but the relentless grudge and hatred of the Bishop and his Cistercian backers, who could reach as far as Pope Innocent III.

They departed Rodez and the Aveyron River with mixed feelings and unease. As they headed south through the wild country of Sauveterre the hunting of wild boar and deer offered them some amusement and an escape from the worries and reality of a fragmented albeit beautiful country. Raymond rode in a melancholy mood as he was approaching the river Tarn and the great city of Albi and the

Toulousain, the heart of his domains. He was trying over and over to find a solution to the unending problems he now had to face. There were not only the Bishops of these busy towns who challenged his power but also the hot-headed Raymond-Roger Trencavel, the Viscount of Carcassonne, who never missed a chance to fight him every inch of the way. There were others such as the Counts of Foix and Comminges who kept challenging him as well. Even the King of France himself was always casting a heavy and threatening shadow over him, although at present he was occupied with John Plantagenet the King of England. Raymond VI was born to be a happy, playful soul and hated that he had to deal with these complex and unpleasant issues. He just hoped that they would go away somehow to leave him to live his life with joy and ease.

As they were approaching the outskirts of Albi what looked like two clouds were rapidly moving on the road towards them as if one cloud was chasing the other. The Count ordered Peire, who rode next to him, and some other knights to charge and surround the insurgents without delay. The squadron formed a wedge between the two groups of riders who looked like clouds from afar because of all the dust they were raising. The nearest group looked, surprisingly, like civilians on horseback, Peire could even see a woman among them. The group behind them was composed of armed guards bearing the insignia of the Bishop of Albi. Both groups were forced to stop on their heels and explain themselves to the Count who had just arrived, placing himself between the armed men and the civilians. Facing the armed men, he shouted,

"What is the meaning of all this? Why are you pursuing these unarmed civilians and by whose authority?"

"These people are heretics and are fleeing from the just punishment of the Bishop of Albi."

"And what exactly is their punishment?"

"Our Bishop found them guilty of heresy and there is only one punishment for heresy: burning at the stake."

"Is that so? Now hear me well; I am the Count of Toulouse and the ultimate authority in this territory. I intend to pass judgment on these civilians myself and until I do they are under my protection. So, go back and tell your Bishop that his verdict is null and void and if he has any objections we can meet at his palace or at the Municipal Square."

The Bishop's squadron, confronted with superior and determined force, turned and galloped back towards the bridge over the river Tarn and the gates of Albi without resistance. In the meantime, the Albigensian civilians had dismounted and advanced with dignity towards the Count and his entourage.

As they moved closer to where he and Raymond were standing, Peire had his first true look at the woman who had caught his eye from afar. His heart skipped a beat when he realized she also carried what looked like a vielle. He immediately felt himself drawn to her. Could she also be a musician? Her long dark hair, wild and dusty from the flight, embraced a beautiful intelligent looking face with deep dark eyes that drew him in. He felt dizzy and confused. Was this lust or something more? She was graceful and poised as she moved forward with the rest of the fugitives. Their eyes met and his breath caught in his throat as she did not look away but returned his gaze. Peire finally had to look away and bring his attention back to the situation at hand.

Having arrived in front of The Count of Toulouse, the eldest of the group addressed him with these words, "Your Excellency, we are true Christians persecuted for our beliefs and because we know that you have a kind and tolerant heart we come to you as supplicants, ready to submit to your justice. We are hard working and honest artisans and like to think that we are useful to our fellow human beings."

"What is your name and of what heresy have you been convicted?"

"I am Nicetas d'Outremer, a master craftsman of musical instruments and other fine things. With me is my daughter Esclamonde who can sing like a nightingale." Peire's heart quickened upon hearing Esclamonde's name for the first time and upon learning that she was a wonderful singer. His eyes were drawn like a magnet back to

Esclamonde's. He could feel his whole being begin to respond to her in a way he had never experienced before. It was so overwhelming that he could hardly hear the elder as he continued, "All the others are carpenters and weavers of silk who share with me a wholesome way of life. They call us heretics because we reject the authority of the Church and its sacraments as being material and therefore evil. We believe in Jesus Christ and the New Testament as spiritual and we reject Jehovah and the Old Testament as material and therefore evil."

"No wonder this narrow-minded Bishop wants to burn you alive. He would have done it for much smaller offences. Nevertheless, although I do not agree with your beliefs, I am opposed to burning people because of their ideas. I will accept you as supplicants and I will protect you from any persecution. However, you will be submitted to the due process of the law in my court, presided over by me and by my good Bishop of Toulouse Raymond de Rabastens. The Bishop of Albi will be given the opportunity to bring his case against you and my friend Peire Cardinal de Campagnac, an ex-canon, will be asked to act as the attorney for your defence. My intention is to clear you legally without appearing arbitrary. I certainly hope for a favourable outcome because I need your craftsmanship and the skills of your companions." He looked over towards Esclamonde with an admiring glance at her beauty and continued, "And I cannot wait to listen to your daughter, Esclamonde, sing."

During this time Peire had continued to secretly watch Esclamonde. He was absolutely enthralled with her graceful demeanour, her calm composure and her beauty, which seemed to glow from within. A very erotic feeling welled up from inside him radiating out to touch the young girl. Esclamonde felt it and turned toward him to meet his eyes. As their eyes met a powerful wave of energy passed between them. Esclamonde remained detached and composed but inside she was spinning. Meeting this handsome man's eyes shook her to the core, for she felt like a lightning bolt had entered her heart and set it on fire.

With this chance to really meet her, Peire realized how slim, supple and shapely her figure was. Her hair waved down her shoulders like the black blue feathers of a raven. Her eyes were violet and her soft skin white as ivory. She wore a rusty-brown unadorned long garment, which was unable to conceal or diminish her beauty. She almost appeared to be an elemental being, a fairy princess come to steal his heart.

Peire could feel a deep, caring and loving energy pouring through him and extending out to Esclamonde. With sudden surety, he realized that he was in love with her as strongly and deeply as the magical powers of spirit and flesh could devise.

Esclamonde felt herself respond to the young man's amorous effusiveness with excitement, awakening her whole passionate self. She was eagerly looking forward to the moment when this handsome young man would begin his consultations in his capacity as their attorney.

Count Raymond of Toulouse could not help but notice the glow of beauty emanating from Esclamonde and the increasing attentiveness of Peire to her. The silent, yet natural, attraction between these two young people was almost physically palpable. He resolved not to take advantage of the power he had over them, possibly, for the first time in his life. Raymond was a well-known womanizer and it was to his credit that at this time he had the strength not to take advantage of his position to taste this rare fruit of paradise that chance brought so close to his grasp. His wisdom and spontaneous sympathy for the young troubadour won over his innate lecherous tendencies and he stood aside watching with interest, yet benevolently, the development of their nascent and wonderful affair.

Peire, by nature, was never too sure of himself in anything, but this time he was absolutely sure that Esclamonde was already his loving mate and that it was going to last for a lifetime.

During his clerical life he had often felt a desire to savour passionate and beautiful women who seemed attracted to him. He knew that the vows of abstinence, he had lived by up to this point, would be very hard to keep. Among the stated reasons for abandoning his ecclesiastical career, a secret deep longing for sensual love, was an additional, important, reason for doing so.

Esclamonde, from the moment she felt her first awakening as a woman, had always dreamed of passionate and cultivated knights and troubadours who could carry her to the high heavens of love and ecstasy. For the first time in her life she was sure that she had found the man she had always dreamed of. Her religious environment was not repressive and yet did not encourage carnal love because it belonged to the dark domain as opposed to the heavenly light of the spirit. Her father, Nicetas, was a spiritual leader and a Perfect of this Christian sect. After her mother's passing he had abstained completely from carnal intercourse. Abstinence was not demanded of Esclamonde. But eventually with age she would be expected to attain the status of a Perfect as well, at which point she would abstain from all carnal pleasures. Until then she was allowed to live a normal life and experience love, and fortunately, love came to her at the right time in the person of Peire.

As the afternoon was fading, Raymond's knights began making camp for the night. They were building fires, roasting meats and setting up tents to the joyous sounds of troubadour songs.

Peire found himself quickly introducing himself to Nicetas and asking for permission to talk to Esclamonde under the pretext of discussing poetry and music with her, at which point he also revealed that he, himself, was a troubadour.

Esclamonde's father, a kind spirited man, found Peire to his liking. After discussing the judicial case with him, and being quite impressed with the negotiating skills Peire was already exhibiting, he shared some of his own story about his skills as a craftsman and his creation of musical instruments.

He finally called out to Esclamonde to join them, saying, "this young man here is not only our defence attorney but also a poet and musician, a real troubadour, and he wants to talk to you about music. As I must meet with the other elders to discuss our case further, I will leave you two to discuss your music." And with that he turned and walked away leaving the young couple alone to talk.

Esclamonde felt her heart beating to the breaking point as the handsome young man before her raised her hand and placed his lips upon it, saying with a gentle melodious voice "Esclamonde is a beautiful name and suits your magical beauty perfectly. I would like to discuss music with you but at this particular moment I cannot talk about anything other than my love for you, which I hope you have noticed glowing through my heart and soul. Esclamonde, I beg you not to hesitate in entrusting and sharing your love with me. I can feel it growing and know it is but waiting to blossom in your heart."

Esclamonde, although taken by surprise by the poetic yet precipitous directness of the young man, was thrilled to feel the incredible impact of his love, which she could deeply sense was true. She hesitated only for a few moments, keeping him in suspense for every second of it, before simply telling him the truth of her heart, "Peire, from the moment I saw you I was drawn to you and quickly realized I love you. The only thing I want in life is to be with you."

A maelstrom of red hot emotions rushed through their souls and bodies urging them to touch each other everywhere to find gates of entry, to taste all possibilities of sensual pleasure but in the midst of the noisy and busy camp they could only hold hands savouring the anticipation of the intimacies of love.

The two, young people were totally absorbed in their world of bliss when Nicetas came back to join them, a knowing smile on his face.

Looking over at Nicetas, Peire wondered if he knew what had just passed during his absence? Peire sensed he did and quickly decided to take the most important step of his life. It was not the only one. Just a few days ago he had cast away his Church cloth and now, with love pouring through his veins, he realized how much he wanted a wife to love and cherish.

Nicetas did not show any surprise when Peire asked his permission to marry his daughter. He was happy for them and yet somewhat sad. Sad for having to let his daughter go but mostly for a road ahead beset with threatening shadows. He said, "My dear boy, I can see in my beloved Esclamonde's eyes a true love for you and such love is not only of the flesh but mostly of heavenly spirit. I can also see the same love in your eyes. Who am I to refuse this miracle of love from realization? Yes, I give you my permission to take my Esclamonde as your wife. According to our true Christian customs no other ceremony is needed. You could consider yourselves married. As a Perfect I have the authority to sanctify your union. However, my dear boy, you are not one of us and therefore you are going to need the sanctions of your world and religion. You must seek the agreement of the Count of Toulouse, who by the way is our protector and we must not provoke his displeasure by ignoring him in any way. He has made mortal enemies in order to save us. Also, my son, you must understand that your association with people like us is going to cause you many serious hardships and dangers. We are a foreign body in your society and we face an open and imminent persecution. Perhaps this is the last corner of earth where we are still tolerated and sometimes allowed to live a normal life, mainly because of the kindness of Raymond VI and the southern nobility. My family were always pure Christians, Cathari, a Greek word for pure, and they came from Constantinople, the capital of the Eastern Roman Empire or the Greek Empire as it is called here in the West. There we were called Manicheans or Bogmils and we were hunted down as animals because of our pacifistic, anti-clerical and egalitarian views. My father immigrated to the beautiful and cosmopolitan city of Narbonne and he gained the protection of the Viscountess Ermengarde because he was an accomplished craftsman of musical instruments. My mother was from a noble family of Narbonne, a Catholic, but she loved my father and he loved her, so they got married, although she never adopted our faith. I was raised as a true Christian, a Cathar and learned my father's profession. Musical instruments were very much in demand in Narbonne, Toulouse, Bezier and many other Occitanian cities and smaller towns where music, dance and poetry filled the air by troubadours and jongleurs. According to our faith the material pursuits of life are impure and belong to

Jehovah the evil God, but music and poetry are an essential part of spirit and therefore are pleasing to the Good God, Jesus Christ. My wife Azelais was beautiful in body and spirit; Esclamonde is the spitting image of her. Also she played the vielle and could sing like a nightingale just like my Esclamonde but she died many years ago as a true Christian to merge with the High Spirit of the Good God. I administered the consolamentum to her to ease her passage. I guess I am talking too much and I might be boring you but soon you will be called to defend us in court and it is useful to learn a few things about us. As for your proposal, if Esclamonde agrees, you have my blessings for your union with my dear daughter." With a glowing smile, Esclamonde quickly agreed to accept Peire's proposal. Nicetas added, "do not neglect to get permission of the Count of Toulouse as well."

That night of the first of September 1200, Peire and Esclamonde slept together in their tent as man and wife in a blissful union. The next day Peire talked to his lord Raymond and obtained his generous blessings. He even offered to stand as best man in the Catholic wedding to take place on the 14th of September in Saint Sernin, the Cathedral of Toulouse.

Before they left Albi, the Count had a shouting match with the Bishop at the municipal palace where curses and threats were heard from both parties. Finally they agreed that the Albigensian heretics would stand trial in Toulouse presided over by Raymond de Rabastens the Bishop of Toulouse and the verdict would be respected by all without appeal. The Count also demanded and got the taxes due to him by the city of Albi.

In a few days the momentous yet exhausting journey came to an end as they approached the rose-red walls of the great city of Toulouse.

Courtly Love 13th century painting

Vielle player and lovers from the Chansonnier Provencal.

CHAPTER 3

A WEDDING, A TRIAL AND A SONG

ny occasion for celebration and rejoicing was good enough for Raymond of Toulouse and his brilliant and merry court as well as for most southern lords, their retinues, friends and hangers on. They were all invited to the wedding of Peire and Esclamonde and all of them were joyfully planning to attend in spite of the modest or even dubious family status of the bride and groom. It was sufficient for them that the Count of Toulouse favoured the couple enough to stand as best man. Also, and most importantly, they were intrigued by the stories told about a love by lightning, about the exceptional beauty of the bride and about the remarkable musical skills of the couple. A troubadour and trobairitz were going to be revealed at this wedding and only this fact carried the highest pedigree of nobility for the bride and groom. However, many clerics, Cistercians and quite a few Abbots and Bishops, viewed this wedding with spite and scorn and not only disdained to attend but blacklisted all those who would. For quite different reasons the Cathars, even Nicetas the father of the bride, were going to be absent. They simply did not want to participate in a Catholic ceremony and a sacrament they rejected as being more or less satanic. Also, they did not want to provoke the Catholics by their presence and thereby embarrass the Count and the nobility who stuck their necks out to protect them.

The obvious contradiction between the satanic nature of marriage and the necessity of performing it for reasons of procreation remained unresolved although they compromised by allowing it for their believers. Those who attained unadulterated spirituality, the Perfects, were celibate, like Nicetas.

Another distinguished group of people who were going to attend this wedding quite enthusiastically were the troubadours; most of them single by choice and inclination. How would the ladies of their adoration feel if they knew that their troubadour, who poured his heart out for them, was in fact married and possibly in love with his wife? They would likely feel cheated. So Troubadours usually felt they had to remain single in order to maintain their credibility and their income. The married troubadours usually turned their poetry and songs to social and political issues by composing sirventes.

On the 14th of September of the year 1200 a great number of illustrious and glittering members of Occitanian nobility turned up in Saint Sernin the Cathedral of Toulouse, followed by rich burghers and colourful troubadours and jongleurs to celebrate the festive event of the wedding of Peire and Esclamonde.

After the ceremony, the festivities continued in the spacious and bright halls of the Count of Toulouse.

The Bishop Raymond de Rabastens was saying to the Count of Toulouse, "Today I overstretched my authority and performed the sacrament of marriage on a couple of questionable faith to the Catholic Church just to please you and I am afraid that I am going to regret it. Fortunately, the heretic father of the bride and his followers had enough sense not to show up. However, I am distressed that the family of the groom did not show up either. Are they displeased to the point of causing problems? You know, the mother of the groom is the sister of the Archbishop of Le Puy-en-Velay who is a person with power and connections in Rome. He is already upset with his nephew having abandoned his career in the Church to become a troubadour. On top of that to learn that he married a heretic, it would test his patience too far. And as if all that isn't enough, you have asked me to preside over the trial of heretics with the intent to acquit them against the wishes of the Bishop of Albi who wanted them burned at the stake. Do you know whom he is planning to send here as the prosecutor? The fanatic

Cistercian Peter Vaux-de-Cernay who hates your guts and possesses the most venomous and able tongue of all the Cistercians put together. What are we going to do?"

"My reverent friend, you worry too much. All is well and under control. The parents of the groom did not have the time to show up for the wedding and they love their son too much to cause any trouble. Please step into the generous spirit and mood knowing that you helped to work this miracle of love. I am sure it is pleasing to a benevolent God who cares little about the machinations and dogmatic avarice of his sanctimonious Church authorities. Also I would like to emphasize to you that this coming trial is not only about rescuing a few unfortunate Cathars but a test of my authority against the malevolent power of interfering clerics. Against this Peter of Vaux-de-Cernay I will pit the agile mind and the hot passion for justice of Peire Cardinal de Campagnac, today's groom. I was planning to employ Guilhalbert de Castres, the Cathar Bishop, but I am not so sure that it is a good idea. His fervour might be viewed as a provocation and have the opposite effect. He also seems to be attached to the hot-headed Raymond-Roger Trencavel who has made it his business to annoy me. I hope you can understand the larger picture and find a way to support me effectively."

"Yes, I can see the complexity of the situation and I will support you, although I cannot help being apprehensive. I am glad I was able to perform this wedding on such short notice and legalize this union before the trial; otherwise your troubadour and defence attorney could have been accused of immorality and discredited. Furthermore we will maintain that the bride was converted to Catholicism before the wedding. I sincerely hope that she will not deny it in court. I know you can be careless sometimes. So, please make sure that all the loose ends have been tied up."

The count nodded reassuringly and walked off to meet the young couple who were holding hands absorbed and enveloped in their emerging love. "My young friends, please descend from the heavens in which you are so blissfully floating for a moment. Come back to the realities of this earth to receive my congratulations and a few words of friendly advice. You know I have been tempted to court your sensuous beauty Esclamonde, but the strong feeling of respect and friendship I feel for Peire prevented me. Of course I might change my mind in the future and come back to claim your heavenly beauty for myself. I am only human and I have done it before on other occasions of lesser temptation."

The two young people, startled at first, received the Count's jests with a flash of smiles although they sensed that he half meant what he said. Esclamonde, who was too much in love to be stirred up by the Count's words replied, "Your Excellency, thank you for all you have done for us. I will not pretend that I am not flattered by your words. However my body and spirit are open only to Peire and none else. I am so happy and so much in love that all other temptations are an innocent breeze refreshing and reinforcing this wonderful love I feel."

Peire, confident of her and his own feelings, felt his concern melt and said, "My Liege, your admiration for my wife flatters me and makes me happy. You should have been a troubadour in my place and I the honoured husband receiving the amorous praise for my beloved wife. For this is the way of our wonderful, wild and free land of Occitania. I am sure there is no other place in the whole world like it."

"Well said, my son, you are a true troubadour through and through and a champion of our way of life and our ideas of freedom, tolerance and patriotism." The Count continued. "Now let's not forget that soon we are facing a trial where our Cathar friends will be accused for heresy and if we want Esclamonde spared this ordeal we must declare that she has been converted to Catholicism. I talked to Nicetas and he agrees that this is the best course to take. Otherwise your marriage would be pronounced null and void and my good friend the Bishop of Toulouse would be in great trouble. But you would find yourselves in much worse trouble. My dear girl do you understand what is at stake here?"

Esclamonde was badly shaken by the terrible dilemma presented to her by the Count although her father had already warned her what the price of her happiness would be. He had advised her to accept conversion. Many Cathars had done the same thing in the past to save their lives. However by doing so her conscience would be soiled and her innocence gone. But she was young, filled with love and not ready for a devastating sacrifice. So she said, "Your Excellency, please try to find a way out of this dilemma but if you cannot I will accept a public conversion."

"My dear girl, I will certainly try to quietly avoid this issue since their malevolence is not quite focused on you but on the older members of your sect and naturally on me. Your attorney, your husband, will try to divert their attention using the skills he learned from them as a canon and the subtleties of his crafty mind."

"You overestimate my abilities, Sir, I am young and lack experience."

"But you are in love and will employ your creative imagination to tip the balance to our favour, and I promise you that I'll do my part."

The festivities continued for a long time and the guests had completely forgotten the wedded couple who had quietly slipped away. The guests did not care why they were there and what they were celebrating anymore. They simply had an uproarious time with relays of songs, food, wine and lascivious dances performed by jongleurs and other performers.

Peire and Esclamonde took up residence in small but pleasant quarters in the Bourg near Saint Sernin where prominent citizens and the nobility of Toulouse had their residences. They managed to immerse themselves in their passionate love although the approaching time of the trial clouded their bliss with understandable worries and anxiety.

The date of the trial had been set for the 8th of November and Peire had a lot of work to do and contacts to make with Nicetas and his people under indictment. All these meetings were done secretly in the Cite' of Toulouse and never where he lived in his anxious efforts to not implicate Esclamonde in the trial. He also met with the Bishop of Toulouse to obtain his friendly advice regarding strategy and tactics of defence. The Prosecutor, Peter of Vaux-de-Cernay was a crafty and a powerful adversary who hated the Cathars and Raymond of Toulouse with a passion. The court would be chaired by the Bishop of Toulouse and co-chaired by the Bishop of Narbonne and an ex-troubadour, the Cistercian Foulques de Marseille. The two bishops were friends with Raymond of Toulouse but Foulques might want to show some excessive zeal to prove his loyalty to the Cistercian's position against heretics. The Court would be held at the Maison Communale situated near the walls separating the Cite' from the Bourg. It was spacious enough to accommodate a large turnout of friends and foes of Cathars as well as many curious nonpartisan spectators.

A few days before the trial began the well-respected Cathar Perfect, Guilharbert de Castres approached Peire with very useful advice, "I do not know how much you know about our beliefs, our way of life and the open and covert hostility we face in the society of Catholics. We try to tread quietly and lightly like cats, although the lands of Raymond of Toulouse and the lands of the Trenscavels, Foix and Comminges are relatively friendly to us. However, the situation could change precipitously for the worse. Our enemies are poking about testing the ground and they can pounce at the slightest provocation. So please do not let your commendable sympathy for us encourage you to offer praise or make polemics that can be construed as provocation towards the Catholic Church. Be aware and wary of Foulques de Marseilles. He is a coiled up snake gathering information and venom against us waiting for his chance and the right moment to strike. Try not to step on him and give him that opportunity. Try to help my friends by emphasizing their innocence and not the correctness of their creed. Please think of what I said and may God help you to help us. Use witnesses who can testify that we are harmless. Mention Saint Bernard who was the first to identify us in Albi and called us Albigensians. He maintained that the only way to deal with us was not through persecution but through persuasion and we agree with him. He was a true Saint and a pure spirit. Pope Innocent III has not decreed differently, at least not yet."

Guilharbert de Castres left quietly and unnoticed leaving Peire impressed and deep in thought.

On November 8th the great hall of the Maison Communale was crowded with nobility, clergy, burghers and common people who had come to participate or watch the trial of the Albigensians. At the head of the hall on a podium was the high bench of the judges, illuminated by the three stained glass windows behind them. At the lower stand below and to the right of them stood the Prosecutor and to the left stood the defences. The accused sat in front and at a distance from the bench. To the left and right from them sat or stood the witness and other interested parties. On a high pedestal to the right of the Bench sat Raymond VI on his throne. Behind the Albigensians to the far end of the hall was the jostling crowd burning with anxiety or curiosity depending on the involvement of each individual.

The Court was called to order and the charges were read out loudly for all to hear. "You are accused of crimes of heresy. What are you pleading, guilty or not guilty?"

Nicetas moved forward and said unassumingly but clearly, "I am speaking on behalf of all the accused and I am saying that we are Christians and we have not committed any crimes. Therefore, we are not guilty as charged. On the contrary we have been evicted from our own property, which has been wrongly seized and despoiled by the Bishop of Albi. The Bishop then decreed without a trial to burn us at the stake in order to justify his unlawful actions against us." There was a subdued whisper among the judges on the bench and a loud protest from the Prosecutor while the Defence was suppressing a smile.

Peter of Vaux-de-Cernay came forward shouting, "Your Honour, it is intolerable to hear the accused posing as accusers. They are heretics and must be tried for this and this only. There are no unlawful actions that could possibly be done against them as they claim because they are heretics and there is only one punishment for heresy, to be burned at the stake! This punishment should have been inflicted upon them in Albi rather than wasting our time here to dignify them with a proper trial."

Peire moved to reply but the presiding judge, the Bishop of Toulouse, stopped him with a slight gesture and turning to the

Prosecutor, he said firmly, "I am surprised to hear you show such a contempt for due process of the law requiring proof of guilt before conviction. I am sure you were carried away by your otherwise commendable religious zeal. Also I assure you that none here considers this trial a waste of time. So, let's get on with it starting with you to state the nature of the charges against the accused."

Peter of Vaux-de-Cernay, flushed by the rebuke, proceeded by stating the case from his point of view, "Albi is a devout Catholic City the spiritual purity of which is threatened by the worst kind of heretics ever known; the Cathars. Saint Bernard managed to spot and expose them for the first time in Albi fifty years ago. So sometimes they bear the name of Albigensians, quite unjustly for Albi, but quite unfortunately this name stuck. However, Albi is not the only town in the Midi cursed to be infected with the Albigensian heretics. In fact, they are more numerous in Toulouse, in Narbonne, Bezier and in countless other towns. So, be aware of the danger. The Albigensians do not believe in the one God but two Gods. So they cannot call themselves Christians as they tell us. They refuse sacrament and turn their back to the Catholic Church and its sacred servants. They are an abomination and as such must be eradicated from our communities. The accused used to live, work and worship their devils in quarters owned by the Prince and Bishop of Albi who until recently ignored their pernicious nature. When he found out he resolved to cleanse his property of their verminous presence by burning them, as any true Catholic Prince should have done. Unfortunately, instead of burning them first the Bishop sent his soldiers to collect their valuable possessions in payment of taxes and rent owed to him. So they got wind of what was coming and managed to slip away on horseback. When he found out that they were escaping he sent a detachment of guards to capture them but the Count of Toulouse interfered quite unjustly and saved them. Later the Count promised the bishop that the heretics would stand trial in Toulouse and now we are here to complete what was started in Albi. I ask the Court to pronounce the accused guilty of heresy and condemn them to burn on the stake until they are dead."

"Do not be so hasty Peter of Vaux-de-Cernay. The due process of law is not yet complete." interjected the co-presiding judge, the Bishop of Narbonne and added, "Let us call the Defence, Peire de Campagnac, to state his position in this case."

Peire moved to the centre of the podium and in a pleasant tone of voice he said, "Your Honourable Magistrates and your Excellencies the Count of Toulouse and the Viscount of Trencavel and the other Lords who considered the proceedings of this trial important enough to attend in person, I say that I am here to defend not only these unfortunate citizens but to defend the truth by hard evidence. In other words, I am not the defender of lies and proven criminals but the defender of innocent people and before your court I will try to prove their innocence by indisputable facts and credible testimony. But let us first examine what the charges are against the defendants. What really are the crimes they have been accused of having committed? Have they murdered any one? Nobody said they did. Have they stolen money or goods from anybody? Nobody said they did. Have they defrauded anyone? Nobody said they did. Have they offended or desecrated our Catholic Church and its sacred servants by observable acts? Nobody said they did. Have they offended the King or their liege lord? Nobody said they did. We have only heard a vague charge that they committed crimes of heresy. By what acts? Against whom? A court like this one can only investigate concrete and observable acts and decide whether these acts are criminal or not. And in this case, there are no such acts. So, what are we supposed to investigate and pass judgement on?"

"The only acts, which were brought forward by the defendants and admitted by the Prosecution, were the acts of the Bishop of Albi against them. Although the Bishop of Albi is not on trial here allow me to mention again that the defendants were dispossessed of their own property and they were convicted without trial to be burned alive."

At this point Foulques de Marseille interjected with subdued indignation saying, "I would like to bring to everybody's attention that the Defence is misrepresenting the essence of this Trial, that being the defendants are heretics. He also seems to claim quite erroneously that they owned their quarter when the Prosecution maintains that this was the property of the Bishop of Albi."

Peter of Vaux-de-Cernay, quite gratified by Foulques' interjection stated in a loud voice, "Thank you, your Honour for coming to the rescue of our Catholic Faith and the sacred rights of the Bishop of Albi. I can hardly control my righteous anger against this protector of heretics and heresy and the protégé of a notorious libertine and sympathizer of heretics, the Count of Toulouse. Also, I have been informed that Peire de Campagnac is a renegade Canon. This is the kind of people we have to put up with in this Court."

The Count of Toulouse kept quiet with a smile on his face but his eyes had turned hard with anger hearing Peter-de-Cernay aiming an unprovoked attack against him. On the other hand, Peire was handling himself quite well and he did not want to spoil this favourable development with an angry retort.

Fortunately, the Bishop of Toulouse took the situation into his own hands by again rebuking a misbehaving prosecutor.

"I call the prosecution to order because it has overstepped its function in this Court by offending the Defence and the Count of Toulouse without just cause and provocation. And just to set the record straight I inform you and the court that Peire de Campagnac is not a renegade but a devout Catholic who was released from his vows as a canon by the Archbishop of Le Puy-en-Velay following the official process. And please, in the future before anyone levels any accusations against anyone, be certain that they are correct otherwise I will pronounce charges against the offender. Now having said that I call the defence to answer the questions of Foulques de Marseille, the co-chairman of this Court."

"The questions raised by his Honour are of great importance and I apologize to him if I gave the impression that I tried to side step them. Now, starting with the question of heresy whether it can constitute a crime by itself even when it is not the cause of recognizable crimes I maintain that this issue has not been established as yet by the ultimate authority on these matters, either Pope Innocent III or the Popes before him. Naturally Catharism has been condemned as an error of dogma, which must be corrected by persuasion and other peaceful means and definitely not by persecution or burning at the stake. A few overzealous Abbots or Bishops followed this non-prescribed course of action quite arbitrarily but I expect the Pope has not sanctioned this course. As you all know, Saint Bernard, who discovered the Albigensian heresy, advocated and employed persuasion and never persecution and burning people alive. The defenders are well known artisans who have shown exemplary conduct in the societies in which they lived and worked. They have never hurt anybody. On the contrary they have often helped their fellow human beings. They are Christians and they have always behaved as true Christians. Now if some good Catholics want to persuade them to follow the path of the Catholic Church they are welcome to try, but persecution and condemnation to burn them alive are far from Christian ways of persuasion."

A general applause and favourable acclamations erupted throughout the great hall of the Maison Communale showing that the people of Toulouse possessed a tolerant and generous spirit such as their Count Raymond VI.

Foulques de Marseilles, the ex-troubadour and now trained Cistercian, was against this exhilarating liberal feeling and he was gradually hardening to the point of adopting intolerant and cruel methods of dealing with non-conformists in general. As an innate politician though, he resolved to keep quiet and pretend that he was in tune with the prevailing mood around him. Obviously, this ex-canon turned lawyer and Troubadour was doing a very good job defending his heretics.

Peire paused until the noise subsided and continued, "As to the second question, I possess here a written document proving that the quarters occupied by the defendants have been donated to them by the Trencavel family who, as you know, own large sections of Albi and of the Albigensian territory. The Viscount of Trencavel is here today to confirm that said document is true and valid. Therefore, the Bishop of Albi took possession of property not belonging to him and he extracted rents that were not owed to him. As for trying to burn them without trial, the prosecutor himself admitted that much. So, it is an indisputable fact. In spite of all this damning evidence, the Bishop of Albi is not on trial here. His victims are on trial here but I would like to ask the reverent court to put an end to their unjust tribulations by pronouncing them not guilty."

Quite a few witnesses were then cross-examined showing a definite positive favour toward the defendants. The Viscount of Trencavel confirmed the deed of cession of the land and buildings, where the defendants used to live. He even demanded a large sum of money from the Bishop of Albi to be spent to resettle these people in Toulouse and Carcassonne. Peter of Vaux-de-Cernay kept fighting like a cornered animal insisting on the subject of heresy being a criminal offence punishable by death and accusing the Count of Toulouse to the Court of conspiring against the Bishop of Albi. Finally, to their great relief, the Court pronounced the defendants not guilty. General jubilation followed but not everyone was happy.

Peter Vaux-de-Cernay kept uttering open threats against the imagined conspirators and raved that their punishment was waiting for them some day in the future. Immediately after the trial though, he left the Midi in disgust to settle back in his homeland of the North, away from this foreign land filled with libertines and heretics.

Peire, helped by some good luck, seemed to have managed not to implicate Esclamonde in the trial. Fortunately, Peter Vaux-de-Cernay remained oblivious of her and of her connection with Peire and the Defendants. Otherwise the trial could have taken a very wrong turn, with unforeseen consequences. However, this secret was not entirely secure as Peire found out in a chance encounter with Foulques de Marseille in a reception held just after the trial in the palace of Raymond of Toulouse. Raymond VI wanted to celebrate the outcome of the trial and had invited all those he considered his friends and among them Foulques de Marseille.

Foulques was an impressively handsome man with subtle abilities to make himself irresistible to women and very popular with the people around him. However, beneath this attractive surface there was something as hard as steel, which at times could show through his intense hazel eyes. He came from a wealthy family of Genovese merchants who settled in Marseille and when he was young he worked in his father's business. His restless and artistic nature though, propelled him to pursue the itinerant life of a troubadour. He moved from castle to castle, singing passionate love songs to the amorous ladies of these castles who often succumbed to his charms. Azelais, the wife of Barral de Baux the Viscount of Marseille was one of them and turned out to be a fatal attraction for him. She ended up breaking his heart, which drove him into deep despair. Possibly for this reason, Foulques suddenly turned his back on his 'songs of damnation' and joined the Cistercian order of the Catholic Church. In the relatively short span of five years his unbridled ambition; coupled with his wounded pride, his unscrupulous opportunism and his calculating mind transformed him into a fanatic champion of the Catholic Church, which was obviously gaining power throughout the Christian world. He wanted to be a part of this growing power and wealth.

When Peire bumped into him, he was greeted with a broad amiable smile and a surfeit of flattering words, "I declare that you have done a marvelous job by proving the innocence of your strange friends through skilful manoeuvrings around and away from the main issue of heresy. You managed to win the wholehearted support and applause of the audience but you humiliated Peter of Vaux-de-Cernay in the process. He will never forgive you for that. He may come back to haunt you one day, or even accuse you to be a heretic. Fortunately for you he did not know that you have recently taken to wife the daughter of a Cathar leader, a Perfect, Nicetas the Greek as some people call him. The true Catholics do not particularly like both Cathars and Greeks. Cathars are considered heretics and Greeks are considered Schismatics. Nicetas happens to have both attributes."

Peire managed to hide his rising alarm and apprehension and he replied with an even tone of voice, "I was under the impression that you supported the verdict of not guilty and if this is so, why are you now revisiting this matter? Do you now feel humiliated as well? You shouldn't have because your part in the trial was impeccable and we did not clash in any way. On the contrary, you actually helped my case with your penetrating questions. And by the way my wedding was sanctified by the Catholic Church."

"It was very clever of you to do so and very surprising regarding your wife, whose father and his associates reject all sacraments. Well, love can work miracles as I used to think when I was living the troubadour life. My dear young friend you should not worry because I know your secret. It is safe with me and in any case it does not matter anymore. I have once lived where you are now and I understand you. I sense that we are very similar although our lives it seems have taken opposite directions, a Canon becoming a Troubadour and a Troubadour becoming a Canon! Still I am convinced that you have made a colossal mistake, which you are going to regret some day. You are trying to swim upstream against an overpowering current of a most powerful river, which is the Church. Perhaps there is still time to change your mind before it will be too late for you."

"Your Reverence, I am not swimming upstream against the current. I am not swimming in the river. I am walking merrily along its banks enjoying the pleasures of its running waters as I do of all the resplendent nature around me. I am still a good Catholic who respects and loves all human beings including you."

"Well put, my friend, well put. You spoke like a troubadour and as for your continued faith to the Catholic Church I will take your word for it."

Saying all that they parted ways, seemingly as friends.

The same day in the Palace of Raymond of Toulouse there was a large crowd of important people from the Southern nobility, from the rich merchant class and from the performing arts. Huddled together were the Viscount of Trencavel with the Counts of Foix and

Comminges speaking with one another in an almost conspiratorial fashion about their grievances against their host. Raymond of Toulouse approached them accompanied by William of Minerve, Raymond of Termes, Pierre Roger de Cabaret and the flamboyant troubadour Raimon de Miraval.

The two groups faced one another with barely concealed animosity bordering on hostility, until Raimon de Miraval broke the ice saying, "The boar withholds its rage against the hounds who also stop in their tracks when the wolves sneak out of the woods."

The young Raymond-Roger Trencavel shook his head in mock puzzlement and said, "It is very appropriate for a troubadour to speak in riddles as a preamble of something my uncle wants to say to us. But let me guess. We are the hounds and he is the boar and only recently I helped him trap the big bad wolf of Albi. Are there any other wolves in the woods threatening to disrupt our quarrels on so many issues and entanglements?"

"Are they ever! Our disputes are nothing compared to the miseries they have in store for us. My dear nephew I am sure we can resolve our mutual grievances amicably. We should really try to stick together! This applies to my brave neighbours of Foix and Comminges as well. I know you are vassals of Aragon but you are on this side of the Pyrenees and we should enjoy this beautiful country together, without constant skirmishes and unpleasantness. What do you say?"

"We wish we could but I am sorry to tell you this uncle, we do not trust you."

"Well, have it your way, but you will regret it. Please remember that."

Raymond of Toulouse turned to the others of his group saying, "Gentlemen, at least we have no problems between ourselves except the competitions for the best songs and musical performances of the troubadours we manage to attract to our castles. Some of them are here today such as my close friend Raimon de Miraval, the illustrious Guy de Cavaillon, the story teller Guilhem de Cabestans, the famous Peire Vidal and the youngest of all Peire Cardinal Campagnac accompanied by his wife and jongleur Esclamonde. It would be a great pity if we do not take advantage of their presence here tonight to listen to their songs and stories."

The great hall was circular with seven bays bulging around its periphery with stained glass windows and numberless slim columns soaring up to support the corresponding vaulted ceilings. A multitude of oil lamps, candles, and torches created a magical, sensuous atmosphere. The performers were moving to the centre and the audience retreated along the periphery and the bays. Men and women were dressed elegantly and some of them flamboyantly. Some of the ladies were exceptionally beautiful and were allowing glimpses of their slim legs and heaving breasts. Lasciviousness and eroticism were coiled up in the air provoking a passionate response from the troubadours. The ladies husbands were standing by them but were rarely the objects of their desire. The marriages had been arranged to serve titles and property interests so love had to be found elsewhere, such as in the troubadours' wooing songs, which often lead to their embraces. The husbands were supposed to be flattered by the attentions offered to their wives and yet certain rules had to be respected otherwise the offender could place himself in jeopardy or even mortal danger. Guilhem de Cabestans sang a canso telling the gruesome but fascinating tale of his eaten heart.

> Long ago, in the Castle of Les Baux
> Hanging over the red valley of Hades
> I set my eyes on sweet Berangere
> The most beautiful and ravishing lady.
>
> So completely I loved, with all my heart and blood
> And she so loved me too
> To taste the mysterious depths of our love
> There was nothing that we did not do

But we went too far, drowned in our joi
Were blind to the malicious lauzengier
Who turned the pride of the lord of Les Baux
Into a jealous and burning rage

Amidst the romance of fair Provence
His bare hands tore out my heart
He kept me alive as he collected my blood
To create my final work of art

Cooking my heart with the rarest herbs
Mixing my blood with his best wine
He served his wife Berangere
These delicacies that were once mine.

She begged him to tell what they were
This delicious meal that she savoured
He told her the whole gruesome tale
Of all his rage filled labours

"So sweet this meat, so pure the wine
None other shall pass my lips"
Said Berangere so eerie and calm
As she ran to the blood-stained cliffs.

She threw herself over the edge.
Falling to death and love
Merging in time eternally
With my song and my blood

But Love makes lovers live again
Continuing their dance
As I passed the gates of Roussillon
I fell once again to her trance

Seremonda our joi shook the castle walls
Without mezura we came undone
And again my heart was torn out and served
My love and I are one

And when the awful truth was revealed
Seremonda jumped the cliffs of Hades
To die and live again, as lovers do
Eternally in the dance of ages.

I heard the brave knights of Aragon
For this stormed down the mountains
Tore to shreds the Lord of Roussillon
But Love cares not for these matters

For now I love her once again
My eternal and fairest lady
But now I'll never reveal her name
To keep her safe from the valley of Hades

But how can we have the bliss of love
Without offering our whole hearts
And how could lovers forever live
Without death to part?

And if you think that I am singing
A canso, a planh or de lonh
It's a fin amor song I'm singing.
Forever and so long…

Guilhem de Cabestans let his rich voice caress, alarm and move his
audience to tears and even some of the ladies to ecstatic heights. Their
husbands who stood behind them felt the tremors in their bodies and
tried to calm them down because they had not understood what was

happening. Guilhem de Cabestans continued playing his vielle for quite some time after he had stopped singing. When his music came to an end the audience exploded into applause and gave a standing ovation.

Guy de Cavaillon and Peire Vidal came forward and embraced Guilhem with tears in their eyes. Guy de Cavaillon half-jokingly said. "You really are a supernatural creature and reverent lover. Your song is otherworldly!"

Peire Vidal, an impressive young-looking yet elderly man turned to the audience with his arm around Cabestans and said. "I was planning to charm you with my love songs but after this unique performance I refuse to compete and come in second. I am hoping that our generous hosts will give us another chance soon."

The Count of Toulouse came forward to the stage and turning to the audience said, "I am disappointed that we will not have the pleasure to hear you sing but I fully understand your vanity, my friend. Indeed, I am inviting you all this coming spring to my palace in St. Gilles. I assure you that my Provençal residence is much more pleasant than here in Toulouse and I am sure it will inspire you to play some more light and joyful songs."

There was an enthusiastic applause from everybody because St Gilles in the spring would be a wonderful place to be. Peire and Esclamonde did not join the great and famous troubadours and grandees on the central stage. They knew their place and did not yet feel sure of themselves in a competitive performance, at least until the spring. They would have plenty of time to prepare for a show to carry the audience to the high heavens, even if they had to compete against Peire Vidal.

Presently they remained enthralled by the performance of Cabestans and the razo of his song. Then Esclamonde broke the silence and said, "In our case, I feel we are safe from jealous husbands who would tear your heart out and serve it to me to eat and wash it down with your blood. A totally revolting idea anyway. And yet by being married to each other perhaps we are missing the ultimate sacrifice and ecstasy of love."

"Well you seem to forget your part of jumping from the cliff."

"Well I am safe from that too."

"Now, what if you passionately love another man and I give you his heart to eat, would you jump off a cliff?"

"I probably would from disgust! But what if you love another woman; I am not sure whether I would tear your heart out or hers. I probably would tear out both of your hearts."

"My dearest Esclamonde, we love each other so much that we do not need cannibalistic excesses in order to feel the glorious ecstasy of our passion for one another."

"My dearest Peire our love for each other is so great that I can not possibly imagine anything greater than this, but we have not been tested yet to see whether a sacrifice would be needed."

Peire and Esclamonde fell silent as they became absorbed in all these thoughts, fears and fantasies.

Footnotes of Chapter Three

1. *Canso : Lyric composition or a song.*
2. *Razo : The subject of a song.*
3. *Motz : The words of a song.*
4. *So : The music of a song.*
5. *Fin' amor : Love for a married woman of high class who might not reciprocate.*
6. *Joi : Lyric word for erotic love. Enjoyment of erotic love, orgasm.*
7. *Lauzengier : A spy, a denouncer, a slanderer, an envious individual.*
8. *Mezura : Conformity to the courteous code, moderation, staying within limits.*
9. *Planh : Lament dirge.*
10. *Amor de lonh : Love lost, love for a far away person.*
11. *Sirventes : A poem put to music dealing with social, religious and political issues and often with current news.*
12. *Tenso : Discussion or dispute in verse and music between two real or fictitious persons performed by two troubadours or a troubadour and his or her jongleur.*
13. *Trobairitza : A woman troubadour.*
14. *Trobar clus : A poem with a hidden or hermetic meaning.*
15. *Vida : A poem or a song telling the life story of a troubadour. A sort of biography.*
16. *Partimen : A lyric poem composed between two troubadours with questions and answers in the form of debate. Something like a tenso.*

Vielle player and dancer with castanets.
From a medallion Limoges 1200-1220, Copenhagen National Museum.

Next Page: Miniatues of the Troubadours Peire Vidal and Bernart
de Ventradorn

CHAPTER 4

COURTS OF LOVE

aymond of Toulouse loved St. Gilles even more than he loved Toulouse because this elegant city on the banks of the western arm of the Rhone River afforded him a splendid and comfortable palatial residence surrounded by friendly burghers and devoted nobility. He loved to spend most of his time here, where he could abandon himself completely to the refined pleasures of love and troubadour songs. Quite often he held Courts of Love in his palace, presided over by his favoured mistresses and sometimes even his wife. These Courts of Love were a cherished custom of Occitania, organized by the lords of the land where a woman was appointed as the Queen of Love and she would organize a grand festival of the nobility where poetry, song and love were celebrated. The Queen of Love presided over competitions between famous troubadours and the victors crowned by her with garlands of peacock feathers, along with rich gifts and money from the Lord of the castle. These were the most important events in Raymond's land at the time and all people of importance would come dressed in their finest silks to enjoy the music and flirtatious atmosphere.

This time though, he decided to invite all the different Courts of Love from the entire Midi to his palace. This would form one united Court, presided over by a Grand Tribunal of the most beautiful and noble ladies of Occitania. The idea was to form a Pantheon of Goddesses eager to be worshipped. They would receive praise and homage from all those who could feel the true tremor of love and express this feeling by the most convincing music and verse. Countesses, Viscountesses and ladies of high rank from Narbonne, Toulouse, Die, Orange, Romans, Les Baux, Anduze, Mairona and many other places came to St. Gilles for this grand occasion.

These Courts of Love were an explosion of colours, sounds and scents. The sensations of touch, taste and sound transported and transformed flesh and matter into spirit through ecstasy. This was now the prevailing atmosphere of the elegant and sophisticated guests who were wandering around the decadent halls and the luxuriant gardens of the St. Gilles Castle-Palace overlooking the placid and sparkling river. They talked, they joked and jested with one another flirting openly or covertly with excitement, with passion or just frivolously. They all wanted to feel and experience life and love as deeply and completely as possible, or even sometimes more than possible. They wanted to experience all the sensations and variations of love in an atmosphere of barely contained wildness and unspoken acceptance. The air had become thick as honey with the voluptuous desires and the erotic vibrations of all these men and women. They desperately needed palpable outlets, or some means of sublimated expression such as the poetry, songs and music expected from the troubadours and jongleurs. The excitement was building, as guests and troubadours alike were getting ready to do just that.

Peire Cardinal, who had been instrumental in helping to organize the festivities of the Courts of Love at St. Gilles for the last two years, was now leaning against one of the soaring pillars delicately checking his vielle and humming a tune. His preoccupation however did not make him oblivious of the burning and leering attentions of many of the guests favouring Esclamonde and even himself. Peire and Esclamonde had become used to the amorous attentions of illustrious men and women during their two years stay in the Court of Raymond of Toulouse and they had learned how to handle these exalted personages without offending them. The art of a troubadour was to create love songs without exposing or offending anybody. It was not easy and often it was very tricky. The young couple was sometimes susceptible to temptation in spite of their love and faithful devotion for one other.

This time the burning arrows were coming from large and beautiful eyes, dark as night, belonging to an exquisite presence dressed in bright red silk shimmering like fire. Her hair was black as a raven's. Her full red lips were smiling with a sweet yet wanton smile that had the feeling of a hungry tiger. This woman was so voluptuously beautiful that she seemed more than human, a spirit, or even the Goddess of Love herself. Esclamonde had noticed her too but was puzzled when she realized that the burning arrows were aimed at her and not Peire. Strangely enough she was flattered and maybe even excited by this deeply erotic call. She was disturbed. Her Cathar upbringing made her believe that she should strive for spiritual purity shunning the material world, which belonged to Belial, the evil God.

Peire had tried to persuade her that there was only one God who reigned over matter and spirit and encouraged men and all living things to transform matter into spirit. Spirit was descending into matter to give it life and Godliness. Although she was trying to understand and accept Peire's version of Christianity she was always coming back to her Cathar beliefs of two Gods, one good and one evil, and sometimes she found the evil God to be very seductive. She was sure that the beautiful lady who was eyeing her was the evil God or rather the Goddess Venus, Astarte or Belial in female form. She felt her saintly father, Nicetas, would have been horrified if he could have glimpsed inside her shifting yet passionate soul which commanded her to live her life in full. Consolamentum could wait for much later, even as late as her time of death.

Most of the Cathar believers enjoyed the pleasures of life until the last possible instant of life when they took the consolamentum as a quick purgative of their soul. Were they really purified or were they just given the consolation, the hope of forgiveness to walk lightly along the paths of the Afterlife? Nicetas was often teaching that all worldly and material enjoyments soiled the human soul, but that the degree of imparted impurity depended on the state of mind, feelings and the object of enjoyment. For instance, the enjoyment of love between pure hearts was the least damaging to the souls involved.

Nicetas loved his wife, Esclamonde's mother, passionately. He was always true to her, as she was true to him. When, after her untimely illness and death, he took the consolamentum, he was already pure enough to become a Perfect and teacher of the true Christian ways. More recently after the trial he had stayed in Toulouse for a while making musical instruments for troubadours and jongleurs. To his son-in-law Peire he gave as a present his masterpiece vielle, the sounds of which were pure and divine. Then he had moved to Fanjeu to be with his friends and spiritual leader Guilhalbert de Castres. This was in order to prepare for the onslaught of the Catholic missionaries who would try to convert them by debate and possibly by other more threatening means. Recently he had set up shop in his natal city of Narbonne, but still commuted to Fanjeu if needed. Esclamonde missed him and his guidance but in this particular moment she was glad he was far away.

Peire was deeply affected by the presence of the stunning woman in red but he did not suspect what was happening to Esclamonde. He simply wanted to impress that woman later with his performance and of course he itched to learn who she was without experiencing any turmoil inside, at least not yet.

The central stage was now occupied by the elderly but still impressive Peire Vidal who had started giving a speech as a preamble to his performance. "Before I offer homage to the noble and ravishing ladies around me I would like to thank his Excellency Raymond of Toulouse and St. Gilles for having organized and made this possible. This is the greatest gathering of all times, the gathering of all the Courts of Love! Since the days of the first troubadour, Guilhem IX of Aquitaine and in the more recent past of his granddaughter Eleanor of Aquitaine and the Viscountess Ermengarde of Narbonne there has never been such festivities as these. I call on all troubadours present to compete in earnest with the most passionate songs and the finest melodies ever heard in our wonderful land of Occitania. All the ladies here are so beautiful that I am certain that for each one of you there will be a passionate song of Fin Amor. I am sorry that good manners will not allow your names to be revealed. Each one of you, I trust, will guess which song is yours. If your consort suspects it too, let him be proud of you."

A loud and joyous round of applause stopped him for a moment, enough for him to take a breath. Then he continued with a beautiful song:

> For what I say and do
> To her, all credit be!
> She gave me art and skill
> And tender reverie.
>
> Her loveliness inspired
> The best of all my verse
> This joyous gift of song.
> Has quenched my aching thirst

Guy De Cavaillon, a grand seigneur and dear friend of Raymond VI took the stage next and played a solo on his vielle without words. The music was so sweet, yet woven with such a deep longing it made the ladies of the court cry and swoon. Obviously words couldn't describe his love and passion; nobody knew for whom he played except perhaps the one who possessed his heart and secrets.

Many troubadours and jongleurs took the stage with songs and music, or only with music like Cavaillon, and emotions were running high but no one was tired and everyone wanted more. Raimon de Miraval, Delfin d' Auvergne, Blacatz, Raimbaut de Vaqueiras, Elias Cairel, Guilhem Ademar and many others paraded in front of an appreciative audience. But the trobairitzes Clara d' Anduze, Castelloza and finally Bieiris de Romans made the greatest sensation because of their directness, their art and their beauty.

Clara d' Anduze put to song her suffering:

Oh, diminishers of youth and joy
The lauzengiers and deceitful spies
Have weighed my heart with suffering
Have made it heavy with unending sighs.

For you, whom I love more than anything
Have been banished from my side.
And since I have no hope of ever seeing you again
Of grief and loneliness, I have died.

Castelloza sang a long song to her lover trying to woo him back by complaining and most predictably did not succeed. Still, many ladies in the audience identified and sympathized with her and they showed it by a strong round of applause.

And then the bright red Goddess who had bewitched Esclamonde and captivated Peire moved to the stage with slow feline steps and sang with a voice of velvet:

My eyes are fixed on you
And I pray if it please you
True love should bring me such relief in your arms.
If it please you, most lovely of creatures,
Then give me that which all, hope and joy can bring
For in you lie my whole heart and desire
And from you unfolds all my happiness.
And because of you I'm sighing
And because of you I'm singing
And because of you my life is in your hands

Bieiris de Romans emanated sensuality and everyone felt it, secretly hoping this mesmerizing music might be sung for them. No one was quite sure where her inspiration came from, except Esclamonde, who felt it all too well. Peire felt strange but he was not sure why.

Delfin the Count of Auvergne asked Guy de Cavaillon in a whispering voice. "Who is this ravishing creature of the night? Her song is a riddle but her voice is magic. It does not rise from her chest but from her dark and moist roots from where she pulls threads of silk."

"I agree with you my lord, she is indeed a creature of the night. They say she is a witch. She is the lady of the Castle of Romans and the widow of a crusader lord. Her life is a mystery and she keeps very much to herself. No one has been able to reproach her for anything though. She has a son, a young boy named Folquet de Romans. I have heard he might become a troubadour himself one day. If he takes after her he must be quite talented.

Meanwhile, Bieiris de Romans kept on singing, rising into a crescendo of thick hot passion.

> My eyes are fixed on you
> To hold you in my frenzied power
> And draw you in the honey of my desire
> I implore you to come to me willingly
> Although I know you already wish
> The same forbidden thing from me

She managed to hold a great many of the audience in her power including Peire and especially Esclamonde, who was feeling dizzy with a lascivious drowning. Then as the song came to a glorious end among applause and approbations, Bieiris de Romans retreated in a gliding fashion and disappeared as if swallowed by the falling night. Both Peire and Esclamonde experienced a sort of panicky sense of loss. Would they ever see her again or had she vanished for good?

There was no time to ponder such feelings and thoughts because it was their turn to take the stage and perform their tenso. A vielle, a bow and a tambourine were the instruments each one of them needed with which to play their music and to accompany their songs. They were waiting until the Countess of Toulouse, Joan Plantagenet, the wife of

Raymond VI, who was presiding over the Court of Love, gave her consent for them to start. All who were present crowded around the stage as they started introducing their tenso with the vivacious music of their combined instruments without the burden of words. Then, when anticipation had reached the highest point, they started singing in turns. When one of them was singing the other was accompanying with vielle or tambourine. Peire took the first turn.

> Peire: In the valleys and the gardens
> So many flowers bloom
> Dazzling me with colors
> Singing beauty's tune.
> Like a butterfly in May
> To their sweetness I am drawn
> But to one rare flower I only go
> Who waits in the rocks alone.

> Esclamonde: If you fancy yourself a butterfly
> Just follow your heart's desire
> Leave this lily of the rocks in peace
> Kiss the flowers you so admire.
> Don't worry this lily won't wither
> Her nectar still throbs and craves
> The touch of so many butterflies
> Who paint the sky with grace.

> Peire: With mere fancy you take offence
> Yet you are so fast, so ready
> To face the dire consequence
> Though your dangerous heart excites me.
> Your impenetrable magic castle of love
> Hides so many deep secrecies
> In hidden halls and corridors
> I'm losing all my certainties.

Esclamonde: In love there are no certainties
    This prison puts love to sleep
    Love catches fire with freedom
    Though it brings us to the brink.
    The ecstasy of joi
    Is the only important thing
    And the more joi Joven brings to us
    The more love can sing.

Peire: That may be true and yet...
    There's a love that lasts forever
    Fin' Amor that makes every lady
    The object of love's desire.
    Allowing lawful partners
    To taste the blessed nectar
    Of pure loves gift of joi
    Sparked by fantasies fire.

Together: Joven seeks unbounded Joy,
    Mezura holds the balance.
    In this sacred play of our love
    With joi we sing and dance!
    Allowing each our freedoms
    To think to feel to pray
    We are alive and we are in love
    Into another day!
    Yes we are alive and we are in love
    With joi we sing and dance!
    Allowing loves sweet freedom
    To give life to our romance, lets sing and dance!

Their burning eyes locked in battle; they ended by playing their viols and tambourines together with purposeful discord, which made their music vivacious and poignant. Their innocence had been swept

59

away by the seductive demands of life swirling around them. Clouds of doubt shaded their love. Yet their passion was still burning unbearably hot exuding and demanding the release of joi.

Their performance was received with a standing ovation. Everyone in the audience found something in the razo to identify with and some were even moved to tears. Then Bieiris de Romans reappeared as suddenly as she had vanished, in a perfectly timed seductive flash of red, to congratulate them. She took both of them in her arms and kissed them on the mouth, first Peire and then Esclamonde where she lingered a little longer. They were both terribly excited by her unexpected reappearance and by her thrilling embrace. Her voluptuous body transmitted to them exquisite erotic vibrations. They were rapidly losing control of propriety and mezura.

Peire managed to say with a slightly trembling voice. "Thank you, my lady, for your kindness, but I must say, your performance put a spell on us. It was magnificent. Still, while you were singing, I had the impression that you were improvising straight from your heart. Is that true?"

"Yes, my friend, I was not only improvising but my eyes were really fixed on someone. Can you guess on whom? Can your beautiful wife guess?"

Esclamonde could certainly guess but she did not dare say it. She only kept staring at Bieiris imploringly. Bieiris put her fingers on her lips then smiled and started walking away, then half turned and said. "Perhaps, the three of us should sing together as a trio. I have a razo in my mind but it would need rehearsing in the moonlight."

The idea sounded too fantastic and unreal to Peire to respond but Esclamonde was eager to follow Bieiris anywhere and she asked gasping. "In the moonlight! You mean tonight! Where can we rehearse tonight?"

"It is not for tonight. The festivities here are not over yet and you should stay but if you still want to, I meant tomorrow night, in my private lodgings somewhere outside of here. I shall let you know."

Having said that she vanished again, leaving them together in excited wonder and anticipation about tomorrow nights promised adventure. Esclamonde mused that it was going to be an unbearably long time until tomorrow night.

The festivities continued with unabated ardour presided over by Joan the Countess of Toulouse who was receiving the amorous homage of many a troubadour and handsome knights while her husband Raymond was engaging in bold advances to receptive beautiful ladies with their escorts pleasantly occupied elsewhere. It was looking as if an orgy of love was in the making. Albas cansos, coblas, sestinas, tensos, partimens were sung and played by troubadours and jongleurs and joined in by the enraptured audience.

Now, Raimbaut de Vaqueiras was singing a descort with his husky and impressive voice using Romance, Italian, Latin, Greek and even Arabic words just for the sound of them. The razo, the meaning of his song was more felt than understood and yet the audience was moved and pleased by it, as was demonstarted by the profuse applause and cheers that filled the air.

After having received congratulations and praises Raimbaut de Vaqueiras approached Peire, took him by the arm and drew him aside from the crowd. He said. "My friend the time for you to fulfill your vows and to take the cross has come. On the 1st of September you must meet me, and others, in Orange by the Roman Arch. We will follow the Domitian Highway to cross the Alps in order to meet my lord Boniface de Montferrat and with him to join the main body of the crusaders in Venice. From there we will sail for Accra in the holy land on Venetian ships."

"Oh my! That is a very short time from now! There are so many things I have planned and need to do for both myself and for my liege Lord Raymond. I guess it can all be worked out. I am certainly happy to fulfill my vows and I'm sure Raymond will understand. I guess we shall meet in Orange then."

The reminder of having to take the cross so soon made him anxious and somewhat cooled the fervor that the whole atmosphere, and especially his encounter with Bieiris, had created. When he spoke to Esclamonde that night about the crusade, she did not seem to be able to focus as she was still under the intoxicating influence of Bieiris's aura and the heated expectation of their next encounter. That night in their quarters she needed his erotic help in order to give vent to her torturing fantasies. He helped her climax again and again but there was no end to her excruciating need. Peire was beginning to realize he could not fathom the hidden depths of Esclamonde who now appeared to him to be an entirely new person.

The next day the Courts of Love were concluding the competitions of poetry, song and music. Crowns of peacock feathers and prizes of silver and gold were distributed to the winners. Among them were Esclamonde and Peire. The festivities continued for the whole day and night because the hosts, guests and performers alike had not yet had their fill of pleasure.

It was evening and Esclamonde was looking for Bieiris everywhere but there was no sign of her. Peire was watching his wife closely and was aware of her rising agitation. Now he knew exactly what was going on in her body, her heart and in her mind because he felt it when he was making love to her the previous night. He knew that she still loved him but he was becoming aware of her need to experience the excitement of deviant pleasures. He had even started fantasizing about being a part of them. He was not intending to follow her though, unless she wanted him to. He waited patiently to see what she was going to do.

Her agitation and nervousness was coming to the breaking point when a non-descript female appeared and asked her to follow. Esclamonde turned towards Peire and beckoned him to accompany her. The female guide smiled implying consent, and all three walked away unobserved. Peire squeezed his wife's hand and whispered to her that he loved her.

The three of them walked for a while along a long corridor, then they climbed several steps, which led them to an allure behind the battlements overlooking the river where several armed guards kept watch. Their guide explained to them where they were going and they continued walking unobstructed to the end of the allure inside a round tower. Through a trap door they climbed down a spiral staircase into an inner courtyard behind soaring walls flanked by another tower with a gate, which was opened to them from inside. They climbed a few steps and after walking along another corridor they stepped into an elegantly decorated and furnished polygonal room with stained glass windows facing the river. Exotic drapes covered the walls, thick rich carpets and countless large and small cushions covered the entire expanse of the floor. Low round tables made of wonderfully carved aromatic woods were dispersed among the cushions and a most intricate chandelier hanging from a wooden ceiling illuminated this most enchanting retreat. There were many braziers, which during winter could provide warmth but presently were burning intoxicating incense and other aromatic substances. The most extraordinary thing was a round, sparkling, emerald pool, fed mysteriously by running water, right in the middle of these sumptuous surroundings. The guide asked them to make themselves comfortable while waiting for Bieiris de Romans and she disappeared.

They did not have to wait long before three scantily dressed servant girls, pretty and enticing like sylphs, approached them. Without a word they helped them out of their clothes and led them into the pool where they proceeded to wash and rub them with scented oils. They totally abandoned themselves to the tender care and caresses of the smiling nymphs, drifting into a seductive dream world woven with colours, sounds, scents, touches and tastes of unfathomable excitement. The nymphs rubbed them dry with warm scented towels and helped them into silk robes. The same or other sylphs, they could not tell, brought them delicate tid bits, fruits and red wine. They were too excited and aroused to think of eating or drinking. They only hungered for the unspeakable pleasures of love they were so eagerly anticipating.

When Bieiris arrived at last they were stunned by her naked beauty showing through her swishing silk veils, falling from her shoulders and down her ankles. She walked towards them slowly like a leopard sure of her kill and when within reach she knelt and kissed Esclamonde deeply while at the same time her long fingers were delicately groping her trembling body. Peire watched for a while transfixed and stunned, before he surrendered to his growing need and moved his body slowly along Bieiris's back and slipped inside her. She welcomed him with intensifying sighs and they made love, the three of them with complete abandon, sweetness and creative passion. Groaning, moaning and exploring the three of them ingeniously used all five senses to open heights of ecstasy and simultaneous pleasure none had experienced before. Lost in an ecstatic trance they continued through the night and into the afternoon hours of the next day when they were finally spent and ready for food, drink and conversation. The three of them slipped into the pool holding hands, savouring their lingering erotic desires and the vestiges of residual pleasures by lightly touching and kissing each other. Bieiris said, with her eyes on Esclamonde, "You know that it is you that I love Esclamonde, Peire is a mere accessory to making love with you but he proved to be a worthy giver of pleasure. I've now grown to love him too. I feel so joyous and fully sated.

I invited you here to form a singing trio and found something much better than that. I intend and hope to see more of you both in the times ahead. Joven, the inspirer of love, the rouser of desires, and the father of Eros and the giver of joi's orgasmic explosion of pleasure, has blessed the three of us with his mighty vibrant presence. I offer my thanks and worship to him or her on behalf of the three of us.

"Dear Bieiris, I love you as an extension of my love for Esclamonde who loved you the first moment she set eyes on you. But also, I must admit that I have experienced unique and indescribable sensations as I merge in so many ways with your beautiful and animated body. I would certainly look forward to repeating this experience but as I am getting ready to go on a crusade I will cherish the memory of our shared experience forever."

"I am disappointed to hear that you will be leaving soon for the crusade but at least I will be consoled by keeping Esclamonde for myself during your absence."

"Dear Bieiris, I know that my Esclamonde will be safe and happy with you during my absence and yet I am afraid that by the time I come back, if I come back, there will be no love left for me in Esclamonde's heart because you would have taken it all. Isn't that true my dearest Esclamonde, my only love?"

"Yes Peire, my love, Bieiris could have taken me away from you and may have eaten me alive with my wholehearted blissful consent. Yet strangely enough I still want to be with you for life as your wife, mistress, jongleur and companion in everything. My dearest love, Bieiris, what you have given me I know will be impossible to experience again with Peire, or anybody else. You are like a Goddess of love and I want to be with you forever, diving into pleasures and sensations that only you can give me. I am afraid though that I could easily lose myself in your magical world and disappear completely. I need my husband in order to keep my identity and sanity. Although he does not know it yet I intend to follow him on the crusade disguised as a male "jongleur".

"Esclamonde, my love, you cannot imagine how happy you make me hearing that you choose me over your strong and ardent desire for Joven's beloved daughter, the Goddess Bieiris. Since I cannot bear to leave you behind, I find your idea of following me on the crusade as my page and jongleur wonderful, although terribly risky."

"It seems to me that I am going to be a very lonely Goddess with both of you running off on a crusade and the wonderful experience we just had together becoming a beautiful fading memory. If you come back one day remember to visit me in my castle in Romans. You know, twelve years ago I followed my late husband on a crusade too, disguised as his page like you are planning Esclamonde. Isn't that strange we both had the same idea? We think and feel the same way, Esclamonde, and in some strange way we even look alike somehow. We have the same hair, like raven's feathers. We have the same hands, feet, breasts and neckline. When I make love to you it is like making love to myself. It is so uncanny and exciting. That is why I loved you at first sight and that is why I know you will come back to me one day. You cannot help it. Anyway, what was I saying? Yes, I joined a crusade under the banner of Richard Plantagenet and I saw action in Cyprus and on the coast of Syria. We had many interesting adventures together. The East is very fascinating and their music is wonderful. I became pregnant, but this joy was shattered when soon after my husband was killed in a battle with the Saracens. I managed to return home where I gave birth to my son Folquet de Romans. Did you know I have a twelve-year-old son who lives in Romans? He has all the graces and the talent of a troubadour! I never married again. I did not want to as I preferred my freedom and was more attracted to women anyway. I spend my time making beautiful things, which serve and glorify the senses. I make perfumes from flowers, herbs, woods and leaves. I sing, write poetry and play the harp and vielle. I can even make love like a Goddess, as you have now experienced. You can stay with me here in St. Gilles for another two days if you like. This is my late father's tower house, where I was born. It is adjacent to Mirapetra, Raymond's stone castle, where the festivities of the Courts of Love took place. Most likely the Count and his friends are still there having fun. You must agree though we are having more fun than them. If you like we can stay together here for two more days. Then I'll sail upstream on the river to my castle in Romans and you two can go back to where you came from. I am sure the Count and his friends will be missing you."

When Bieiris finished talking, she took Esclamonde in her arms and stroked her hair ever so tenderly like a mother would do to her daughter. Then the tenderness turned into the urgency of passion and Peire joined in the melee of timeless lovemaking. Only short intermissions of food, drink and relaxed conversation broke their sensual trance.

When they finally were back in Mirapetra, Raymond's stone castle and palace, they had been absent for four whole days. Four days, like a lifetime, they would never forget.

Medieval Love Scene (Joi)

Boniface elected as leader of the Fourth Crusade 1201.
Painting by Henri Decaisne

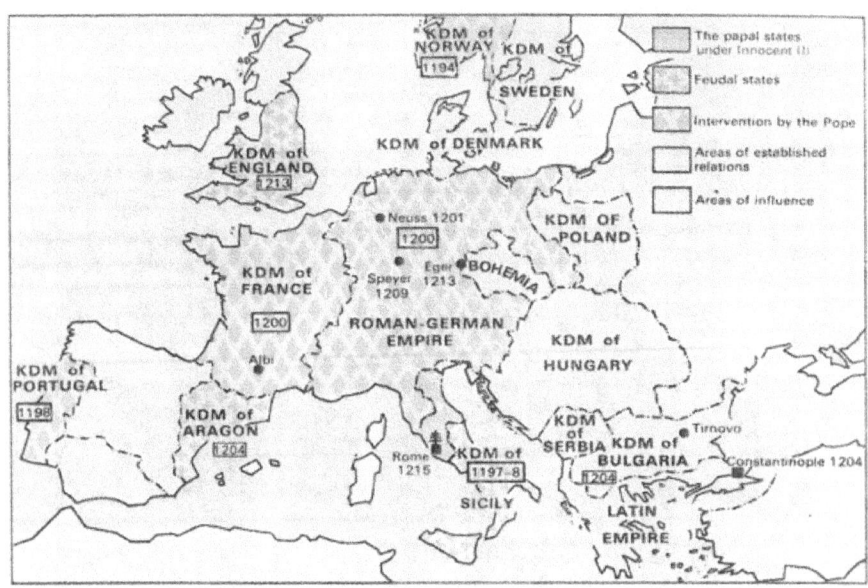

The Influence of Pope Innocent III

CHAPTER 5

A CRUSADE GONE ASTRAY

 nder the old Roman Arch by the Provencal city of Orange a multitude of knights, lesser warriors and camp followers had gathered, ready to march east on the Domitian Road, which would take them across the Alps. Boniface de Montferrat had just arrived from Soissons where he had been proclaimed the leader of the crusade. Many illustrious French, Flemish and Occitanian noblemen, knights and troubadours, followed him. The vast crowds, bearing the cross on their chests or on their shoulders, received him enthusiastically. By the side of Boniface rode the crusader troubadour Raimbaut de Vaqueiras and close behind him rode the troubadours Peire Vidal, Gaucelm Faidit Arnaut de Mareuil and Peire Cardinal de Campagnac with his handsome page and jongleur, Esclamond.

Esclamonde had been disguised, quite convincingly, as a good-looking page who carried Peire's musical instruments and attended to all his needs. Boyish, pleasant looking pages also attended other noblemen and some troubadours so she easily blended with them without attracting attention. Prominent among the crusading nobility was the dour looking Simon de Montfort, Baldwin of Flanders and the Marshal of Champagne, Geoffrey de Villehardouin. The Marshal's nephew Geoffrey and his friends Champlitte and Otto Dela Ross from Burgundy were also there, along with many more martial looking knights, like Turc de Mairrona, the husband of the trobairitz Na Castelloza. Na Castelloza loved and composed songs for the troubadour N'Arman de Brean. It was quite an eclectic crowd of warriors, artists, adventurers and lovers who gathered in the shadows of the Roman Arch getting ready to travel east. A crusade in those days was not just a fanatical religious war designed to take back the holy land from the Saracens. Though officially it was just that. Underneath it was also a grand adventure, an excuse to see the world, to learn, travel and especially to many, a way to pocket some wealth.

The crusaders had set up camp around the Roman Arch with their multi-coloured tents, banners and shining armour filling the luscious countryside with additional splendour. The sounds of knights practicing, laughter and song could be heard in the spacious red and silver tent of the crusade's leader, Boniface de Montferrat, where an important meeting of the magnates was in process. They were presently discussing the important matters of transportation and financing of the enterprise. An embassy from Venice, led by Marino Dandolo had arrived to offer proposals of the rich Republic concerning these crucial issues. Marino was the nephew of the Doge of Venice Enrico Dandolo and he was empowered to speak on his behalf. After intense deliberations he convinced the crusaders to march against the Dalmatian City of Zara in exchange for their transportation to the holy land. Zara was a dangerous maritime competitor of Venice but the crusaders could easily eliminate it. The crusaders needed Venice's help quite badly so they agreed to make this small diversion, which could also prove quite profitable for them.

Only one of the warlords objected vehemently to this diversion, the grim giant Simon de Montfort. "I remind you all that our purpose here is to liberate Jerusalem from the infidels and not to attack Christian cities, for profit. If we start doing that we will become a menace to the Christian World and we will surely lose our souls in the process."

Baldwin the Count of Flanders stood up and said. "My brave friend, we all here understand and share your pious objection but you obviously do not know that Zara is the hiding harbour and launching place of godless pirates who prey on Christian ships and Christian coastal towns and villages. Please do not waste your sympathy for such people. By subduing them we are becoming the Champions of Christianity and at the same time we earn our passage to the holy land."

"Well, for now I must take your word for it, but if I find out that Zara is a normal Christian city I will not be a part of this crusade."

Simon de Montfort was a formidable and experienced warrior and the leaders of the crusade felt they needed him, as his departure would decrease their strength and most importantly would have damaged the moral content of the enterprise. They were relieved that he decided to stay, at least for the moment.

Peire who was near the scene was saying to Esclamonde. "Although I tend to agree with this Simon de Montfort I cannot help feeling apprehensive about him to the point of getting goose bumps."

"My feelings are even stronger. I am terrified of him. He looks like an executioner."

Marino Dandolo, a tall and strapping young man nearly thirty years old, who happened to be near enough to overhear them said; "He is not that bad. He is a valiant warrior of renown, but he is one of those self-righteous Northerners of inflexible piety who are unable to understand the dire necessities of life."

"And I guess these necessities of life include our needs for money and for the means of transportation which your mighty city can provide to us in exchange for our mercenary services."

"Yes, you could put it that way. My city would not have become mighty if she were in the habit of giving away her services for free and by letting opportunities slip away."

"Is this Zara really a hideout of pirates as the Count of Flanders claimed; obviously instructed by yourself."

"You seem quite astute for your age and for your profession as a troubadour and a poet. Zara is in fact a lair of pirates but most importantly it is damaging the commercial interests of Venice and is too close to us for comfort. Sooner or later we would have to deal with Zara; better sooner than later and this crusade is the opportunity we were looking for."

"Would you join this crusade after Zara is dealt with?"

"Most likely I will. My uncle the Doge of Venice, Enrico Dandolo, has ambitious investment plans for this enterprise."

"You call this crusade an enterprise?"

"Yes, for Venice, all crusades are enterprises. That's how Venice has become great and wealthy."

"What kind of people are you, Marino Dandolo, who are investing in the Christian fervour and sacrifices of others in order to amass wealth and power?"

"We are gentlemen merchants who value our lineage and know how to take advantage of opportunities. I'm sure this combination will help us last for many generations to come. We know how to deal with realities. Stick with me and you will learn something more than just scholarship and poetry."

The following day the crusaders broke up camp and moved forward along the Domitian road. They began by heading south and then west towards the Maritime Alps passing through or around Avignon, Aix, Nice, Savona and Genoa. Within two weeks they were camping by the Adige River outside of Verona to await instructions from Venice. Verona had grown wealthy and powerful by taking advantage of the heavy traffic of people and goods between Germany and Italy. All the German emperors with their armies were advancing or withdrawing to and from Italy stopping by Verona, making it wealthier with every passage. Verona was also closely associated with Venice and its commercial activities. At the time Ezzelino da Romano was the Lord of Verona, making sure it remained prosperous.

Also in Verona lived Renier, the brother of Peire's father Gaucelm de Campagnac. Renier had become wealthy as a merchant and administrator. He belonged to both the city nobility and the merchant class, which was quite normal in Italian city-states like Verona. Peire's uncle Renier, who was absolutely delighted to have them visit his tower house, received Peire and Esclamonde very warmly.

"My dear nephew, as soon as you come back safely from this crusade, you should stay with me and help me with my commercial activities. It is quite prosperous here and you would love all the culture

Verona has to offer. Since I have no children of my own I would treat you as my very own son."

"My uncle, thank you very much for your kind offer, I am happy to know that I can always find a place with you here in time of need. For the present I am on a leave of absence from the service of the Count of Toulouse, Raymond VI, and after the crusade I intend to join him."

"From what I hear the Count of Toulouse is pursuing his pleasures in the midst of troubles with his vassals and worse with the Church. He has been accused of protecting heretics and Pope Innocent III has fixed a baleful eye on him. Our patrimony of Campagnac might fall into evil times in the near future with all these conflicts and turmoil around it. I am only hoping to be proved wrong in time and that you will carry on a happy and creative life in the beautiful country of our origins. If things go bad though, there will always be a place for you and for your family here. Now, concerning this crusade, I am hearing many strange and disturbing rumours about it. An exiled Prince of the Eastern Roman Empire has been visiting the German Emperor asking him to help regain the throne of Constantinople for his imprisoned father and himself by overthrowing the present emperor there. His name is Alexios Angelos. From what I hear he is a loudmouth and schemer who over-emphasizes his situation making promises he cannot keep. The German Emperor referred him to the leaders of the crusade just to get rid of him. Boniface de Montferrat, an impressionable man, seems to be paying heed to his reckless proposals, which more or less are to divert the present crusade to Constantinople. I am sure the crafty old Doge of Venice, Enrico Dandolo, would secretly encourage the crusaders to satisfy the foolish wishes of Alexios Angelos. You see, when a frog invites the stork to help him against another frog the stork will gulp down both frogs and become the master of the pond, rewarding himself by eating all remaining frogs. I understand this is a Greek fable from which the Greeks have obviously not yet learned a thing!"

Peire was left wondering whether he should continue with a crusade that might go astray, or to take Esclamonde and turn back to

Raymond of Toulouse and Bieiris of Romans in the merry land of love and songs. His vows to take the cross could certainly not hold him bound if this crusade would not ever reach the holy land. He talked to Esclamonde about it but she wanted to continue as she was more taken by the spirit of adventure rather than concerns about his vows and other such ethical questions. Deep inside he was similarly inclined so finally they both decided to follow the crusade no matter what happened.

A few days later the crusaders were transported southeast by Venetian ships to the rocky coast where the maritime city of Zara was perched behind strong walls and towers. Red crosses were painted on the ramparts to remind the crusaders that Zara was a Christian city and thereby deter and shame the attackers. Embassies had come from the King of Hungary to whom the city of Zara belonged to protest the attack on his city but to no avail. Even Pope Innocent III, the mastermind of the crusade, dispatched an emissary ordering the crusaders to desist from harming the Christian people of Zara. He was ignored and told that they were not Christians but godless pirates preying on Christians and Christian ships. Siege engines were set up, and after repeated and furious attacks the city was taken. The inhabitants were slaughtered so thoroughly that no one was left alive to declare whether they were Christian or not, pirate or not. All evidence was wiped clean and Zara became a Christian city under the ruling power of Venice.

Pope Innocent III, who was a stickler for legalities, issued excommunications to a few of the Venetian leaders, including the octogenarian Doge Enrico Dandolo just for appearances. These were lifted soon afterwards when some specious explanations were given and grants were made for the Church. The booty was plentiful and the crusaders were gratified that the enterprise was proving to be so profitable so soon. Their appetite was now whetted for more pickings and more blood and carnage ahead.

Peire, carried away by the general mood, sang an old song by Bertrand de Born, a troubadour of the last century,

Maces and brands and painted helms,
Escutcheons hacked and stabbed with holes,
All this we'll see when battle joins,
And many a baron trading blows.

Horses in panic flee,
Their masters dead or wounded.
And in the fury of the fray
Valiant knights rewarded

With savage toll of heads and limbs,
Ransom blood and spoils
Preferring death to life in chains
Our valiant blood it boils

The bystanders joined in and repeated the last strophe with hoarse fury and one of them was Simon de Montfort, whose valour and war skills had been crucial for the capture of Zara. This forbidding and dour man obviously had a soft spot for certain songs and particularly those of the warlike troubadour Bertrand de Born. His momentary elation, however, was fated to change soon when he joined the meeting that had already started in the main hall of Zara's municipal palace.

The imposing octogenarian Doge of Venice Enrico Dandolo was speaking, "Noble companions-in-arms and dear friends I congratulate you and thank you on behalf of Venice for your great success of rescuing the City of Zara from barbarity and delivering it to civilization. Such a deed is sometimes as holy as the Christianization of a Saracen city. Furthermore, it was quite profitable to do so. You have earned your fare for your next destination, which could be Accra in the holy land, unless you are ready for another immensely profitable stop over."

There was a stir in the audience of crusaders raised by the greedy excitement of the majority and the angry apprehension of the small minority. Among the latter was Simon de Montfort who nevertheless kept quiet, waiting for Enrico to finish.

Dandolo took stock of the crowd's reaction and continued, "I understand you are eager to do battle with the whole Saracen World in the holy land and you will in time after you have become wealthier and have obtained reinforcements. This will increase your chances to win the holy land. We have been promised a fabulous wealth if we stop over in Constantinople to reinstate Isaac II and his son Alexios on the imperial throne, which is rightfully theirs, and expel the usurper Alexios III Angelos. We Venetians are in a position to know that Alexios III is a corrupt, foolish and weak emperor with faltering support. Valiant warriors such as you will have very little trouble in accomplishing this absolutely just and relatively easy venture. The Most Serene Republic of Venice will cover all your traveling expenses. As soon as Isaac II and Alexios IV are reinstated as Emperors of the Eastern Roman Empire we will receive 200,000 marks of silver which is a fabulous sum of money."

A round of applause and enthusiastic shouts filled the air as soon as this immense reward was spelled out. Enrico Dandolo continued," And for those who doubt our intentions to continue with our crusade to the holy land, I can reassure you that we will continue after getting reinforcements from the Greeks and the Bulgarians. With these reinforcements our success in the holy land will be assured."

At this point Simon de Montfort stood up and shouted. "You are weaving webs of disgusting deceit, old man. I do not believe anymore that you even intend to reach the holy land. Your intentions seem to be to pillage Christian Cities by diverting our pious energy and resources. You are deceiving our Christian faith. I am not going to be a part of this hideous deception! I warned your accomplices back in Orange that I would abandon a crusade which is no longer a crusade but a pillaging expedition." The other leaders of the crusade tried hard to change his mind but he ignored them and marched off in disgust.

Simon's retinue and a few others, who also shared his views, followed him to return to their homelands, mainly in Northern France.

A few others like Samplitte and the young Villehardouin decided to reach the holy land by themselves, for they did not want anything to do with another diversion but were determined to fulfill their holy mission. The bulk of the massive crusading army enthusiastically embraced this new adventure and soon set sail for Constantinople. The Venetian ships carried over 20,000 crusaders, complete with their horses, weapons, equipment and supplies around the Greek peninsula. They sailed between countless ethereal islands, which seemed to beckon to Peire and Esclamonde like nymphs of the sparkling blue sea.

They stopped at Karystos on the island of Evia to hold a council of war. There they decided to divide the fleet into two. A large fleet would sail directly for Constantinople under Enrico Dandolo. A smaller fleet under Boniface de Montferrat, who had with him Alexios Angelos, would go to the wealthiest islands to demand tax money and submission to the new Emperor. They started at Andros and Chios. After they completed their mission they joined Enrico in Scutari, which faced Constantinople across the Straits of Bosporus.

The great city was indeed a wondrous sight; behind the red brick walls the golden domes, marble palaces and ornate arches appeared suspended above a wispy mist. It struck the hearts of the beholders with admiration and covetous animosity. The capital of Eastern Christianity was reputed to have accumulated fabulous treasures over the centuries. So far no invader had ever succeeded in entering and taking possession of them. From what they had heard from Enrico Dandolo and by the looks of the pretender to the throne Alexios Angelos, who did not inspire any respect at all, Constantinople and the Eastern Empire with all its treasures was ripe and ready to fall into their lap. Alexios III, the Emperor inside the city, who was the uncle of the pretender to the throne Alexios Angelos outside the city, tried to buy out the crusaders by offering huge amounts of silver marks. His offer was ignominiously rejected. Instead, a redoubtable war galley was rowed back and forth under the walls of the Voukoleon palace, the residents of Alexios III Angelos, in the sea of Propontis.

On the deck of the galley stood the younger Alexios. Enrico Dandolo and Boniface de Montferrat flanked him while Peire and Esclamond were behind them singing an aggressive sirventes as loudly as they could.

> Worthless knaves stop your strutting
> Our brave hearts hold no terror
> Stop ruffling up your feathers
> And behold your lawful Emperor.

They sang it in Romans, in Italian, in French and in Greek so that those inside and the insurgents outside the walls could understand. On July 5, 1203 the fleet attacked the sea walls and towers. The suburb of Galata, across the Golden Horn inlet, was taken. The fleet invested the city along the Golden Horn and Propontis. The land forces concentrated mainly against the northwestern walls under the Imperial Palace of Vlachernae. At first a combined Greek and Varangian force, under Theodore Laskaris managed to check the crusaders' land attack. Later Alexios III lost his nerve and shamelessly ran away, precipitating a rout of his army.

Alexios III was one of the most hated and despised men of power of all time. Ten years earlier he had blinded his own brother Isaac II in order to usurp his throne. Ever since he had continuously and cruelly suppressed, dispossessed and overtaxed his helpless subjects, while scheming constantly against his adversaries. At this crucial moment of battle he secretly decided to top his cowardly life by collecting his valuables and fleeing under the cover of night, through the Golden Gate, which was not yet invested by the crusaders. He simply vanished into thin air, not daring to ever show his face again. Unfortunately for the Greek Empire, these despicable traits circulated in the blood of the Angeli family. The claimant to the throne turned out to not be any better.

On July 18, 1203 Isaac was let out of prison and his son Alexios was invited sit on the throne in the city as Co-Emperor with Isaac II.

The leaders of the crusade informed Pope Innocent III of the successful conclusion of the enterprise and of the imminent union of the two churches under the primacy of the Pope. This development surely appeased Pope Innocent III who had been angry, particularly with the Venetians, that had led this holy crusade astray.

Now, Alexios IV saw his dream come true. Though the realization of this dream turned out to be a nightmare. Not only for him but also for the people of Constantinople and for the once mighty Eastern Roman Empire. Alexios IV was unable to fulfill his exorbitant promises. He only managed to collect a portion of the money he had promised by extortion and outright robbery, thus earning the hatred of his former supporters and of the whole population. His plans to subjugate the Orthodox Church to the Pope were met with violent resistance by everyone without exception. This pusillanimous, incompetent and foolish man had put himself between the hammer and the anvil. He had tried desperately to extricate himself through procrastination and persuasion, but he couldn't get away with it.

In November 1203 the crusaders sent Peire Campagnac and Conon de Bethune to demand the immediate fulfillment of all the agreements.

Peire Campagnac spoke first. "Your Majesty, the leaders of the crusade empowered us to remind you of your obligations to the Republic of Venice and to all the crusaders which are the immediate payment of 150,000 marks of silver and the union of the Churches. Obviously, we have kept our part of the bargain to place you on the throne. We demand your immediate compliance with the terms of our agreement."

Alexios IV retorted with suppressed anger "I have given you 50,000 marks of silver, which is more than enough for your help. I regained my throne by the efforts of my countrymen and not by your efforts. Although I am for the union of the Churches, I have tried my best but cannot make it happen as soon as Pope Innocent III wishes."

"Your Majesty, I am surprised to hear you saying that you intend to repudiate our agreement. I beg you to reconsider because otherwise you will face very unpleasant consequences."

"I am not afraid of your implied threats because you could also face worse consequences yourself."

At that point Conon de Bethune, red in the face from his rising anger shouted, "My colleague has been more polite than you deserve but Enrico Dandolo instructed me, in case you should become reluctant to fulfill your commitments, to tell you this 'We pulled you out of shit once and back to shit we will drop you for your ingratitude.' Your majesty, please take this statement as a declaration of war."

Peire and Conon left Alexios livid with anger and trembling with fear. He did not even realize how much his fear was justified. Enrico Dandolo knew from the start that this foolish man would not be able to keep his promises and so he would have the excuse he needed to take Constantinople by force. Indeed this was always his secret purpose, to take the mighty Constantinople for the glory of Venice.

The siege started with the crusaders closing in with their ships along the Golden Horn and Propontis, the land forces stretching from Vlachernae to the Gate of Sylivria. Alexios was paralyzed with fear. Although the crusaders were suffering from a very severe winter and a lack of food, he was not able to repulse them.

Peire and Esclamonde suffered along with the others in their own private quarters in the Latin town of Galata. They were always part of Boniface de Montferrat's retinue and enjoyed some small privileges, together with Raimbaut de Vaqueiras and a few other troubadours. The most important of these privileges was that they could enjoy some privacy, at least during the night. Two people knew about the disguise of Esclamonde but understood and kept silent. Boniface de Montferrat was one and the other was Raimbaut de Vaqueiras. Although they secretly desired the beautiful jongleuritza they did not take advantage of the opportunities offered during the campaign but instead had managed to transform their amorous inclinations into a paternal affection and protectiveness towards both Esclamonde and Peire.

The two men were highly respected for their military skills, their bravery and their moral and social conduct. Vaqueiras was also idealized for his entertaining, heroic and political sirventes, which inspired Peire. Peire and Esclamonde themselves were also gaining popularity among the crusaders for their entertaining performances. Yet they were also gaining some notoriety for their bravery during the frequent skirmishes outside the walls of Constantinople. The legal and scholarly training of Peire made him useful to the leaders of the crusade for secretarial and diplomatic work, such as his recent mission to Alexios IV Angelos. Geoffrey de Villehardouin, one of the leaders of the crusade and also a scholar, had often employed Peire's services for his chronicles on the 4th Crusade. All of these connections and activities formed a protective shield around the young couple, who otherwise would have been exposed to the various appetites and challenges of an uncouth and often murderous mob of crusaders.

January 1204 was freezing cold and miserable for the besiegers and besieged alike. The difference was that there was optimism outside the walls of the city while despair and anger grew inside. The optimism was often crowned with heroic and satirical sirventes, while the despair and anger were culminating into riots.

Peire remembered the fable of the stork and the frogs. His uncle Renier had accurately predicted the current situation. He composed a satirical tenso, which he performed with Esclamonde, in front of the leaders of the crusade in Boniface's residence. They switched over from stork to frogs and back making everybody laugh uproariously including Enrico Dandolo, even though he recognized himself as the stork. While they were singing and laughing someone came in running to announce that the rioting Populace of Constantinople had deposed Alexios IV and placed Alexios V, Murjuflos, on the throne.

"Who is he and what happened to Alexios and Isaac Angeli?" Asked Baldwin of Flanders. The messenger, who was Marino Dandolo, replied. "He was a general and a relatively good fighter. His real name is Alexios Doukas but because he scowls a lot they call him, Murjuflos, the scowler. As for Alexios and Isaac, God forgive their sins, they were murdered."

Boniface de Montferrat crossed himself and said humorously. "Well the new Emperor will have ample cause to scowl a lot from now on."

"I guess he will," said Enrico Dandolo and continued, "Now, this is another frog I have to gulp down. I hope there will be no others because I do not particularly like eating frogs."

There was loud laughter from all present, but Enrico Dandolo signalled for silence and continued. "Let us be serious because we have a lot to do in order to take Constantinople. Today is January 25 1204. By the end of March, at the latest, we will have finished the new siege engine towers and special ladders. By mid-April we must take this city."

The walls along the Golden Horn were not very high and had also been damaged during the operations against Alexios III the previous year. Under these walls the Venetian ships were so closely arranged that they were forming a solid platform. The besieged, no matter how hard they tried, could not burn or damage them in any way because the crusaders had protected them with wet hides, which were almost impossible to burn.

On April 12 smoke canisters were catapulted to the ramparts creating a thick and suffocating smokescreen along the whole length of the city walls. Many of the defenders stepped back, blinded and choking and those who tried to stand fast couldn't see what was coming. Ladders were suddenly lifted from the floating platform to hook firmly on the ramparts. A multitude of fierce crusaders climbed the ladders jumping on and surprising the blinded and confused guards. They were hacked to bloody pieces by all the frenzied insurgents and the survivors retreated in panic.

The tall figure of Enrico Dandolo could be seen on the largest galley directing the operations by shouting orders and gesturing sharply to everybody around him. This man, who was over 80 years old, commanded such a demonic energy that all the crusaders were inspired to move forward and do his bidding. Those who scaled the Golden Horn walls quickly climbed down on the other side and opened some of the gates to let the mounted crusaders into the city before the smoke cleared. The mounted crusaders rushed through the cobbled streets like demons, pursuing combatants and non-combatants without mercy. Boniface de Montferrat and his knights and sergeants galloped towards the Great Church of Saint Sophia and the Great Palace of Voukoleon. Raimbaut de Vaqueiras, Peire de Campagnac and Esclamonde galloped with them. When they reached the grounds of Saint Sophia an unbelievably obscene spectacle awaited them. A large number of crusaders had arrived before them and were in the process of slaughtering a crowd of men, women and children who were trying to find sanctuary inside the great church. The poor citizens seeking sanctuary in Saint Sophia couldn't conceive that the crusaders were already inside beheading, dismembering and disembowelling with satanic pleasure. Obviously, the Catholic crusaders were not observing the sanctuary of the Church. They convinced themselves it was not valid for schismatic Greeks in a schismatic Greek Church. Boniface, who was a chivalrous and honourable man was thoroughly appalled and he shouted orders to stop the carnage but the crazed demons continued the orgy of bloodshed without paying any attention to him.

Boniface understood that he was powerless to interfere and continued with some of his knights and soldiers towards the Great Palace of Voukoleon in the hope of saving some people and salvaging any treasures they could find intact. Other of his men joined their comrades in Saint Sophia for profit and the pleasure of slaughter.

Fortunately, Boniface was the first to arrive at the Palace and the few Varangian and Greek guards left admitted him with relief. There he discovered, hidden and terrified, two beautiful and regal looking women. Amazingly it turned out one was the widow of the late Isaac II, Margaret of Hungary. The other, perhaps even more amazingly, was the widow of the late Emperors Alexios II and Andronicus I, Agnes Capet, who was also the sister of Philip Augustus the King of France. Naturally he offered these two important women his protection and managed to calm them down with his kindness and affability. Both women were still young and beautiful enough to excite the desire of a handsome womanizer like Boniface. Margaret, the daughter of the

King of Hungary Bella IV, responded whole-heartedly to his chivalrous and amorous attentions and an erotic rapport quickly grew between them. This was a relief for Anna-Agnes who had been the mistress of Theodore Vranas after the violent death of her last husband the Emperor Andronicus I in 1185. Theodore Vranas, acting as her protector, was there with her and took the opportunity to ask Boniface to stand as his best man in their long delayed wedding.

Boniface agreed and looking meaningfully at Margaret he said. "It seems to me that we will be looking forward to two weddings as soon as Saint Sophia is cleared up and turned into a Catholic church."

Theodore Vranas nodded submissively. Margaret, shaking with emotions, that were quickly turning from fear into joy, said, "My Lord, if by your gallant statement you are asking me to marry you, I gladly accept."

Boniface knelt and kissed her hand passionately and then turning around he said in a serious voice, "Raimbaut de Vaqueiras and Peire de Campagnac please be my witnesses to the official proposal of marriage I am making to the graceful Lady Margaret of Hungary. Since I must return to complete the conquest of Constantinople I would also ask you to stay with my future wife and Agnes of France to protect them during my short absence. I will leave behind many of my knights to guard this palace against any insurgents. I am sure Theodore Vranas and his men will have ample reason to defend the palace as well."

He galloped away with the rest of his knights towards the Palace of Vlachernae at the northwest corner of the city, where he expected to find Enrico Dandolo and the other leaders of the crusade. He purposely avoided passing through the grounds of Saint Sophia because he couldn't stand the shameful and horrid sight of the wanton slaughter, which was still on going. However, as he was traversing the city from the southeast to the northwest corner he was not spared the frequent and disgusting lurid scenes of bestial atrocities. Many crusaders were cutting throats or strangling their victims while performing sexual acts of unimaginable perversity on them. The gutters were overflowing with blood and assorted pieces of human flesh to the point that the streets had become very slippery for pedestrians and horses alike. In the looting and pillaging of palaces and churches, stores and houses of the rich and poor, a large number of the city's populace of have-nots, of the dispossessed and of the downtrodden had joined in with the disgusting ugly mood of vengeance. Boniface and his knights, feeling sickened by all this, studiously avoided being involved unless provoked and rode on until they finally reached the fortified palace of Vlachernae.

As they entered the Great Hall of the Palace they saw Enrico Dandolo, Baldwin of Flanders, Geoffrey de Villehardouin and the other leaders of the crusade in the process of debating the division of the spoils and the high offices of the Eastern Roman Empire.

Boniface de Montferrat faced them all and said. "Are you aware of the atrocities being committed right now against unarmed citizens unnecessarily? All resistance has melted away and Constantinople is ours. Why are our Christian soldiers killing innocent Christian women and children? And if you do not care about the killing of innocent people surely you should care about the loot taken away from us in such an uncontrollable fashion."

Geoffrey de Villehardouin stood up and said. "I must remind you that according to our custom a conquered city can be left to the mercy of the conquerors for three days and three nights. We must allow this to continue for another whole day. We must somehow take revenge for 1182 when Andronicus slaughtered our own people mercilessly in Constantinople. You must remember this since even your own brother Renier and his wife were among the victims."

"I know very well what happened then but I also know that the Sicilian Normans exacted a suitable retribution by sacking Salonica in 1185. If we are going to govern this city we should not exterminate all its population because we cannot just replace it all with Catholics. We must stop the killings and the looting right now!"

Enrico Dandolo interjected by saying. "I think that the Schismatic Greeks deserve what they are getting but we should not allow the common soldier to get rich at our expense. We must order all knights and soldiers to deposit their loot at the Hippodrome so that we can redistribute it in the proper way"

In the end it still took a whole day to stop the violent chaos and return the city to a semblance of proper and orderly ways. At least a good portion of the loot was deposited in the Hippodrome and it was redistributed with the lion's share taken by Dandolo and the other Venetian magnates.

In the same way the whole Empire was divided up. Again, the crusaders who were indebted to Venice were forced to cede the largest share to them. Venice had been controlling everything from the start and had now become the Emperor maker and the beneficiary of the whole enterprise.

Boniface de Montferrat was the obvious choice to become the new Emperor but he was too popular, too capable and his seat of power too close to Venice. This made him too much of a perceived threat to the Venetians to be chosen. Instead, the mediocre Baldwin of Flanders was crowned Emperor. Boniface was surprised and very disappointed but was consoled by being instated as the King of Salonica.

Before Boniface left for his new Kingdom he organized brilliant festivities to celebrate his marriage to Margaret of Hungary. The wedding took place in the splendid church of Saint Sophia together with the marriage of Agnes of France and Theodore Vranas. Both weddings were officiated by the new Catholic Patriarch of Constantinople Thomas Morozini. Thomas was another Venetian appointed by Enrico Dandolo and only later, after the fact, was he accepted by Pope Innocent III. In the end, the cleverest Pope of all time was outwitted by the craftiest person since the time of Ulysses.

The joint celebrations and wedding festivities took place in the Great Palace of Voukoleon. There was music and song from the famous troubadours and their jongleurs who had accompanied Boniface de Montferrat in this 4th Crusade. Raimbaut de Vaqueiras and Peire Cardinal had their day performing together and separately. They sang cansos in praise of love for Agnes and Margaret. They sang sirventes to glorify the bravery and magnanimity of Boniface and the

Ulyssian cunning of Enrico Dandolo. All these wonderful and heartfelt celebrations were a very stark contrast to the background of horrifying suffering and devastation in the once glorious and proud Constantinople.

Esclamonde was overcome with sadness amidst the general jubilation and had retired to a balcony overlooking the Sea of Marmara where the sun was setting in the West. Feelings of disgust for all she had recently experienced watching the great Constantinople fall combined with nostalgia, for her country, her father and Bieiris. She was also feeling many unsettling premonitions about the future, which invaded her whole being, troubling her deeply. Having to experience the most horrifying dark and satanic actions of men in the name of the Church tore at her heart knowing what her people were facing at home. She ached for her father's reassurance but only felt intense concern for his safety. It felt as if everything she knew was crumbling around her and this grand victory she had been a part of did not feel like a victory at all. It felt instead like a much bigger evil march of power, destroying all in its path. Silent tears streamed down her cheeks as she fell into deep and complex emotions.

Over the next two years Peire spent his time helping to rebuild the new city and its political infrastructure. It took a lot of delicate work to keep everything in order and Peire's particular skills were needed once more. He worked alongside Geoffrey de Villehardouin administering the city and fighting many skirmishes with the Greeks, who never fully capitulated. They created a new center for themselves in Nicea. Peire's favourite activity during this time, though, was helping Geoffrey work on writing his chronicles about the fall of Constantinople. There truly was a lot to do to complete all the tasks at hand. Esclamonde did not take much of a part in all these activities and became withdrawn during this period. She continued to support Peire and love him deeply in private but she could never feel comfortable in this foreign land, which had been taken so violently. Esclamonde longed for her homeland, longed for her father, longed to feel the purity of a love she felt she had lost witnessing such atrocities. Recently Esclamonde had a new reason, which was much greater than nostalgia to want to return home. Peire, who had noticed her moody behaviour of late asked. "Esclamonde, my love, what is preoccupying you these days? You are withdrawn and don't even accompany me to perform anymore."

"Peire, it is time for us to go home. A new life is starting in my womb and we must take care of it." She burst into unstoppable tears. Peire held her tenderly and whispered, "Oh my love, this is wonderful news! It will be ok, do not worry. This is a great reason for us to end this bloody crusade and return home."

Bertran De Born, Troubadour of War

Attack on Zara.

The Second Conquest of Constantinople, by Domenico Tintoretto1580-1605

Conquest of Constantinople by the crusaders in 1204. Miniature from a
French illustrated manuscript, 15th century

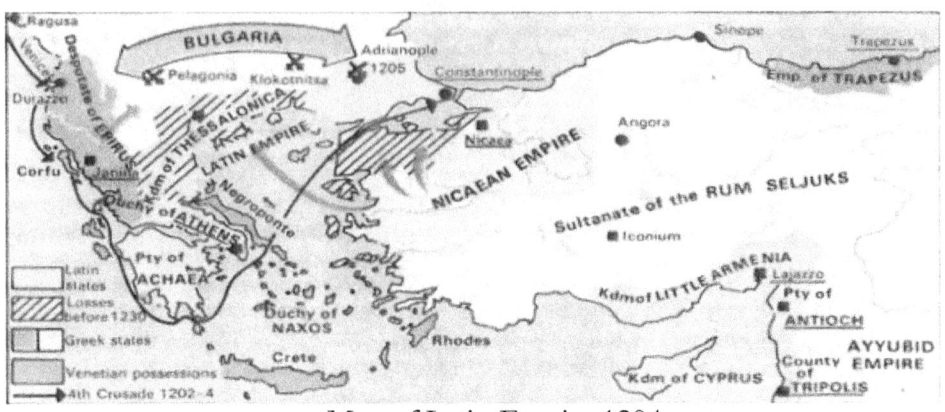

Map of Latin Empire 1204.

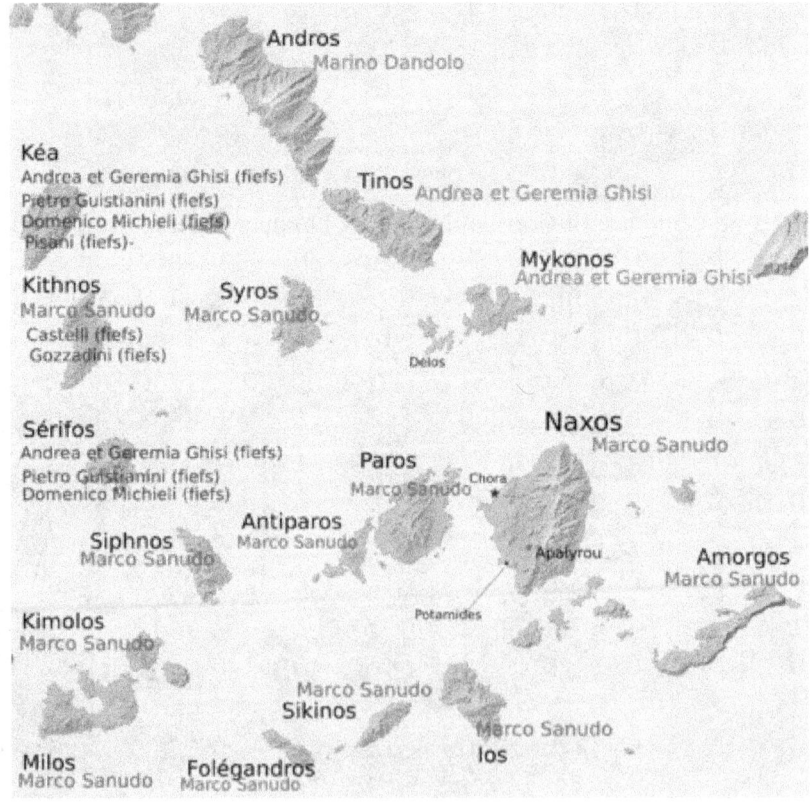

Andros and the islands of the Duchy of Naxos.

CHAPTER 6

A STOPOVER ON ANDROS

arino Dandolo was getting ready to set sail to the island of Andros, which was assigned to him by his uncle Enrico Dandolo and the High Council of Venice. He would have to take possession of it by force or by peaceful means depending on the mood of the inhabitants. He was to be accompanied by his brother Marco Dandolo, his friend Giacomo Querini, the quarrelsome cleric John and the scheming Jeremiah Ghizi. After some negotiating Peire managed to free himself of his obligations so that he could join them. Both Peire and Esclamonde were offered passage on Marino's ships. They would get to stop over on this purportedly beautiful island before continuing with Querini to Venice. From Venice, it would be easy to travel by road to Verona and then on to the domain of Raymond VI of Toulouse.

The weather was good that June and a mild breeze from the North East filled the sails of the seven galleys gliding across the sparkling blue Aegean Sea, carrying them effortlessly to their destination of the island of Andros. The mountain flanks of Andros, brown with patches of green, were sighted, giving at first no indication of a safe bay to anchor.

Peire was on the bridge of the ship talking to Marino Dandolo as they were gazing at the rugged coast.

"This island looks quite arid and desolate from here. A poor prize for your valour and position, why are you so keen to possess it?"

"My friend, appearances deceive sometimes. In this case, you will be shocked when you discover the paradise that is hidden behind this rugged coast. There are lush green valleys filled with fruit trees and vineyards that are watered by countless fountains of the most pure water you can imagine. Most importantly, there are endless groves of mulberry trees, which feed millions and millions of busy silkworms. The native Greeks are industrious and possess the skill to produce silk materials of superior quality, which can fetch high prices in Venice, Verona, Narbonne, Toulouse, Paris, London and elsewhere in the West. We Venetians have the means to transport these valuable products safely to the most lucrative markets and sell them at the highest profit. The Greeks of the Eastern Empire kept the secret of making silk to themselves for six hundred years until the Sicilian Normans extracted it from them by force sixty years ago. They had appointed Richard de Linghev, a Narbonese nobleman, as Count of Andros, to control the silk business on their behalf. He made an agreement with the Greek Tourmarch, Governor of Andros, to exploit the silk business together so that the island could continue producing and selling silk unmolested. In the meantime, the Sicilian Norman's ties to the island slipped away and now the grandson of the Tourmarch, Manuel Aladinos is his name, is the most important person on the island. With the Linghev gone, Manuel Aladinos does not have the means to transport his silk anywhere very easily and so he must sell it at a reduced price. As you can see, I intend to become his benefactor and beneficiary. I understand he is married to a noble Lady from Narbonne who is the granddaughter of Ermengarde, the Viscountess of Narbonne. Alamanda is her name. I am actually eager to meet them."

"I am surprised that you already know so much about the place and the people of the Island you are about to conquer. No wonder the Venetians are admired and feared at the same time."

"Knowledge is power my friend. Venice has been ploughing these waters for more than two hundred years gathering wealth and information to take advantage of further opportunities."

As they were talking the galleys rounded another cape and came into view of a magnificent green valley behind a semi-sheltered bay. Six of the galleys glided behind the northern mountainous branch of the bay to shelter there in case of wind, although that day the sea was calm. Dandolo's head galley manoeuvred between a small rocky island and an overgrown peninsula with steep sloping flanks. On the south side, the bay continued, interrupted by another but smaller peninsula until it ended by the foot of the mountain range that traversed the island from the east to the west. Dandolo must have truly known the island quite well to be able to perform such a difficult manoeuvre in such a tight spot. He also knew that the northeasterly wind could gather force quite suddenly and smash his proud galley against the rocks. For this reason, inflated sheepskins padded his vessel from all sides. With strong ropes he tied it securely on a makeshift rocky dock, between the island and the peninsula. His experienced eyes saw that this small island could form the basis of a castle and become the seat of his authority. The adjacent peninsula would become the ground of a town to gather his faithful knights, artisans and merchants who would build his wealth. He and his men landed on the plateau just across the island where they built a temporary wall and made camp inside it.

Without delay he sent an armed foraging party on a surprise attack to a tower house perched on the mountain to the south. They managed to enter it and capture the resident owner, Dimitris Vrahnos, whom they brought to Marino Dandolo for questioning. From him, he learned that Manuel Aladinos was, indeed, the first archon and the most important land owner on the island and that he commanded the respect of all the other landowners and commoners. Therefore, he was the man to negotiate with concerning the new order to be established on Andros. There were other archons like Varangis with property on and behind the mountain range of Yerakones to the south, Logothetis, with estates on the green slopes of Petalon, the northern mountain range, and Dardanos, with extensive lands and flocks to the north of the island near Gavrio. Vrahnos himself owned extensive property in the valley and mountain slopes directly south from where Marino Dandolo and his men were camping. All these archons except for Vrahnos of course, were gathering in the four-tower manor house of Aladinos discussing the course of action concerning the Frankish landing on their Island. The Greeks called all Western Europeans Franks, from the time of Charlemagne onwards, Venetians included.

The four-tower manor of Alandinos was on the northeastern slopes of the lush valley. His estates extended to most of the middle and eastern part of the valley and a good part of the southern valley behind the Yerakones mountains, which he had given as present to his beautiful wife Alamanda. All of these Greek archons commanded silk producing establishments and were very anxious lest they be deprived of their lucrative business. All these details Marino Dandolo learned from the frightened Dimitris Vrahnos who eagerly offered to mediate for a peaceful arrangement between the Andriots and Dandolo. So Dandolo sent Vrahnos to Aladinos to mediate while Dandolo held his tower-house and family as hostages lest he played foul at some point.

In the four-tower Manor of Aladinos the archons, after having listened to Vrahnos, debated whether to accept Dandolo's offer for a peaceful takeover or to confront him militarily. Dardanos, driven by his fierce temperament, shouted that they should rouse the people to fight against the Franks and not lie down like sheep to be slaughtered. Niketas Honiates countered that they did not have a chance against experienced and ironclad warriors. He was present when Constantinople had fallen in the hands of the crusaders and he had witnessed the wholesale destruction of the greatest city of the world and the horrible massacre of men, women and children. He did not wish to see the same thing repeated on this lovely island. He managed to escape to Athens where his brother, Michael Honiates, was the Bishop. After a short breathing space, Otto de la Ross, one of the leaders of the crusade, invaded and conquered Athens as well. The two brothers exiled themselves to Andros, where they were given some land in the valley south of the Yerakones Mountains. They called their new home Hones to remind them of their birthplace in Asia Minor. Niketas was clearly in favour of a peaceful arrangement so that he and his brother Michael would not have to run away again. He needed peace and quiet to write the chronicle of his troubled times and to concentrate on other scholarly pursuits. Perhaps later they could seek patronage from Theodore Laskaris the self-styled Emperor of Nicea, the newly formed Greek Empire in Asia Minor. Logothetes suggested that they should turn to the Genovese for help, who were now hovering around the Aegean Islands hoping to pick up some spoils from under the Venetian's noses.

"Why? So that we can fall from Scylla to Harybdis and suffer worse in their rapacious hands? Can you forget Gaffore, the Genovese pirate, who only recently devastated Andros and many other islands?" Niketas countered.

While his guests were debating what to do, Manuel Aladinos had turned his back to them and was gazing out with melancholy at the beautiful green valley below and to the east from the open window of the tower. He had lived well with his beautiful wife, Alamanda, and his fifteen-year-old daughter, Feliza, on this beautiful estate. His peers and the common people to whom he provided sustenance and protection respected him. The silk business was still doing well although the old routes of marketing his goods were disrupted and costs had increased. Venice was now the prevailing power with whom he would have to come to terms. If he wanted to keep at least part of his wealth and his style of living he would have to negotiate a peaceful agreement with Marino Dandolo, otherwise he would lose everything

He turned to face his guests and said, "Dear friends, I am sure you can see that there is no alternative but to negotiate peace with Marino Dandolo. We do not really have the means to fight him and I believe that he needs our support and our ability to produce silk. We also need the means of transportation, which he can provide. Vrahnos told us that Dandolo intended to build a new fortified town on the Peninsula and the rocky islet down in the bay. This would suit us well as chances are he will likely leave us alone in our tower manors since his knights would most likely live down there."

The archons had to agree, albeit sullenly, that Aladinos was pointing out the only course with minimal danger to their lives and estates. Having secured their consent, Aladinos continued on addressing Vrahnos, "Go tell Dandolo that we agree to discuss his offer with him and invite him to visit us here with a small retinue of his followers."

Vrahnos ran back to deliver this message to Dandolo, desperately hoping for the most harmless outcome possible. Meanwhile, Marino Dandolo had summoned all his notable companions, on the flat ground at the end of the promontory right across from the rocky islet, to discuss his plans to take over Andros.

"As you all know, the island of Andros has been assigned to me and my descendants to rule and exploit its resources. I owe allegiance to Marko Sanudo, the Duke of Naxos and of the Archipelago, and naturally to the Emperor of Constantinople Baldwin, to the King of Salonica Boniface de Montferrat and ultimately to the most Serene Republic of Venice." So many liege lords could only mean that Marino Dandolo was virtually independent and yet protected against other potential claimants. There were smiles and whispers of understanding and approbation among the audience, although a few sour faces concealed disappointment and envy. Among the latter were Jeremiah Ghizi and the reverent John, appointed Bishop of Andros by Pope Innocent III.

Marino Dandolo continued. "This island is fertile and most importantly, it can produce silk of good quality. For those of you who stay here with me, we could have a comfortable life provided we manage its people and resources wisely. I intend to build a castle stronghold on the island across this channel and a town on the peninsula to serve our needs and our comfort. You can build your tower houses here, surrounded by artisans and merchants. The flat terrace where we are now will be our future meeting place and the channel, Riva, will be extended to the north and south with stone and wooden embankments to shelter at least two galleons from the winds. A stone bridge will join the new town to the castle and the whole island will be ruled from here by our feudal system. The present land owners and leaders of Andros are willing to parlay with us for a peaceful takeover by which we will become their overlords."

Most of the assembly showed their enthusiasm with applause and approbation with one of them shouting. "Dandolo should be the name of the new castle and city to honour our brave and wise leader."

A new round of applause and redoubled clamour seemed to confirm the choice and leadership of Marino Dandolo. However, there were a few who were envious or simply disagreed with his plans. One of them was Jeremiah Ghizi who stood up to express his dissent. "Why waste time building castles and new towns when we could attack these schismatic Greeks and simply take all their lands and goods and divide them among ourselves. It will be more satisfying and profitable for all of us."

There were murmurs of some approval in the assembly, when a knight with a sword at his side and a vielle on his back stood up to speak. "I am one of the crusaders, like many of you here who took part in the siege and capture of Constantinople. I have witnessed the complete destruction of that city and the hideous massacre of men, women and children indiscriminately. A great city was depopulated and reduced to penury overnight and the new Emperor Baldwin of Flanders inherited destitution. He is now having problems fighting the Greeks to the East and the Bulgarians to the north. Do you really wish to subject this beautiful and prosperous island to the same fate as that of Constantinople? We would then inherit a burned-out rock to rule over and instead of revenue expect only undying hatred of the Greeks all around us. For me, Andros is only a stopover on my way to the domains of my Liege Lord Raymond VI of Toulouse. I personally stand to profit from a quick pillaging operation but my heart bleeds when I envisage the rape of this Island Paradise. Better to have less for a long peaceful period, than to receive more for a short time but then get nothing in the future except troubles. Therefore, I concur with Lord Dandolo's proposal for a peaceful takeover."

The assembly was favourably impressed and was swayed again to the viewpoint of peace when the presumptive Bishop of Andros shouted full of venom. "From the crow's mouth only a crow comes fourth and from a renegade canon like Peire Cardinal subtle poison concealed in the honey of peace. This man abandoned the Holy Church to join the heathen Raymond of Toulouse who protects Jews, Mohammedans and heretic Cathars in his domain and soon he will face the punishment of God. Do not listen to him, instead destroy all the establishment of the schematics."

Peire Cardinal managed to control his well-justified anger and quickly retorted, "It is true that I was trained to be a canon in Saint Marie of Puy-en-Velay but as soon as I discovered my true calling for poetry and music I respectfully left my ecclesiastical career without abandoning my faith. I became a troubadour and a knight in the service of Raymond VI of Toulouse and fulfilled my pledge to take part in a crusade, which by no fault of mine went astray. Let us not go astray here as well and resort to destructive violence, rather let us follow the true Christian ways of peace. My Liege Lord, the Count of Toulouse, follows the ways of peace in his domain and because of his tolerance and love of joy and beauty his principality enjoys freedom and prosperity. It would be a very good idea to imitate this present-day David who glories God by singing and dancing rather than perpetuate the intolerance of excessive religious zeal causing misery and destruction."

At this point Marino Dandolo stood up tall and majestic, and with authoritative finality said, "The words of this noble troubadour express my views exactly on establishing a peaceful government here. The building of the castle and city of Dandolo, as some of you called it, will start immediately and those of you who are feudal overlords are invited to build their tower houses in it. Our reverent Bishop of Andros should start supervising his new metropolitan Church and learn to control his religious fervour against the schematics, as he calls them, and direct it towards peace. As for my companion in arms, Jeremiah Ghizi, I would like to remind him that his territory is not Andros but the islands of Tinos and Skyros where he can apply his high-handed methods, if he wishes. In the meantime, he can vent his martial impetuosity against the Genovese galleys, which for days now, have been hovering out there like vultures ready to seize pieces of what is ours, not theirs. My esteemed friend should rest assured that he will have his share of our enterprise here, as will all those who have helped us but intend to move along to other destinations. Tomorrow myself and a retinue of a several knights will visit Manuel Aladinos at his tower mansion to arrange our takeover of the Island."

Everybody in the assembly, friends and dissidents alike, were overawed by the authoritative decision of their leader and dispersed to perform their prescribed business.

Peire and Esclamonde followed Dandolo's mounted detachment, which in single file meandered through the lush valley full of beautiful old trees including many mulberry trees and cultivations. Just before noon they reached the eastern terraces where the four-tower mansion of Manuel Aladinos stood. The scenery reminded them of some of the mountain valleys in Rouergue and Gevaudain back in Occitania. It made them feel nostalgic and yet at home.

When they all finally sat down for lunch in the spacious and elegant hall of Aladinos, Peire whispered to Esclamonde, "Aladinos has made a great effort to please us and yet everyone is so tense as if they are nervous of breaking something unawares. Thank God Jeremiah Ghizi and the Bishop are not with us to cause trouble."

"Aladinos seems to me to be an amiable and reasonable man who wants to save as much as he can of his estate and that of his peers using his knowledge of silk and his friendship as his main bargaining advantage but Marino Dandolo is hedging."

Suddenly, and without warning, the door opened and a beam of light entered the room silhouetting two figures, which broke the light into two strong beams. As the figures entered the room the uncertain and tense atmosphere in the hall was broken by the appearance of two beautiful women, an older one of around forty and a younger of fifteen. Aladinos, somewhat taken by surprise, stood up to greet them and took them by the hands introducing them to his guests, "here they are! My wife Alamanda and my only daughter Feliza who wanted to meet you."

The guests stirred with admiration for the sublime beauty of the two women but Marino Dandolo and Giacomo Querini were unable to hold themselves back and jumped up from their seats advancing towards them simultaneously. They both knelt to pay their amorous respects to the two beautiful ladies who looked at them with delighted surprise. Feliza was immediately flattered by this demonstration of both men although she felt pulled toward the blond Querini over the robust Dandolo. An imperceptible biting feeling of jealousy passed between the two friends. Dandolo felt compelled to make a rash decision. He took the hand of Feliza while sending a severe glance to Querini and then turning to Manuel Aladinos said, "My Lord, the sudden appearance of your daughter has caused a fierce eruption of love in me for her. I ask your permission to have Feliza as my wife."

Everyone around them was dumbfounded by this turn of events, most of all the parents and Feliza, the object of desire. Alamanda was thrilled by the intensity and audacity of Dandolo's feelings and wished for a speedy and happy conclusion.

Manuel was feverishly calculating in his mind the unexpected advantages of such a marriage and after a few moments of reflection responded, "Your Excellency, I am deeply honoured by your impetuous proposal, and as I can see my wife is more so, but I would like to hear my daughter's response."

Feliza, whose hand was still in Dandolo's grasp, knew very well that she had to accept the life-binding proposal of this powerful man. After an imperceptibly quick glance of sad farewell towards Querini, she said with a serious tone of voice, "I am deeply moved and honoured by your proposal and although our acquaintance was extremely brief I accept and will become your wife."

Marino beside himself with overflowing emotion kissed both of Feliza's hands and said, "I declare for all to hear, that this is the happiest moment of my life. Now that I have experienced it, love does not need more than an instant to conquer a ready heart, my heart in this case."

Giacomo Querini, dumbfounded by the sudden turn of events, was holding the hilt of his sword uncertain of what to do next. Had he just lost an opportunity or perhaps he had never had a chance?

Peire Cardinal who had noticed the pent-up drama turned and whispered to Esclamonde, "The older lion got the prey while the younger one wonders whether to pounce now or bide his time."

"The young lady is so much like the women of our country who marry one and love another, so that they can always dream of love ahead. Young Querini will certainly be the love ahead."

"In any case, the negotiations reached an unexpectedly happy conclusion for both parties and for this island. I am so divided inside of me. I would have liked to have stayed here and yet I yearn to return home."

"As for me I want to go back to our beautiful and lively country of song, dance and love, where fate awaits us."

"Do not worry, Dear Esclamonde, we will be returning there for the birth of our child, whatever our fate might be."

The wedding was celebrated in the ancient Greek monastery of All Holy Mary in the presence of the Greek Orthodox Bishop and the furious Catholic Bishop John. He was furious because he had to officiate in a Schismatic Church but he was given no choice since Dandolo could not wait for the new Catholic Church to be built in his new capital city. He had promised to repeat the wedding as soon as the first Catholic Church was built sometime next year. Giacomo Querini was compensated and honoured as the best man with Feliza's firm insistence. Marino Dandolo could not refuse her anything at all, even something so blatantly risky for him.

The festivities continued in the four-tower manor of Aladinos. The Catholic crusaders and the Schismatic Greeks abandoned themselves together in the joy of eating, drinking, song and dance. The two styles of merry making of East and West were practiced side-by-side. As time went on they began to blend quite nicely together.

Alamanda, Peire Cardinal and Esclamonde joined together and performed the troubadour acts of their country, cansos, coblas and tensos. Everybody around them became silent and listened, enthralled by the magical beauty of their art.

"Where did these people come from?" somebody asked and Niketas Honiates, the scholar, volunteered to inform him. "The land of the Visigoths is their country, out West between the Alps and the Mediterranean Sea, and Carcassonne is their ancient capital city." His words sounded outlandishly impressive although meant very little to those who heard them, including the neighbours and natives of that area.

The marriage of Marino Dandolo to Feliza signified peace and prosperity for the principality of Andros. Some of Dandolo's companions inspired by his happiness began to look for native brides of their own from the notable Greek families. The process of matchmaking started even during the wedding festivities. Niketas, who had noticed this happening, turned to his brother Michael and said, "Now that Marino Dandolo married Feliza like Alexander who married Roxanne, the Persian, his companions might follow his example to marry Greek girls like Alexander's warriors married Persian girls. It would be wonderful if that happens, for everyone concerned."

"You know, my brother, you're over exaggerating enthusiasm endeavours to compare two events that cannot be compared because of their immense difference in scale and importance. I advised you to moderate your enthusiasm because disappointment might be around the corner."

The wedding festivities went on for days with joyous participation of both the high and low-born alike. This way the island of Andros slipped sweetly and peacefully and almost unaware into the era of the Franks.

CHAPTER 7

BACK HOME

oon after the wedding Peire and Esclamonde took ship with Giacomo Querini and sailed back to Venice. From Venice, they traveled to Verona on horseback where Renier de Campagnac received them with great warmth. Renier, once more, repeated his offer to give them a wonderful home and abundant life in Verona.

"Dear uncle, I thank you again for your kindness, but as you know, I am obligated to serve my Lord Raymond of Toulouse and, furthermore, my wife Esclamonde is expecting a child soon. We both feel that we want to be back home for that.

"Dear Peire I understand your reasons, yet I must tell you that according to my intelligence Pope Innocent III is putting relentless pressure on Raymond VI to subjugate himself to the authority of the Church and eradicate all heresies from his land. The Pope is threatening excommunication and even a crusade against him. Raymond is unwilling to change his ways and he seems to have adopted delaying tactics by effectively ignoring the demands of the legates of the Pope."

"I thought that the Pope supported the methods of persuasion used to convert the so-called heretics back to the so-called correctness of the Catholic Church."

"I detect some kind of irony and scepticism for the ways and methods of our Church. This is somewhat surprising for someone who was trained to be a canon. To answer your question, I must inform you

that the famous Catholic orator Dominic de Guzman tried to persuade
the Cathars in Pamiers using solid arguments of theology, only recently,
and he failed. There was a debate between him and the Cathar Bishop
Guilhabert de Castres but it was a debate between two deaf people.
After that, Dominic de Guzman concluded that persuasion is useless
and the Pope decided that other, more drastic, methods should be
employed in order to re-establish the authority of the Church in the
lands of Toulouse, of Foix and of the Trencavel. I have heard that the
Pope is trying to persuade the King of France, Philippe Augustus, to
lead a crusade against the Cathars in the South. The Northerners are
thirsty for loot, land and blood. Fortunately, Philippe Augustus is at
war with John Plantagenet of England. He is not likely to travel south
on a crusade but there are others who would. In short, I am worried
for you and that you are walking far too nonchalantly into deep
trouble."

"Dear uncle I know firsthand how horrible a crusade against other
Christians of different denominations can be. Therefore I do not take
your caring warnings lightly. However, I must go back home for now
and if things take a turn for the worse we may have to return and hope
that you will still be open to having us join you then."

"As long as I am alive you can consider my house in Verona open
to you and your family."

Peire and Esclamonde rode west along the ancient Roman Road,
the Domitian Way, towards their homeland. All this new and unsettling
information weighed upon their hearts while images of their experience
in Constantinople still haunted them. With all this uncertainty they felt
very grateful to Renier for his heartfelt and comforting offer of his
home in case of trouble. While crossing the domains of Montferrat,
some more very sad news awaited them; their dear friends Boniface de
Montferrat and Raimbaut de Vaqueiras had been cruelly slaughtered
somewhere in Bulgaria. There were none to sing their exploits and their
unquestionable valour. Even their remains could not be found, as they
were most likely carelessly tossed down some nameless crack or crevice
in the hostile mountain vastness.

They continued along the Domitian Way in a deep dark mood because of their friends' deaths and a growing apprehension of what might be in store for them at home. As they approached the Roman Arch in Orange, travelers told them that Raymond VI of Toulouse was in Saint Gilles and in terrible distress because of his recent excommunication and his fruitless negotiations with the Papal legate Peter of Castelnau.

Peire was in a quandary whether to run immediately to his liege lord or take care of his wife, who was due to deliver anytime now. Campagnac was too far to travel to and Saint Gilles too unsuitable for delivering babies. Bieiris de Romans was close enough and ultimately the perfect person to take care of Esclamonde with the tender loving care she needed.

So they traveled to Romans and Bieiris was more than thrilled to see them after so many years apart. She was as beautiful as ever and, in spite of Esclamonde's advanced pregnancy and the anxiety of lurking dangers, or maybe because of them, the old passions they all had once felt for each other were rekindled and blazed again.

Even before the customary exchanging of news or even explaining their need of a safe delivery they fell upon each other with gentle passion. All was intuitively felt and as Bieiris began kissing Esclamonde's pregnant belly they could not help but respond to her outpouring of love wholeheartedly. They made sweet love without thought of the future and all their worries melted away for a time.

A week later, into this love filled atmosphere, a baby boy was born with the help of Bieiris' knowledge of herbs and healing. They called him Nascibon. Bieiris took care of Esclamonde and Nascibon with all of her loving heart like a mother, sister, and lover, like a true friend. This enabled Peire to feel safe enough to leave them in order to join Raymond in St. Gilles.

It was late December of 1207, almost Christmas, when Peire reached Raymond's palace in St. Gilles. The weather was still pleasant as it usually is in Provence. All was in turmoil though, with mixed activities as preparations were under way for Christmas celebrations, while the gruelling negotiations with the Papal legate Peter de Castelnau and his retinue were proceeding relentlessly.

Peire was admitted into the conference room in the midst of a heated argument between Raymond and the Legate. Peter was a tall ungainly figure with a constant hard-unyielding expression on his face and a posture of authoritative arrogance that could make anyone bristle with anger, let alone Raymond who could hardly control himself.

Peter was saying, "You have been protecting heretics and, quite possibly, are one of them yourself. You have been employing foreign mercenaries to fight your private battles and bully the Church. You have violated the truce declared for the great feast-days of the Church. You have appointed Jews to public offices. You have pillaged monasteries and turned churches into fortresses. For these reasons and many others our Holy Father has charged me to read out to you his letter.

"Do not forget that life and death themselves are in God's hands. God may suddenly strike you down and in his anger deliver you to everlasting torment. Even if you are permitted to live, do not suppose that misfortune cannot reach you. You are not made of iron. You are weak and vulnerable like other men. Fever, leprosy, paralysis, insanity, incurable disease may all attack you like any other of your kind. Are you not ashamed of breaking the oath by which you swore to eradicate heresy from your dominions? Are you already so mad that you think yourself wiser than all the faithful of the universal Church? The hand of the Lord will no longer be stayed. It will stretch forth to crush you, for the anger which you have provoked will not lightly be evaded!"

Raymond, pallid and shaking all over by the unjust violence and by the haranguing of the highest authority of the Church, pronounced by such an unworthy minion, remained silent for a long time. He was in a quandary whether to strike this cleric dead or try to reason with him. The consequences of his excommunication could mean that his vassals were released from their oaths of homage to him and that neighbouring rulers could invade his principalities to depose him and take over with the blessings of the Pope.

"What do you want from me in order to lift my excommunication?"

"You know very well that you must submit to the Church by accepting its terms unconditionally. You heard the terms. Didn't you?"

"I am willing to submit but give me some time to enforce your terms."

"I will return the second week of January next year. Make sure you have complied by then."

After saying that, Peter de Castelnau and his retinue turned abruptly and walked out of the conference hall with a show of majestic arrogance. This infuriated the Count and all the people around him, including Peire.

The Count slumped in his chair exasperated. As he looked absentmindedly around he recognized Peire Cardinal and revived.

"Back from the crusades after five years, at last, while the whole world and its Church is crashing down upon my head. I guess you must have noticed that I am in serious trouble. I have been excommunicated and am facing the possibility of being invaded and destroyed by a crusade of Northerners, organized by the Pope and his Cistercian wolves. You have been away too long at a time when I desperately needed you. What am I going to do?"

Peire shivered with guilt and compassion on seeing and hearing the helplessness and despondency of this man who used to be so full of life and joy. This once great and handsome man now seemed diminished as if shrunk by his recent calamities. He needed the help of his friends. Peire wanted to help him but how could he? He only managed to say.

"My dearest Liege Lord, I cannot give you false hopes just to make you feel better. You are walking a tightrope between total destruction and total subjugation with self-inflicted castration. I took part in a crusade, an unjust crusade, against the Schismatic Greeks and witnessed the total destruction of the greatest city in the world. It was not about the glory of faith but of shameless pillage and rape. If there is a crusade against us, it will be in order to depose and dispossess you. The eradication of heresy is only a pretext. You cannot openly fight against it for the Church is too powerful. On the other hand, if you give in to their demands, you still will lose everything. There is no alternative but to keep walking and balancing precariously on the tightrope as you do now, and pray for the best. As for me, I will be with you all the way on this tight and tragic rope, singing or fighting, if necessary."

"My dearest troubadour and knight, your words of truth have made me feel better already because I know now that it is not all that bad to walk on a tightrope. It has its charms and after all, a worthy life is walking on such a rope. It is the art of the most exalted jongleur of all. Life and circumstances will be the troubadour and composer of my act of rope dancing."

Everybody around applauded his words and show of poetic defiance. A few secretly cried. Peire did both.

Heavy clouds were gathering from the East and from the North over the lands of the carefree. In this land of the troubadours where love reins supreme, imperceptible feelings and thoughts of fear and shame to enjoy life started sneaking in. The Southern knights were getting angry and thirsty for bloody battle with anyone who would threaten their Lords, their land and their way of life. The songs of Bertran de Born, the warrior troubadour, were heard again.

> Maces and brands and painted helms,
> Escutcheons hacked and stabbed with holes,
> All this we'll see when battle joins,
> And many a baron trading blows.
> Horses in panic flee,
> Their master's dead or wounded.
> And in the fury of the fray
> Valiant knights rewarded
> With savage toll of heads and limbs,
> Blood, ransom and spoils
> Preferring death to life in chains
> Our valiant blood it boils

But the emissaries of the Pope, the choleric Cistercians, the power-hungry bishops, were not warriors but weavers of sticky spider webs of guilt, fear and hell mongering.

The songs of love, the cansos, gave way to the political anticlerical sirventes. Peire Cardinal composed one to feed the anger of Raymond VI of Toulouse and his retinue of knights:

> Emperors and monarchs
> Dukes and Counts and Lords
> Together with the Knights
> Are wont to rule the world.
>
> But now I see that priests
> Have gathered all the power
> With theft and treachery
> They've plucked most every flower
>
> By preaching and by force
> By twisting all that's true
> With sly hypocrisy
> They'll take the world to rule
>
> Like Judas' betraying kiss
> Their will is being done
> Behind the scenes they pull the strings
> There's nowhere left to run
>
> Soon all will be theirs
> If we don't wake up my friends
> The storm is looming all around
> But we can rise again
> Come together change the weather
> We can rise again…

Everybody around shouted and stamped their feet in a very ugly mood and sang again the songs of Bertran de Born.

> "Each valiant-hearted knight
> Takes savage toll of heads and limbs
> Preferring death to life in chains."

The clerics were not going to fight by themselves. They were plotting to employ the bestial valour of the northern knights the likes of which Peire had seen storm and sack Constantinople during his recent crusade. The Southern knights did not lack in valour but they were impulsive, explosive, disorganized and not very focused. The worst part, though, was that the Southern knights had not been able to truly unite. Unfortunately, they often worked at cross-purposes to each other. The Count of Toulouse, The Viscount of Trencavel, the Count of Foix and the Count of Comminges constantly suspected each other for real or imagined trespasses and coveted each other's possessions. Nevertheless, they all shared the same culture and language. They also cherished the same carefree way of life and religious freedoms.

Enthroned Church debating with Heretics. 13th century miniature.

Seal of Raymond VI Count of Toulouse

Statue of Raymond VI in the Toulouse City Hall.

Arnaud Amaury and his gang of Cistercian Abbots, presided by St.
Dominic crushing helpless Cathars underfoot
(Print Adrian Melaer, 1633-1667)

CHAPTER 8

HELL BREAKS LOOSE

arly in January 1208, Peter of Castelnau and the Bishop of Couserans returned to St. Gilles at the invitation of Raymond VI, who was presumably ready to offer his submission in exchange for having his excommunication lifted. At the beginning of the process the Count appeared sincere in being willing to accept all the terms set forth by the legate. It seemed the whole affair was going to end peacefully. Peter of Castelnau was, for once, pleasantly surprised that his mission was going to have a successful conclusion. However two of the Cistercians of his retinue did not seem to share his feelings. They had withdrawn into a dark corner and were muttering between themselves, obviously disappointed by the turn of events.

"It looks like the snake is going to slip away again, when everything was underway for crushing his poisonous head. The Pope needs a credible cause to mobilize the pious North against the impious and heretical South."

"There are quite a few hot-headed knights who could provide 'a credible cause', or even someone who could appear as one of them. A paid assassin perhaps? All for the glory of God and his Church, of course, and Peter would attain sainthood and a worthy Cistercian would inherit his Bishopric of Citeaux. What do you think?"

"Arnaud-Amaury would be gratified and grateful. Let us not waste time. Let Hell break loose."

The two Cistercians scuttled away and disappeared through the many dark passages of St. Gilles Castle.

The Count and his people were dissatisfied and troubled by the humiliating agreement with the Papal legate and yet somewhat relieved that the ugly head of war was averted. The Southern knights mumbled among themselves in an ugly mood, unable to bear the humiliation imposed upon their Count and themselves. Their customary anticlericalism welled up to a murderous hatred against all the Cistercians and particularly against the legate himself who was considered to be the engineer for the systematic degradation of their pride. Threats and rants were bantered about and duly noted by the Cistercians and their spies. The Cistercians added to the fire by spreading a rumour that the Count had changed his mind and was ready to cancel the agreement, moved by his fickle nature and his hatred against the Church. The rumour they circulated implied that he had threatened to imprison the legate and even take his life if the terms were not cancelled. These rumours were so preposterous that not even extreme fickleness could explain and support them.

The Count heard these rumours circulating and was extremely concerned about what his enemies were up to. He summoned Peire Cardinal to get his opinion on it all.

"Peire, what do you make of these rumours. Do you believe them? Most importantly, do others believe them?"

"I certainly do not believe them by the mere fact that it's against your interests to act this way but unfortunately many people on both sides believe them. Your enemies have been prepared for war and it suits their purposes to spread these rumours and, naturally, they pretend to believe them. Unfortunately, many from your own side want to believe them because they hope to get even and regain their pride. Their emotions have clouded their reason."

"I realize you belong to the minority who understand they are lies propagated by our enemies. It saddens me that only a minority stands by the truth and serves my true interests! I feel besieged by enemies and by my own people alike. Something evil is at work here."

On 14 January 1208 Peter of Castelnau and his party were about to cross a branch of the Rhone River going east just after leaving, St.

Gilles, when a mounted man with a spear galloped furiously towards them and pierced through the legate killing him instantly. Without a word or a shout the assassin galloped away melting into the countryside leaving no traces behind him. No one knew his name, or had seen him before. No one saw him after the incident or heard of him ever again. There was no heroic pride, no war cry, not a trace of anything but the cold reality that Peter of Castelnau had been murdered.

The Cistercians raised a clamour of holy indignation and accused the Count of having organized the assassination as soon as the legate hit the ground, without any investigation whatsoever to prove Raymond's guilt. The prominent Cistercian Arnauld Amaury started, with all speed, for Rome to inform the Pope of the indisputable guilt of his archenemy the Count of Toulouse. The pope fell speechless for three days. Not that he was in doubt of Raymond's guilt, but to meditate on the enormity of the malicious deed and to determine a punishment that would restore the dignity and authority of the Church. When Pope Innocent III regained his speech, he excommunicated Raymond VI. He then proclaimed a relentless crusade against his dominions and against all the dominions that harboured the heretic Cathars, which included the Trenscavels, the Foix and Comminges.

Arnauld Amaury traveled North to the Court of the King of France, Philip Augustus, and to the adjacent duchies of Burgundy and Flanders to spread the word of a holy crusade. He promoted the crusade with fervour advertising the rich rewards to be gained from conquering the South with the added benefit of plenary indulgence, which would absolve the crusaders of all sins undertaken during the crusade. Philip Augustus, as a practical man, had always considered crusades a waste of time and money. With regret, he now had to offer his blessings to whoever wished to join this crusade. It was the best he could do at this point, as he was busy fighting John Plantagenet of England. It was in this way that Arnauld Amaury was finally successful in gathering together a large number of Grandees and knights from France, Burgundy, Champagne, Flanders, Germany and even Auvergne to form a holy crusade to conquer the South. All this despite the fact that most of this land of Occitania was still fully Christian.

In his palace at St. Gilles, Count Raymond called a meeting of his vassals and friends to try and find ways to confront or avert the terrible threat of this gathering storm. The young Viscount Raymond-Roger Trencavel said to Raymond for all to hear, "You brought this threat of a bloody crusade upon us all by assassinating the Pope's legate, not that I grieve for that arrogant cleric, but it was a stupid thing to do. As far as I am concerned I am prepared to defend Carcassonne and my cities only if the crusaders attack them. Otherwise I'll stay out of this mess of which I am not responsible. You deal with it by yourself."

A clamour of protest went up from Raymond and his close friends. As it finally quieted down Raymond said with a quiet intensity, "Trencavel, your enmity towards me has allowed malicious rumours and false accusations into your heart. Our common enemies, who hate our way of life and covet our lands, have propagated these rumours and accusations. I am in no way responsible for the assassination of Peter of Castelnau, with whom I had reached an agreement. This agreement would have averted a crusade against us. Now, we must be united against them and not let them divide us. You are a fool if you think that you can avoid our common fate by following a separate way. The only real excuse they have for this crusade are the Cathars who live in your land as well as my lands. They also live, peacefully I might add, in the lands of Foix and Comminges. Mark my words Trencavel, your independent ways will be your undoing."

Most people in the meeting were deeply impressed by the Count's address but not Trencavel, who blinded by his arrogance, stomped out as irreconcilable as ever. The Count shook his head with resigned sadness as he realized his countrymen were splintered and not ready for a concerted effort against the gathering storm. Many of them did not even quite believe there was something to worry about and felt they could deal with whatever happened when it happened. Planning ahead of time was not in their Southern nature. It put a damper on their pleasure-loving style. With all of these realizations weighing heavily inside him Raymond secretly resolved that he had to make his peace with the Pope and the Church before this hellish crusade was unleashed upon him and his people. Under these circumstances did he even have a chance, or was it already too late?

Peire, noticing the heavy atmosphere and tense silence amongst the Count's guests, pulled out his vielle and began playing an improvised melody. He played the mood of the room in a deep melody filled with pathos and slowly picked up the energy transforming the hopeless atmosphere into a righteous and timely sirventes:

> Whoever killed the Pope's legate
> Couldn't be thinking very straight.
> Or was he serving the warmonger?
> Who stealing our land and joy grows stronger.

> Toulouse wants peace to love and play
> But Rome needs heresy to make us pay.
> Are we just pawns in a dangerous game?
> Spilling blood in Gods name?

> There's nothing sacred anymore
> To the priests who are wanting more and more.
> So, hold on brothers! Let us come together!
> In love and freedom, for forever.

Most people were carried along by the magic of the music but they could not or would not truly open up to the terrifying reality of the lyrics. Other troubadours and jongleurs began singing passionate love songs and cansos, but somehow their effect was not penetrating through to hearts already preoccupied with these recent worries.

Raimon de Miraval sadly noted in song:

The flowers are fading
There scent is spent
Love finds no entry
In a frightened heart

The Count of Toulouse knew that he had no time to lose. He had to go north to plead with Arnauld-Amaury, with the King of France, Philip Augustus, with the German Emperor, Otto, and with anyone else who had the power to stop this crusade. He was prepared to suffer any humiliation in order to save his country from the horrors of an invasion by religious fanatics and plunderers.

Soon after the meeting Count Raymond VI and his retinue of faithful knights traveled north along the Rhone River. Peire Cardinal accompanied him until near Romans where he took his leave to join his wife Esclamonde and their infant son Nascibon in the Castle of his dear friend Bieiris. The stone castle, forbidding on the outside, was sumptuously feathered and voluptuously warm inside providing all the simple as well as the subtle pleasures required by the hostess and her guests. Nascibon was well cared for and an exceedingly happy child. Esclamonde was glowing, fulfilled as a mother and enjoying her deepening love of Bieiris. Seeing Peire again was at first a little awkward but it didn't take long for them to get reacquainted and rekindle their passion. Bieiris gave them some space for a while but eventually couldn't resist her excitement at seeing Peire and Esclamonde's passion and love reignited. Rather than feeling jealous it made her feel more attracted to them both as she slowly moved to join in. Before long, they found themselves falling into a familiar, erotic dance that they had all secretly missed very much. In this voluptuous oblivion of the lotus-eaters the rest of the world and its cares did not exist at all. Peire, unnerved and anxious from the meeting at St. Gilles, needed this pleasurable oblivion more than ever and so he chose not to mention a word of the terrible troubles about to erupt all around them. The bad news did eventually find a way to sneak into their carefree retreat. When it did, the strange thing was that everyone already knew about it but had kept quiet in order to prolong whatever was left of the goodness of life.

Bieiris looked at them sadly and said, "My dear friends, thank you for the love you have given me, which was a life saving force for me. I hope that I have returned to you as much love as I possess. Unfortunately, the world around us is galloping towards hatred, war and devastation. I am afraid we cannot remain unaffected. The Count of Toulouse was not successful in his heartfelt effort to stop a crusade already decided upon long ago by the powers that be. The only thing left for him to negotiate in order for him and his domains to remain unmolested is his participation in the crusade. This is a humiliating, dangerous and disgusting situation! Unfortunately I feel this is what he will probably be forced to do in the end. In the meantime Arnauld-Amaury has managed to muster a huge army of French, Flemish Burgundian and German crusaders who are granted plenary indulgence to be cleansed of all their sins past, present and future as an inducement. They can kill women and children with an easy conscience because the Church sanctions it! Can you believe it? Champagnard, Auvergnat and even Provencal are joining them. Most of the bishops, abbots and churchmen from our lands have sided with them as well. I am terribly concerned as this army is travelling down the Rhone River as we speak! I do not know if they will pass through my lands. Romans is not exactly on their way south, but you never know. You can stay with me, if you want, but I am not sure you would be safe here. We are now in a time of war and, sadly, all good things must come to an end. I am so sorry." After saying this Bieiris embraced them and cried uncontrollably. Both Peire and Esclamonde joined her with tears of their own.

Finally, Esclamonde stopped and said. "I am terribly worried about the safety of our little boy, Nascibon. Maybe we should have left him in Verona, in the care of Peire's Uncle. We should have listened to him then. It seems that it is too late now to travel to Verona safely but maybe we can get to Campagnac and Peire's family? I am also very concerned about my father who lives among his brethren somewhere in Saissac or Carcassonne. I haven't seen him for so long. I must go to him now in his time of need or I may never get a chance to see him again. All these years I had forgotten that I am a true Christian, a Cathar, even though since my marriage I have not followed their ways. Quite the opposite, it seems, since I am attached so strongly to the pleasures of the flesh. I do not repent this fact and yet I am a believer nonetheless. What do you think we should do Peire?"

"I am sorry, too, that we must go so soon before the crusaders get to the south. They know I am Raymond's man and they may find out Esclamonde is connected with the Cathars. Bieiris will be compromised if they find us in her castle. I will not allow this to happen by staying with her. Bieiris must remain blameless for her own sake and for ours. At a future date, when the area is not overrun with crusaders, we may return. In the meantime, we must go to my parents in Campagnac, which is somewhat out of the way. My mother is known to be a devout Catholic and is related to the Bishop of Le Puy. We will be safe there, at least for a while. We can travel west and southwest, crossing the Rhone River at Montelimar and then to Aubenas. From Aubenas to Campagnac it is difficult terrain. We must traverse the Cevennes Mountains, skirting the mountain Auberac and go through Causse de Sauveterre. I'm sure we can manage it, though, as I have been there on hunting trips during my adolescence. I know our son is only 18 months old but he is healthy and strong. I will carry him on my horse. Esclamonde will ride her horse like she used to when she disguised herself as a man during the crusade in Greece. If we can get a strong mule to carry our supplies we will be ready. In three days we can be in Campagnac. It is late March now and the weather is fair with the prospect of getting better. As for your father Nicetas d'Outremer we will find a way to meet him after we get settled in Campagnac. Let us not forget that eventually I must join my liege lord the Count of Toulouse. For now, let us travel safely to Campagnac."

On the day of Annunciation, the 25th of March 1209, Bieiris bid her tearful farewell to her precious friends. She advised them to be cautious on their perilous trip that not only crossed mountains and overflowing rivers, but where wolves and brigands could also harm them. She insisted they take with them two armed escorts from her household. After many protests they finally agreed to accept them with gratitude.

The group of five traveled with caution and speed, avoiding towns and hostels as much as they could and, hopefully, evading the people who might think to rob them or worse. They traveled across the wild countryside sleeping in caves and makeshift tents. They were all used to hardship and even the baby did not mind very much. The weather was good and within four days they arrived at the Campagnac Castle safely.

They were received with mixed feelings. Peire's father, Guilhem, was unreservedly happy to see him after so many years, to meet Esclamonde and particularly to hold his grandson, Nascibon. His mother, Bieiris, had reservations with Esclamonde because of her Cathar origins. They were living in dangerous times and her family could be accused for sheltering heretics, apart from the fact that she hated heresy with a passion. His brother Bertrand was not sympathetic to the Cathars. At the same time he was worried that Peire might eventually claim his share of the family estate.

Peire understood right away that their stay in the Campagnac castle would have to be a short one. However, he was determined to implore his parents and brother to keep Nascibon for a longer time as the child needed a stable home, rather than being dragged around the country in a time of war. As for Esclamonde, she would have to part with their child and follow him wherever he had to go in order to join Raymond of Toulouse. Maybe, in that vicinity she might find her father, Nicetas. His mother understood that Peire had justifiable doubts about his welcome because of Esclamonde and even for Nascibon's welcome. She wanted to clarify matters and said, "I have never been happy with your marriage to a heretic woman and, particularly, now that the Church has proclaimed a crusade to cleanse our Christian country. Don't you understand that you are putting us in jeopardy by being here with her? This does not affect or include my grandson, Nascibon. We love him and we will keep him with us for as long as we live. Campagnac is his home."

"Mother, I must say I am quite bitter that you have rejected Esclamonde, my love of her and my life choices, although I do understand your reasons. I am very grateful to you, though, that you love and will protect my son in these troubled times. I do feel your love in these caring actions. Thank you. I have heard that our relative, the Bishop of Le Puy, is mustering a Crusading expedition against Rouergue because it is in the Count of Toulouse's territory. For my wife's safety and for yours we will rid you of our presence here."

So early in June of 1209 Peire and Esclamonde left Campagnac to join the Count of Toulouse. Their departure turned out to be a very sad occasion with feelings of rejection and guilt mixed with genuine parental and filial love. Nascibon was crying inconsolably to see his parents leaving but he was still young and there was plenty of time to forget them. Esclamonde was broken by grief but her tears dripped like poison inside her and did not show in her eyes.

After a two-week journey through a land that was already showing signs of changes due to the fear of impending war, they finally arrived at St. Gilles. They immediately met with Count Raymond VI and found him a changed man, diminished physically and psychologically. He turned to Peire and said in a sad tone. "Where have you been while I was suffering one humiliation after the other? In Valence, I capitulated to their debilitating demands. I gave them seven of my best castles. I handed them three city councils, which were loyal to me. I promised to persecute loyal and industrious people because of their beliefs. I have virtually become a crusader like them. I have been stripped of my powers. I am still alive though and hoping I might find an opportunity in the future to strike back and regain a semblance of my old strength."

"I am sorry, my Lord. I had to deal with my own problems, but I am back and ready to serve you."

"Yes, I still need you, not as a troubadour but as a secretary and a negotiator. I want you to manage my humiliating losses by minimizing them, as best you can. On the 14th of June, the crusade gathered all its forces in Lyon and they will soon be here to finish me off. Raymond–Roger Trencavel rejected my appeal to join forces with me. The fool does not realize that they will eat him alive for protecting heretics. He had a chance to survive the coming massacre by standing with me and I had a chance with him, but he mistakenly thinks the crusaders have a quarrel only with me and not with him. Fool! Now he will have to face the beast alone and does not know what is coming. I wish I could change his mind. I feel so saddened by all of this but now I am too busy feeling sorry for myself to feel sorry for him anymore."

"I will certainly try to negotiate the execution of whatever decisions you were forced to accede to; but what are you expecting to happen when the crusaders arrive?"

"Most likely they will make me submit to the final and ultimate ordeal."

The huge army of crusaders soon came and their multitudes filled the grounds around St. Gilles at a radius of many miles. Their tents, rich and poor, spread their colors in the fields, as far as the eye could see, like a vast field of evil flowers. Arnauld-Amaury was the effective leader of the crusade as Philip Augustus had declined the honour that had been offered to him. He had other wars to fight near home against John Plantagenet of England and the German Emperor Otto.

Among the military chiefs, the most prominent in valour and ability was Simon de Montfort. Peire remembered him with trepidation from Zara at the start of the 4th Crusade. He was a fierce and able fighter, who had abandoned the crusade, then, on moral grounds for being manipulated to crusade against fellow Christians. Peire wondered what his moral grounds were now for being an ardent leader in this crusade against his fellow Christians. Peire had often observed in his travels that people's actions were full of puzzling contradictions. Beliefs and postures often conflicted with a person's deep and un-confessed needs and desires and this would manifest in contradictory behaviours and actions. All religious zeal aside, deep inside Simon de Montfort there must be a burning desire to become a landed magnate and in the present crusade this desire had a strong chance of being satisfied at the expense of Count Raymond VI and the other southern magnates.

On 18th June, Count Raymond VI, stripped to the waist, was led up the steps of St. Gilles abbey, where three Archbishops and nineteen Bishops were assembled. He swore to obey the instructions of the Church and its legates and to redress a long list of accumulated grievances; such as his favour of heretics and Jews, his hostility against the Church, his use of mercenaries, his setting up of tollgates, and on the list went. Strangely enough, he was spared the humiliation of having to admit that he had ordered the murder of Peter de Castelnau. The legate then pulled him into the Church flogging him with a switch. When they felt the humiliation and suffering complete the Archbishops finally pronounced Raymond's absolution at the Altar.

Peire, who was watching the humiliating ceremony close at hand, cried bitterly with sorrow and suppressed rage. The Count looked at him and whispered. "Do not cry. There was no other way to rescue a glimmer of hope for my people and for us to stay alive."

Four days later, on 22nd June, Count Raymond VI was forced to 'take the cross' and join the crusade.

Peter of Vaux-de-Cernay turned to Peire Cardinal and said with venom. "Your master, the subtle cunning serpent managed to slither away again."

"You shouldn't complain. We are on the same side this time."

"We are and we aren't and you know it."

Vaux-de-Cernay, Peire's old opponent in trial at Toulouse, was now one of the leaders and the historian–troubadour of the crusaders. His former animosity against the Count and the Southern way of life had now grown into a murderous passion and a malevolence supported by the obvious military supremacy of the invading army. He had not forgotten his defeat at the trial and he had been contemplating his hour of revenge. The Count's manoeuvre to repent and join the crusade had thwarted his grasping expectation to see him broken and crushed together with this renegade priest turned troubadour, whom he would gladly torture before burning alive.

Peire was aware of the mortal danger confronting him and counted his blessings that Esclamonde hadn't been exposed at the trial and, therefore, she was not yet a target of this evil and revengeful crusader—troubadour. However, her father, Nicetas was in immediate danger, as he resided in the domains of Raimon—Roger Trencavel, who was now the main target of the crusaders' rapacious fury. Trencavel had counted on his short—sighted notion that the only victim of the crusade would be his uncle Raymond of Toulouse. The Count, though, had managed to dexterously sidestep the rapacious onslaught, and the northern bull was now charging upon Trencavel, as he was the most obvious next target. In vain he pleaded, but Arnauld—Amaury dismissed him out of hand. All this effort and expense could not be made in vain, so the crusaders began venting themselves on the brave but foolish Trencavel, the Viscount of Bezier and Carcassonne. After the humiliating submission of Count Raymond VI, the entire army of crusaders, without waiting to be sidestepped again, marched without delay against the prosperous City of Bezier to quench their thirst for blood and booty. The young Vi—Count hardly had time to reach Bezier and warn its citizens of the immediate danger, which even then he greatly underestimated. He asked them to hold on until he could get reinforcements from Carcassonne and elsewhere by riding there and back at top speed. Again, he had overestimated his resources and his ability to muster them in time.

On the 21st of July, the crusaders crossed the river Herault, which marked the eastern boundary of Raymond—Roger's lands. Servian and other small cities surrendered without resistance and the crusaders advanced up to the eastern bank of the river Orb where Beziers was situated on a strong encampment. The siege train, composed of sappers, carpenters and military engineers, was busy taking position and with sorting out the problems of a difficult siege. The knights and their assistants were trying to figure out a strategy of attack while the multitudes of camp followers were milling around the grounds facing the southeastern city gate.

On the 22nd of July, an old bishop from Montpellier was sent to demand that the citizens deliver two hundred heretics to the crusaders in order to save themselves and their property. The Citizen Council refused and the hostilities began. A sortie of citizens rode out with white pennants, uttering blood–curdling yells, and releasing a shower of arrows on the crusaders. A knight who had ventured onto the bridge below the wall was cut down and for a moment it looked as if the citizens had the upper hand. However, the sight of premature triumph exhibited by the citizens greatly enraged the camp-followers who then rushed the city in a furious mob, using clubs and tent poles to maliciously attack without reason. Their fury and numbers were so great that they flooded over the walls and the gate of the city. They were intoxicated with success and inflamed by fanaticism and greed. They had been indoctrinated by the preachers that the Southerners were instruments of Satan, protectors of Jews and heretics and immeasurably rich. Once they had penetrated into the streets, this evil howling mob rushed through the city killing everyone they could find. Appalling scenes of destruction and violence followed. The heavily armed knights could not believe their eyes that their underlings, the scum of the earth, had succeeded in three hours taking a city that they could take only after a long siege! It was disturbing for them to discover that their pre-eminence by birthright had been challenged in such a vulgar manner. Belatedly, the knights, not to be undone in pursuit of plunder, charged through the gates and invaded the houses, shoving aside the camp–followers with cudgels and seizing valuables from their grasp. The camp–followers, frustrated in their hopes of a rich booty, spread through the city filled with a lust for the destruction of anything they could not take for themselves. They invaded the churches and slaughtered the terrified citizens who had gathered there for safety. Priests, women and children were cut down indiscriminately. Of the crowds, which had packed the cathedral of St. Madeleine for sanctuary, no one survived. Finally, they set the whole city alight in a blazing fire, which quickly swallowed everything and everybody. Even the invaders had to withdraw to the surrounding hills with all their loot.

On the Hill, overlooking Beziers under attack, friends and foes stood watching together. The prelate Arnauld-Amaury, with a glimmer of cruel triumph in his eyes, had assumed somewhat by default the authority of the leader of the crusade. He was attended by Peter of Vaux-de-Cernay and many other bishops and clerics. The true military leaders and their knights were busy pillaging and killing. The only secular leaders and knights belonged to the entourage of Count Raymond VI who stood nearby silent and quietly horrified. He was under supervision and watched closely. Certainly, he was not trusted to participate in the military action, something that suited him just fine.

Peire Cardinal was standing next to him, saying in a whisper, "My liege, we are forced to witness and take part in this unholy butchery of our own people. This is becoming worse than the carnage during the 4th crusade. There, at least, we were killing schismatic Greeks while here we are killing our brothers and sisters and our own children. This crusade is an abomination designed for the enjoyment of Satan and his minions, who by the way are gloating and leering a few paces from us."

"Dear Peire, my great-grandfather Raymond IV was the leader of the 1st Crusade which gave Jerusalem back to Christianity by wiping out all its Jewish and Saracen populations. Now, four generations later I am punished by another crusade that is going to wipe out not only a large number of my countrymen but also our culture! For what? For the power and glory of a self-righteous, sanctimonious, hypocritical and increasingly evil Church? I have been humiliated and desecrated just to gain some time hoping against hope that our luck, might change for the better. In the meantime, let us be extremely careful. Keep your wife hidden as much as you can, particularly from Cernay, from Folquet the Bishop of Toulouse and from Satan himself, Arnauld-Amaury."

All three of them were busy giving shrill orders to messengers and knights who were running up and down the hill, assisting with the continued massacre in Beziers. One of the knights was pestering Arnauld-Amaury with the redundant question, "How can we distinguish the heretics from the true Catholics and spare the latter." Arnold replied with a subtle yet sinister laughter, "Kill them all; God will recognize his own."

Simon De Montfort

Mass burning
of Cathars

CHAPTER 9

SIMON DE MONTFORT

he crusaders were elated with their unexpected success in Beziers, which was now drowned in blood and burned to ashes. Yet they were still not satiated. Everything was too quick and too little for them. They wanted much more blood and booty so they advanced immediately up the valley of the Aude River to the majestic and powerful city of Carcassonne. They chanted, with raucous voices, the 'golden sequence' of the Cistercians, the Veni Sancte, Spiritus, which was becoming the anthem of the crusade. To the Southerners they appeared like packs of wolves with red eyes, salivating at the mouth and thirsting after their blood, property and souls. The citizens of the city of Narbonne, terror stricken by the prospect of suffering the same fate as Beziers, offered their complete submission to Arnauld–Amaury, the spiritual leader of the crusade. They undertook to deliver all known heretics to the legate immediately, with all the property owned by the heretics and its large Jewish population. It was infinitely better for them to decide who will live and who will perish than the crusaders, who would certainly kill them all and let God recognize his own among the dead. In addition, they promised to supply food to the army and to pay a tax towards the expenses of the crusade. On these terms Arnauld–Amaury offered his and the crusaders' protection. In this way Narbonne was saved.

Esclamonde, who was hiding in the baggage train of Raymond of Toulouse, was mortally worried on her father's account, for he could be one of the heretics sacrificed by the Narbonnese. Peire tried to calm her fears but as he could not get any reliable information he was not too reassuring.

"You know, my love, the Count cannot help us as he is so closely watched. I cannot get information from anybody else without compromising ourselves but I hear that many Perfects and believers are too wary to stay in one place so they are constantly moving to safer places in the Count's domains. I am sure, Nicetas, as aware as he is, would know how to evade persecution and capture."

"No place is safe anymore, anywhere! The Count himself is virtually a hostage. Through all of these years with you I have been happy and contented in spite of our hardships, to the point of forgetting that I am also a true Christian. I accepted a life in which good and evil were mixed but now I see again that they are clearly distinct, and evil, now in the form of the Catholic Church, is rearing its ugly head and striking out at goodness. Peire, you know I love you but this time my place is with my father, who is a holy man near martyrdom. If they take him, I will declare myself and stand next to him."

"My dearest Esclamonde, please do not say things like that. We have our son and we should live to give him our protection and love. Please do not lose hope. Your father, I am sure, is safe and in any case, he would want us to stay alive because life is the most precious thing there is."

"Peire, our son is not with us to make us a complete family. He is in hiding because of me. The safest place for him would be in Verona. This means we will never be together as a family. I am tired of hiding and disguising myself as a man. Still, I will persevere a while longer, at least until I find my father again."

On their march up the valley of the Aude River to Carcassonne, they passed through a succession of ghost towns. Their garrisons and inhabitants had fled to the forest or they had joined the growing crowd of hungry, penniless refugees at Carcassonne. The advance guard of the army arrived outside Carcassonne on the evening of 28th July, as the bells of the city were ringing for vespers. Carcassonne was incomparably the strongest city in Raymond–Roger's possession. It was built on a steep escarpment some six hundred yards from the marshes of the river Aude. Its strong walls were the work of the Visigoths of the fifth century. Twenty-six towers and the castle of the Trenscavels reinforced them and three large suburbs embraced them. Two of the suburbs, the Bourg to the north and the Castellare to the south, were surrounded by walls and ditches of their own. The third, the suburb of St. Vincent, which included the Jewish quarter, lay unprotected to the west between the city and the river.

On the 1ˢᵗ of August, the main body of the crusade arrived. At once, they began their siege on the city by capturing first the unfortified suburb of St. Vincent and attacking the Bourg and the Castellare. These were taken and regained many times through fierce fighting. At this indecisive stage of the siege, Peter II of Aragon arrived in the crusaders' camp with an escort of a hundred knights, undecided whether he wanted to rescue Raymond–Roger or simply mediate on his behalf. What he actually wanted to do was confirm his suzerainty over the Trencavel domains in case any of the leaders of the crusade would try to claim them for themselves. The garrison, who hoped that he had come to reinforce them, was quickly disillusioned. The only thing he could do for them was to negotiate their surrender on reasonable terms, but he did not even do that for he suddenly departed for Barcelona in the middle of negotiations. He ended up achieving nothing of his muddled purposes, leaving Carcassonne to its own devices and Arnauld-Amaury as the master of the situation. In the meantime, pitiable trains of Cathars were herded into the area from Narbonne and elsewhere, in plain view from Carcassonne, as human fuel for the first cleansing fire to take place soon. Arnauld–Amaury and the crusaders waited for the citizens of Carcassonne to decide whether to deliver their own Cathars or follow the example of Beziers. On the 14ᵗʰ of August, Raymond–Roger and nine of his knights were given safe conduct to negotiate with the crusaders in the Count of Never's tent. He agreed that all the inhabitants were to walk in single file out of one gate, wearing only their shirts and breaches and leaving all their possessions behind them. As soon as the terms been agreed upon by both parties Raymond Roger and his retinue were suddenly seized and taken away in chains in flagrant breach of their safe conduct.

On the following day, the 15th of August, the remaining inhabitants left Carcassonne in accordance with the agreement, carrying nothing but their sins, as Peter of Vaux-de-Cernay crowed. To the great relief of Esclamonde and Peire, one of them was Nicetas. Peire, with great difficulty held Esclamonde back from rushing to embrace her father, whispering to her at the same time.

"Not yet, not now, my dearest. They are all around us watching like hawks ready to pick you up and to throw you into the prison camp and from there, to the pyre. Your father was lucky to escape this time. We will soon find out where he is going to hide, in Toulouse most likely. When we do, I promise you we will meet him."

Esclamonde, who could hardly control her sobs, retorted through clenched lips. "Would he be safe in Toulouse? The Count is not reliable as a protector anymore and the new bishop, Folquet de Marseille, is allied to the crusaders' cause and is a ruthless persecutor of my people. I am intensely worried. What can we do?"

"My love, I agree that the Bishop of Toulouse, Folquet, is dangerous to us, but we know it and will be careful so that both of us and your father will be safe. Toulouse is a big city and we have friends there as well as enemies. The Count simply plays a very delicate game and cannot be involved openly, but he can help us discreetly if needed. In the meantime, control yourself and be patient. You will see your father at the right time and place and when it is safe to do so. Right now, we must stay close to the Count of Toulouse and observe what is happening around us without attracting attention."

The crusaders had taken Carcassonne intact and as the Viscount Raymond–Roger was in prison and out of the way, there was a lot of commotion, consultations and discussions as to who among the leaders of the crusade would inherit the Trencavel possessions.

All the leaders of the crusade had gathered in the Trencavel palace and Arnauld-Amaury addressed them.

"I have done enough to set the will of God in motion but now that this important city is in our hands it is your turn to decide who will be the master of this principality and the chief leader of this crusade. The heretics and their sympathizers have not yet been crushed. They are lurking in many unconquered fortified towns of this and of neighbouring principalities. I must turn first to the Duke of Burgundy, to the Count of Nevers, and to the Count of St. Pol as the most exalted of all our nobility who took part in the crusade. Who is willing to take the burden off my shoulders?"

The Duke of Burgundy stood up and spoke first. "I feel honoured by the offer but I must decline because I am needed in my Duchy. I am sure that the Counts of Nevers and of St. Pol will have the same reasons for declining this honour." He turned and looked at them, who nodded in agreement with him. "So," he continued, "The only man, among us, who has proven his worth in this campaign and on many other occasions and is one of the most pious and ardent Catholics, is the Baron Simon de Montfort. I see him demurring but we will not take no for an answer from him. It is an order."

Peter of Vaux-de-Cernay moved towards Simon, a herculean man, and pushed him to stand up and accept the position offered to him. The grim giant finally stood up growling. "I am only a soldier of Christ, I never expected to be given this responsibility. I will accept it, though, on certain conditions. You must make sure that the Pope confirms my new title and that Peter II of Aragon accepts my homage. I will also need a steady supply of good soldiers and money. This crusade has only just started and we have a long way to go yet. To start with, I need you to stay here with me longer than the customary forty days. You know very well that I abhor heresy with all my heart and I will never find peace or give any peace until all heretics and deviants are burned alive. Heresy spoils the harmony and order provided by God to our society and I will make sure to re-establish God's order in this sinful land. Some of you are getting ready to return to your homes but I, for one, never intended to go back to my home until my work here has been completed. You want to make me Viscount of the burned town of Beziers, of the empty town of Carcassonne and of many more towns I still must conquer! I need money and trusted soldiers to give meaning to my new noble title. I will need your constant support in all these things I have asked of you. Are you prepared to do this?

The Duke of Burgundy looked in turn, dark and with meaning, to the Count of Nevers, the Count of St. Pol and to the legate Arnauld Amaury. He finally faced Simon de Montfort and said. "How right and astute of you to demand solid guarantees before you undertake the thankless job of conquering and cleansing this cursed land. It is true that the Count of Nevers is leaving us, taking all of his army with him. It is a pity, but his forty days of obligatory service are up and there is nothing we can do to prevent him from departing. Even I must depart soon as I also have a duchy to govern and protect, but I promise you that I, and my army will stay with you until you are properly installed in your dominions. After my departure, I will be taking all of the necessary measures to ensure that fresh and experienced troops, as well as money, will be sent to you for as long as you need them. I am sure that our holy father the Pope will confirm you as Viscount of Carcassonne and Beziers through the ministrations of our reverent abbot and the legate Arnauld-Amaury."

The legate of the Pope promised right then and there that he would secure from Pope Innocent III the confirmation and indulgences for the future crusaders who would join the army of Simon de Montfort. Simon was finally satisfied by the promises made and accepted the leadership of the crusade.

Simon's first act as the new leader was to organize a huge bonfire, where hundreds of heretics, men, women and children were burned alive. This offered a fantastically lurid spectacle to the crusading army and to the terror-stricken inhabitants of the area. Esclamonde and Peire were in the crowd and the effect on them was devastating, particularly on Esclamonde, who was shaking uncontrollably all over.

As the bodies caught fire, horrible and agonizing screams of pain began filling the air getting louder and more intense. Then slowly there were fewer and fewer screams until crackling and whistling were the only sounds issuing from the raging fire. The bodies could be seen distorting, melting and falling apart as a hideous stench filled the air. This went on for a long time offering thrilling sensations to many crusaders, particularly to the clerics. Arnauld-Amaury and Peter of Vaux-de-Cernay were experiencing a divine, or rather satanic, exhilaration. Simon de Montfort watched the burning impassively but without pity. Terror was going to be one of his methods of achieving the abject submission of these unruly and perverted inhabitants. And, in fact, many fortified towns were opening their gates to him delivering more heretics and sympathizers in order to appease the beast and save themselves. Even the brave Count of Foix accepted onerous terms in order to save his skin and property.

On the 10th of November 1209, Raymond–Roger Trencavel died of dysentery in his prison near Carcassonne. His death was undeniably convenient for Simon de Montfort, who would now sit more securely on the chair of his Viscounty. Soon afterwards a letter came from the Pope confirming his conquered title.

Arnauld-Amaury, who was now the Bishop of Narbonne, was saying to his friend Vaux-de Cernay. "This unfortunate young man was the victim of his uncle's predicament, from which the Count of Toulouse had been unable to escape except by diverting the crusade against Trencavel's domains. But his turn will come soon."

"I will not rest until I see him burn." Cernay retorted with a sinister passion.

"In fact, the process involved in tearing him down is already in motion. I have sent a long list of heretics and their sympathizers to the consuls of Toulouse asking them to be surrendered immediately along with their property. The city fathers refused my demand saying they are good Catholics and upstanding citizens. So, I have been able to lay an interdict upon the city."

"But still Raymond escapes us because of his hypocritical submission to the Church. Why are we so careful and so hesitant to punish him as he deserves?"

"I am ready to excommunicate him on account of the promises that he did not keep, and know, for sure, that they will be too hard for him to keep. Namely, the persecution of heresy, the abolition of toll-gates, the dismissal of mercenaries and Jewish administrators, which cannot be achieved quickly without inviting the disintegration of his government. Did you know he actually employs Jews to run his government? What kind of Catholic would do that? A heretic!"

"But of course we are not concerned about such a disintegration. On the contrary we will be glad to see it happen. His inclusiveness to all these non believers and heretics has dug his own grave."

"For sure, but his Holiness the Pope is a stickler for legal formalities and he believes in the idea of justice even when it hurts us. He demands that accusations must be completely supported. So, we must be careful how we handle matters and how we present them to his holiness."

"What about the assassination of Peter de Castlenneau. Isn't he guilty of this?"

"Peter of Castlenneau proved to be a saint. When we opened his grave, he emanated an odour of sanctity. The Cistercian brotherhood decided that this assassination has fulfilled its purpose and there is no need to pursue it any further lest any investigation turn against us. Unfortunately, there is no proof that Raymond is guilty of it."

"Then who is guilty? Did we ever find the assassin?"

"The assassin has not been found and I do not think he will ever be found."

In the meantime, through the winter of 1209 Simon de Montfort was engaged in conquering castles and fortified towns along the river valleys and the hills on both sides of the Aude River. He showed remarkable military skills, ruthlessness and terror, often bluffing to appear stronger than he really was. Most of the crusaders had left him for their Northern homes and only a few loyal troops had stayed with him. However, his inexhaustible energy made him appear everywhere at the same time, always having the initiative against his enemies. He experienced reverses in both the military and the diplomatic fields but that left him undaunted. The principal author of his troubles was Peter II of Aragon, who repeatedly refused to accept his homage and who encouraged the Southern barons to put up a stiff resistance.

The leader of the resistance was Pierre–Roger, Lord of Cabaret. He was an old man; but age had not diminished his formidable physical powers and glamour, which were praised in the songs of the troubadour Raimon de Miraval. Simon's forces were unable to take any of the fortified keeps of Cabaret and Bouchard de Marly, Simon's kinsman. Fifty of his soldiers were ambushed and captured. Still, Simon managed to be the master of the area and to burn all the heretics he could find. The stench of burning flesh pervaded all of the land from the Black Mountains to the foothills of the Pyrenees, instilling terror in the hearts of all the inhabitants. When he captured the city of Bram, for instance, the entire garrison had their eyes put out except for one, who was spared to lead the wretched column to Cabaret.

Terror upon terror was spreading like wild fire across the land, yet still there were centers of unyielding resistance other than Cabaret. Minerve on the ravine of the Briant River and its lord William, Termes dominating the river valley in the Corbiere Mountains and its lord Raymond de Termes, Montréal and Laurac and their Lord Giraude de Laurac. They all fought desperately and spiritedly against Simon de Montfort and his crusaders. These leaders of resistance stubbornly protected their Cathar citizens, although they themselves were Catholics, simply because of the injustice and brutality of the crusaders and the sanctimonious cruelty wielded by the Catholic Church.

For eight months the fighting went on, tenacity against tenacity, grim determination against bravery and heroism, bluff against privation, hunger and thirst, terror against desperation. Simon de Montfort, most of the time short of money and soldiers, used all means available to him in order to break the walls and the morale of the defenders. He employed the most advanced siege engines, like trebuchets, operated by experienced engineers. These new weapons were immense mechanical slings mounted on wooden frames and equipped with pivot and counterweights instead of the old twisted rope springs.

Simon's largest trebuchet, a monster called Malevoisine, wreaked havoc on the walls of Minerve and forced its surrender on July 24 1210. William of Minerve delivered his city together with 140 Cathars who, when asked to renounce their faith and return to the bosom of the Catholic Church replied, "Why preach to us, we care nothing for your faith, we deny the Church of Rome." The thick smoke of their burning flesh merged with countless other smoke clouds coming from countless pyres burning throughout the former Trencavel domains. Pierre-Roger of Caberet lasted until February 1211, encouraged by the heroism of his people and the songs of his dear friend Raimon de Miraval. Finally, another ex–troubadour, his old friend Folquet de Marseilles and Bishop of Toulouse, persuaded him to surrender.

Simon de Montfort made himself respected by his warriors and ecclesiastic supporters and feared by his enemies and victims, although his successes were mixed with reverses and his resources were limited and often uncertain. The crusaders rarely stayed with him for more than forty days and during the winter months he was left only with his faithful friends. There were times when he was desperate for help but, fortunately, was lucky to have a devoted and energetic wife, Alice de Montmorency, who always managed to find money and fresh recruits for him. She even joined him during the campaigns. She was a tall and majestic woman, an excellent match for a towering warrior such as him.

After a long time apart Simon and Alice met again at Pezenas. They embraced each other with true feelings of love and passion, so hard to imagine between a pitiless man and a calculating woman, but obviously they were made for each other. A couple of hours later she gave him a report of her efforts on his behalf.

"Simon, I have tried very hard to get help from Philip Augustus but he is preoccupied with John Plantagenet and Otto, the German emperor. He cannot give us all the money and knights we need. However, the Cistercians were very supportive and they finally convinced him to let me raise some money from his vassals and recruit a small number of knights who wanted to take advantage of the indulgences offered by the Church. This is how I managed to bring you some knights and this sum of money."

"My dear Alice you have been more than a wife to me, you are a true comrade in arms, an adviser and an ambassador. I do not know what I would have done without you. My struggle here in this land is enormously hard and a thankless one. These Southerners are not a bit like us in the North, they are at the same time recklessly brave, disgustingly cowardly, fickle, treacherous, lecherous, depraved and undisciplined. They are like slime and often appear to me like moving sand. When I win a castle or a city, I am never sure that they will stay mine when I turn my back on them. They are just like their Count, Raymond VI of Toulouse. The heretics among them believe in the most unbelievable and contradictory things you can possibly imagine. They call themselves true Christians, but they believe in two Gods, the God of Good and the God of Evil. They maintain that only their spirit belongs to the good God while their body together with all matter belongs to the evil God, Satan or Jehovah. They equate Jehovah of the Old Testament with Satan. Can you imagine such a sacrilegious notion! They consider carnal love as an evil act and yet they get married and procreate. So, what are they when they do that? Probably satanists. Yet those among them who abstain of all carnal pleasures, the Perfects, are considered holy men and are revered by all the heretics and their sympathizers, who most Southerners are. Really, I cannot fathom their perverted beliefs but their rejection of our Church and its sacraments is intolerable to me. All these Southerners are so disgusting, no more than vermin in my mind. I often contemplate burning them all and repopulating this land with Northerners. People we can understand and accept. When I took the cross, I did it because I wanted to cleanse these Southern lands and return them to the Christianity of the Catholic Church. This is what I am doing now, but my only allies here are the Cistercians and the Bishops. All the others are my open or secret enemies."

"My Lord, my love, do not get worked up like this with your religious fervour. There are other things to think about. Do not forget that we come from the small baronage of Montfort-l'Amaury, which cannot possibly contain and sustain our innate worth and greatness. Now, you are in the process of conquering the Trencavel territories of which you already have the title of Viscount. I know that this is not enough for you and for our family. You must eventually conquer all the domains of the Counts of Toulouse, Foix, and Comminges, which, by the way, harbour the vast majority of heretics. I know for sure that Arnauld-Amaury has started the process of eroding the legal defences of Count Raymond VI by indictments and threats of excommunication. Soon the gates will be open to invade these territories. Eventually you must build a large and strong principality to comprise all Languedoc and Provence. You deserve it. Keep in mind that you should not be carried away by your dislike of all Southerners because you may end up with a land without subjects and instead of deriving an income you will need to borrow money to maintain it. We need wealth and glory at the same time in order to have the exalted status we deserve among the nobility of Europe. Our son, Simon, almost won the Earldom of Leister in England but John Plantagenet took it away from him. Now we rely on the King of France, Philip Augustus, to defeat him so that Simon can take it back. Simon is strong and competent like you. I am sure that he will manage to get his earldom back. Our other son, Amaury, is a good man but he does not possess your strengths and abilities. Try to live long enough until we are blessed with competent grandchildren."

"My dear Alice, your ambitions are even greater than mine and your plans exceed my imagination. Let me point out to you that there are serious obstacles in the realization of such plans. The most serious obstacle is Peter II of Aragon who, as you know, hasn't even recognized me as Viscount of Beziers and Carcassonne, let alone as Count of Toulouse, Foix, Comminges and Provence. He will never recognize anyone so near his border becoming so powerful. If it were not for the Church that supports me, he would have raised a war against me already. Twice he has shown his face threateningly around here but he did not dare go against the Church and he left empty-handed. Furthermore, if I overreach myself, even my present-day friends might turn against me, including the King of France and the Pope, let alone the Dukes of Nevers and Burgundy. You know very well that the Grandees would not take kindly to an upstart growing to their size. Therefore I must tread very carefully towards such a grandiose objective, which, between us, is very dear to my heart."

"Well, I understand your prudence and I am glad that my plan is dear to your heart as well. If sometime in the future you find an opportunity to defeat Peter of Aragon, it will be a giant step forward towards achieving this objective. As for Count Raymond VI of Toulouse, he is more of a nuisance than a threat to you. This is what I think."

"I do agree with your ideas and assessments but the major issue right now is my unending need for money to carry out my present campaigns, as what you brought to me is clearly not enough. I have decided to enter into an agreement with Raymond de Salvagnac, the Knight Templar, who is immensely rich. I have agreed to borrow money from him and then repay him with the treasure collected in Montréal and Lavaur, which I have yet to conquer."

"Simon, this agreement with Salvagnac might solve your immediate economic problems but, in the end, it will tie you down and take your gains away unnecessarily. Please try to stay away from the Templars. God only knows how they managed to hoard so much treasure! We are blaming Count Raymond VI for dealing with Jews while we are instead dealing with the Templars, who are ultimately doing the same sort of money lending schemes."

Finally, with Simon's might and the Templars' money Montréal and Lavanur were taken by storm. All of the inhabitants were slaughtered or burned depending upon whether they were Catholics or Cathars. The leaders of the resistance, Aimery, and his sister Giraude de Laurac, both Cathars, were killed gruesomely by torture while the crusaders got nothing for their pains since the Templar, Salvagnac, took all the treasure for himself as per their agreement. Simon continued his inroads into the territory of the count of Foix, uprooting vines, cutting trees, burning villages and people, and spreading terror everywhere. The Count of Foix was surviving between submissions and retaliations but Simon de Montfort always emerged triumphant.

While Simon was dominating the scene with his grim might, the Count of Toulouse was skirting around the fringes of the military operation by putting up an anaemic show of collaboration and good will with the Crusading cause. Arnauld–Amaury was applying relentless pressure on him to deliver Cathars, to disband his mercenaries and his Jewish administrators, to raze his castles to the ground and to do an endless list of things that the Count was not willing to do. Finally, Arnauld-Amaury excommunicated him but the Count appealed to the Pope by presenting himself to Innocent III for a final judgment. Peire Cardinal went with him to Rome leaving Esclamonde hidden in Toulouse with friends. Nicetas was nowhere to be found as yet and Esclamonde was frantic with worry. It couldn't have been a worse time to leave her alone in such a state but he had to. Esclamonde felt abandoned and betrayed by everyone, including now her only true support and love, Peire. While he was away, she fled from her hiding place and joined an underground group of Cathars without, however, locating her father, Nicetas.

Meanwhile in Rome, Pope Innocent III granted an audience with Count Raymond VI and Peire. Simultaneously, though, Arnauld–Amaury's agents, led by Peter of Vaux-de-Cernay also showed up to make sure Raymond couldn't slip away this time. Peter was invited to speak first and as he was expounding on his venomous accusations against the Count of Toulouse, Peire had the opportunity to observe the appearance and reaction of the Pope. Innocent III was a youngish, good-looking man with a scholarly and austere demeanour. While Vaux-de-Cernay was haranguing the Count with an excessive passion full of hatred, Innocent III was growing visibly impatient. At certain points, he asked him to conclude but he just kept raging on. Finally, Innocent III gave the floor to Peire Cardinal, who in contrast, spoke in a subdued and melodious voice. "Your Holiness, my Liege Lord, the defendant understands and concurs with the aims of the Church to eradicate heresy but this cannot be done overnight. He should be allowed the time already agreed upon. Heresy is a sickness of society, which we agree needs to be cured. It is not advantageous, though, or morally correct to destroy a whole society, especially one which is Catholic and under your spiritual dominion, in order to eliminate this sickness. Give us the time to cure this sickness. This is all we are asking. It must also be said that Raymond has delivered many of his castles to the Church and razed many others to the ground as was demanded of him. It is not reasonable under these circumstances to ask him to deliver all his possessions without adequate justification simply because some warlord from the North covets them. As for his alleged complicity in the assassination of the legate Peter of Castelnau, I maintain that my Lord is innocent. No proof whatsoever has been put forward and no investigation has ever been undertaken to reveal the truth. As for the assassin, we never learned his whereabouts or his name. All we know is that his hideous act has triggered this crusade."

The Pope smiled benevolently and said. "My son, you serve your Liege Lord very well and I hope that you are serving the truth as well. You, Raymond of Toulouse, will be given more time to prove that you are a true child of the Church. Written instructions will follow with my legate Theditious, who will assist my first legate Arnauld–Amaury. I can see that my first legate sometimes tends to exceed his authority. I am sure this is simply due to his excessive zeal and love of Christ. You can go now with my blessings."

The Count of Toulouse was relieved that he managed to shake off an excommunication and gain some additional time of relative peace. Peire was congratulated for his success and he enjoyed the Count's favour but inside he felt uneasy because he was sensing that this good turn would not last long. Arnauld-Amaury was held back for a period by Theditious and by the inhibiting instructions of the Pope, which afforded them some relief. Slowly over time, though, he did begin renewing his pressure on Raymond encouraged in part by the military successes of Simon de Montfort around them. He demanded new flesh to burn on his pyres but the Count, again, did not comply.

In the meantime, Folquet de Marseille, the Bishop of Toulouse, had organized storm troopers inside the city to hunt for heretics. They wore white robes with red crosses and called themselves the White brotherhood. Supposedly they were after usurers, which made them popular, but in fact they actually hunted out Cathars and Jews. They stripped them of their property, which they then divided amongst themselves and the crusaders, who burned the dispossessed victims outside the city. The Count of Toulouse could no longer bear the pressure and pretend to be a crusader against his own people and against himself. He had reached a turning point and felt that he needed to declare himself openly against Arnauld-Amaury, Simon de Montfort and the crusade. With his encouragement, those in the city who hated the activities of the White Brotherhood organized the Black Brotherhood and a Civil War started in Toulouse.

In the midst of all this chaos, Pierre returned to find Esclamonde missing. He started a frantic search to find her, but in vain. She was nowhere to be found. The Cathars did not trust anyone to divulge any helpful information and what made things more difficult still, was that Esclamonde herself did not wish to be found by Peire. He guessed her feelings of bitterness and rejection toward him and a heavy sense of guilt burdened him, mixed with the devastating pain of loss."

When the Count of Toulouse showed his face on the battlefield clearly against Simon de Montfort, old enemies like Raymond-Roger, the Count of Foix, and many other Southerners joined him hoping for the first time that they might drive the crusaders out of the South. On the old Roman road southeast of Toulouse, their superior but undisciplined forces clashed with the inferior but disciplined army of the crusaders at the fortified town of Castelnaudary. Simon's garrison yielded and regained the town several times. The Count of Foix fought bravely and obstinately but the Count of Toulouse remained timidly inactive behind a palisade on a hill while his siege engines remained unused.

Peire Cardinal fought desperately and bravely in Castelnandery trying to anaesthetize his pain with the fury of war. The unexplained timidity of his liege lord puzzled and embarrassed him. He must have his reasons, he thought. Still, if Raymond had thrown his forces into the fray, when he had the chance, together with the Count of Foix, they would have won the battle and, who knows, they might have driven the crusaders out of their country. Simon knew how to take advantage of all opportunities with his superior military skills and would never hesitate in being recklessly brave. He managed to slaughter most of the southern army and put the rest to shameful flight while Raymond and his forces melted away, leaving behind their siege engines. They all fled to find shelter in Toulouse. Fortunately, Simon de Montfort and his troops were too few and too exhausted to pursue their victory by storming and taking Toulouse. Peire, as soon as he was back in the town, resumed his desperate search for Esclamonde.

Folquet Bishop of Toulouse

Esclamonde (creative depiction)

CHAPTER 10

ESCLAMONDE

rom the rambling mansion of the Maurands spread out a maze of workshops reaching all the way down to the Garonne River, criss-crossed by twisting alleys with frequent dead ends. The Maurands were one of the wealthiest patrician families of Toulouse and they owned most of these shops and tenements, where some of their wealth was produced. The crafty bishop of Toulouse, Folquet, always suspected that many heretics were hiding in that district but his storm troopers of the White Brotherhood could not easily venture there because they could be trapped and hacked to pieces by their opponents of the Black Brotherhood. Even a friendly visitor could not easily find his way in the twisted alleys of the St. Pierre de Cuisine quarter, let alone those looking for trouble. The Maurands were unwilling to cooperate with the heretic hunters of Folquet and they were too rich and powerful to be interfered with, particularly when they were so generous to the Church and to the Bishop himself. Folquet needed someone, a traitor, to guide his minions surreptitiously to where the heretic enclaves were hiding. Traitors could always be found, provided there were sufficient rewards to be gained. There was a bloody civil war in Toulouse and Simon de Montfort's supporters, the Bishop Folquet and Bernard Capdenier, the nouveau-rich and vulgar politicians of the Cite', fought against the supporters of Count Raymond VI using the White and the Black Brotherhoods respectively as their military arms. White robed raiders, while they were breaking into the citizens' homes to kill, kidnap

and pillage, would have to clash with their black robed opponents causing chaos and fear in the streets of Toulouse.

The enveloping darkness of night had fallen on the chaotic neighbourhood of Saint Peire de Cuisine swallowing all its irregular shapes and turning them into a formidable black cavern. Three dark figures moved stealthily along the sooty alleyways toward an archway that lead into a hidden courtyard where they knocked conspiratorially at a low inner door. No sound could be heard and yet intense activity was happening behind that door, a long flight of steps below. The three mysterious people were admitted and led down the steps into a spacious basement, lit by a fireplace and candles. Near the fireplace crouched an elderly man who quietly addressed the group of men and women, who were crowded around him. The three newcomers, as they approached the others by the fireplace, dropped their hoods and revealed themselves to be young women. One of them kept herself in the shadows agitated by subdued emotion as she intensely watched the elderly man speak.

"My brothers and sisters, we are experiencing the most agonizing possible times, with trials and tribulations which test the purity of our spirit as it struggles against the relentless assaults of the impure material world all around us. We have seen our brethren and our friends burn like torches by the hundreds and thousands, burned together on huge pyres. Quite likely the same fate is in store for us, as we are also being hunted like animals to feed the insatiable hunger of the crusade for blood and burnt offerings. I hear that Simon de Montfort has conquered the entire South except for Toulouse and a scant few towns and castles. Arnauld-Amaury is often in the city demanding, from the consuls, our flesh and soul and money as well. Folquet the Bishop, mediates so that he is satisfied with less money in exchange for more of our flesh."

"Someone in the group said, "Why should we care if they burn us? By burning us they would liberate our spirit, which would gain its freedom from the tyranny of our flesh. Isn't this what we want?"

"It depends whether you are ready for the separation of your spirit from your flesh. If you are, take the Consolamentum and accept death without fear, whenever it comes and in whatever form. Most of the believers are not ready yet; even some of the Perfects are in the process of learning how to purify their spirit from the clinging flesh. Whoever is not ready fears death, and most of us are not ready yet. Therefore, we must find ways to save ourselves in order to find the time to get ready. Our hiding place, here in the property of Guy Maurand, our protector, is safe for now but it will not be forever. We must be prepared for a sudden departure if needed. A very good friend of mine, Ramon de Parella has built our ultimate hiding place on the Pog of Montsegur in the foothills of the Pyrenees south of Foix in the territory of Foix. Unfortunately, not everyone can go there. Only the Perfects of the Perfects would have this privilege. The rest of us must learn the hard way to become a Perfect of the Perfects by prayer, practice and confrontation with our worst fears. This is the process of purification that we must follow in order to reach Perfection. Even if we do not manage to reach and gain entrance in Montsegur, we might find a better place directly in heaven, the dwelling place of the spirit, if we are pure enough. If we are not, we will be reincarnated again and again until we finally become pure enough. In the meantime, be good and try to stay out of harm's way."

One of the newcomers, who was still sitting in the shadows, addressed the speaker saying, "The Perfects of the Perfects have no need of Montsegur because they have nothing to fear. But we, the mere believers, need this ultimate hiding place in order to have a chance to reach purity. Perhaps there is not enough space for all of us and they decided to admit not the most needful but the most deserving. So, what should the most needful do? Turn into renegades or jump into the fire? Also, what do you mean by saying the Perfects of Perfects? Do you imply that there are Perfects that are not perfect enough? What can we hope for? The kingdom of Heaven or an escape from Hell?"

While she was speaking the elderly preacher was shivering with strong waves of emotion as recognition was dawning on him. Yet he chose to address her question before rushing to embrace her. "My daughter, your voice sounds familiar and more so, your inquisitive mind. For the sake of everyone here let me answer your questions first; Montsegur is only a temporary resting place before the inevitable martyrdom, and not Heaven on earth. It is a place where our Perfects can achieve their final purification by prayer and good deeds to their fellow men and women. It is true, there is not enough space for all, but goodness receives goodness and some believers who are judged to be worthy of salvation could be admitted there. It is true that no Perfect is perfect enough as long as he resides in his material shell and must always devote his efforts to purify himself and become Perfect of Perfects. A believer like you is free to live like anybody else on this earth and experience all the pleasures of the flesh but he or she differs from everybody else because he or she possesses the knowledge that flesh is evil and the spirit is good. He or she can always choose their direction towards one or the other principle. These present-day terrors help us choose more easily one or the other because Hell has revealed itself right here on Earth where it belongs in all its glory. There is no Hell in the Spirit World but only in the material world. What we see today is Satan unmasked and revealed in its true form, its material form, which is the only form it possesses. The Catholics maintain falsely that Satan is spirit and that Hell is spiritual. There is no hell elsewhere but in the material world, where Satan rules supreme, but he has no other kingdom to rule. Surely you can choose to become a renegade and reject our beliefs without punishment from us. Your punishment will be the consequence of your choice. Surely you can choose to jump into the crusaders' fire or commit suicide in any other way but this is only a desertion or dodging battle. This would interrupt the process of purification and might condemn you to go through an unfavourable reincarnation in the material world. We may call this an unwelcome delay from achieving true spiritual freedom. The only thing we can hope for is a chance to purify ourselves from the pollutions of matter and earthly hell and eventually achieve and reach the Spiritual Heaven, possibly by progressive reincarnations, by shedding all our material garments. I can only hope that I have answered your questions. At least the best way I could. Please come to me now, Esclamonde my daughter, so that I can hold you in my arms after so many years of separation. I sensed your presence as you entered and hid in the shadows, but when you spoke I recognized you without the slightest doubt. Please come to me because I have missed you so much."

Esclamonde ran to her father, Nicetas, and embraced him tightly kissing him between sobs and tears. "For the last two years I have been hiding in the quarter of the Pergaminieres, the parchment makers shop, south but not far from here. I was looking for you but no one could give me your whereabouts until Alaman de Rouaix, our protector, gave me news of you. My friend Arnaude de Lamothe offered to be our guide to find you here. My third companion Dulcia insisted on coming with us for the benefit of listening to your teaching as she said, but I am a bit uneasy about her as she is asking too many questions."

"What kind of questions?"

"Who are our protectors and if she could visit other cells because she is bored hiding for such a long time in the same place. She does not know about Alaman de Rouaix, as I myself evaded her questions."

"Most likely you are unnecessarily suspicious. Anyway, let us not worry about Dulcia. Tell me about yourself and your husband Peire. Where is he and why are you are not with him?"

"It is a very long story which I will tell you as soon as we have some privacy."

After the secret congregation had ended Esclamonde and Nicetas slipped off to Nicetas' tiny room where, by the warm glow of an oil lamp, they began to reconnect. Esclamonde began. "In the twelve years since I last saw you so many things have happened. Pierre and I were in Constantinople with the 4th crusade, where we had a foretaste of the horrors that are now happening here. Five years ago, we had a son, Nascibon, who lives in Campagnac with Peire's parents. I haven't seen my son for more than three years now and I haven't seen my husband for eighteen months. In fact, I left him because I decided to join our people, where I belong. The suffering of our people is so terrible that I am feeling irresistibly drawn back to them and to you, my dearest father. Peire could not and should not be here with me. He has a separate mission to follow and I do not wish for him to share my fate."

Nicetas was listening quietly and with deep sadness to the long story that his beloved Esclamonde was telling him. Between tears she filled in all the details concerning the events, thoughts and feelings, she'd been through in the past 12 years. As the tale came to an end, a long pause followed interrupted by her sobs. Nicetas took his daughter in his arms and tried to console her with caresses and sweet words. Finally, he asked her. "Do you still love your husband and your son?"

"I love them very much but for their own safety I have chosen not to be with them. I also cannot be dragged behind a man whose strong loyalties bind him to the Count of Toulouse and his ambiguous movements and policies. I want to stay with you and eventually become a Perfect like you. I know that my nature tempts me towards the intense pleasures of the flesh and I can easily fall into the steaming pit of iniquity, where Belial reigns supreme. I have done it before in my travels but I want to redeem myself by taking the arduous steps towards perfection, under your guidance. I am prepared to earn my passage to Montsegur."

"I am very sad to hear your decision to stay away from your husband and your child, although I should have been gratified that it conforms with our faith. Most of our brethren go through the process of purification together with their families and so they reach perfection with serenity. It seems that you intend to take the path of salvation with turmoil in your heart. How do you propose to do that? How can you become pure with such a heavy burden?"

"I will learn how to swim in the heavy seas with two stones hanging around my neck. That is how. Please show me how to swim and I will swim."

"My dearest Esclamonde, it will not be easy in your case but I will try, since you are determined to take the path. You already know the theory of our Faith but now you must visualize the essence of your spirit, entangled as it is by your material desires and attachments. Eventually, but systematically, you must shut away these desires and attachments so that your spirit can shake off its bonds and fly away free. I am afraid you must go through Abstinentia for one or two years in order to help yourself in your efforts to visualize your inner world. While you will be abstaining from the pleasures of the flesh you will undergo the Apparelliamentum comprising of confessions and meditations. At a certain point, you may feel ready to go through the ceremony of Conveniencia where you must make a sincere promise to take the Consolamentum before you die or preferably earlier. By the Conveniencia you will become a Perfect. I told you, it will not be easy, and keep in mind you will be experiencing temptations every step of the way and may even relapse into the pleasures of the flesh. If you do, then you will simply have to start all over again. It is not easy but this is our path of liberation. As long as you know what you are up against you may start right here with me and I will support you all the way through. As you know, I come from an old line of true Christians that goes back to the land of the Greeks. Although I have had a long training through trials and persecutions I have even had relapses myself. You are the wonderful product of a relapse, when I met and married your late mother. Maybe we are meant to experience relapses and struggle with the pleasures of the flesh. By the way, I understand you had the opportunity to visit the greatest and most beautiful city of the world, the city of my origin, Constantinople. How did you find it?"

"I, unfortunately, did not see it in the glory it must have once been. I saw only its brutal destruction and obliteration by the crusaders, and am ashamed that, officially, I was one of them. It was extremely upsetting and haunts me still. All that is in the past, though, and I am now ready to start a new life with you, under your guidance."

Esclamonde stayed with Nicetas, together with thirty Cathars, who worked as workers and artisans in one of the factories belonging to Guy Maurand, their employer and protector. Arnaude returned to the parchment making shop in the Cite, where she and her family and twenty other Cathars worked under the protection of Alaman de Rouaix

The last of the 3 newcomers who arrived that night, Dulcia, slipped off to the mansion of the mayor, Bernard Capdenier, who was holding her entire family hostage, forcing her to be his mistress and act as a spy and informer against her own people. She entered through the back door and the mayor himself admitted her immediately.

"Did you manage to get any useful information?"

"Yes, I discovered a very important hideout of heretics in the quarter of St.–Pierre de Cuisine. A well-known Perfect is among them, Nicetas d'Outremer and his daughter Esclamonde is with him. She is the wife of the famous troubadour Peire Cardinal, who is also the adviser and secretary of the Count of Toulouse."

"Can you guide our storm troopers there?"

"Yes, I can, provided you keep your part of the bargain, to release my mother, father, brother and sister immediately. They are much less valuable to you than the Nicetas group. I will remain as your hostage until this mission is successfully completed."

Bernard Capdenier knew that the offered catch was a very valuable exchange of favours and money from the Bishop Folquet and the legate Arnauld-Amaury, who only recently had demanded 1000 livres of gold from him and the city counsellors. The legate would agree to extract much less money in exchange of such a valuable catch of heretics. Bernard released Dulcia's family and kept her as a hostage. He then rushed to meet Folquet in his Episcopal Palace and informed the Bishop that he could undertake a clean-up operation in Maurand's workshops as soon as he gave his blessing.

The handsome Bishop smiled sardonically and said, "This is good news my friend, I hope to assuage the hunger of our carnivorous legate, Arnauld-Amaury, and convince him to be satisfied with 500 livres instead of his original demand of 1000 livres. I may even convince him to take even less with more heretics of renown. By the way, did you say that the wife of Peire Cardinal, Esclamonde is with them? I wonder what happened. Regardless, we will soon find out, although I am not going to strike quite yet. Simon de Montfort is busy conquering, pillaging and devastating the principalities of the Counts of Foix and Comminges and that of the Viscount of Bigorre, which is bound to create a conflict with King Peter II of Aragon. The King of Aragon was recently victorious against the Moors in the field of Las Navas de Tolosa and now he has crossed the Pyrenees with angry complaints against Simon. I have heard that he has met with Count Raymond VI and Raymond the younger, quite possibly to form an alliance against the crusade. King Peter II maintains that the crusade has outlived its original purpose to eradicate heresy, that there are no longer any heretics and that the crusade is now being used by Simon de Montfort to carve out a mighty principality for himself and his descendants made up of the territories of the Counts of Toulouse, Foix, Comminges and of the Viscounts of Bigorre and of Beziers–Carcassonne. I understand that his emissaries are remonstrating his case with the Pope in Rome, who I am sure will take his side as he has started to mistrust Simon de Montfort's extravagant ambitions and the high-handedness of his legate, Arnauld-Amaury. The Pope is a stickler for due process of the law and he is unwilling to disturb the legal rights of the established nobility for the sake of an upstart like Simon de Montfort. Peire Cardinal has joined Peter II's ambassadors as Count Raymond VI's representative and I know for sure that he possesses extraordinary powers of persuasion. On the other side Simon Montfort is too sure of himself and is bound to ignore even the Pope's admonitions and rebukes hoping to create a fait–accompli of his supremacy in the area, which even the Pope would have to accept. At present, he is master of all the territories between the Massif Central and the Pyrenees with the exception of Toulouse, Montauban, and the hill towns of Rouergue. Raymond's brother Baldwin has defected and joined the crusaders' cause and that has been an additional blow against the prestige of the Count of Toulouse. It seems inevitable that Simon will be the winner but I would rather wait a bit longer until the situation becomes clearer. I will keep the heretic hiding places under close surveillance so that none of them can escape. At the appropriate moment I will strike to capture them all and offer them to Simon and Arnauld–Amaury in order to get the maximum benefit."

In early June of 1213 the white robed raiders suddenly burst into the hiding places of the Cathars of St. Pierre de Cuisine and captured, unawares, two hundred of them before the Maurands and the Black Brotherhood had a chance to react. They were herded and locked up in the subterranean prison of the Episcopal Palace, where jailer monks asked them to abandon their faith and become good Catholics. Very few did but their repentance was judged to be insincere and they were condemned to burn at the stake. The crusaders needed victims and not repentants. The Perfects had started to administer the Consolamentum to their fellow believers when a jailer–monk grabbed Esclamonde forcibly out of Nicetas's arms before she had a chance to take the Consolamentum or even say goodbye to him. She was taken to the Bishop of Folquet for questioning. Folquet was a very handsome and irresistibly charming man who knew how to play with the minds and feelings of those whom he wanted to persuade or seduce. His Episcopal office did not prevent him from being an intensely active womanizer and a very effective one at that. He knew how to conquer the senses and souls of women.

Esclamonde found herself confused for in spite of her agitation concerning the fate of her father, her companions and herself she was being affected by his charm. Folquet looked at her kindly and said, "My dear child, I understand and am sympathetic with your terrible plight. Please believe me that I will try my best to rescue you and your father. It is beyond my power to rescue the rest of your companions from the grasp of the leaders of the crusade though."

"Your Excellency, thank you for your kindness and willingness to help me and my father. How can you be so kind after having abducted and imprisoned us in your own prisons? What do you want from my father and me in exchange for our rescue? Be sure that we are not inclined to deny our faith."

"I will never force you to deny your faith, but I may try to persuade you by theological and common-sense arguments, the same way St. Benedict had done long ago."

"And why should you go to all this trouble?" she asked.

"Because you are worth saving and because you are an accomplished poet and musician like I used to be, and because your father is a craftsman of musical instruments. It would be a terrible waste to burn your exceptional talents at the stake. Twelve years ago, Peire Cardinal, your husband, managed to save your people in court where I had acted as the litigant against him. I was very impressed by his argumentation then and I also like him as a fellow troubadour. By the way, why aren't you with him, instead of risking your life in a Cathar cell?"

"Thank you for your noble sentiments, which prompted our rescue. As for Peire Cardinal, I have chosen not to burden him with my presence because of my faith. Furthermore, I do not want him to know my whereabouts and circumstances."

"I admire you for your stance and attitude. Peire Cardinal will not learn from me anything about you."

After this strange interview Esclamonde was given lodgings in a comfortable cell apart from Nicetas, who was also taken to a separate one. Esclamonde was profoundly affected and puzzled by conflicting thoughts and feelings. She was undoubtedly charmed and impressed by the personality and words of Folquet and yet there were disturbing contradictions in the whole setup.

Shortly after her interview she was allowed to meet with her father in his cell. He was gravely pensive. "My dear daughter, the Bishop visited me and offered his unconditional hospitality and safety under his roof until the end of the storm, as he said. He could not do the same with the rest of our brethren because they are officially the prisoners of the all-powerful legate Arnauld-Amaury and of the leader of the crusade, Simon de Montfort. I told him that I could not live in safety when my people are condemned to be burnt alive. My life has run its course and my place is among my people now."

"In that case, my place is next to yours in the pyre! I have been away from you for far too long a time. Now that I finally found you, I want to die with you and have the same glorious end!"

"Listen to me, my dear Esclamonde, you must accept the Bishop's offer and live. You still have a lot to learn and experience before you achieve purity and perfection. If you rush to your death right now you will be condemned to reincarnate unfavourably. It is not your time yet. Please take his offer and live. Your perfection awaits you at Montsegur. Go there and seek the protection and guidance of Ramon de Parella.

Esclamonde protested and cried for a long time but in the end, she had to accept her father's reasoning and advice. They embraced each other for a long time knowing it was for the last time. Esclamonde locked herself in her cell and Nicetas went back to the prison with the other Cathars. A few days later all of them were herded out of Toulouse to Castelnaudary, where a magnificent ceremony was about to take place.

On the 24th of June 1213, the crusaders gathered at Castelnaudary to witness the knighting of Simon de Montfort's eldest son Amaury. Tents were erected for the spectators in a meadow outside Castelnaudary and an altar was placed in an open pavilion at the summit of a hill. Here the Bishops of Orleans and Auxerre stood, splendidly robed, while Amaury was led toward them by his father and mother to be presented with his sword and belt before the altar. The surrounding clerics broke into the Veni Creator Spiritus. At the same moment on an opposite hill the two hundred Cathars from Toulouse were consumed in a gigantic ceremonial conflagration, signifying to the people that the original purpose of the crusade was still a burning issue. It was a burning answer to Peter II of Aragon who claimed that the crusade was no longer necessary and to Pope Innocent III, who had almost believed him. Amaury, with the fire reflected on his face, turned to receive homage from the crusaders as his father's heir. In this way, Simon de Montfort was confirming himself and his family as the hereditary princes of all the Southern lands and the leaders of a religious crusade with the burning purpose of eradicating heresy. Peter of Vaux-de-Cernay wept, overcome by the religious significance of the knighting ceremony and elevated by the cleansing fires of burning heretics. While Peter was raving about the triumph of the Church and the crusade over the serpents of heresy, Thedisius, the legate, was talking to Folquet. "Your contribution of two hundred heretics was extremely valuable and timely to the cause of keeping the crusade alive. As you know, I was in Rome trying to prove to the Pope that the crusade is needed and that Simon de Montfort should be acknowledged as the Prince of all the Southern territories and the champion of the Church. The embassy of the King of Aragon, assisted by the emissaries of the Count of Toulouse, had convinced his Holiness that Simon was using the crusade to promote his ambition to gain a principality for himself and that there were no more heretics to worry about. The Pope had decided to disband the crusade, to withhold the indulgences and to forbid the invasion of the territories of all the Southern Princes including those of the Count of Toulouse. As you know, without indulgences no new crusaders can be recruited and without permission to conquer Simon would wither away. It took us two months to change the Pope's mind and to make him declare to the Aragonese embassy that they had played deceitfully on his ignorance, that protectors of heretics were more dangerous to the faith than heretics themselves. Finally, Innocent III forbade Peter II of Aragon to interfere with the crusade. However, he did not sanction Simon's takeover of Foix, Comminges, Bigorre and Toulouse. He has always been reluctant to disturb the established order in favour of upstart powers because he feels he should protect the permanence and stability guaranteed by the old nobility. As we know, Innocent has a tendency to change his mind quite often and much depends on the fortunes of the war."

"You are quite right; the fortunes of the ongoing War can have an impact on the Pope's decisions but to whose favour we cannot tell." Folquet responded. "Right now, the city of Toulouse is in turmoil and the majority is going against us. They blame me, and rightly so, for the Holocaust we are witnessing right now but they will not dare attack me of yet. Count Raymond VI comes and goes like a cat and conspires with his loyal friends in Toulouse. He plays hit and run with Simon's occupation forces and he tries to form an alliance with Peter II of Aragon and the counts of Foix and Comminges. An army of dispossessed southern knights, known as Faidit, has gathered around him and his son Raymond, ready for any desperate action. But they are not a match against the disciplined army of Simon de Montfort, at least not yet."

"Who are the Faidit and where do they come from?" Thedisius asked.

Folquet, who had his slippery fingers in everything, said "They used to be the lower and middle gentry of Languedoc and Provence but they lost their estates and castles to the Northern crusaders, who have now taken their places. Last year at Pamiers, Simon and the Church issued the statutes legalizing this takeover and establishing the legal customs of the North including Primogeniture, by which the first-born inherits all and, therefore, there is no division of the estate. This is the new social order, which would sustain and consolidate Simon's power in the South. The ceremonial knighting of Amaury today crowns this new social order and burning the heretics demonstrates the devotion of the new dynasty to the cause of the Catholic Church. As for the Faidit, they are like angry wasps forced out of their nests. Their sting could be fatal. Somehow they do not seem to be angry with me as I do tend to their basic needs for food and medical care from time to time."

"So, Folquet, you can serve as a mediator if needed. My main concern is Peter II of Aragon, right now, as his prestige as the victor against the Moors makes him extremely dangerous as the leader of the Southern cause against us. What do you think, can we persuade him to stay loyal to the Catholic Church?"

"As long as the Catholic Church sides with Simon de Montfort and his ambitions to take over all of the Southern principalities, the King of Aragon will fight against us. He feels arrogantly confident that he will defeat us. His issue is not against the Church but against Simon's ambitions. I am fortunate to have the good will of both sides. For this reason I can be useful as a mediator provided that some of you, like the hard headed Arnauld-Amaury, are prepared to listen to my advice. I hear that he plans to put pressure on the people of Toulouse for more hostages, for more heretics and for more money. I have advised him against it but he is not listening to me. Please, Thedisius, try to make him understand that in the end he will alienate all the citizens of Toulouse and thereby strengthen the Count and his son who, by the way, shows signs of vigorous ability and courage, unlike his father. Please do something to dissuade him from his unreasonable and extortionist plans. It has been a pleasure discussing these important matters with you Thedisius but now that the ceremony and its accompanying festivities are winding down I must get back to Toulouse. I have been gone now for over a week and must make sure I do not lose my influence."

In the Episcopal Palace, Esclamonde was crying inconsolably and had not been eating any food for days. She kept telling herself that she should not have listened to her father's advice, that she should have thrown herself into the pyre with the others. What was the point of staying alive after having lost everything? Now she was left with only this unbearable loneliness.

As soon as Folquet returned from Castelnaudary he went straight to Esclamonde to find her in this pitiable state. He sat next to her and took her in his arms whispering soft words of consolation, which dripped like warm honey straight into her vulnerable heart and made her feel somewhat better, in a confused kind of way. It was not what he said but the sound and warmth of his voice that began to change her mood. She suddenly felt like washing herself and began to feel a desire for food returning. As her sobs subsided she began to feel a familiar tingling sensation returning to her as well and it scared her. Folquet was a master of persuasion and charm even without resorting to elaborate talk and poems. His personality alone had a magnetic power with sensuous tentacles that enveloped and enticed without coercing his object of desire, or victim. Folquet visited Esclamonde again and again offering just consolation without making direct or implied sexual demands on her. Esclamonde began looking forward to their encounters with an increasing feeling of urgency until one day the inevitable happened and they merged together in an explosion of deeply erotic enjoyment. From that point on Esclamonde forgot who she used to be and all her Perfect goals. Instead, she became totally immersed in the land of lotus-eaters during her love affair with Folquet, the Bishop of Toulouse. There were times, when Folquet was away, that disturbing thoughts assailed her mind. According to the two principles of her faith, she must be experiencing the sensations of absolute evil in the unclean mire of flesh. Here in this world of flesh and pleasure, it seemed, she kept returning to drown with ever increasing passion and joy. As for the spiritual heaven, she seemed to have lost all her inclinations of aspiring to it. She sometimes even thought that her father, Nicetas, and her brethren were deluded to see Heaven instead of the world of flesh. Folquet himself now appeared to her as the God of all flesh and a miracle worker of sensual pleasures.

Folquet was a womanizer but a discreet one because of his office. In this case he had felt a very powerful infatuation with Esclamonde. He had seen her long ago, at the time of the trial, and her image had penetrated his mind, stuck there until she fell within his grasp. He had engineered this whole setup in order to seduce her and keep her for his own private pleasure but when he finally experienced love with her he was totally captivated by her unleashed eroticism and her insatiable need. At times, he saw her as a demon of a sensual Inferno, Lilith herself, undoubtedly, or the goddess Venus, who was the same spiritual entity anyway. According to his Catholic Faith, what he was experiencing with Esclamonde was a mortal sin and Esclamonde herself was an emissary of Satan thrown onto his path for his spiritual damnation. However, all of these thoughts made his passion for her burn all the more fiercely. Most likely one day he would find in himself the spiritual strength to be rid of her by throwing her into a cleansing fire together with other Cathars. Until then he couldn't stop loving her.

At one point, after a long, intense erotic session, she asked him. "Where is all this leading us? What do you think will happen to us in the end? What could the end be?"

"I do not really know and, as a matter of fact, I do not want to know the end."

"Who is foolish enough to want to know the time and the manner of his or her death?"

"Not I, for sure."

"Do you really feel that the end of our love will be something like death?"

"Most likely worse, so let us enjoy the preciousness of our limited time together in this world."

He took her in his arms again and they made love desperately to push the end as far away as possible.

Then she asked him again, "Can our love continue after death?"

"Our love? Most likely in hell."

"You know I am a Cathar. I do not believe in Hell."

Folquet was certainly a wonderful lover but at the same time he was a man of God, the Bishop of a very important city in fact. Yet, first and foremost, he was a politician and a very good one at that. He always knew that Esclamonde could be a mortal danger to his prestige and power. Her attachment to him made her even more dangerous because if she ever felt rejected she could reveal their affair with disastrous consequences. He was finding his own attachment to her blurred his judgment and weakened his will to act for his own good. Obviously, he had to do something about it and do it fast as the events were galloping past him. This middle-aged man badly needed this young woman who made him feel alive, with a red-hot youthful vigour. It was not easy for him to send her away or let her perish. In the Episcopal Palace, everybody was led to believe that Esclamonde was his orphan niece under his protection and care. No one questioned it or suspected anything else. In order to legitimize her presence, he had assigned her to his valuable library as a scribe and a copier. She had also joined the choir of the adjacent nunnery, where her exceptional voice was greatly appreciated. Having minimized the danger by these precautionary measures he finally decided to keep Esclamonde near him, at least for the time being. So, the months went by and Esclamonde, who never sensed his private thoughts, was happy to be with him and perform her appointed tasks. However, from time to time she remembered her father with sorrow and her husband and child with a sharp pain of guilt. She pushed these thoughts away as quickly as she could so they couldn't spoil her present joy in life. As for her spiritual journey to Montsegur, she had put it aside without, however, cancelling it entirely. The Abstinentia she had started in the Cathar cell before her capture was entirely forgotten and replaced by an orgy of intense sensuality, not only with Folquet but also with her fellow librarians and even with some nuns of the choir.

She had never forgotten Bieiris and her forbidden but ravaging exotic practices either. During her choir practices, she used her beauty and charm to seduce two nuns similarly inclined. Folquet was often away on diplomatic missions for Simon or for the Church, giving her the time and the opportunity to enjoy her erotic side-activities. When she confessed her indiscretions to him, instead of getting angry he was enormously aroused and loved her all the more. Whenever he thought it was safe, he participated wholeheartedly in orgies of fantastic depravity. She was going further and further in the thick recesses of the old Goat Belial and she loved every minute of it.

She never ventured outside the Episcopal Palace walls and she ignored or blocked any noises, rumours, proclamations, announcements, debates and the clamour of war, which were hitting her protective walls like ebbing and flowing waves.

There were times when she wondered whether she had done the right thing by deserting her husband and child in order to join her Cathar brethren, whom she had deserted as well later. Her reasoning and justifications for doing so were no longer valid, except that she did not want to be dragged along behind the pointless wanderings of Count Raymond VI and his retinue, where Peire was attached.

When the heavy smoke from the burning of Cathars would sometimes reach her behind the palace walls she felt an overpowering hatred for Simon de Montfort and his crusade. At these times she felt an overpowering urge to bolt and join her people again.

Siege on the castle of love. A 14th century depiction of a popular analogy of the time; the concurring of a heart to achieve love and joi.

The four stages of courtship 14th century ivory.

Peter II King of Aragon and his Arms

CHAPTER 11

HOW LOW WE HAVE FALLEN

n the gloomy hall of the Chateau Narbonnais which guarded the Southern gate of Toulouse, Count Raymond VI and his friends were rejoicing with the news that Peter II of Aragon had crossed the Pyrenees with one thousand knights. The good news had given an occasion for Raimon de Miraval to sing a hopeful triumphant sirventes.

> The King is coming over the mountains
> To fill the fields with fluttering banners
> Hauberks, helmets, lances and swords
> The King is coming to raise our pride
>
> Pride that has perished at the hands
> Of the French freebooters from the North
> We who have fallen will rise again
> For justice is at our side

Peire Cardinal caught by Miraval's Enthusiasm continued with one of his own sirventes.

> Our Count, the Southern princes
> And the multitudes of Faidit
> Will join with the brave King,
> To release our land of the free

To crush the head of the evil wolf,
Who now devastates our land
Who drinks our blood and burns our flesh,
Its time to make our stand

We will rise again,
To claim back what is ours
To raise our flags, regain our pride
To reclaim our southern towers

Now the time has come
For retribution and demands
To corner the wolf, to crush his head,
Its time to make a stand

To regain our pride and claim our land,
Its time to make a stand!
Its time to make a stand,
Yes, its time to make a stand!

The Count, in spite of the general jubilation, had remained pensive and at certain point he said, "I am very happy that, at this critical time, our people and our Southern princes have finally united against our common enemy, the wolf Simon de Montfort, his crusaders and all the other wolves of his entourage. I warn you, though, that it will not be easy to defeat these wolves, even though the victor of the Moors, Peter II of Aragon, is coming to lead us. We should not underestimate them because they are cunning and fierce fighters. I suspect that the King of Aragon will try to win a quick victory by risking everything in one battle. I think we should hold back some reserves and build some defences just in case.

The Count of Foix jumped to his feet and shouted. "We have seen your cowardly ways in Castelnaudary and I for one intend to attack the enemy and not hide behind palisades."

The young Raymond moved angrily against Foix but his father held him back firmly and said, "We are not here to fight among ourselves but to find the best way to fight united against our enemies. My dear Foix, do not mistake caution for cowardice. I have managed to keep my forces intact to fight many more battles until I wear the enemy out.

The Count of Comminges replied. "The King, Foix and I prefer the headlong attacks that win or lose battles and despise your boring tactics of defence. Regardless, the immediate plan is to meet the King at the fortified city of Muret a few miles south of here and upstream of the Garonne River."

"Yes, I know. My forces and a large contingent of the Toulousain militia will board barges and navigate them upstream to Muret, which we must capture right away before the main battle begins."

Peire Cardinal, who had also secretly hated and been embarrassed by his Liege Lord's behaviour in Castelnaudary, had now started seeing Raymond's tactics with a more understanding eye. Raymond was advocating a war of attrition, which perhaps was the most realistic way to fight against Simon de Montfort and his crusaders.

On the 10th of September 1213, Peter of Aragon and his knights joined forces with the smaller armies of the Counts of Foix and Comminges along with an enormous mob of militiamen from Toulouse. These last were not highly regarded as soldiers, but they had brought with them provisions, arms and six siege engines in a fleet of barges, which they towed upstream from Toulouse. Raymond's forces rode close by with their equipment and provisions. The total mounted strength of the Southern coalition was about twice that of the crusaders assembled forty miles away at Fanjeaux. Peter II of Aragon, cock sure and arrogant as usual, did not doubt for a minute that he would conquer Simon's crusaders. At that most inopportune moment Raymond of Toulouse proposed to him that they should fortify the camps with palisades and repel the crusaders with crossbows if they attempted to force a battle. Simon could be starved out at leisure.

The Aragonese knights guffawed at this plan and Peter said with disdain, "Am I, the King of Aragon and the Moor slayer, to dishonour myself by the kind of cowardice which has brought you to your present pitiful state?"

Raymond retired to his camp on Perramon Hill to sulk, humiliated, in his tent while the King and the Counts of Foix and Comminges drew out their troops on the North of the plain one mile from the fortified town of Muret. In the meantime, the Toulousain militia assaulted the battered walls of Muret and invaded the lower town, furiously pursuing the crusaders of the garrison through the streets and killing several of them. Peire, who had joined the Toulousiains, overpowered and captured one of these crusaders and by doing so he managed to save him from the murderous fury of the militia. His name was Guy de Sommerive. Peire took him to Raymond's camp on Perramon Hill. Soon afterwards, in the midst of the chaos, Simon's army appeared on the far side of the Garonne River. Panic seized the ill–trained militiamen and they withdrew in confusion to their camp allowing Simon to cross into the town without resistance.

Because of the lack of an adequate chain of command an important opportunity had been lost to capture and hold Muret. When a King's knight questioned the militia leaders about their cowardly action, they said. "Sir, by doing so, we have trapped Simon and his entire army inside Muret where we can starve them."

The knight galloped away to his King thoroughly disgusted by this hasty and irrational rationalization. Several bishops had followed Simon and Folquet. One of them tried desperately to negotiate a peaceful arrangement because he feared the prestige and the superior numbers of the King of Aragon. The King, sure of victory, disdainfully rejected their proposals. The King of Aragon even refused to coordinate with Raymond's forces which were barricaded one mile south west of his own.

"This victory will be entirely my own and I will not share it with unworthy and cowardly allies", he said to Peire Cardinal who had come to offer Raymond's assistance."

In the meantime, Simon de Montfort prepared his troops with grim determination knowing very well that he had to win or perish. He formed three squadrons, the first under William of Contres, the second under Bouchard de Marly, and the third a reserve under Simon's own command. The first two were to attack like spears one behind the other and the third was to flank the Southerners by picking its way through a broad marsh.

Peter II of Aragon had passed the previous night with mistresses in an intense orgy of erotic dissipation and on the day of the battle he was so exhausted that he was unable to stand upright during the reading of the Gospel. Still, he drew up his troops at the summit of a gentle rise, with his right flank protected by a stream, and his left by Pesquies Marsh. He exchanged his distinctive armour for that of an ordinary knight and placed himself at the frontline. Peter had the advantages of numbers and terrain, but he exploited neither of them. Each knight was allowed to place himself in the line, with his equerry and mounted sergeant. A confused mass of horsemen, without infantry, without orders, waited for the French charge. The result was a rout, not a battle. Simon's first squadron charged a mile across the plain and struck the Aragonese Calvary with overpowering violence throwing them aside "Like dust before a gale". As they fell back, the second squadron of Bouchard de Marly hurled itself into the gap. The King was trapped in the thickest of the fighting and was struck to the ground, crying out "I am the King", but too late to be spared or taken alive. By now Simon himself had joined the melee with the reserve, picking his way along a path across the marsh and falling on the Aragonese left. He fought with his sword and his fists spreading terror in his wake like a legendary giant warrior and hero. The entire Southern line had broken up, and as the news of Peter's death spread, they turned and fled headlong in all directions pursued by most of the French army. The battle had lasted scarcely half an hour. The French foot–soldiers, who had stayed behind to hold the town, swarmed across the plain to finish off the wounded and plunder the dead. Simon sought out the body of Peter II of Aragon and found it had already been stripped naked by pillagers. Folquet, who actually truly cared for his fellow citizens and parishioners, tried to warn the Toulousain militia of their imminent danger but they did not listen to him. When they finally learned about the Aragonese defeat, it was already too late as the crusaders fell upon them, mowing them down in a terrible slaughter. Only a handful of them reached the barges moored by the Garonne River. They were practically the only survivors left of the great host of brave militiamen, which had left Toulouse three days earlier.

Meanwhile, in the fortified camp on Perramon Hill, shortly before and during the battle on the plains below, a heated discussion was taking place. The Count of Toulouse was saying, "The Royal fool of Aragon, who dreams of exclusive victories, hasn't got a clue what he is up against now that he is about to meet Simon de Montfort in the battlefield. He is calling me a coward because I am taking the only possible course of action, a war of attrition, a hit and run skirmishing war. Believe me, gentlemen, we have no alternative but to continue fighting in this manner. If we are fortunate enough to get away with an orderly retreat we might yet win the war in the end.

Guy de Sommerive stepped forward and said, "As you know I am your prisoner and am reluctant to speak my mind but, if I have the Count's permission, I must declare that Simon de Montfort is a formidable and almost invincible figure. I have been one of his knights for the last three years and I know that you cannot defeat him in an open battle. The Count's way is the only way."

Young Raymond, the son of Count Raymond VI, a tall handsome man of 21, stood up and said, "I am terribly disappointed that the King of Aragon has declined our help. I was looking forward to have this chance to prove my worth as a knight in glorious battle. I am a Toulouse and a Plantagenet and my blood demands an opportunity for victory. While we are talking here… Wait, I think I can hear a noise like the hewing of a forest of trees, mingled with confused war–cries.

Comminges! Aragon! Montfort! My God! The battle has started! Or, oh my god, has it just ended?"

Everybody ran to the edge of the Perramon Hill to try and understand what was happening. A few minutes later somebody cried out. "My God! The King's banner has already fallen and it is downtrodden. There is a rout of the Aragonese. Oh my God, all is lost! The pride of Aragon has fallen. Our last hope is gone!"

The Battle of Muret

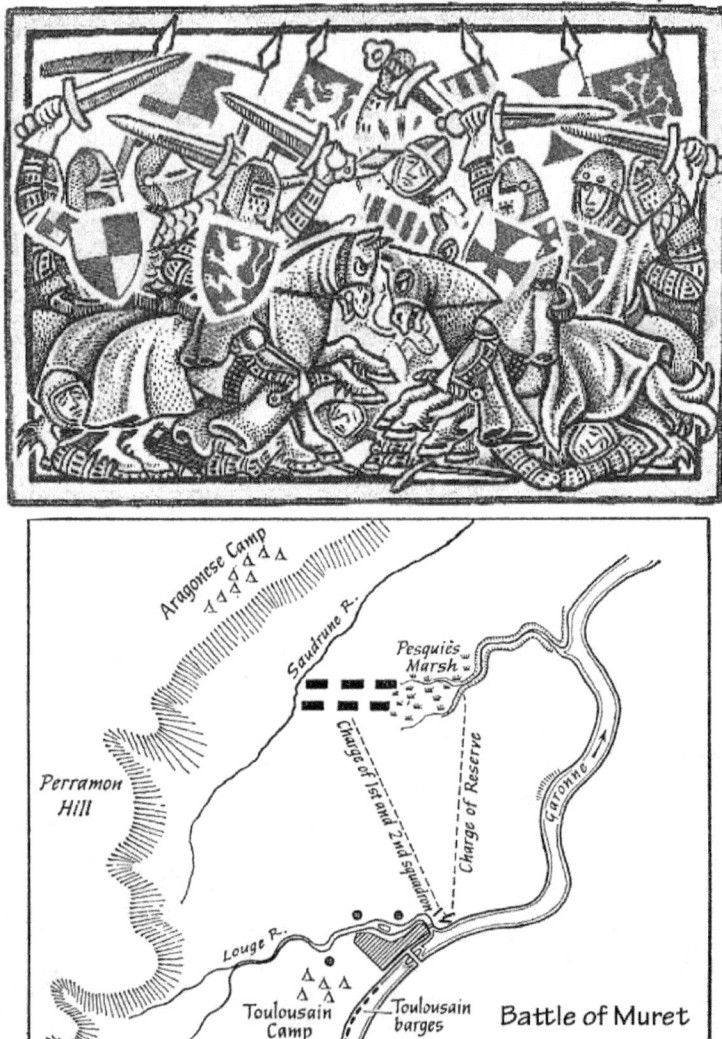

Soon afterwards the terrible defeat of the Southerners was confirmed and Raymond organized an orderly flight back to Toulouse. As they were galloping along the west bank of the Garonne, Raymond said to Peire and Guy Sommerive, "It is ironic that Peter II of Aragon was killed here fighting against a French crusade only a year after leading a Spanish one to victory. It is such a pity that his life was wasted here when after having defeated the Moors he had a golden opportunity to the south of his kingdom. Unfortunately, this foolishness and carelessness combined with arrogance and snobbery are endemic diseases in the South. No wonder we are in trouble! By the way, I have noticed that you're still with us Guy. You are no longer our prisoner as there is no one left alive to exchange you for anyway. You must know you are free to go?"

"Thank you for your kindness in this difficult time your Excellency. Indeed, I am with you only for the ride at this point, until we reach Toulouse anyway. I am sick of fighting my innocent countrymen and I intend to ride on to Verona to join my brother who is prospering there. Ultimately I have a dream to eventually go to Moreas, a place that was conquered by my countrymen during the 4TH Crusade. I understand, Peire, you were in the 4TH Crusade yourself. Do you remember this place?"

"Yes, I was there, but we have more in common than that it seems. My uncle actually lives in Verona and I am planning to go there soon to find a peaceful shelter for my only son. Perhaps we could travel together?"

Raymond looked at them both with a sad expression and said. "Well, after the present disaster I might have to seek the hospitality of King John, my wife's brother in England, for my family and myself. We all may have to go in exile temporarily or permanently it seems. Although I don't want to abandon hope yet, I am determined to stay in Toulouse for a bit longer to see how things develop. I am still hoping that, beyond all probability, we may have an opportunity to regain our pride sometime soon."

Count Raymond VI was followed at a short distance by the dejected refugees of the battlefield, including the Counts of Foix and Comminges, all fleeing to some relative safety behind the mighty walls of Toulouse. Simon de Montfort did not follow up his victory by marching on Toulouse, as many feared he would. Perhaps his force was too small and too tired for siege and perhaps the true extent of his victory had taken some time to dawn on him. However, on the day after the battle the Bishops hailed it as a miraculous victory against overwhelming odds. The body of Peter II of Aragon was mournfully carried back to Toulouse after the battle, to find a temporary resting place in the priory of the Hospitallers of St. John. There was a sullen and dark feeling in the air and the citizens and leaders of Toulouse alike wondered what would come next.

Peire was thinking obsessively of Esclamonde but he no longer searched for her as all indications pointed to the sad conclusion that she must have perished in one of the countless pyres where Cathars were being burned at an alarming rate. His mind was now concentrated on Nascibon and whether he would still find him in Campagnac with his parents. There were rumours that the whole Rouergue was in turmoil. The Count of Rodez was fighting a losing war against the Bishop of Rodez who was supported by Simon de Montfort's troops. The Castle of Severac changed hands several times over and was now occupied by Simon's knights. His brother, he had heard, still held Campagnac, but for how long? He had to go there soon and rescue his son. Guy Sommerive, who was quickly becoming a faithful friend, volunteered to go with him and help out in case of trouble.

With a growing feeling of urgency Peire and Guy hastily gathered a few attendants and supplies and started for Campagnac as quickly as they could. They went towards Montauban, which was still loyal to the House of Toulouse. They had to be careful because the soldiers of Simon de Montfort were patrolling the area and clashing with desperate and unruly bands of Faidit. The Faidit were not necessarily friendly either, even to those who claimed allegiance to the house of Toulouse, because their desperate state inclined them against anyone who appeared fair game. Their sudden complete destitution, hunger and anger made them extremely dangerous and extremely difficult to handle even by their own leaders.

Peire and Guy traveled by circuitous routes, avoiding any possible encounters with anyone. It made Peire very sad to think that this beautiful land of freedom and love had descended into such a terrible state. A land that was so recently blessed with flourishing culture, tolerance, song and joy. Now there seemed to be no joy anymore, the people they saw from a distance all seemed to be living in fear and focussed only on surviving. When they finally arrived in the neighbourhood of Campagnac, after stealthily avoiding any encounters, they found themselves facing, head-on, the terrible conflicts of the time anyway. As they entered Campagnac they found Peire's family and castle were under siege by a band of desperate Faidit who, in turn, were under attack by the Bishop of Rodez!

Peire and Guy carefully approached the Captain of the detachment from Rodez to find out what was happening without concealing their identity. The Captain, a hardened soldier would not say much until Peire told him it was his family's Castle and his young son was in there. Finally, the Captain, convinced of Peire's distressed sincerity, obliged them with a reply, "This rabble of Faidit were chased out of Severac by the crusaders and after gathering more of their kind attacked Campagnac because they wanted a fortified place for themselves. Gaucelm de Campagnac asked the Bishop of Rodez to help him and that is why we are here. Alas, the Campagnacs are too few and the Faidit have managed to occupy the gate and the flanking towers. As we speak there is a raging battle going on to defend the two other towers and the Keep. We are outnumbered and we will not be able to beat them off and be of any help to the defenders. I am sorry to hear from you, sir, that it is your own family and your own son in such great peril in there. We expect some reinforcements soon from either Rodez or Severac. Frankly speaking, you should hope that the help comes from Rodez and the Bishop, rather than the Northern crusaders from Severac. The crusaders may save you from the Faidit but their rapacity will likely lead them to dispossess you after as well."

"Captain, I have an idea as to how to save the castle and my family right now. If some reinforcements arrive later, I pray from Rodez, all the better, but we must act now! Your horsemen should try to draw them out by fake attacks against the main gate. At the same time, my detachment and your foot soldiers will try to enter the castle through one of the back towers from a secret access that I know well. I will go first to warn my family so that they won't attack us by mistake. Then, I will quickly return to admit the rest. This way we can attack them from both sides and may be lucky enough to beat them off. I agree with you that any help from the Northern crusaders could be much worse for us than these hungry Faidit."

The Captain reluctantly agreed with Peire and quietly divided his forces for the execution of the plan. Peire and Guy moved unobserved into the northeastern tower. After a quick discussion with the guards about the plan the entire detachment, under Peire and Guy, secretly entered the tower and joined the few defenders of the castle. Gaucelm and Bieiris were overwhelmed by the intense emotions of their reunion even under the extreme urgency of the situation. The fight was going on unabated but now the odds had turned around and the defenders were quickly gaining the upper hand. During the night, the Campagnacs and their new allies managed to dislodge the Faidit from all of the towers and pushed them through the main gate and out of the castle where the horsemen of Rodez were waiting for them with their lances. The battle continued through the next day when, finally, some reinforcements appeared from Rodez and Severac. The ragtag army of Faidit quickly withdrew towards the southwest but managed to take with them Bertrand de Campagnac and Nascibon as hostages. Peire, in a state of terrible anguish and despair, galloped after them followed closely by Guy de Sommerive and their attendants. He had managed to save Campagnac but he was losing his son and his brother. The Faidit were always ahead of them, just out of reach. In any case, what could they have done? They were highly outnumbered and terribly vulnerable. They would have surely been captured as well and tortured to death for having thwarted the near-capture of Campagnac. They decided just to follow the Faidit unobserved until an opportunity was presented to them to try and free the hostages either forcibly or by negotiations. The Faidit were now approaching Lolmie in Quercy with some definite purpose in mind. Peire and Guy watched them unobserved from a short distance. They were obviously up to something as they also were taking precautions to not be observed by those inside the castle of Lolmie. Quite a few more faidit from around the area had joined them, taking cover as well. On the night of 17th of February the whole ragtag army of Faidit were secretly admitted into Lolmie. The small northern garrison of crusaders was surprised and overpowered. The subdued squeals of slaughter could be heard from where Peire and Guy were hiding. They eventually discovered that Baldwyn of Toulouse, the renegade brother of Count Raymond VI, had been surprised in his sleep and taken alive by the Faidit. He was to be carried off in triumph to Montauban to await the Count's pleasure. The small contingent of Peire and Guy followed the unwieldy procession of Faidit towards Montauban unobserved. They began to notice the attention of the Faidit was completely concentrated on their big catch. They no longer seemed to care about their other prisoners very much. Many of them managed to escape here and there but Bertrand and the child were not among them.

When the gates of Montauban finally opened to admit the Faidit, Peire and his friends managed to sneak in as well. Inside the city they were greeted by an absolute chaos of wild jubilation. A court had been quickly set up in the central square, with the Count of Toulouse and the most august of the Faidit presiding alongside co-magistrates the Counts of Foix and Comminges.

Baldwin of Toulouse was pulled by chains and thrown at the feet of his judges. He looked frightened and stupefied. Count Raymond VI addressed him, "You once came to me and begged me to give you Brunickel, one of my castles. I offered it to you as a brotherly gesture not knowing that you had already made a pact with the devil, my archenemy Simon de Montfort. You knew he had come from the North to dispossess and destroy me under the disguise of a crusader! You tricked me then and you have been my enemy and a traitor to your own blood ever since. I feel repulsion for individuals like you who are helping to destroy our beautiful land and our peaceful way of life. I am duly horrified that you are my own brother whom I have been nothing but kind to all these years. I can see no way of mercy left for those of your kind in times like these. With great pain I must condemn you to hang by the neck until you are dead and gone."

Baldwin of Toulouse was given no more chances to defend himself and was manhandled by one of the knights of the late King of Aragon and taken to the gallows, assisted by the Counts of Foix and Comminges. It was a pitiable act of retribution against the painful blows which fate had dealt them leading to the destruction of all they held dear.

The sight was so dismal and disgusting that Peire composed a lament.

> My lord,
> How low have we fallen?
> When brother must kill brother
> to offer pitiful revenge.
>
> Love, our truth, is now hanging
> Leaving nothing left to gain
> All these lands once filled with laughter
> Now drowning in blood and pain
>
> Against a bitter fate we've been fighting
> Holding on to these shreds of pride
> Can we still keep our faith alive?
> In these dark and dangerous times?
>
> For still another day we must keep dreaming
> Holding our love deep inside.
> For still another day we must keep fighting
> Holding onto our pride.

An obscene rejoicing followed that lasted all night. Peire and his friends stayed out of it because the general mood made their stomachs turn but also because they wanted to take advantage of the prevailing disorder in hopes of finding Bertrand and Nascibon. They searched desperately through the crowds but as they left the festivities behind they spotted a man in rags holding a child by the hand scuttling towards the River Tarn. Peire ran towards them and grabbed his brother by the arm. "Bertrand, do not be afraid. It is your brother Peire. We have been on your trail since the Faidit took you from Campagnac. I am so happy to find you both alive and unharmed!"

"Thank God you found us! When we escaped I wasn't sure we could survive the trip home in these desperate times. Thank you for helping save our home and for following us all this way! In these dark times it seems rare to have a faithful brother. Here is your son, Nascibon. He has been a very brave boy throughout this nightmare."

Peire took his seven-year-old son in his arms and looked at him with tears in his eyes. The boy stared back at him unblinkingly and said, "Are you really my father? I have never seen you before. A horrible looking, smelly and mean man took me away from my home but my uncle just rescued me from him. Are we safe now?"

Nascibon was a tall sturdy boy who looked very much like his mother, Esclamonde, whom he would never get to see again. Peire reflected on his son's cruel fate, which had kept them apart, and sobs struggled through his chest. Unfortunately, there was no time to indulge in such emotions of self-pity. He would have to save them both from further calamities. He would have to seek the Count's protection, for whatever it was worth. He took his son by the hand and they all walked brazenly through the crowd to where the Count of Toulouse and his entourage were holding court. Raymond saw them and signalled Peire to approach.

"I am happy to see you again in this most unhappy of all times and to see that you have found your son under these horrible circumstances is truly a miracle indeed. I see your brother is with you as well and I am happy for you. At least your own brother is not your mortal enemy, as happens so often these days. What do you want from me Peire? As you can plainly see, I am not at my best and as a matter of fact I am fighting for the last scraps of what Pope Innocent III is preparing to leave me of my former estate."

It was true that Raymond was dejected and a faded remnant of his former brilliant self. His unending struggle against overwhelming odds to save at least a part of his estate and his way of life had taken a huge toll on his being. Fortunately, his successor, the young Raymond, cut a much more hopeful and vigorous figure than his father. Apparently, the Plantagenet blood from his mother Joan, filled him with energy and optimism, something that injected some pride and hope in the empty shell of Raymond VI. All was not yet lost. Pope Innocent III, had no intention of allowing the chance of the battlefield to disturb the due process of law. He had no intention of granting Simon de Montfort all that he had won and wanted, which would destroy completely the vanquished of Languedoc. In order to exact the submission of all, he would never allow one of them, and particularly the upstart Simon de Montfort, to become all-powerful. He would exercise mercy to the vanquished and admonish humility to the victor. He had, therefore, given the most precise instruction to his six legates to wait for the decisions of the coming ecumenical counsel, taking place on the 11th of November 1215, in the old Lateran Basilica. The two Raymonds knew about this and were hopeful that their luck might take a better turn.

So, Raymond looked at Peire speculatively and said. "You need my help for a short while at least to keep you safe from the Faidit while you are still in this troubled land. I heard that they abducted your son and brother and that they may still claim them in order to get a ransom. They will not do any such thing under my watch. In return though, I ask that you be in Rome for the ecumenical counsel to help argue for my cause. Until then you have ample time to find a secure place for your son. As for me, I intend to seek hospitality from my wife's brother, King John of England, since my possessions and income have been reduced to almost nothing. I even had to cede my family castle, the Château Narbonnais, to Folquet, the Bishop of Toulouse. Montauban remains vaguely mine in quickly diminishing proportions. My friend, let us hope for better times and as you can see I need all the help I can get in Rome."

"My liege lord, I will certainly attend the ecumenical council on your behalf and will do my best to restore your former rights. Since it is not yet the spring of 1214, I have plenty of time to take my son to Verona where my Uncle Renier de Campagnac has offered us his hospitality. My new friend, Guy Sommerive, has proven to be a loyal companion and will be our fellow traveler. I promise, when the time comes, I will go to Rome. Perhaps I will meet you there accompanied by the young Raymond, my future liege lord."

"That is all I wanted. You have always been such a great help to me reasoning with the Church. Thank you. What is your brother going to do now?"

Bertrand replied. "I do not have the luxury of running to Verona because I am desperately needed in Campagnac to defend it against all the insurgents, crusaders and Faidit alike. I would have been the happiest man on earth to have you as my liege lord, but after the battle of Muret the Count of Rodez switched his allegiances to the King of England to save himself from the northern crusaders. After that the Bishop of Rodez filled the gap and became the overlord of Campagnac. You understand we had to accept this arrangement as the least damaging to us in order to survive. The Faidit are leaderless and therefore more dangerous than the disciplined forces of the Bishop."

"I fully understand. Please do not overexert yourself explaining and finding excuses for submitting to my enemies. This is the rule of the day. When a time comes that we can provide leadership again, I want you on my side."

"When the time comes, the Campagnacs will march under your or your son's banner. This is a promise."

So sometime in March 1214 the Raymonds left for England. Bertrand rode north to Campagnac and the party of Guy de Sommerive and Peire Campagnac took the road of exile to Verona. Simon de Montfort was left to dominate the now desolate lands of Languedoc, where he continued to obsessively try and cleanse it of Cathars and the desperate Faidit with only partial success.

Medieval Verona (Liber Chronicarum)

Ezzelino da
Romano,
on the right,
in front of
Frederick II
(From
Chronica)

CHAPTER 12

BETWEEN VERONA AND ROME

ith a heavy heart and an unbearable sadness Peire crossed the Alps along the Domitian Roman Road travelling east to Italy. He had left behind him his wonderful homeland of joy and song that in merely five years had been relentlessly transformed into a hell of congealing blood and burning flesh. His only consolation was that he was holding the hand of his seven-year-old son and that he had a chance to really get to know him for the first time. He found that he could actually relate to him with all his heart and mind.

Nascibon wanted to know about everything and asked unending questions. "Why were you not with me in Campagnac?"

"I was in the war and had to leave you in a safe place. Weren't you happy there?"

"I was alright but I wanted my father and mother. All the other children had a mother and a father but I did not know mine. Where is my mother?"

"Your mother was lost in the war."

"What was my mother like? Did she love me?"

"Your mother was beautiful. You look like her."

"Did she love me? If she did, why did she leave me?"

"Your mother loves you and she did not leave you. She was lost in the war."

"Why is war always around us?"

"Because there are bad people who want to hurt other people."

"Are we the bad people or the good people?"

"Mostly we are the good people."

"What do you mean by 'mostly'?"

"It means that sometimes even the good people do foolish and bad things, and we have done that."

"I do not understand. I want to be a good person and do good things always."

"Always think this way my son."

"Who were these bad people that took me away from Campagnac?"

"They were desperate and angry people."

"So, they were not so bad?"

"No, they were not so bad."

"Why didn't you take me back to Campagnac with my grannies, my uncle and my cousins?" Are they safe?"

"They are safe for now because they have strong friends but I wanted you to be with me. Aren't you happy with me?"

"Yes, I am happy with you but where are we going?"

"We are going to stay with your Grand-Uncle Renier in the magnificent city of Verona."

"Would he like me? How big is Verona? Is it like Campagnac?"

"Your Grand-Uncle wanted you to stay with him even before you were born. He would certainly love your presence now. Verona is much bigger than Campagnac. It is as big as Toulouse, which you have seen."

"Are you going to stay with me this time?"

"I will stay as much as I can but I may have to go away from time to time. I am a troubadour and a troubadour cannot stay in one place because many people want to hear his songs in many places. I will always come back to see you because I will always love you."

Nascibon became pensive and he stopped asking questions. Perhaps he was tired or perhaps he had understood what was in store for him in the future.

Guy Sommerive, who had overheard the questions and answers between Peire and Nascibon, could not help but feel warm-heartedness towards them. After a while he commented, "I am happy for you, Peire, for having such a clever boy as a son. I wish I had a son myself. I left Sommerive without any memories to hold me or regret to stop me. I am going to Verona to find some close relatives like you. I joined the crusade as a fortune hunter but Simon de Montfort did not favour me with a fief and I caused grief to many people who were not my enemies. The truth is that I was glad to be captured by you in Muret, which enabled me to escape the devastation with you"

"I am also glad that you are my companion by choice." Peire responded. "You helped me greatly in delivering Campagnac and then, later, with the rescue of my son and brother. I want you as my friend and am grateful for your companionship in these desperate times. Maybe you will find a nice girl in Verona to love and give you a son to inherit your good name and your good nature."

Guy smiled as he heard the sincere sentiments of his new friend and said, "As a matter of fact, my relatives in Verona have plans to match me up with a comely girl of noble birth. I feel quite ready for that, although I also have plans to travel to Greece and join the Champagnan nobleman Villehardouin to whom I am somewhat related. I understand he has become the Prince of Moreas and he needs French knights to help him. I sound like an adventurer and a fortune hunter but in reality, I simply want the opportunity to build my own noble house and secure a good posterity."

"Most crusaders, it seems, want the same thing as you. I seem to be an exception for I am happy simply being a wandering troubadour. Perhaps Nascibon will decide to build something for his and my posterity. When I was in Greece with my beloved Esclamonde I entertained with her a fleeting desire to settle on the island of Andros but our desire to return home was much stronger then. Perhaps you will have the opportunity to visit this beautiful Island. Its Lord is my friend Marino Dandolo. Perhaps you will meet him one day. He is a very amiable and remarkable man."

Sometime in May of 1214, they reached the resplendent city of Verona with its forty-eight magnificent towers and the many mansions of its noble merchants and administrators. The city commanded the only access of the German emperors to Italy and from there to the commercial wealth of the East. Because of this, and the enterprising spirit of its people, Verona had become fabulously rich and powerful, a close second to Venice itself.

At the mention of his uncle, Peire and his company were given permission to enter the city. Renier de Campagnac or Renieri Campagna, as the locals called him, was thrilled to learn that Peire and Nascibon intended to stay with him for an extended period this time. From the very first moment, he loved his seven-year-old grandnephew, Nascibon, and offered to become his legal guardian, something that Peire accepted as a favourable arrangement for the future of his son. The hopeless situation back home and the disappearance of his wife Esclamonde, now presumed dead, had made him hope for such an arrangement. Nascibon would receive an excellent education, a comfortable life and a prosperous future as the sole heir of his uncle and his fortune. The only, but serious, problem would be the absence of a mother for his son. Surely, there were many females around in his Uncle's mansion, and some of them had children who could be playmates for his son, but the absence of a compact family was a concern. For as long as he could be around and close to his son, he would do anything he could to be a good father. He was determined to do that with all his heart.

Renier suggested that he should marry again to a young and beautiful girl from one of the noble families of Verona but Peire had his objections. "Dear uncle, I know it sounds like a good idea to marry again for Nascibon's sake and mine. I am prepared to stay with you for a while but I cannot stay forever. I am an itinerant troubadour and I still have loyalty to the House of Toulouse. In eighteen months or so, I must go to the ecumenical council in Rome to defend the rights of the House of Toulouse. It sounds crazy that I still want to do this but my mind and heart are attached to my ruined country and devoted to the two Raymonds, father and son both."

"Your fixation with lost causes is puzzling to me, to put it mildly. Simon de Montfort is in undisputed control of Languedoc and Provence although the Pope does not recognize his claim on the territories of the House of Toulouse yet. I guess what you will be trying to do in Rome will be to convince the Pope not to dispossess the Raymonds entirely. If this is your desire then I wish you good luck. You are certainly going to need it. In the meantime, you could be occupied right here in Verona much more profitably by managing some of my business affairs. Verona has grown rich because German merchants, crusaders and the armies of the German emperors have to go through our city to serve their greed, religious fervour and ambitions in Italy, the Eastern Empire and the holy land. We hold the key to their deepest desires and we are blessed with clever burghers, able and brave knights and exceptionally strong leaders like Ezzelino da Romano. Ezzelino II is the Lord and ultimate authority of Verona and he happens to be my friend and supporter. So, you can understand that you are very lucky to be in Verona right now. You will be able to not only earn your living but to accumulate your own wealth over and above my wealth, which is always at your disposal. The longer you are able to stay in Verona the better it will be for you, your son and for me. When I met you ten years ago, I was very impressed by the beauty and personality of your wife Esclamonde. Alas, she has passed away, a victim of the cruelties of war. It is a great pity but you must go on and build your life again by marrying a worthy girl, and there are many worthy girls in Verona. I understand your friend Guy Sommerive is going to do that himself. Why don't you join him?"

"My Uncle, thank you so much for your love and the fabulous opportunities you lay at my feet. I declare to you that I intend to take advantage of what you are offering me for as long a time as I can manage. I am not ready to get married again yet, though I am sure one day I will be."

"I'm very happy that you have decided to stay with me in Verona at least until the Ecumenical Council in Rome which gives us more than a year together. There is much to experience here."

Peire dove right into his Uncle's business, from which he derived great pleasure, satisfaction and considerable wealth. It was the perfect distraction for his aching heart that had not yet healed from the loss of his beloved, his country and his way of life. During this time, he had the added pleasure of getting to know his son better. He was grateful that Nascibon would now receive the education and training of a scholar, of a merchant, and of an urban knight.

Guy married a beautiful and wealthy bride with whom he had a son by the name of Leone. Guy was quickly becoming too rich, powerful and comfortable in Verona to contemplate any of his planned adventures in Greece. His son, Leone, though was destined for great things in the East and in time would, one day, fulfill his fathers' dreams by having many successful adventures in the principality of Moreas, Greece.

In the meantime, much news was drifting in from France, Languedoc, England and Germany. Simon de Montfort was busy suppressing the unending resistance of the Faidit with their hit-and-run tactics. The Faidit had nothing to lose but their lives and they did not seem to care much for that anymore. Simon could never be sure that he had won a battle or even if he had truly taken a castle or fortified town because as soon as he moved elsewhere to fight somebody else, the Faidit, who were beaten, would come back again to claim what they had lost. The Faidit were always losing and yet they were always around to kill isolated crusaders and to reoccupy their own burned villages and castles. Simon was exasperated fighting against these beaten beggars who would never concede defeat. He couldn't kill them all although he was trying his best to do just that. The continuous war had dried up his sources of income and he was always short of money. He borrowed from the Knights Templar and from the common usurers using as collateral the pillaging and revenue of conquered towns. This situation would have been untenable if he hadn't formed a strong alliance with the bishops and abbots of Languedoc and Provence.

The Bishops and the Cistercians were serving their interests by supporting Simon because with his help they had usurped the lands and the power of the lay nobility. They supported his claims to become Count of Toulouse, of Foix, of Comminges and of Bigorre, in addition to Bezier and Carcassonne. For a while the King of England, John Plantagenet, disputed Simon's claims by a show of force in the borders of Agenais and Quercy in the West but his main concern was his war with the King of France, Philip–Augustus. Simon did not have much to worry about from the English at least. The Anglo-German alliance against France, however, could have turned things around but, fortunately for France and Simon de Montfort, it was smashed in the great battle at Bouvines in September of 1214. With this victory Philip–Augustus became the most powerful monarch in Europe while John Plantagenet was no longer of any account in the affairs of Simon de Montfort. After the death of the German Emperor, Otto IV, Frederick II Hohenstaufen became the Emperor of Germany as well as the King of Sicily. Frederick II was to soon play an important role in Italy and particularly in Verona.

After his victory at Bouvines, Philip–Augustus was completely unchallenged and felt safe enough to allow his son and heir, Prince Louis, to make a show of force and to assist Simon de Montfort in Languedoc. Just to show his power and authority he demolished the walls of Toulouse and Narbonne to the applause and exhilaration of Peter of Vaux-de-Cernay who exclaimed, "Finally the pride of Toulouse has been humbled to rubble and dust." Surprisingly, only Arnauld–Amaury, now the Archbishop of Narbonne, was angry with Simon de Montfort calling him "an ungrateful dog." Times had changed; Arnauld-Amaury was no longer the Cistercian with the single purpose of destroying heresy but a comfortably settled Archbishop who saw the walls of his city destroyed by his chosen son, Simon de Montfort. All of a sudden, he identified with the Southern nobility.

Times had changed, indeed. In the palace of Ezzelino II da Ramano, the Potentate of Verona, the archons of the city and of neighbouring cities had gathered to celebrate the many victories of their Lord and particularly his unexpected and great victory against the Venetians. Many rich burghers, foreign visitors, ambassadors and troubadours, including Peire Cardinal and Guy de Cavaillion, were present.

Ezzelino, a sturdy red-haired man, was saying. "The Venetians were not satisfied with their immense spoils from the Greek Empire and their riches from their commerce in the East, they also wanted a share of our commercial traffic with Germany which has been ours from time immemorial. So, they incited the Paduans against us, but we drove the Paduans into the dirt. Then, they stirred up the Lombard League against us but we crushed the Lombards as well. After running out of willing allies, they had to show their greedy faces against us and we humbled them as well in bloody battle. This was an important victory for us because we secured our commercial interests and our possessions in Treviso Bassano, Vicenza and Romano. Venice will have to stay quiet for a while and leave us to our own lucrative business between the Germans and the Italians as we have always done. Indeed, I see among us the German ambassador, who, I am sure has important news and messages to bring us."

The German ambassador bowed and said, "I have greetings from Frederick II, Hohenstaufen, the new Emperor of the Holy German Empire. Otto IV, after his shameful defeat at Bouvines by the King of France, is no longer our Emperor. His friend and relative, the Plantagenet King of England, was also, unfortunately, defeated alongside him at Bouvines. The new Emperor, Frederick II, looks forward to the traditional friendship of Verona and to the personal friendship of the Lord of Verona, Ezzelino II da Romano. He will soon pass through your city on his way to his kingdom of Sicilies. What shall I say to my Emperor?"

"To your Emperor, Frederick II, you shall say that Verona and myself personally, Ezzelino II da Ramono, are his devoted friends. He is most welcome to our hospitality. He can be sure of a safe passage through our city to his Sicilian Kingdom. Naturally we are looking forward to his friendship and military alliance against all our enemies in Italy as well."

"I am empowered to promise the Emperor's assistance for the protection of Verona. German knights have already fought with you in your recent victorious battles and they will continue doing so as long as we remain friends. The Emperor knows that your friendship with the Holy German Empire has cost you, in the past, the displeasure of the Papal authorities. We assure you that the new Emperor Frederick II has no intention of antagonizing the Pope but intends to cooperate with the Vatican in every way he can."

"Your reassurance concerning a lasting friendship with the Vatican is extremely important to us because it would reconcile the factions of the Guelfs and the Ghibellines, which have caused many civil disturbances in the past, in our city."

The impressive German ambassador withdrew with the usual reverence and Ezzelino de Romano, obviously satisfied by the official business just conducted, was now inclined towards a more casual discourse to entertain his guests and announced, "We have among us two illustrious poets and troubadours, Peire Cardinal de Campagnac, who also happens to be the nephew of Renieri Campagna one of our noble peers of Verona, and Guy de Cavaillon who also happens to be a Knight Templar of noble birth. I ask them to honour us with their melodious poetry."

The elderly but still handsome Guy de Cavaillon and the young Peire Cardinal de Campagnac advanced gracefully into the middle of the great hall, holding their viols in their left hands. They stopped and bowed to Ezzelino II, who sat before them on the princely throne of Verona.

Peire spoke for both of them, saying "Your Excellency and noble guests, Guy de Cavaillion and myself have prepared for your entertainment, a partimen, a musical dialogue, as a commentary of our troubled times. We certainly do not presume to offer instruction to our learned audience but to provoke some feelings and thoughts."

Guy de Cavaillion played a nostalgic and sad tune on his vielle for a few minutes and then sang accompanied by Peire's instrument. Afterwards, Peire sang accompanied by Guy's vielle and so it went on as they continued alternating roles.

> Guy: Praises I offer
> To the victors of the day
> Like David's Goliath
> Victory we made
> The falcon of Verona
> Mightily swooped down
> On the lion of Venice
> And put her to the ground

> Peire: This victory's beyond measure
> But measure always prevails
> Our falcon now flying high
> With the lion must reconcile
> Before the lion remembers
> His power and his strength
> And fuels the fires of dark revenge
> Igniting war and death.

> Guy: A young eagle has risen
> Far into the North
> Who surely will soon swoop down
> Upon his claims in the South
> Flying with our falcon
> Against the enemies of our land
> The lion will be cowering
> Let us rejoice, sing and dance

> Peire: Eagles and falcons

Fly as they please
Following prey and fancy
Fortunes changing with the breeze
Each must use his chances
Swooping down when time is right
Finding peace in their dances
To greater things take flight

Guy: For once there was a dreamland
West beyond the mountains
Where love and joy danced and bloomed
Not ruled by eagles, or falcons
Ruled by a loving unicorn
So wild and carefree
Full of life full of love
Free to feel and be.

Peire: But all around lurked dangers
Creatures no longer human
With empty space where hearts should be
The fear of God would summon
Packs of wolves with crosses and swords
Killing love, and pleasure
The Unicorn then lost his horn
To hell he is now tethered

Guy: Burning freedom, burning joy
Fire possessed the land
Yet deep within this darkness
The Unicorn still stands
Young and brave, a bright new horn
Shining in the night
Heralding a coming dawn
Of darkness taking flight

Peire and Guy sang the last verse together of their partimen and, for their efforts, received a standing ovation from the distinguished audience.

The Prince of Verona remained pensive for a while and then commented, "I guess you must refer to the Young Raymond of Toulouse as the Unicorn with the 'bright new horn' because his father has certainly lost his horn permanently. I hope you will argue well for his cause when you go to the ecumenical council in Rome. There will be many matters to be resolved in Rome and some of them will even have to do with our own disputes with our neighbours. Although you did not presume to instruct us, you did give us your advice under the guise of verse. Rest assured that it was well taken. The Venetians intend to approach us for reconciliation to the mutual advantage of Venice and Verona and we will be willing to negotiate with them. Verona will certainly stand to profit from the friendship of Venice. The falcon would show respect to the lion provided that the lion understands our worth and that the eagle is our friend."

The council, which Pope Innocent III had been planning for two and a half years, opened in the cavernous gloom of the old Lateran Basilica on the 11th of November 1215. Four hundred bishops, eight hundred abbots and a mass of lay magnates, ambassadors and officials had gathered to deliberate on the items of an immense agenda of which the Albigensian Crusade was but a small part. The presence of almost every participant in the great struggle for Languedoc, though, ensured that it would be a vigorous debate. Eighteen southern bishops attended, and among the northern bishops' present twelve had taken part in the Albigensian Crusade at some time in the past six years. Count Raymond VI, the young Raymond, the Count of Foix and several of the more important Faidit appeared in Rome for the occasion. Among them and next to Count Raymond VI stood Peire Cardinal Campagnac. Simon de Montfort was represented by his brother Guy. King John had asked two English prelates to press his claims on Agenais.

In the midst of their maelstrom of conflicting ambitions, Pope Innocent III raised his voice and said, "I wish to make it abundantly clear that this ecumenical council must uphold justice as the measure of all its decisions. Therefore, we should not allow the fortunes of the battlefield to disturb the due process of law. If we want to be respected as the highest authority in Christendom, we should be known for justice abiding in our minds and hearts, and for our willingness and capability to deliver it."

Guy de Montfort and Folquet the Bishop of Toulouse came forward. Guy spoke, "I wish to remind your Holiness that my brother's victories in the battlefield enabled the Church to regain control over an unruly and heretical country. My brother rightfully claims this land for himself as the Count of Toulouse, Foix Comminges and Bigorre in addition to his official title as the Viscount of Beziers and Carcassonne. I also wish to remind your Holiness that Simon de Montfort has used his victories and his might to ensure that all the bishops of the land have regained their rightful possessions and that they promote the policies of the Catholic Church."

Folquet, the Bishop of Toulouse, moved in to speak and forestall Guy from saying anything more which could compromise Simon's case. "Your Holiness, Simon de Montfort is a faithful servant of the Church, entirely devoted to your cause. He has put up with hardships and exhaustion, thrown himself into the battle against heretics and mercenaries. Giving Simon the confiscated property of heretics is mere hypocrisy, if your Holiness does not declare that the Counts of Toulouse and Foix are heretics. They are proven heretics and therefore, Simon de Montfort must confiscate their lands. He, in turn, must then be given the title of the Count of these lands. Your Holiness, you must not fall into this torturous piece of sophistry whereby you offer Simon the property of heretics and then say they are not heretics so he can't have their property. You may as well openly dispossess Simon and have done with him but this would certainly be a flagrant injustice."

At this point Peire Cardinal asked for permission to talk. He countered with, "The Bishop of Toulouse has conveniently assumed that the Counts of Toulouse and Foix are proven heretics in order to justify the usurpation of their lands and titles by Simon de Montfort. There is no proof of such a preposterous allegation whatsoever. In fact, it is quite the opposite. The Count of Toulouse has shown repeatedly that he is a faithful son of the Church and has always given to the Church everything he was asked to, including his own palatial castle, the Château Narbonnais, which in fact is in the possession of Folquet the Bishop of Toulouse, my esteemed litigant. The Count of Foix has also ceded his own castle to demonstrate his loyalty to the Church."

Bishop Folquet shouted before Peire had finished. "The Count of Toulouse and the Count of Foix have been fighting against Simon de Montfort and the crusaders actively demonstrating their hostility to the Church. They have been hiding and protecting heretics all along. In fact, Raymond–Roger, the Count of Foix, was responsible for the massacre of crusaders and pilgrims at Montgey. Furthermore, everyone knows of his notorious sister, Esclamonde, who is herself a prominent Cathar, a Perfect in fact. How much more evidence do we need in order to confirm that the two Counts are heretics?"

Raymond-Roger jumped in angrily, "The so-called victims of Montgey were not pilgrims but brigands, traitors and perjurers who had come to destroy me under the sign of the cross. Why are you bringing up my sister into this argument? I can only be counted responsible for my own actions and my sister is responsible for her own. Am I to be ruined for my sister's sins? And who are you, Folquet de Marseilles, now Bishop of Toulouse, that you presume to be a censor and judge in matters of morality? You are a former troubadour and notorious libertine and singer of songs whose sound is damnation. I hear that even now you maintain a harem in your episcopal palace and you indulge in lecherous activities. You are certainly not clean enough to judge me!"

Raymond-Roger stopped as he ran out of breath and Peire rushed in to continue his previous discourse, "The Count of Foix was quite eloquent in defending himself and by so doing he presented the true picture of our situation. The Count of Toulouse has only fought against Simon de Montfort reluctantly and indeed only when it was absolutely necessary to protect his life and property, not for protecting heretics. Your Holiness, what was he supposed to do, let himself be slaughtered by brigands, traitors and perjurers, because this is exactly what many of the crusaders really were. Simon de Montfort and his crusaders are masking their ambitions with shallow pieties, wreaking murder and destruction on an innocent Catholic population. They simply covet our properties and titles hiding their greed and rapacity behind a cross, which they themselves have soiled. I maintain that it is completely justified for the Count of Toulouse and for the other Southern Counts to be allowed to keep their properties and titles. In any case the young Raymond was only twelve years old when the crusade started. He is completely innocent on any account whatsoever."

There was a pleasant surprise when the Archdeacon of Lyon leapt to Raymond's defence and so, ironically, did Arnauld-Amaury, who in his new capacity as Archbishop of Narbonne had come to see a greater menace in Simon's strength that in Raymond's weakness.

The Pope agreed with them and he chided Raymond's enemies by saying, "Preachers of suffering and discord. Even if Raymond is guilty of heresy, which I believe he is not, why should his heir, the young Raymond, be dispossessed? Since Simon now controls the land, no power of mine could take it away from him so let him guard it well, for if he loses it, he will not have my help in getting it back."

The council's decision was published on the 14th of December 1215 and stated: Count Raymond VI, on account of his inability to govern his domains in accordance with the faith was to lose everything that the crusaders had occupied. He was to live in exile, out of Languedoc, on his wife's dowry and a pension of four hundred marks a year. Those of Raymond's lands, which the crusaders had not conquered, were to pass to the young Raymond. In practice, this meant only the Marquisate of Provence east of Rhone. As for the Count of Foix, he would have his castle at Foix restored to him. The only title that was allowed for Simon to have was that of the Trencavels while the young Raymond became Raymond VII Count of Toulouse. Raymond VI was a shadow of his former self and a broken man with a vacant stare, which distressed his son, his friends and especially Peire.

When they met, Raymond VI embraced Peire and cried. "Thank you, my friend, for defending me so well. Listening to the Pope I had the impression that I was going to be reinstated but the majority of the Bishops influence the final decision, at least partly. Regardless, I should be happy that my son will have a chance to recover all of the family estate in the end. He has the title of the Count of Toulouse and that means a lot to me, because he can legally claim all the territories of my family. Simon can only keep it so long as he has the military power to do so. The Faidit have become numerous and determined and now they have a brave leader to follow to victory in my son. Peire, it saddens me that I cannot be that leader but my son is a much better soldier than I. He is like his grandfather, Henry Plantagenet, and not like me. I used to be a loving, yet pleasure-seeking, man full of joy. I was a good Lord for my people in the time of peace. Sadly, I became useless in this time of war and Simon brushed me aside as he took all my estates." Raymond fell into a heavy silence for a while then out of the blue he drew Peire close and said with some agitation, "By the way, I noticed that Folquet did not use the information that your wife was a Cathar against you and yet I know he knows it. He is not the type to spare his enemies with damaging information. Something is amiss here. Be careful of him. Soon there will be important developments in Languedoc and Provence. Be on the alert and please follow my son when you are summoned."

"My Liege Lord, I am ready to follow your son with complete loyalty to the house of Toulouse anytime I am summoned. In the meantime, I will go back to Verona to my Uncle's business and to my son, Nascibon. As for Folquet, I am glad he did not bring up Esclamonde because I would have been very upset to be reminded of her burning."

After the ecumenical council Pope Innocent III fell sick. Maybe it was from exhaustion or perhaps from devastating disappointments with the people around him. Their greed, dishonesty, hypocrisy, indifference to justice and their self-seeking purposes, hurt him deeply and certainly added to his stress and weakness. On the 16th of July 1216, he succumbed to his sickness and died, although he was only 55. He was a brilliant Pope who made the institution of the papacy respected and feared by all. He was a man of law who tried single-mindedly to uphold justice, although he let himself be dragged into unjust Crusading wars, which brought untold misery and destruction. He realized it in the end but by then it was already too late. His intelligence and love of justice did not help him win the respect of the people around him. It was a very sad fact that when he died his body was left to rot unburied and eaten by rats. Everyone around him was too busy competing for office and spoils and trying to elect a new Pope to even care for his remains. Many thought he deserved it but there were a few who knew him and thought otherwise.

Peire Cardinal, when he heard about this desecration, said, "Priestly flatterers, cringers and wolves used him when he was alive and strong but when he died they did not respect the empty shell because of their own emptiness."

Pope Innocent III.
Pope from 1198-1216

201

Seals of Raymond VII

CHAPTER 13

THE MARCH OF THE FAIDIT

he decisions of the ecumenical council were interpreted in completely different ways by Simon and by the young Raymond. Simon, satisfied that the status quo was condoned, embarked in a triumphal visit to the court of Philipp–Augustus to do him homage for the County of Toulouse.

The Young Raymond landed in Marseille to claim the entire estate of his father using the Count's title just granted to him.

Simon was received warmly by the King and with enthusiasm by the Northerners singing, "Blessed is he who comes in the name of the Lord."

The young Raymond was receiving the homage of all the Southern nobility and an army of Faidit was flocking to his standards under the Roman Arch at Orange.

Simon was still receiving the plaudits of the North when a messenger brought him the disquieting news that the young Raymond had laid siege to Beaucaire, and the lower town had already fallen. In the citadel, the northern garrison were approaching the end of their resistance. Peire had joined the Raymonds and their numerous and increasing followers under the Roman Arch in Orange. Count Raymond VI had put himself willingly and gladly under the command of his son, the younger Raymond, who was now deservedly acclaimed as the Count of Toulouse, Raymond VII. The young man showed all his respect and love to his father but he was now the undisputed lord of the South. He was the only hope for the dispossessed gentry, the Faidit, and all the nobility, merchants and commoners of the South. Under the Roman Arch he delivered a rousing speech, which demonstarted all his political charm and value.

"I have heard that this land we live in, or some of us used to live in, was a happy land where we had our homes and derived our livelihood, either large or small, from it. A land where we enjoyed the good things in life, our freedom, song, good food, love… I do not remember any of this because I was too young then. All I can remember is the waves of Northern crusaders destroying our country and our lives. They have taken our homes and property away and systematically turned this once fair land into a living hell. I can see before me the brave Faidit, you who were despoiled of all your properties and left to roam the country as penniless beggars. I can see here the gallant nobility who were forced to do the bidding of the tyrant hoping that they might keep some scraps of their former estates. I can see here, with a pleasant surprise, a few clergymen who finally understood the hypocrisy behind this unholy crusade. I can see the multitudes of townsfolk and country folk, who have in some ways suffered the most living in constant terror. I am sad to admit I that I have seen only war and destruction in my boyhood and adolescence. Nevertheless, I have learned from this and, now that I have come of age, am ready to help you take back from these greedy invaders what is rightfully ours. With your help, we will throw them out of our beautiful Southern lands, and make it a happy land again. We must fight a merciless war against Simon de Montfort and his unholy crusaders until all of them have gone back to their cold Northern towers where they came from or are killed if must be. At last we are going to fight back with everything we have, knowing our war is just. Our victory will mean that we will get back what used to be ours and possibly even more. There will be no more Faidit but an honourable gentry that will hold our country together. All our people will live in peace and prosperity in a country that will be free and happy again. I have come to give you hope. Forward to Victory."

The immense crowds gathered under the Roman Arch went crazy with enthusiasm and shouted. "Victory!"

The march of the Faidit had started behind this young brave leader who gave them a sense of purpose, strength and hope. The march proceeded to Avignon growing in numbers while gathering more and more force and enthusiasm. When they arrived in Avignon the city had prepared festivities in anticipation of deliverance and the beginning of the liberation of Provence and Languedoc. It was there Peire realized that unlike his father and most of the Southern nobility the young Raymond was not only a charismatic leader but also a prudent and highly organized general. Peire approached him to offer his allegiance and his genuine devotion.

The young Raymond responded by saying to him. "I know you have been a faithful friend and a good counsellor to my father. You were very effective in Rome on our behalf. I am very honoured to have you stay at my side and help us free our land. Still, we must not forget to celebrate and, whenever we can, manage to enjoy some festivities. Let us not forget that you are blessed with gifts that made you a troubadour. Today is such an occasion for those gifts."

"I feel very privileged to offer a song to you and our liberation army, poised to soon strike down our mortal enemies."

I remember the gentle days
of love and joy and song
When we were blessed by the magic airs
of a carefree Unicorn.

But the buzzing crows of envy
Stirred up the Northern dragon.
Who always craved for gold and power
As he thundered down the mountain.

Through the land of felicity
Smoking ruins left in his wake.

Seven years of plunder
Left despair and heart-break.

The darkness became so black
Only light could be born.
Breaking through the darkest night
In the shape of the Unicorn.

The Unicorn of old
Was gentle and so kind.
But the dragon blew his fiery breath
And left no light to find.

Now the Unicorn is coming back
Full of passion love and art.
To drive his shining horn right through
The dragon's fiery heart.

Everyone present acclaimed the song enthusiastically, especially the young Raymond who identified himself as the Unicorn reborn. A banner was fashioned with a silver white unicorn charging from the two-thirds black background to one-third bright orange background of sunrise and hope. This became the banner of the new liberation army, which was largely composed of angry Faidit bent on revenge against the crows, vultures, wolves and especially the dragon himself, Simon de Montfort. Peire Cardinal de Campagnac had become the national poet and troubadour of the South striking back against its hated oppressors.

There in Avignon, by chance, he came upon Bieiris de Romans who was still as beautiful as ever, accompanied by four graceful female attendants. They embraced intensely and cried from joy and sorrow. Bieiris learned for the first time that Esclamonde had perished at the stake burnt alive as a heretic.

"Did you see her die?"

"No, I did not but I know for sure that she and her father were in the large group of Cathars who were burnt outside Toulouse a few years back."

"Peire, if you did not witness her burning by your own eyes, there is a chance she may be still alive."

"If she were alive someone would have known and none ever whispered such thing. Please, Bieiris, do not scratch my old wound with unfounded hopes."

"Sorry, Peire, but as for me, I will always hope as long as I am alive. I loved her and I still love her. This feeling alone keeps her alive for me."

"You know I loved her too, but I refuse to torture myself by hoping beyond reality."

"Peire, please come to my quarters, even if just for old time's sake."

Bieiris was as irresistible as ever and they fell into each other making love passionately and ingeniously but something was missing and they both felt it. It was not the same without Esclamonde. Still they promised each other that they would meet again.

The liberation army of Faidit was marching to Beaucaire and so was Peire under the black and orange banner with the silver unicorn. The citizens opened the gates of the town to the army of the Unicorn while the crusaders fought their way to the castle on a cliff to the north of the town and to the triangular tower known as Redorte. The Redorte did not survive for long. Overlooked by the Redorte on the north, hemmed in by the town on the south, and cut off from the Rhone by a fleet of boats from Tarascon, the garrison of the castle looked out on a powerful Southern army barring the road to the west. The prospects of resistance seemed small and yet they held out for more than four months. During this time Simon de Montfort had come with his troops to besiege the besiegers. Yet the young Raymond had built a wall around the western side of the castle, so as to bring it within the fortified enclosure of the town. The result was that the defenders could not make sorties into the besiegers' ranks, and neither could the main body of the Crusading army get close enough to relieve them

Peter of Vaux-de-Cernay remarked to Simon. "It looks as if you are trying to besiege all of Provence."

"You are right, unfortunately the situation has become untenable for us. Still, it is my duty to help those in the castle."

On the 24th of August 1216, Simon had to accept terms. The surviving crusaders of the castle were allowed to leave with full honours and Simon withdrew with his army, leaving the young Raymond in possession of Beaucaire. There was a celebratory feeling in the air for this was the first victory of the Southerners after seven years of successive defeats. However the young Raymond remained cool and concentrated after his victory. He kept his motley forces disciplined, busy and in high spirits. His plan was to consolidate his hold on Provence by relying mainly on the nobility, the burghers and the common people. He was determined to antagonize, as little as possible, the monastic orders and the bishops who were supporters of Simon de Montfort because of their material self-interest. On some occasions, he managed to even make a few friends among them by guaranteeing them privileges.

Peire Cardinal was always wary of the clergy because he knew them well. On a warm evening in Avignon, where the young Raymond now held his court, he sang his old song.

> Emperors and monarchs
> Dukes and Counts and Lords
> Together with the Knights
> Are wont to rule the world.
>
> But now I see that priests
> Have gathered all the power
> With theft and treachery
> They've plucked most every flower

By preaching and by force
By twisting all that's true
With sly hypocrisy
They'll take the world to rule

Like Judas' betraying kiss
Their will is being done
Behind the scenes they pull the strings
There's nowhere left to run

Soon all will be theirs
If we don't wake up my friend
Their will must not be done
For we can rise again
Their will must not be done
For we will rise again

The young Raymond applauded with all the others but he said, "Do not be too hard on them. They are not all that bad. Many of them are changing sides and we should not antagonize them. Even Arnauld-Amaury, now the Archbishop of Narbonne, has become Simon's enemy."

"I understand your need for diplomacy, as long as you are not carried away by their false friendships. As for Arnauld-Amaury, the butcher of Beziers and the maker of Simon's original might, he is presently worried that Simon might pose a great threat to him. Therefore, he simply changed sides, not on moral grounds but because of his miserable self-interest. Please allow me to sing another song."

The priests would shepherds be
But are hypocrites all
Beneath their holy airs
I can see Satan's fall.

When I see how they act
I call to mind the tale
Of Master Ysengrin
Who entered the sheeps vale.

Fearing attack by dogs
As a sheep, he disguised
Then devoured all the sheep
Escaping the dog's eyes.

"I assure you, my dear Peire, that I will never be that 'sheep'."

"Unfortunately, no one can be sure until one is devoured, yet I know that you will be very careful."

"I am, and your admonitions in verse and otherwise are taken seriously in view of the serious tasks ahead of us. As you know, my father is busy recruiting an army in Spain in order to attack Simon from the Southwest and join with the citizens of Toulouse who are up in arms against the Montfortists. In the meantime, I am sending many small groups of Faidit for hit-and-run warfare to the west against the scattered patrols and garrisons of crusaders. These groups of Faidit will eventually converge on Toulouse and enter it to reinforce its citizens, who are friendly to us. I am hoping that Toulouse will become ours in the end and our banner of the Unicorn will fly proudly on the top of the Chevet of Saint Sernin."

"I have been hearing that Simon is putting an intolerable pressure on the citizens of Toulouse in order to extort unrealistic sums of money from them, to gather more and more heretics for burning and, ultimately, is trying to dominate the whole city. His friend, that snake the Bishop Folquet, is playing his customary treacherous role of peace and bridge maker, not unlike that of Master Ysengrin."

"Yes, I know, but whatever Simon is doing there is helping our cause. His unwitting barbarity, instead of terrorizing the citizens to submission, is cementing solidarity among them against him and favouring our designs. What I want you to do, Peire, is to join one of the Faidit detachments and go directly to Toulouse as a messenger to provide the inspiration for raising their morale and their patriotic fervour against the unholy crusaders."

So Peire and his group of Faidit left for Toulouse, arriving in the spring of 1217. At about the same time Simon was returning to the Rhone Valley to deal with the young Raymond. The situation in Toulouse was desperate but not hopeless. An occupation force of crusaders was terrorizing the population and imposing heavier and higher taxation. The prison cells of the Chateau Narbonnais were full and the excess prisoners had been dispersed in small groups among the various castles of Languedoc to be held as hostages against the city's good behaviour. Yet the citizens, having been treated with deception and brutality by both Simon and Bishop Folquet, were beyond caring of the fate of hostages and of any other consequences. They were fuming with anger and seeking bloody revenge. So Peire and Raymond's agents had no difficulty organizing the resistance and raising the morale and the fighting spirit of men, women and children. crusaders were ambushed and murdered daily. Alice de Montfort, after the departure of her husband, did not have enough reserves to confront this, as of yet, undeclared uprising. Therefore, she barricaded herself in the Château Narbonnais, her headquarters. During the previous months Simon de Montfort had managed to antagonize not only the citizens of Toulouse but also all the Pyrenean principalities. Going against the decisions of the ecumenical council in Rome he invaded Foix, Comminges, Couserans and Bigorre and he conquered their castles. With Bigorre, he committed the ultimate affront and folly by forcing the Countess Petronilla to marry his son Guy de Montfort, although she was already married to Nuno Sanchez, a cousin of the young King of Aragon. Nuno Sanchez withdrew to Lourdes, the strongest fortress of the region, from which he continued to control the southern highlands of the country.

As soon as Simon committed his next folly, by feeling strong enough to return to the Rhone Valley, the Pyrenean warlike counts and their knights overthrew Simon's garrisons and were ready to march on

Toulouse to take their revenge. In mid-September of 1217, Raymond VI launched his long-awaited invasion of Languedoc. His force was small. Some volunteers recruited in Aragon, the Pyrenean Counts with their contingents and a good number of Toulousain urban knights whom Simon had expelled from the city the year before. Raymond VI retained the advantage of surprise to the last by keeping to the minor valleys and crossing the Garonne at fords, not bridges. Therefore, they were within twenty-five miles of Toulouse before they met any resistance. By the time the news of their coming reached the garrison in the Château Narbonnais, Raymond was already in the city. He had entered by the ford of the Bazacle under cover of a thick autumn fog. At the same time the various groups of Faidit, those who originated from Provence as well as some from elsewhere, converged and entered the city with them. Huge crowds gathered quickly, and with hysterical enthusiasm, celebrated their open uprising. They then turned to the gratifying business of avenging themselves upon the crusaders and their collaborators. Those that could be found were massacred in the streets. Others, including the Bishop Folquet, fled in terror to the Château Narbonnais bringing the first news to the startled Northerners there.

Alice de Montfort asked Folquet for an explanation. "Who are these rebels who have taken over my city?"

"They are the followers of Raymond VII and the Pyrenean mountain warriors. The young Raymond has also flooded your city with great numbers of Faidit. Among the banners I can see silver unicorns in black and orange backgrounds signifying their open revolt against us. If we do not act immediately they will overrun us."

"What went wrong? Yesterday everything was going so well."

"Never was everything going so well. Their anger was gathering force and now all is out of control. We need reinforcements immediately from Guy de Montfort in Carcassonne and from Simon himself in the Rhone valley."

Alice dispatched messengers to Guy and Simon asking them for help. However, Carcassonne was nearly sixty miles away and by the time Guy had arrived with a hastily assembled force of garrison troops, the Toulousains had barricaded the streets and Guy's men were repelled with heavy losses. Towards evening, the noise of celebrations could be clearly heard by the demoralized tenants of the Château Narbonnais. The crusaders captured in the afternoon's battle were being dragged behind horses to the gallows.

In the Rhone valley, Simon de Montfort was trying to re-conquer Provence from the young Raymond by rallying the Bishops and the new Papal legate, Bertrand, to his cause and by terrorizing the nobility and the burghers of Provence. He was successful with the Bishops and the legate but could make no headway with the nobility and burghers who remained deeply loyal to the young Raymond and continued to resist him. When the messengers arrived with the alarming tidings from Toulouse he, at first, did not seem to appreciate the seriousness of the situation so he wasted more precious time in futile negotiations. As a result, he did not reach Toulouse until October, nearly one month after Raymond's return.

The Toulousains had made good use of the precious respite. Simon had efficiently destroyed nearly every yard of wall in 1216, but the churches had been left intact and these were now converted into fortresses. Crossbowmen were lodged in the towers and pinnacles of the cathedral and the Abbey of St.-Sernin. On the edge of the city, volunteers worked day and night to construct makeshift fortifications around the vulnerable southeastern quarter.

When Simon arrived with the crusading army, a continuous line of walls and trenches extended from the Garonne to the cathedral. Behind these homemade defences stood an army that was growing daily in strength. Toulouse was organized with an iron discipline for the duration of the siege. Those who were not fighting at the walls were directed to watch-duty or trench–digging. Rich merchants and civic dignitaries alike hauled rubble through the streets. Women worked the siege engines. Taxes were imposed to pay the wages of the professional soldiers, and the property of known Montfortists was sequestered.

Simon was now confronted by an extremely difficult situation. He dreamed of building a new city west of St.-Cyprian with fresh, loyal immigrants and of making Toulouse and its inhabitants disappear into a huge inferno. In fact, he did intend to level Toulouse to the ground and exterminate all of its inhabitants. He started by trying to occupy the unfortified suburb of St.-Cyprian but he met with such unexpected resistance that after several weeks he had achieved nothing. On the opposite bank of the Garonne his son, Amaury, was pushed back by determined sorties from the town. The crusaders passed the rest of the winter of 1217 to 1218 wretchedly huddled on the south side of the city unable to penetrate even once into the streets. Their morale was becoming low as there was no money to pay their wages and there were rumblings of deserting Simon and his cause.

Alice de Montfort, accompanied by Folquet the Bishop of Toulouse, travelled north to ask for money and fresh crusaders. Alice went as far as to offer the crusaders rich lands in Quercy when the rebels had been defeated. In May 1218, Bishop Folquet and Alice de Montfort returned in triumph with a fresh army and some money. However, Toulouse had also been reinforced; particularly from Quercy and Perigord, where people were infuriated that Alice had offered their land to the crusaders.

Whatever advantage Simon gained from his new recruits was quickly wiped out by Raymond's new reinforcements. From Perigord arrived the notorious couple Bertrand and Jezabel de Cazenac, leading five hundred warriors. Bertrand and Jezabel were as notorious for their successful exploits in battle as they were for their insatiable sexual appetites demonstrated in frequent wild orgies. What mattered, however, was that they were mortal enemies of Simon de Montfort. Soon afterwards the young Raymond, leading the main army of Faidit out of Provence entered the city in triumph. Now all the actors had gathered on the stage of Toulouse to play their final act.

By May 1218, Simon was unable to occupy the west bank of the Garonne and his troops were driven back and forced to pitch their tents at a safe distance, a humiliation which was keenly felt by him. Suddenly there was a terrible rainstorm and the Garonne broke its banks, carrying away both of the bridges of Toulouse and filling the trenches around the suburb of St.-Cyprian with slime and debris. Simon took his chance and immediately occupied the suburb with a fleet of boats, preparing an amphibious assault on the city. The crusaders tried to enter the city from the Pont-Neuf Bridge but they only managed to occupy its western tower and were stopped before reaching its eastern tower. For days, the two sides fought tenaciously for control of the river. In the end, the Toulousains, together with their allies, tightened their grip on the west bank and the crusaders were forced to retreat in disorder. The western arm of Simon's planned double assault had to be abandoned, but the eastern arm was still taking shape. A wooden "cat," a mobile shelter, enabled an assault party to approach the base of the eastern walls at Villeneuve. However, as this monster approached the walls, a trebuchet firing a large stone from inside the city scored a direct hit against it and smashed it to pieces. Then, on the 25th of June, the crusaders were taken by surprise as the Toulousains launched a sudden sortie from two points. Simon came to the rescue and tried to block the Villeneuve gate from which the Toulousains were still pouring out into the melee. From a platform behind the walls, a group of women were firing heavy blocks of masonry from a trebuchet. One of them, a crazed amazon of wild beauty, spotted the object of their collected hatred, Simon de Montfort, moving toward the gate like a dragon. She took aim and released a heavy stone from the trebuchet scoring a direct hit on the dragon's head splashing his brains upon the battlefield. The invincible Simon de Montfort had suddenly, almost inconceivably, been killed!

Peire, who was fighting at the ramparts above the Villeneuve gate, witnessed this momentous event and something else besides, which shocked him to the very core. As he turned to see who had launched the stone he recognized what looked like his beloved Esclamonde being hailed with howls by the other maenads of the trebuchet. He called out to her and tried to reach her but by the time he had climbed the platform she had disappeared and the other women were unwilling to help him in any way.

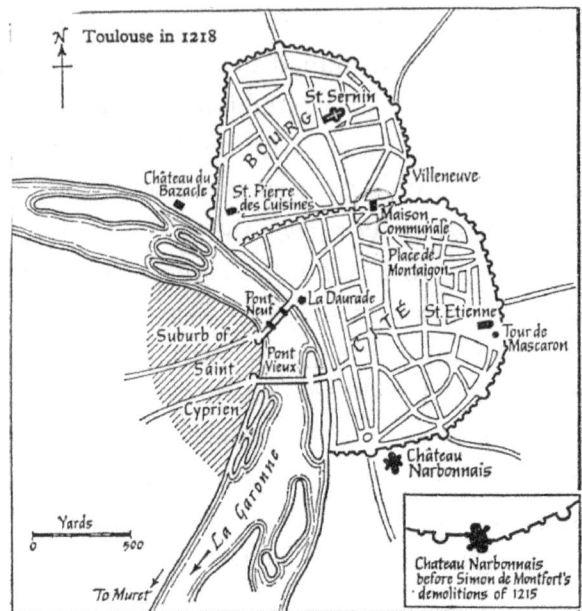

Battle of Toulouse

Death of Simon de Montfort
From 'Cassell's Illustrated Universal History' - 1882

CHAPTER 14

THE RETURN OF THE UNICORN

he sudden ghost-like appearance of Esclamonde after so many years and under such fantastic circumstances, where she played the avenging tyrant-killer, shocked Peire out of his wits. If it was her why was she avoiding and hiding from him? Or was he the victim of hallucinations and was all that he had seen, or rather, thought he had seen, not real at all? He felt he was going mad. Yet all could see that a large stone had definitely smashed Simon de Montfort's head, thrown by a woman, killing him instantly. His remains were taken to the Château Narbonnais where his wife Alice, his relatives and his friends held him as a saint and a martyr.

At the same time, the news of Simon's death was received in Toulouse with frenzied rejoicing. Church bells rang out. Happy processions of citizens danced through the streets to drums, cymbals and trumpets, while in the large City Hall the higher-ups held their equally jubilant celebrations.

Bertrand de Cazenac was saying in a loud voice, "I hear that in Château Narbonnais, the monster's broken remains have been converted into Holy Relics by the priests and quite possibly some abbot, bishop or even the Pope will declare him a saint."

Peire Cardinal, forgetting Esclamonde for a moment, was carried away by repulsion against the idea of Simon's sainthood and improvised this sirventes:

If killing men and shedding blood,
Destroying souls and murdering,
Heeding false counsel, lighting fires,
Debasing barons, and plundering

Seizing lands by violence,
Causing pride to mount on high,
Kindling evil, quenching good,
Slaughtering innocent life.

If for all this one can indeed,
Win a reward from Jesus.
If that is so, I must concede
Simon de Montfort can wear a crown
And sit in the glory of Heaven.

Enthusiastic laughter and applause broke out, demonstrating the agreement of everyone present. Peire remembered Esclamonde again and what he had witnessed at the Villeneuve gate and he continued with another new song:

I used to know a Lady fair,
Burned at the stake by Simon,
But at the Villeneuve gate.
I saw her flash like lightning,

An avenging angel born of flames
Striking him down at the gate.
Did I see right? Did I see wrong?
Simon struck down by mystic fate.

The applause had not quite died down when from the back of the great hall a woman's voice, sweet and strong, began singing to his melody:

No ghost and not an angel
It was I at the gate, my friend.
Your eyes did not see wrong
We used to sing together then.

Cansos and partimen
But not even an alba
When we were torn apart
No songs we sang together.

At the gate, the dragon's head
I smashed it with a stone
To welcome the return
Of the gentle Unicorn.

Peire and everybody else turned and saw a wild yet beautiful woman dressed in plain clothes, boldly staring at all of them smiling with a bittersweet smile. Peire, for a second time recognized Esclamonde, and ran to her. They embraced, crying in front of everyone.

"Why did you run away and what were you doing all these years?"

"All in good time and not here where everybody is celebrating our deliverance."

While they were talking a woman of striking and harsh wanton beauty was watching them with interest. She was Jezebel de Cazenac, who finally said with a loud voice for all to hear, "Let us not forget that we all owe our deliverance and the new age that is soon coming to a woman fighter and poetess, the lady Esclamonde. Let us all give her the generous applause and ovation she deserves."

They all shouted and sang praises while drums, cymbals and tambourines were banged along in the background. The patriotic fervour was unmistakably mixed with erotic undertones. Jezebel and

Esclamonde became sources and magnets of the wild excitement emanating from all the men and women around them.

Among the shouts, obscene abuses against the departed Simon de Montfort, his wife Alice and all his brood were heard with increasing frequency and intensity to the point of indecency. The Pyrenean Counts and knights among many others competed in desecrating their dead enemy.

Peire was saying to Esclamonde in disgust, "Even an enemy must be shown respect when dead. Dishonour is ours, not theirs, if we heap upon them too much abuse and zeal for their death."

Count Raymond VI who had held aloof until then came forward and said for all to hear. "My dear friends. I have thanked all of you for your valour and sacrifices, which brought about this glorious victory at last. However, let us be satisfied that we have managed to overcome a remarkable opponent and not to allow ourselves to abuse him now that he is dead. As a matter of fact, Simon de Montfort had all the qualities of a good prince: courage, foresight and remarkable perseverance."

It came as a great shock to the audience to hear such magnanimous praise from Count Raymond VI, the man who had suffered most by the policies and the military actions of Simon de Montfort.

The young Count Raymond VII, although surprised, understood his father's honest admission and hastened to add. "Since I was twelve years old, I have been following my father from campaign to campaign, from defeat to defeat and from humiliation to humiliation pursued by Simon de Montfort and his crusaders. My father was always trying to save as much of our nation and our way of life as possible. He did that not by hating his archenemy but by learning from him. Because of his efforts we are able, today, to see the commencement of our liberation. Esclamonde's fatal blow to Simon's skull is a fantastic and significant event, however it wouldn't be enough to regain our freedom without my father's patient work and ability to appreciate his enemy's strengths and learn from them. Fortunately, Simon's successors do not seem to possess any of his good qualities and soon, I am sure, we will be able to take back from them all that used to be ours."

Count Raymond VI had tears in his eyes upon receiving so much love and understanding from his son. He realized that he was much luckier than Simon. He was blessed with a great successor who was very valiant, courageous, understanding and wise.

However, Raymond's admiration for Simon de Montfort fell like a wet blanket on the enthusiasm of the crowd and Raymond-Roger the Count of Foix jumped to his feet to voice his objection. "I am amazed to hear praise for the monster who turned our country into a wasteland where we can still smell our blood and our ashes. We are certainly not going to admire this monster. We are going to hate and despise his memory, not only in our lifetime, but also for as long as human history lasts and tells the tales of horror perpetrated by him. We should not feel ashamed to desecrate and abuse his revolting carcass. Young Raymond, you sounded apologetic for the preposterous admiration of your father for his worst enemy and rightly so because it was embarrassing to say the least. What did Simon do? Kill, burn and destroy life, because his ambition was not compatible with life. And what did he manage to achieve in the end? To roam rapaciously over a principality which yielded nothing to him. So, he and his dragon wife, Alice, had to beg their relatives and Philip–Augustus for loans and grants for their keep and for their famished crusaders. Must we really admire such a monster? I say no, and I prompt you to continue raining abuse on that departed monster."

William de Puylaurens, the chronicler, tried to say that Count Raymond VI meant to admire only the military virtues of Simon de Montfort and nothing else but nobody paid attention to him and the celebration continued unabated giving vent to the pent-up feelings of anger and desperation accumulated in the last nine years of war and devastation.

Esclamonde looked at Peire and asked him. "What do you make of all this? Do you agree with Raymond's opinion or would you rather go along with the feelings of the Count de Foix and of most of us here?"

"My sirventes describe my genuine feelings and opinions about Simon de Montfort. The Count of Toulouse is growing old and he looks it. He likely wants to be known in posterity as someone who was up against a strong and worthy opponent."

"You are not so kind to your Liege Lord. Do you mean that he did not really believe what he was saying?"

"No, I did not say that. I have been near him enough to know that he really did admire the military skills of Simon de Montfort but right now he cares about his own posterity as well. As far as he is concerned, his real enemies have always been the bishops, the Cistercians and most of the clergy. I have never heard him say any kind words about them. But there were times I was disappointed with him, sometimes to the point of despising him, because I felt he was fainthearted and tended to dodge a battle. Later, I reasoned that he did not want to risk everything in a battle that he could not win. He always tried to give himself the opportunity for a better day. Finally that day came and he showed everyone he could fight like a brave man. This battle of Toulouse was the better day he had been preparing for, and you my love were its crowning glory!"

"Yes. Perhaps his conduct can be justified, perhaps not. But he is an old man now and whatever he had to give, it has been spent. The young Raymond is our hope and he seems to be a good leader for his people. He has a chance to give them back the lives they used to have."

"I am sure he will do well. He is already being called the Unicorn, a new hope for the people of this ravaged land. But what about us? Are you coming back to me or do you intend to disappear on me again? Why did you run away in the first place? What on earth is your story?"

"You ask me too many questions but I cannot answer them until you hear my whole story which is not at all easy to tell. There are many demons hidden in me and it is painful and embarrassing to let you see them. Most likely you will not want me back after my story is told. Let us go to your quarters where we can speak in private."

Toulouse was in ruins and there were hardly any houses standing for shelter and privacy but Peire had managed to find quarters in the deserted Abbey of St. Sernin where the entourage of the Raymonds were also staying. They were not comfortable but they had privacy.

Esclamonde started by asking about her son, Nascibon, and was relieved to hear that he was safe in Verona albeit sad because he was so far away.

"You should have been with your son in Verona instead of doing whatever it was you have been doing. He was asking passionately about you because he needed his mother. By the way, he looks a lot like you and is a very clever child."

Esclamonde started crying uncontrollably and finally she managed to say, "You make it very difficult for me, Peire, reminding me where my place should have been, as a mother, and although you did not say so, as a wife to you as well. I am sure you are wondering where our love has gone and whether there is any of it left. Let me tell you my story from the beginning since I left you. In my way, I had warned you that I objected to being dragged behind you while you were doing errands for Raymond and that I could never remain in Campagnac where I was not welcome or in Verona outside my natural habitat. I know that Nascibon had to be safe somewhere but I could not be there myself. I was sure that you had understood my problem then but I also understood that you could not find an acceptable solution. Our whole society at the time had sunk into black despair and my people; my father's people in particular, were hunted like animals and burnt systematically by the hundreds. I felt compelled to find my father before it was too late to ever see him again. I didn't want to drag you into my search, pulling you off your path and important obligations. So, I quietly slipped away while you were gone. I joined some of my people in that tenement near St. Pierre des Cuisines by the Garonne River, where they were hiding. I submitted myself to the disciplines of the Cathars and I lived a life of abstinence with the purpose in mind to become a Perfect. I was fortunate to find my father and receive love and spiritual instruction from him, which gave me consolation and peace. I knew you were looking for me and I even saw you a few times but I was determined to stay hidden and reap the benefits of a warm spiritual life that only a Cathar community could give me. For a while I was oblivious of what was going on around me in Toulouse and in the entire South until one day one of our own betrayed us to the White Brotherhood. We were all gathered up and thrown into prison cells under the Episcopal Palace. Surprisingly, Folquet came to our rescue, although he was the one who had imprisoned us in the first place. He did not seem to want anything in return and I opted to save my life. Though my father could have been saved with Folquet's protection he chose death alongside his brethren. I wanted to as well but he insisted I try and save myself for our son, you and my spiritual work. Later, in my devastating loneliness and suffering, I allowed myself to be seduced by Folquet, not under duress but with my confused consent. It turns out I again willingly chose Belial, the God of the infinite pleasures of the flesh, over the Spiritual God because it seems this is a deep proclivity inside me. For a long time, perhaps years, I was lost in a thick warm silky spider web of excruciating pleasures woven by the expert and subtle embraces and protection of Folquet."

Frustrated with confusion and anger Peire tried to interrupt but Esclamonde placed her hand on his shoulder and continued. "Please let me finish before you have your say. Listen to my story, which is my bare and painful truth, through and through. Try to understand it with your full heart and an open mind before you protest and rain recriminations down on me. Do not forget our wonderful experience with our friend and lover Bieiris de Romans. She opened a new road of pleasure for both of us, quite possibly a road without return. In his episcopal palace, Folquet continued what Bieiris had started and he helped me to discover within myself an ocean of passions and needs for all kinds of pleasures. According to the beliefs of my Cathar brethren, what I had discovered was the realm of the material world with all its pains and pleasures and I felt happy and fulfilled to be in that realm where Folquet or Belial or Venus or Astarte held the supreme power. I felt as if I was Lilith embodied, the demon of erotic gratification. I know that according to the beliefs of my people there is no salvation in the realm of the flesh and salvation can only be in the spiritual realm. Yet there is so much pleasure in the realm of the flesh. One day, just over a year ago I ran away from the palace and joined the uprising in Toulouse. I did that not because I repented for my evil ways but because I was disgusted with the double dealings and betrayal of Bishop Folquet against the citizens of Toulouse for the benefit of himself and Simon de Montfort. He was always behaving that way as it turns out but I was oblivious of anything else except my own hidden life of pleasure. When he betrayed the trust of the Toulousains and led them into a devious trap Simon had laid for them, I suddenly woke up as I witnessed their imprisonment and their slaughter. I now saw Folquet in his true colors and he disgusted me. He was no longer the fascinating lover but a repulsive creature of absolute evil. I managed to escape his seductive clutches and ran away with information concerning the designs of Folquet and Simon against the citizens of Toulouse. I think in all this madness I was actually able to help the citizens of Toulouse successfully retaliate in part because of my intimate understanding of Folquet's twisted mind. The tables had now been turned and the crusaders who were found looting houses and shops and those who had been brutally policing the streets were roughly gathered, tied behind horses and dragged to the gallows. The people of Toulouse, finally having an opportunity to express their pent-up rage, cut many to pieces in cold blood on the streets and I joined in this orgy of death and devastation. For the first time, I massacred other human beings and even felt some pleasure in it. In the span of about a year I learned to handle all the weapons and war engines. I became particularly skilful with catapults and trebuchets, as I have recently proven by killing our archenemy and destroyer of our country, the invincible Simon de Montfort. For one year I fought on the ramparts and the trenches of Toulouse against the crusaders like an Amazon and when I was not fighting I still looked for pleasure wherever I could find it. I let Lilith rule my flesh and senses. Then, I joined the Cazenacs, driven to them by mutual attraction. I shared the same perverse passions with them and I tasted the thrills of even more new sensations in their orgies. Bernard and Jezebel are brave and fierce warriors and they considered me as their comrade in arms, which flattered me and made me feel good and somewhat whole again. As you can see Peire, I have tasted with my own flesh and heart unspeakable experiences that according to your religion condemn me to the everlasting fires of Hell. According to the beliefs of my people though they only prevent me from reaching my spiritual salvation while I give them power. I could simply die as a creature of flesh going through the process of corruption. However even at the last possible moment I could reject Belial and embrace the Spiritual God. If I am sincere and take the consolamentum I still actually have a chance for salvation. However, right now I am not yet ready for that. This is what I am, or what I have become. Peire, now that you have heard my story would you really still want me back? Or even love me at all?"

As her tale was unfolding his initial rage, jealousy and revulsion were gradually being replaced by a growing feeling of arousal. This was his true love, after all, and her candid and uninhibited exposition of her sensual experiences affected him deeply. He was left speechless from all his intense and conflicting emotions so he simply took her lovely face in his trembling hands and kissed her passionately and insatiably, munching her lips, sucking her tongue, inhaling her breath and exhaling his breath in an intense and uncontrollable erotic explosion. They undressed with a heated haste and their limbs intertwined with a tender ferocity, convulsing in a forever embrace.

Much later when they were able to speak again, Peire remembered to reply to Esclamonde's last question. "Yes, I want you back, Esclamonde, although I will never forget your tale. The question is whether you want to come back to me?"

"Yes, Peire, I am with you now, although I am still the woman of my tale."

Meanwhile, a new banner of a silver unicorn was quickly becoming a rallying symbol for the entire Midi, which was now up in arms against the crusaders and their new leader. For on the day after Simon's death, the crusaders had met in Château Narbonnais and elected Simon's 18-year-old son, Amaury de Montfort, to succeed him. He was not without courage and resourcefulness but he had none of his father's personal charisma and none of the fanatical self-righteousness. The only charismatic figure left in the politics of the Midi was the 21-year-old Raymond VII who was increasingly admired and worshiped as their redeemer. Amaury ordered a last, desperate assault on Toulouse but failed miserably and was forced to raise the siege. He retreated and barricaded himself in Carcassonne taking the remains of his father with him while being pursued by the young Raymond's Southern army.

Peire and Esclamonde fought in the ranks of the Raymonds, animated by patriotism and the rekindled love they felt for one another. At this time, the Unicorn was leading them from victory to victory and creating an exhilaration not experienced in many years.

Amaury de Montfort, in a desperate attempt to save his father's conquests all at once, committed the fatal mistake of dividing his forces. The young Raymond and his allies could then pick them off one by one. Neutralizing the Crusading army by slaughter, capture and putting them to flight. Many towns changed hands or their allegiances, and the South was gradually returning to the good old times before the crusade. Amaury's situation was becoming extremely difficult and untenable and he would have been killed or expelled if the majority of the Bishops, the Cardinal Legate, Bertrand and the new Pope, Honorius III, did not support him. In order to save themselves, Alice de Montfort with the Legate himself and a number of Bishops traveled urgently to the French Court to ask for help. Pope Honorius III issued plenary indulgences for a new crusade against the South and finally Philip Augustus reluctantly allowed his son Louis to lead it sometime in May 1219. By June, Louis appeared before the Walls of Marmande leading a horde of crusaders, which included thirty-three counts with an enormous throng of knights and foot soldiers, apart from twenty bishops and a swarm of Cistercians and Benedictines.

Marmande was a fortified outpost of the Agenais in the north west of Languedoc coming under the sway of the young Raymond. It was guarding the waterway of Garonne and so it was of strategic importance for the invasion of the Midi. Louis immediately stormed and took the outer defences. The garrison, remembering perhaps the fate of Beziers threw itself on Louis's mercy. They were spared and joined the crusaders. The punishment planned for them was visited on the innocent inhabitants of the town. They were slaughtered to the last man, woman and child, and the town was left in flames as the army continued its march towards Toulouse.

It looked as if the return of the Unicorn was only a short and fleeting visitation and the liberation of the Midi a shaky parenthesis. And yet, the bloody holocaust at Marmande and the sinister invasion of Louis and his crusaders, instead of striking terror in the liberation army of the Unicorn, just strengthened their resolve to resist and even overcome the might of the Northerners

Toulouse was making feverish preparations by taking in supplies and strengthening the walls and barbicans. The young Raymond had gathered a large garrison. Esclamonde and Peire had joined the team handling the siege engines at the Château de Bazacle. They were the first to spot the crusaders when they arrived from the northwest on the 16th of June 1219. Louis did not waste time but ordered a massive assault at this point hoping to surprise and overrun the defendants and take Toulouse. However, his troops were beaten off by a constant rain of missiles from the engines and by fierce hand-to-hand fighting at the walls and barbicans below the Château de Bazacle. After a second and third attack had failed miserably, Louis deployed his large army to completely encircle the city of Toulouse and his host sat encamped before the walls. There were more attacks against the gates of Villeneuve, Mascaron and elsewhere but they were easily repulsed leaving many casualties behind.

William of Puylaurens standing next to Peire said to him as he watched the enemy from the walls, "Prince Louis hasn't got a chance against our brave knights who fight under the inspired leadership of our young Raymond. I think he is wasting his soldiers and his time."

"I agree with you, sir, that he doesn't have a chance now. He spread himself too thin encircling us. We have supplies and plenty of water to last for a long time. His army is too large to feed and water easily under the increasing heat of summer. When forty days are up his feudal levies will want to go back to their homes, which he can't do anything about."

That was exactly what happened when in early August, forty–five days after his arrival, Louis suddenly burned his siege engines and marched away with his army. After the initial shock of disbelief, the garrison and all the other inhabitants of Toulouse threw themselves into a wild triumphant rejoicing. They rejoiced for their bravery and military skills. They rejoiced for the sudden retreat of Prince Louis's enormous army. They hailed their leaders as victors and saviours but mostly they hailed the young Raymond as the returning Unicorn bringing them justice, peace and joy again.

In a gathering of the leaders, though, more sober voices were heard. The young Raymond was saying, "I certainly feel proud of our great victory but also relieved to see the dust behind the last northern soldiers returning to their homes, hopefully as far as possible from here. However, we should not forget what Prince Louis did to Marmande because he could have done the same to Toulouse and anywhere else in the South if we had let him or in the future if we ever let our guard down. He still left 200 knights behind to reinforce Amaury de Montfort against us. We must deal and finish with Amaury as soon as possible and should not waste time with premature celebrations."

The Count of Toulouse, Raymond VI, looked gray and old but also proud as he watched his son. He also said, "Be wary of the cold fire burning inside Louis Capet. He is a capable leader who knows how to cut his losses short at the right time. His present retreat is not necessarily a defeat. Just pray he will not ever come back. However, keep up the hails of victory. They are good for our morale. We need them. Yet, also be wary of the bishops and the abbots. They can be the stepping stones for future crusades as they have been in the past."

The Count of Foix who was nodding his head in agreement added, "A few of these bishops, with the blessing of Pope Honorius III, are promoting the idea that Amaury de Montfort transfer his thankless inheritance to King Philip-Augustus. Can you imagine the sinister implications of such a transfer? French troops will be coming down here to rule the land exactly like Prince Louis did. Fortunately for us, the old king is reluctant to consider such an idea. Still, what of his successor, Louis, who has tasted our blood? As for me, I am rushing down to my country to clear it of whatever northern vermin remains there. I suggest that each one of you return to your own lands and rid it of any Northerners still lurking about. My dear boy, Raymond, do not lose any more time. Chase Amaury de Montfort out of this country before he involves the French Throne."

All the gentry present agreed with this assessment and mobilized for the complete recovery of their feudal holdings. The Pyrenean Counts rushed south, the Cazenacs and others galloped west and northwest to Perigor but most of them followed the young Raymond to Carcassonne and the adjacent territories where Amaury de Montfort was still holding out. Peire and Esclamonde traveled west to Romans for a reunion with Bieiris.

Esclamonde had been behaving like a proper wife to Peire and their love had only deepened with the time they spent apart. However, Esclamonde was also expressing an ardent desire to meet with Bieiris again. Peire understood that he had to take her there before she became too restless. The truth was he was also quite happy with the idea of getting together with their old friend who had always filled their lives with so much pleasure and love. He had originally tried to convince her to visit their son instead but Esclamonde, it seemed, was not ready to deal with the explanations he would obviously demand. Perhaps she did not have within her the inherent instincts of being a mother, so natural for other women. Perhaps it was simply convenient that Nascibon was tucked away safely in Verona, in order for her to pursue her other natural instincts. Inside she was feeling terribly guilty but, instead of confronting and solving her problem, she was postponing it with Peire's mute concurrence. Quite often this inability to take care of family responsibilities has been the shortcoming of many philosophers, troubadours, libertines and other free spirited vagabonds.

They arrived at Romans with pounding hearts from the anticipation of meeting Bieiris again and were received with intense excitement. Bieiris was beside herself with joy at seeing Esclamonde alive and told her she had always felt that she was not dead, despite hearing she was. As they entered the castle they did not fail to notice that Bieiris seemed even more attractive and sensuous with age. They found themselves pouncing hungrily on each other and fell into ecstatic union together. The air was filled with delicate sucking, gurgling, squealing and gasping sounds composing a divine music of love. Only when their triple passion was assuaged somewhat, an exchange of questions started trickling in concerning the time they had been apart. Finally, Bieiris learned the whole story and an excited amazement flashed on her face.

"Peire, my dear, your wife is truly Lilith. How can you handle such a demon? You will never know what she is going to do or where she might go next to follow her heated fancy."

"I am aware that she may have to fly away again whether following spirit or flesh. However, she is here with me now and I love her beyond my own desires. This love is all that matters in the end."

"Well, Esclamonde is certainly with us now and we should be very happy for that! Is there really anything worth having that is truer than what we have now?"

"I have no intention of going anywhere. Everything I want is here with me now and now is forever. But enough talk of my future fancies, the last time I was here your son, Folquet de Romans, was with you. Where is he now?"

"My Folquet chose to become a troubadour and is now in the court of Frederick II, the German Emperor and the King of Sicilies. Most likely, he will attend the Emperor at his coronation in Rome next year. Frederick is a gifted and enlightened personality and is encouraging those who can exercise the fine arts and sciences successfully. He has been a generous patron of troubadours and since the conditions here have not been conducive to poetry and music, many of our best troubadours including my son Folquet, Guilhem Figueira and others have flocked to his court in Palermo. By the way, Peire, do you really think that the terrible winter is retreating to the north and a long sparkling spring is coming?"

"The spring is coming, for sure, and the good and balmy weather will be with us for a while but I cannot say for how long. Our Lord, the young Raymond, is brave, wise and loved. Unfortunately, I saw what Louis Capet did to Marmande and it was truly horrible. When he realized he could not do the same with Toulouse, he retreated without being defeated. What I saw there made me shiver."

"Is this your sirventes for the coming winter?"

"I hope not. I am not as gloomy as people think."

"I do not think you are gloomy. I think you have pronounced an oracle of gloom. Yet, everything is going well in Provence and Languedoc, returning back to normal again. Some of our troubadours are even coming back from Italy and Spain to sing in their homeland once more. As for the clergy, they are shrinking back into their shells and some of them are even trying to reconcile themselves with our secular nobility. Many fortified towns have been restored to our Southern nobility. By the way, I hear that your hometown of Campagnac has transferred its allegiance to the Count of Rodez, Henry, to whom it used to belong. This, I believe, was your brother's choice, counter to that of your parents who preferred the Bishop of Rodez."

"Oh heavens, what is going on? I had better go to Campagnac myself to find out what is happening. I am sure you both will not mind if Esclamonde stays with you while I am away?"

So Peire hiked through the mountains alone and in two days he was in Campagnac. His brother Bertrand was not in the best of moods as his choice had angered the bishop and upset his parents who were of the opinion that it was safer for them to be under the protection of Bishop Gaucelm. His father and brother were still arguing about this turn of events endlessly. "I remind you that the Bishop saved us when the Faidit attacked us and carried you and Nascibon away with them."

"May I remind you that Peire, with the support of Count Raymond VI, rescued us from the Faidit who were behaving like brigands then but are now under the control of the young Raymond. Our bloodline runs back to the bloodline of the Counts of Toulouse. I am simply honouring my bloodline and my original allegiance."

Bieiris Cardinal de Campagnac cut in sharply, "Get it through your heads, all of you, that the Bishop will prevail in the end over any local secular power because the Pope and the King of France are behind them. What is your opinion, Peire?"

"Bertrand was right to give his allegiance to the Count of Rodez but all of us must try to placate and befriend the Bishop even by offering him some compensation. That will be my father's job while my mother should seek the assistance of her brother, the Bishop of Le Puy-en-Velay. I cannot dismiss the possibility of another crusade descending upon us at some time in the future so we must be able to survive as a family. Here, we can use our disagreements to our advantage.

Campagnac was not at the center of Peire's life but it was certainly a reference point, a place he could always come back to. He was very glad to see his family united by the time he left. He did not go back to Romans right away. Instead he joined the young Raymond, who was besieging Penne in the Agenais, to share in the elation of victory. Penne was one of the few cities left in the hands of Amaury de Montfort. Across the Midi most castles were restored back to a generation of Faidit owners and Southern princes as it was in 1209. A Count of Foix ruled in Pamiers and a Trencavel in Carcassonne. The sons of the Lord of Cabaret held court there once again. Toulouse had replanted its vines and rebuilt its bridges. After the capture of Penne, Amaury de Montfort returned to his ancestral home in the forest of Rambouillet near Paris. Peire returned to Esclamonde and Bieiris at Romans and stayed on for a few more blissful months until the news arrived that Count Raymond VI was dying. Without delay they rushed to Toulouse in the hope of seeing him alive.

They found the Count of Toulouse on his deathbed surrounded by his friends and relatives. At his side holding his hand was his son and heir, soon to officially become Raymond VII.

The approaching death had transformed the once glamorous man into a fading shadow of himself, who retained though, a lucid mind and a clear voice. "My real enemy was not Simon de Montfort, and not even the common clergy but the power hiding behind the Church which wants to control our minds and our souls. Now that I am about to cross the gate of Heaven, I know that they cannot bar my way, simply because I do not recognize their authority. I have been excommunicated countless times and I guess my excommunication still stands since I can see no priests around here to administer the last communion to me. No matter. I can still cross to the other side without their blessing. They will be held accountable for this omission when their time comes. My son and heir, please do whatever is necessary when I am gone for the dignity of my dead body. In a very short time and at a very young age you managed to win our freedom and to restore the good name and the glory of the House of Toulouse. Keep up the good work but also be prepared against any adversity. In my time, I have remained flexible in order to survive. Too flexible perhaps, and have been blamed for that. However, flexibility can also be a virtue at times. Please don't judge me too harshly as you may need to be flexible yourself sometime, you never know. I am very tired now. Farewell and bless you."

In July 1222 Raymond VI died in Toulouse after a reign of twenty-eight years. The Church pursued him to the grave not allowing him an official Christian burial on the grounds of being an excommunicate. However, an unofficial Christian burial took place in a secret location somewhere on the grounds of St.-Sernin in a nameless grave. Raymond's body had been moved into another coffin while the original one, filled with heavy clothing stood outside the priory of the Hospitaller's awaiting permission for burial, which never came. For years it sat there in spite of the continuous, albeit pretended, efforts of Raymond VII with successive Popes. Folquet, the Bishop of Toulouse actually helped Raymond VII in a crucial way for the secret burial of Raymond VI, thus earning his gratitude and reconciliation and his own return to Toulouse after four years of exile.

At this time, during his comings and goings, Peire bumped into Folquet quite by chance and although unwilling he couldn't avoid talking to him. "Well, Peire Cardinal, we always seem to meet at the most crucial times. In the past we have been opponents, although I have actually helped you even then without you knowing it, but now I am a friend of Raymond VII, and so I am your friend as well."

"I guess one must often be grateful for dubious favours better kept unspoken. God has burdened us with deadly secrets, each one of us. I guess peace is maintained by mutual discretion." Peire said with disguised anger

"I couldn't have put it better myself, I who am supposed to be an accomplished politician and a diplomat. In any case, I honestly ask you to consider me as your friend and not hesitate to ask for my help in times of trouble."

"Thank you Folquet, you can consider me your friend then."

Peire left troubled by this encounter yet he never spoke of it to Esclamonde.

Life was very pleasant for Peire and Esclamonde for two more years. Their time was spent mostly in the court of Raymond VII with short visits to Campagnac and Romans.

Then two significant events occurred that together shook the unbroken serenity of the Unicorn's pastures. In August 1223, Philip Augustus died and was succeeded by Louis VIII, a small lean man, cold, unemotional and prematurely aged at thirty-six. Like his father he had unbounded ambitions for his dynasty, but unlike Philip he was a man of very profound piety with a horror of heresy. In February 1224 Amaury de Montfort surrendered his rights in Languedoc to the new King, Louis VIII. This development became a thick black cloud encroaching on the blue skies above the Unicorn's pastures.

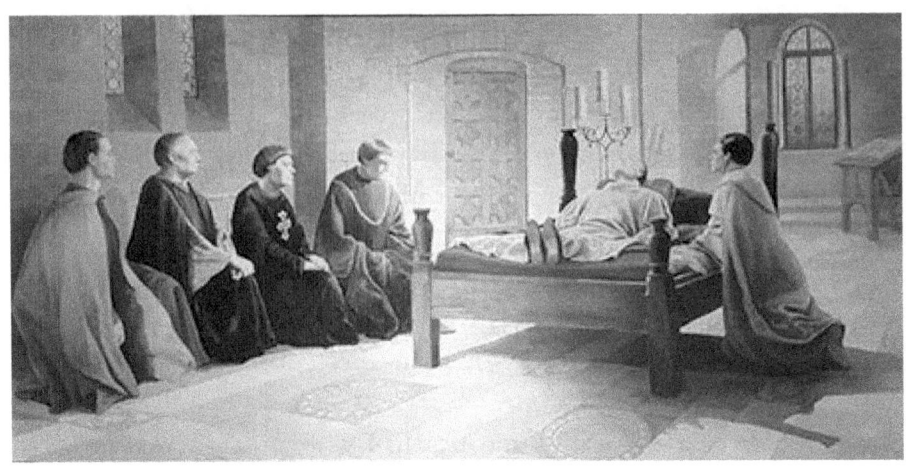

Raymond VI Count of Toulouse' Death

Various pictures of troubadour life at the time

Frederick II engraving, 19th century

The Court of Emperor Frederick II in Palermo. Arthur Georg vonRamberg

CHAPTER 15

LUCIFER

fter long and often painful discussions Peire managed to convince Esclamonde to cross the Alps and visit their son Nascibon in Verona. Sometime in November 1224 they made their appearance without warning at the mansion of Renieri Campagna. This caused mixed feelings of surprise, embarrassment, guilt and growing joy to their seventeen-year-old son, their aging uncle and themselves. Nascibon was a strapping and exceptionally handsome young man with a striking resemblance to Esclamonde, who was standing there speechless in awe in front of her son. He was the first to break the silence. "I am very happy to meet you, mother, and I am truly relieved that my father managed to find you and bring you to me at last. I am sorry that I have not learned to love you and that the only sentiment I can express is my admiration for your beauty. I will not ask you why you have been away from me for as long as I can remember, because you cannot possibly give me any satisfactory answers. However, I am glad you are here now and at least I may have the opportunity to get to know you a little, although I am already a grown man with plans and a life of my own. As for you father, although you have spent some time with me in the past, you have been away for eight years during which I have grown to manhood without you. I have a very full life now, of which you are not part of. In a few days I will be knighted. Did you even know this? Ezzelino III da Romano in the presence of Emperor Frederick II, who will soon be passing through Verona, will knight me. My life feels very unimportant

to you both but I suppose I should be glad you are here with me now especially at this auspicious moment.

Esclamonde was crying, Peire was trying to comfort her and old Renieri cut in with a trembling voice. "My dear boy, do not be so hard on your parents. They wanted you safe with me here in Verona, where you could enjoy the comfort and the excellent prospects that my position and our prosperous and enterprising city could offer you. In the country of our origin, an insane and merciless war has been going on and you would have suffered untold miseries and hardship, and quite likely you could have been killed accidentally or intentionally. Your parents were obligated to live there by the force of duty and choice. They couldn't be in both places at the same time. Your father used any chance he got to be here with you even if for just a short time. Your mother did not have such a chance. It is very unfortunate, but this is how it has been."

"My grandfather, you know that I love and respect you because you raised me and stood by me in everything. You have been my father, my mother and my grandfather, but this did not mean that I did not long for my real mother and father. Now that I finally meet them as a man, I cannot help but to express my bitterness for their absence. I know that they must have had valid reasons for being absent. I am also old enough to know about the terrible situation of our homeland. It is the same old story of a conflict between the Pope and the local nobility using some pretext, like heresy for instance, and the weapon of excommunication. We have similar problems here whenever the Pope clashes with the German Emperor or some other potentate, dividing the land into two warring camps. This has been the reason Verona has had to constantly fight the Lombard League, as we all know. Fortunately, we are too enterprising and wealthy here in Italy to be ruined by such wars as in the case of the trans-alpine lands. I am very sorry to have hurt my father and especially my mother, who is still in tears. My initial bitter surprise is now replaced by much warmer feelings towards you, mother."

As he said these words, Nascibon approached and embraced Esclamonde with genuine warmth. She responded by kissing his hands and his cheeks smearing him with her tears, and then she managed to say. "My dearest Nascibon, my handsome son, in spite of what I have done or what I have not done, I am your mother who loves you no matter what because you came from inside of me and you are the flesh of my flesh. I have no other sons or daughters, just you, only you. Please do not forget that. Do not ever forget that. Please do not ask me why this and why that, just love me as your mother, if you can."

Her strong emotions overpowered his original reservations and conquered his heart. He held her in his arms for a long time oblivious of anyone else until finally he felt his father's hands grasping his shoulder. Then he turned and embraced Peire saying, "It is wonderful to finally be in the arms of my father and mother at the same time, at long last."

"Yes, it is wonderful for us too. Nascibon, please know that I am proud of you for having grown so strong, so bright and handsome, and for the words you have spoken today, which show knowledge, awareness, wisdom and compassion. We feel very lucky that we have arrived at this time and are able to be here for the momentous event of your knighting by Ezzelino III in the presence of such an illustrious personage as Frederick II, the Holy Emperor. By the way, I have brought with me as a gift to you the escutcheon of our family bearing our crest. It would be most fitting to carry it with you on the day of your Knighting."

"I would be proud to. But what is the meaning of this crest?"

"It is a version of the Tree of Life containing the mysteries and secrets of life itself, which are revealed to us gradually and unexpectedly. It shows the struggle of two opposing forces and an establishment of equilibrium between them. One might say that they are the forces of good and evil, of spirit and matter, fighting one another. It is up to the individual to establish the balance inside him, inside you. Perhaps it is too early for you to understand it right now. It will help you gain wisdom as you progress in life. I haven't even reached its full understanding myself yet. At this point, it is important to know that our family is the guardian of such a crest, which is a code of wisdom."

"Father, I am perhaps too young to understand the meaning of what you have just said, but I already feel proud to bear your gift, the escutcheon of our family."

Esclamonde had stopped crying and, listening to Peire trying to decipher his family crest, she focused on its symbols of good and evil which reminded her of the two principles of her own creed. In her own life, she had experienced both principles and had found great enjoyment in each of them separately. She needed to meditate on all her experiences, those of Spirit and those of flesh and all those she could not seem to place in just one principle or the other. The reunion with her husband a few years back and the reunion with her son now, though beautiful and heart warming, had also left her feeling extremely confused and vulnerable, stirring up deep inner turmoil. Esclamonde was having a difficult time reconciling all her feelings with the precincts of her creed. Perhaps her father would have had an explanation if he were alive to give it. Peire would have maintained that the two principles could sometimes come to terms and establish a balance as in his family crest, for instance. But how does oil mix with water?

In late November 1224, The Emperor arrived with five hundred German knights. Celebrations began with much pomp and circumstance in a special area, which lay outside of Verona. Ezzelino III, the new Lord of Verona, welcomed the Emperor and renewed his alliance with him. This in effect gave the Emperor unopposed passage to Italy and to his Sicilian Kingdom, and prestige and power to Verona. The celebrations lasted three days with jousting, music, singing and dancing and near the end of the festivities several young men were knighted, Nascibon among them.

Frederick II was a man of a magnificent physique and manly beauty, very much like a God of antiquity. His eyes were full of light and intelligence often with a roving tendency towards beautiful women. Esclamonde felt his roving eye penetrating deeply into her, awakening once more the demon Lilith, which she felt come alive in the center of her womanhood and pleasure. At midnight after the celebration she allowed herself to be whisked off to Frederick's quarters quite unnoticed by anyone, including her husband who was fast asleep. There, she was engulfed again in the exquisite pleasures of the second principle, that of all flesh. She was sliding further and further away from the first principle of the spirit, or so she thought at the time.

"My dearest Esclamonde, perhaps you may know that I have invited your husband to accompany me, together with you of course, to Palermo. He has accepted my invitation providing that you have no objections. Do you have any objections?"

"No wonder, they call you Lucifer or even the Antichrist. I have many objections but how could I resist the Emperor and the master of seduction? You know that my husband admires you unreservedly as the most enlightened monarch of this era. You have taken advantage of his blindness, caused by your splendour, in order to ravish his wife."

"His wife, who was passionately willing, I must add. You say they call me Lucifer and the Antichrist but those who call me that are hypocritical clerics and superstitious peasants deep in darkness, who are frightened by the divine light of truth, of science and freedom. I do not mind being called Lucifer because the meaning of this name is the bearer of light. However, I object vehemently to being called the Antichrist because I have the deepest reverence for Christ as the embodiment of ultimate goodness and love."

"I am impressed and happy to hear you speak in this way. You are very much like my husband, no wonder he admires you so much. Still, I must confess that the sinister implications of those names excite me, possibly because of the passionate demoness, Lilith, living inside me."

"Lilith excites me too, not because she is evil but because of her powerful, intelligent and lascivious nature."

"Perhaps you should know that I was brought up as a Cathar and, for the time being, have chosen to follow the Material Principle of all flesh and am now happily wallowing in it."

"So I noticed. Yet, I also think that you are deluded to think that good and evil, spirit and matter are separate entities. They are not. They are entwined."

"Again, you think and speak like my husband making me feel less unfaithful to him. Also, there is one other matter. Only recently I met my son after many, many years of absence. How could I leave him now to go off with you to Palermo?"

"You will not be leaving him, he is coming with me as well to do his service as one of my knights."

"You have thought of everything! Do you want them for their worth or because of me?"

"Because of their worth and because of you."

Early in December 1224, the reunited family bid goodbye to Renieri and followed the Emperor and his army to his Sicilian Kingdom. Renieri was in tears and complained, "It is ironic that after a tearful reunion I have to suffer this terrible separation."

"My dearest grandfather there is no need to cry. I am only going to do my service as a knight for the Emperor and will be back soon. Regardless, I have obligations to the Lord of Verona, Ezzelino da Romano as well."

"I hope to see you soon unless Pope Honorius III persuades the Emperor to go on a crusade to deliver Jerusalem from the Saracens, in which case I will be out of luck. I am already too old, you know."

Esclamonde interrupted to say, "My dear uncle, I do not think that the Emperor would be inclined to take the cross, at least right now. I am sure he is more interested in putting his Southern Italian Kingdom in order first."

Peire, who was blindly happy to have joined his idol, Frederick, added, "Esclamonde is right, the Emperor is eager to consolidate his Italian kingdom and his vast German-Italian empire rather than scamper off in wasteful crusades. He is a man of arts and science who wants to build a civilized world liberated from the evil influences of soul-eating clerics."

"Do not get too carried away, my nephew, expressing such revolutionary ideas because all this does is to put yourself in mortal danger. I hear they call him the Antichrist. You should not risk being thought of as the disciple of the Antichrist. It is a consolation for me to know that the chances of a crusade are slim. After all, how could the Pope entrust a crusade to the Antichrist!"

The Imperial Army proceeded on its way south and within a few days reached Rome where Frederick paid his respects to Pope Honorius III. It was the third time that Peire had visited the Lateran. This time he had been included in the Emperor's retinue and had the opportunity to observe the new players in the Papal entourage. Honorius III was a frail old man with a manic obstinacy in his eyes. The usual self-righteous Cardinals and other officials surrounded him. There was one who stood out among the others by his magnificent stature and the severity of his demeanour. He was Romano Frangipani Cardinal of St. Angelo, a member of one of the great Roman families.

The Pope addressed the Emperor without preliminaries; "I am holding you to your word that you will soon lead a crusade to recover Jerusalem for Christendom. However, I have heard that you are frivolously occupied otherwise."

"I have a kingdom and an empire to organize and run, your Holiness, and I must do that first before I mobilize a crusade. Nevertheless, I will keep my promise, be sure of that."

"I hope so, my son. The Holy Church is facing two great problems right now, the recovery of Jerusalem and the eradication of heresy in Occitania. I am relying on you for Jerusalem and on the King of France, Louis VIII, for Occitania. I have appointed Romano Frangipani, here, as my legate to guide Louis VIII against the heretics."

Peire felt a cold shiver run down his spine as he watched Frangipani, the future tormentor and tyrant of his people.

The Pope continued on with his pet subject, "I understand that you are the Suzerain of Provence and therefore you are involved in my crusade against the heretics as well."

"So, it seems," Frederick said, not pleased with the idea.

As Frederick and his retinue were leaving, Frangipani turned to the Pope and said, "We think that Raymond of Toulouse is the protector of heretics but I smell a much worst rat in the wake of Frederick II. Mark my words; this emperor will be a tricky problem for the Church one day. There are rumours that he is the Antichrist you know."

"My dear Romano, your religious zeal makes you see heretics and enemies of the Church everywhere. I remind you that our Church has to rely on its two secular pillars, the King of France and the Emperor. I have appointed you as my legate to guide the King of France. Hopefully soon he will finally stop haggling with us for money and get on with the crusade against Toulouse. At least Frederick intends to finance the crusade himself that he promised to lead."

"When and if he is going to do it. By the way, I noticed a notorious troubadour and venomous critic of our church among his followers, Peire Cardinal. A few years ago, he was here arguing for the cause of the excommunicate Count Raymond VI. The Emperor is surrounded by many such individuals and worse. In his opulent Court of Palermo, he is spending his time in perverse pleasures with his harem and in the company of troubadours, sorcerers, heretics and Saracens. No wonder many pious Christians think of him as Lucifer or the Antichrist."

"As I told you, Frederick is our ally. Please stop tearing him down and concentrate on your mission. You should leave immediately for France."

As for Frederick, he and his army arrived in Palermo just before Christmas 1224. Palermo was the capital of the former Norman Kingdom of the two Sicilies, which was comprised of Sicily and a large part of southern Italy. Frederick had succeeded the Norman Kings and inherited the cultural mosaic of Norman-Italian, Byzantine-Greek and Arabic components. He intended to rule it in a way that would create maximum advantages for the economic development and the quality of life of his Kingdom. His court in Palermo shone with opulent splendour and reflected his ideas and wise policies as an enlightened monarch. He was certainly a consummate libertine given to resourceful erotic pleasures but he was also a keen student of the arts and sciences and an ardent patron of troubadours. To the majority of the clerics and to the coarse and superstitious secular masses, he appeared as a disturbing and threatening personage to whom they could easily attribute the characteristics of Lucifer or the Antichrist. Even some perverted individuals in his immediate entourage wanted to identify themselves as disciples of the Antichrist. They even organized covens for him to supposedly preside over. Occasionally his curiosity pushed him into their trap and an atmosphere of unwholesome sorcery had developed around him providing juicy ammunition to his clerical enemies.

Esclamonde was fascinated by the erotic environment of the Court and abandoned herself to the luxuriant pleasures abundantly provided all around her. The gardens, the aery architecture, the pools, the perfumed baths, the soft carpets and softer beds, the delicate taste of foods and wines, the intense light of the day and the discreet candles and torches at night, the attractive figures of men and women moving about seductively and sparsely dressed, all this and more intoxicated her senses. In Occitania there was a playful eroticism but here the erotic mood was heavier and much more intense. She loved it. She did not consort with Frederick as often as she had thought she would because he was often busy with the affairs of state and with many other pleasures of his own. She did not mind. She had time and the opportunity to taste other pleasures herself including Peire's company. She had always cherished him and consorted with her husband with an unusually strong passion. This passion felt even stronger after Frederick had made love to her. It was surprising but true.

Peire had been happy as well, composing all sorts of poems and songs, which were greatly appreciated by Frederick and his cultivated entourage. He also had an affair with the beautiful and learned Lucrecia, who actually informed him of Esclamonde's affair with Frederick. He was not upset but smiled and said, "Lucrecia, you are the delight of all my senses but Esclamonde is not less, no matter what she does. I have been with her for countless years and we have been through many experiences together and separately. We have always valued our freedom and we did not love each other less whenever we exercised this freedom. She enjoys being with Frederick and perhaps she loves him but I do not love her less and she does not love me less because of that. You know I love you, but I do not love her less because of that."

"Peire, I have never come across a man like you before and although I feel terribly jealous, I admire you and love you more for feeling the way you feel. Yet tell me, now that you know, what are your feelings for Fredrick. Do you hate him?"

"No, I certainly don't hate him! I used to admire him and now I do not admire him less. Frederick is the most gifted and most free of men on earth. Esclamonde was lucky to be with him."

"How do you mean? He is surely the most free of men on earth because he is the Emperor."

"I mean he is free in mind and spirit. There are emperors, kings, dukes, counts, bishops, cardinals and popes who are slaves of their religious doctrines, of their prejudices, of their superstitions, of their rapacity, of their avarice, of their need to control and oppress others and of their obsessions and the fear of death. The king of France who plans to invade my country is a supreme example of this enslavement. The Pope is another. Frederick is certainly ambitious but he is not a slave to his ambitions. He is authoritarian but not controlling. He is open to the good teachings of Christianity and of other religions but he does not blindly obey the dictates of any soul-smothering dogma. He is open to all thoughts and feelings that breeze his way and open to the new and delicate light of dawn. He actually is Lucifer with the original and good meaning of this name. He is not the Antichrist that some stupid and malignant clerics call him because the anti-dogma would be as bad as or worse than the soul smothering dogma itself."

"I am enthralled by the sound and poetry of your words. You seem to me, with this unusual viewpoint, to be a man of profound freedom yourself. However, let me ask you this. Does your son, Nascibene, know of the antics and misbehaviour of his parents or is he too young, too vigorous and too attractive to women to worry about such things."

"Well, you have given the answer to your question yourself. Nascibon or Nascibene as you Italians call him, does not know of our "antics" unless you have a mind to inform him yourself, you who seem to know everything that is going on in Palermo. The point is whether such information would endear you to him or not."

"Nascibene is preoccupied with his service as a knight of the Emperor and is most likely going to hate me for giving him information that he is not at all ready to receive. I only hope that he is not going to hear it from somebody else. Yet if he does, he will not believe it and the informer would certainly be in trouble with him. I guess there is no need to worry about it."

"You are clever and perceptive enough to see that I am not at all worried about it."

In the early summer of 1225, Frederick II was married by proxy to Yolanda, the Queen presumptive of Jerusalem, which also made him King of Jerusalem, although the Holy City was in the hands of the Infidels. This was an added reason for him to have to lead a crusade in the near or not so distant future. In the meantime, magnificent celebrations were organized in Palermo for this most glorious event. The celebrations lasted one whole week and the most illustrious lay and clerical magnates were invited to listen to enthusiastic speeches and admonitory sermons. They also enjoyed an unending show of famous troubadours, exotic dances and the acrobatics of skilful and beautiful performers. The foods and drinks were plentiful and even the most jaundiced clerics were happy to be there.

Of course, quite a few abbots and cardinals did not miss the opportunity to whisper to each other that the Emperor and his entourage were more pagan than Christian, and possibly worse. They called Frederick a heretic, a sorcerer and the Antichrist, and that the time of reckoning was around the corner for him. In a louder voice, they praised the King of France, Louis VIII as the most pious and saintly disciple of the Church, and his wife, Blanche of Castile, as a staunch Catholic bringing up her many children by strict Catholic rules.

Frederick, hearing all these praises, commented inaudibly to Peire who was standing nearby, "I am surprised that this frozen royal couple has managed to produce so many children. By Immaculate Conception no doubt."

"And yet, he is preparing to conquer the country of my origin by taking the Cross. It may be that these so-called products of Immaculate Conception may end up inheriting it one day. By the way, as a crusader against heretics he will be allowed to conquer Provence as well, which is Imperial territory, your territory."

"If you are trying to involve me as an ally to Count Raymond VII of Toulouse you are out of luck. I cannot go against a crusade, even an unjust one, when I am supposed to lead another one, myself, although under duress. I even married by proxy in order to prove my genuine intention of taking the Cross in order to gain time. Otherwise I run the risk of excommunication. I am cornered, you see. Raymond VII is in a much worse position than myself. I will not be surprised if he is already excommunicated. They usually do that in order to legitimize their unjust invasions. I understand that Raymond of Toulouse is pleading with Louis and Frangipani at Bourges, where a council of Bishops and Archbishops is in session, to spare him in exchange for his total submission to the will of the Church and its instrument, the King of France. I am sorry that I am giving you all this bad news and that I am disappointing you by admitting my helplessness against the true Antichrist, the Church!"

"My God! The story of Simon de Montfort is repeating itself and Raymond VII is going to suffer like his father Raymond VI."

"Not quite, the situation is much worse now. Simon was just an ambitious individual with a vacillating Papal backing, Louis VIII, the King of France, is a lasting institution with the unwavering support of the Church. Raymond of Toulouse is a good friend of mine, but he does not have a chance. Regardless, nothing is going to happen this year, Louis is too methodical to do anything rash. He will first make sure that the Church will finance his crusade and that the titles transferred to him by Amaury de Montfort are signed, witnessed and authenticated before he starts. In one year's time, he will be invading my vassals in Provence. Please do not be in a hurry to run from my court, in fact, I advise you not to go there at all. There is very little you can do to help poor Raymond of Toulouse. He is a brave and resourceful young man but the forces pitted against him are too formidable and insidious to deal with. I am facing the same predicament myself but I still have room to manoeuvre and gain time before they pounce on me. They will never tolerate a free spirit like mine and they will turn heaven and earth upside down until they finally smother it. My crusade is only a ploy to beat them at their own game but they have figured me out and have been applying intolerable pressure on me to begin this crusade with the implied or direct threat of excommunication.

"In my life, I have always been seeking the patronage of enlightened persons and have been lucky to find them in the courts of the Counts of Toulouse and most certainly in yours. Enlightenment and freedom have always been the supreme virtues and the major attributes of Universal Goodness. The enslavement of the spirit, and the avid need for power and obscurantism are some of the worst attributes of real evil. Unfortunately, our Church seems to be consorting with the black core of evil and persecutes all the disciples of Light. I find this situation incredibly difficult and cannot find any peace with it. For the time being I will stay with you but next spring I will be obligated to serve Raymond VII, my Liege Lord, to give him moral and legal support, and my sword for whatever it is worth."

The days passed sweetly and swiftly in the Court and all their cares were forgotten for a time. Frederick's enthusiasm for Esclamonde was fizzling out as he was increasingly preoccupied with the Lombard League, the Pope and his pledge to take the Cross, aside from the fact that his always renewed harem provided ample diversion for him. Esclamonde was deeply hurt as a woman but she did not show it in any way, or to anyone. Once, she had planned to confess her affair to Peire but now she couldn't bear to talk to him about it. Peire, who had guessed her silent drama, did not want to embarrass her by questioning her. He was simply affectionate with her and she was grateful for that. Lucretia remained a very good friend to both of them in more ways than one and she kept her mouth shut.

Nascibon was busy with military expeditions and diplomatic missions as part of his service to the Emperor. By March 1226, Frederick decided to send him back to Verona at the head of a detachment of knights in order to assist his ally Ezzelino III against the Count of Verona, Richard of San Bonifacio, who was threatening his hold on the city of Verona.

Peire and Esclamonde grasped at this opportunity to bid goodbye to Frederick and follow their son back to Verona. Frederick was truly sorry to see them go and expressed his wish to see them return to his court one day soon.

Louis VIII

CHAPTER 16

THE SECOND COMING OF DOOM

hen Nascibon and his entourage arrived in Verona, the city was in a state of civil war. Richard of San Bonifacio, a descendent of the old Counts of Verona was now head of the Guelfs. The Guelfs, supported by the power of the Pope, were now trying to overthrow Ezzelino III and the Ghibellines who held the city as allies of the Emperor Frederick II. Behind the Guelfs were Milan and the Lombard League as well as the secret hand of the Papacy. The arrival of the Imperial detachment under Nascibon tipped the balance and gave a clear victory to Ezzelino who regained absolute control of Verona. A significant series of events followed Ezzelino's victory. Nascibon married Cunizza, Ezzelino's daughter and their wedding became an illustrious part of the general victory celebrations. Cunizza was a gracious and very sweet woman, unlike her father who was as ruthless as he was a brave and an effective ruler.

Shortly after the wedding Renier died of old age, happy and content. Nascibon inherited all of his substantial estate, which together with Cunizza's dowry made him one of the richest men in Verona. Peire and Esclamonde were very happy for Nascibon's good fortune but deep inside were uneasy and sad because they had to soon return to the unhappy land of their origins. The news had been drifting across the Alps that King Louis was getting ready to lead his crusade against Provence and Toulouse. He would start from Bourges and proceed south down the Rhone valley.

Esclamonde also had her own melancholic reasons for feeling warn out and drained of all her formerly abundant energy. On one hand, she wanted to stay with her son to help him raise his family and on the other hand she wanted to run away from a place in which she did not really belong and from her unsettling memories. Also, her recent promiscuity could come back to haunt her in the conservative society of Verona and cause a grave embarrassment to the presently elevated status of Nascibon's family. Peire's considerate discretion, although comforting, also felt hurtful to her, as if she was being judged and patronized. Peire on the other hand really did not want to hear any more confessions from her for they hurt too much, so quiet understanding seemed the most loving thing he could do. Esclamonde felt she had to keep moving in the hope that she might find some new fresh air to breathe, and perhaps some peace. Peire felt that he had to go back home, due to a sense of loyalty to the House of Toulouse at the time of its greatest need, as well as to see his parents for the last time as he had heard they might be close to dying. Recently he had met his old friend Guy de Sommerive and Guy's fifteen-year-old son Leone. Guy tried to convince him to stay in Verona in peace and prosperity rather than going back looking for danger and hardship. Leone was hoping to find adventure in Greece under William of Villehardouin, the Prince of Moreas. There were many opportunities there for enterprising young knights. Leone kept saying that as soon as he was knighted he would head east to find adventure and ultimately a fief. Nascibon had playfully shared this adventurous dream with him in the past when they were boys but now he was a wealthy young man married, commited to his business and content establishing his important position in Verona. Maybe one day he could at least visit, as he had become good friends with the family Sommerive and Leone.

Goodbyes were said, arguments made and tears shed as Nascibon's parents took the ancient Roman road heading west to the lands beyond the Alps. Soon after their departure from Verona, they acquired, as fellow travelers, a group of Franciscan monks with radical convictions. They maintained that they practiced the true teachings of Saint Francis of Assisi without the deviation or compromises used by the established order. They called themselves Spirituals because they claimed to have access to the Divine Spirit which permeated all living things, human, animal, plant, even earth, air, water and fire. They lived in decent poverty and were always ready to help and love their fellow human beings. Esclamonde identified with these gentle monks immediately because they reminded her of her father's ways and her Cathar origins. They seemed to understand the turmoil inside of her and offered her consolation. She even confessed to them that she was a Cathar believer, who had deviated to the material principle. Not only did they accept her completely, as she was, but they enveloped her with deep understanding and love. These Spirituals were very much in line with Peire's own spiritual feelings as well and he was extremely grateful to them for giving Esclamonde the consolation she needed. However, watching them talk together his sixth sense warned him that Esclamonde might drift away from him again some day soon.

It was early in May 1226 when Peire and Esclamonde began their crossing of the Alps and had to part ways with the good and friendly Franciscans. After a week's trek they descended from the Alps entering the Rhone valley and their familiar homeland once more. While crossing the Rhone River at Beaucaire they received the alarming news that King Louis VIII and his Crusading army were approaching Avignon from the North. Most cities were surrendering to him one after the other without a fight. Raymond had charged all of his subjects to resist to the last, but they were wearied of an unending war and disinclined to ruin themselves for what appeared to be a hopeless cause. So they deserted Raymond in indecent haste and some went as far as making a shameful declaration of submission. The Lord of Laurac sent this message to the king: "We long to rest under your protective wings and live under your wise government."

Peire and Esclamonde, with their small retinue, galloped along the Domitian road in all haste to join Raymond and his army in Toulouse.

In Toulouse, they found a great gathering around the Count of Toulouse, Raymond VII, and the Count of Foix, Roger-Bernard. Many

Southern Lords were also present, Comminges, Cabaret, the young Trencavel, and even some bishops, like Folquet. They were in the process of deliberating what to do to stop the King's crusade from destroying them all.

Raymond was saying, "The King seemed to have an unopposed promenade down the Rhone River with most cities and southern lords falling head over heels to see who would welcome him first. Even Beaucaire, where our liberation started, surrendered to him. The irony is that I had mortgaged Beaucaire in order to get a loan to fight the coming war. I have just had recent news, though, that Avignon has decided not to let him pass. Now the king is getting ready to start a siege. I am hoping he is delayed there long enough to give us the time to organize our resistance."

The young Count of Foix, Roger-Bernard, stood up and said with an ardent tone, "We have beaten them before and we will beat them now. I venture to guess that the King's downfall will be here in Toulouse, unless he is beaten first before the walls of Avignon in which case he will be going back to his gloomy Kingdom to sulk."

"If he is going back at all, I mean alive!" Richard of Cornwall interjected and continued, "Our court astrologer predicted to my brother Henry III, the king of England, that Louis will die on this expedition and chaos will reign in his kingdom. So, let Louis conduct his crusade in peace and let God claim his own."

Richard of Cornwall had just arrived and his appearance and words had made an exhilarating impression on the gathering, many of whom acclaimed him with enthusiasm.

"If I understood you correctly, my royal cousin Henry had no intention of sending me any reinforcements against our common enemy King Louis. This is disappointing news indeed. Whether Louis dies or not, I still need reinforcements because his Capetian House could claim my legacy as his. I am not up against an individual like Simon de Montfort as my father was but the Royal House of France! Behind King Louis is the iron Queen Blanche of Castile and her counsellor, confessor and most likely her lover Cardinal Romano Frangipani, the Papal legate."

Folquet, the Bishop of Toulouse, now visibly aged but still impressive, took the floor and said. "Our count is right in his realistic assessment of the situation. The House of Capet is an institution and one of the strongest in Europe because it is favoured with the unswerving support of the Church. The Count and the Southern nobility must come to terms with the King of France before it is too late and total disaster falls upon us."

Folquet paused and fixed his eyes on Esclamonde who held his gaze unflinching and then said, "The Count and the Southern nobility must help the King eradicate heresy from this land. After all, this is supposed to be the reason for his crusade. By helping him to do that, you could disarm him."

There was a mixed response in the audience of subdued approval and somewhat louder disapproval when Esclamonde made herself heard with her clear and sonorous voice, "I am sure that our Southern customs allow a woman to speak to an audience like yours, especially if this woman has earned the right to stand as equal among men of value. Eight years ago, I was handling the siege engines of the city and one of my stones crushed Simon de Montfort's head delivering us all from the Northern yolk and terror."

There were wild acclamations and applause. Once the crowd quieted down, she continued, "In the time of our ancestors up to the days of Raymond VI and prior to Simon's crusade, there was joy and freedom in this land. The people were free to feel, to think and to believe whatever they liked until the crusaders came to take all these good things away from us. Then, for nine years there was darkness interrupted only by the fires of burning Cathars and their sympathizers. I was captured then together with my father. My father was burned but I was rescued and allowed to live. I will always be grateful to the person who saved me, though I will not reveal this person's identity as a gesture of gratitude. For eight years we have lived freely again, enjoying our wonderful way of life in our land where the Unicorn reigns. But now a second coming of doom is looming upon us. Our Bishop prompts you to submit and return back to the dark days of Simon de Montfort and perhaps even darker days to come. Our Bishop prompts you to deliver your lambs to the coming wolves in the hope that they will spare the rest of you. As you can see, I am one of those lambs myself. I offer myself to you as a sacrifice in case you decide to submit to the King in order to save your lives and perhaps your estates. As for me, I would rather fight for our beautiful and just way of life."

After a short silence of abated breaths, the crowd exploded by crying hooray and by shouting Esclamonde, Esclamonde, Toulouse, Toulouse, Foix, Comminges, Trencavel... Long live the Unicorn, down with the Capetians and his crows. Freedom or Death!

Peire took Esclamonde into his arms and kissed her with ardent emotion welling up through his whole being. He was so proud of her.

Folquet kept quiet without losing his composure and Raymond of Toulouse took to the floor and said, "Thank you Esclamonde, our heroine, for reminding us that we must fight for our precious freedom and our way of life. I promise you that we will soon be ready to confront the King here in Toulouse, which has always been the downfall of tyrants. Long live Avignon for resisting him. We wish them victory, which will be our victory too! As for our good Bishop, I assure you he means well and I will remain his friend. But I will never agree to deliver any of my subjects to the King and his crows because of their creed or their views and convictions. This is a land where everyone is free to live as he or she pleases provided that he or she does not harm our society. This has always been one of the reasons for our happiness and prosperity. We intend to fight for this and for our freedom. Only recently we won back our stolen estates and we do not intend to lose them again."

The crowd cheered their leader loud and clear for Heaven to hear and when the din abated the troubadour Guilhem Figueira of Toulouse stood up and said "I am sure you all remember Arnauld-Amaury, the Abbot of Citeaux and the legate of Rome, who burned Beziers. Now, another legate, the evil crow Romano Frangipani, guides the King into another wave of butchery and the burning of our cities. He is surely behind this second coming of our doom. Guilhem then began playing a rousing and poignant melody, which soon was adorned by his powerful voice singing:

> You arch-deceiver Rome,
> The root of all our ills
> False and perfidious!
> Rome, you have decked your head
> With caps of infamy
> You and your own Citeaux
> Who wrought at Beziers
> That monstrous butchery
> Rome, vile and corrupt
> Your heart has become rotten
> Your avid greed will make you burn
> In flames eternally.

By the time Figueira had finished singing and haranguing, the gathering had degenerated into a wild orgy of dancing and singing. Folquet had managed to slip away but not without a brief, furtive conversation with Peire and Esclamonde. "Your declaration of heresy and poetic bad mouthing against the Church will only bring you closer to the coming doom but, in any case, I will remember the favour of your noble discretion."

Peire replied to him in a low voice, "I am not sure whether to be revengeful or thankful to you. So, discretion is our solution. Good and evil are so entangled within you, which makes you different from most crows. Perhaps you are a raven."

"A raven! Well, I am flattered." He whispered and was gone.

Peire looked deeply at Esclamonde and asked her, "Do you still have any feelings for him now?"

"I only have distant memories but no feelings. For you I have many feelings and memories but please stop asking questions from jealousy."

"For some time, though, you have seemed to be retreating further and further away inside yourself. What is happening to you?"

"It seems I am returning back to my roots again as a believer of the two principles. For a long time I served Belial and I've been identifying with Lilith but now I yearn for my father's ways and thoughts, for the spiritual principle. Often, I find myself swaying like a pendulum between the two realities of Spirit and Matter, and I am waiting for the pendulum to find its resting place."

As she was talking, three elderly men approached them and introduced themselves as Guilhabert de Castres, Bernard de Marty and Ramon de Parella.

Guilhabert de Castres, the oldest of the three, spoke first, "We are very proud of you, the way you spoke, and your brave deeds. We used to know your father. He was a good man and pure. He died like a martyr and he is now with Jesus Christ our savoir. He likely has served his thirty third reincarnation and he is now fully in the world of spirit"

"Thank you for your kind words although I do not deserve any praises. I am the most impure person you could possibly imagine."

Ramon de Parella smiled and said, "My dear Esclamonde, no matter how impure you may think you are, you can be redeemed by only one sincere commitment to purity."

"My father, Nicetas, spoke to me about you and urged me to seek you out in Montsegur when the time comes. Would you accept me there when this time does come?"

"Yes, my brothers and I will welcome you when your time comes, as you said."

"Thank you, father, I will remember your open invitation to Montsegur."

The news from the front in Provence was encouraging. The Avignonese were putting up a stubborn and effective resistance and King Louis and his troops were stuck outside the city walls. The summer was particularly hot. Dysentery, spread by huge black flies, took a heavy toll on Louis's troops. Discontent mounted in the royal army and several of the barons in the camp were suspected of plotting against him. An assault, ordered by the King and led by the Count of St.-Pol, was subjected to a murderous crossfire and the Count himself was killed. The defeat was attributed to the treachery of some of Louis's barons, particularly Tibald Count of Champagne. In the end Tibald left the camp without leave and returned to Champagne. The army's morale could not have been lower.

In the meantime, Richard of Cornwall was attacking La Rochelle in the West and the Count of Toulouse was feverishly preparing his resistance in Toulouse. It looked as if the King's crusade might just peter out in dismal failure.

During that time Peire felt he could visit his parents without being missed by Raymond of Toulouse. Accompanied by Esclamonde they arrived in Campagnac in early August of 1226.

His parents had very little time left. He was fortunate to have arrived when he did for they were both already on their deathbeds. Bieiris recognized him but Gaucelm couldn't. His Mother called him to her side and said, "You were too gifted and too restless for your own good and for ours. You are an illustrious vagabond without a home and without a family. Your father and I have grown tired of missing you. Gaucelm is past caring now, but all his life he was deeply saddend that you were not next to him. Fortunately, Bernard, though not as gifted as you, possesses the earthly qualities that can keep our estate intact and safe. Furthermore, he has filled our house with descendants. You? You only had one son and he is not even here. Why has Esclamonde not given you any more children?"

"Our son, your grandson Nascibon, is well established in Verona as a nobleman. He is married to the daughter of the Lord of Verona and he may have children of his own as we speak."

"This is good news indeed, Praise to God. Nascibon may yet redeem your wasted life by leaving behind him worthy descendants. One more thing; again, you are wasting your time and talents by serving Raymond of Toulouse. His is a lost cause. The King of France and his descendants will win in the end and they will take everything, mark my words. The South will be theirs. Please try to understand this.

Now, I am tired and I have to close my eyes. You were always my beloved son and I bless you."

She closed her eyes and she never opened them again. Gaucelm, her husband, passed away a few days later without a word of farewell or blessing as he had lost touch with this world a long time before. They were buried within the walls of the Campagnac Castle in the grounds of St. Michael's chapel. The funeral was attended by Bertrand and his large family as well as by friends from the neighbouring manors.

Peire had a long talk with his brother, Bertrand, on family issues and mainly on the repercussions of the King's crusade on Campagnac.

"Peire, I am now responsible for the family estate and I cannot risk losing it by sticking my neck out for Raymond of Toulouse. The King is going to win in the end because he commands the resources of the strongest Kingdom in Europe. I like Raymond and I owe allegiance to him but the odds are piled up too high against him. The Count of Rodez is fraternizing with the Bishop of Rodez in order to ingratiate himself with the King. What am I supposed to do? Out of necessity, I am going to lie low, hoping that I will not attract attention. I will give you some of my men to take with you when you return to Toulouse to fight for the Unicorn, which in my opinion is a lost cause. If I do not give them to you they would likely desert me anyway, although most of the desertions these days are happening in the opposite direction. I have heard stories that make me sick! Sicard de Puylaurens for instance, a former Faidit who had fought against Simon de Montfort at Castelnaudary and defended Toulouse against Louis himself in 1219, has now prostrated in front of the King saying, 'I am drunk with delight at your arrival and am rolling in the mud to kiss the toe of your glorious majesty. I bathe your feet with my tears, illustrious Lord, and I crave the privilege of being received as a slave beneath your protective mantle.' Isn't that disgusting? Could you compose such poetry yourself my brother? When I heard these words I learned them by heart to remember how low we have fallen."

"Indeed, I could not. I ask you, my brother, could you have not learned better poetry to remember? Nevertheless, I understand your position and thank you for the volunteers. I have also heard of mass defections, submissions and surrenders. Apparently, Avignon is in the process of negotiating surrender to the King. I must return to Raymond in Toulouse and hope that I will meet with him in time."

On their way back to Toulouse, Peire asked Esclamonde. "You heard my mother wondering on her deathbed why you did not give me any more children. For a long time now I had meant to ask you this question myself. Can you tell me now?"

"When I got pregnant with Nascibon, I did want a child very much. Since then I have not wanted any more children. Our itinerant life, my dualist convictions, my sexual appetites and my free spirit are not really compatible with childbearing ways. As you know, I value truth, sincerity and freedom more than anything, and in your own way you do too which is why I love you and stay by your side."

"I do understand and accept you and I love you for all that you are. May I ask how you manage it though, not getting pregnant?"

"We, the believers in two principles, possess the secret knowledge of avoiding pregnancy while enjoying lovemaking. Courtesans, ordinary prostitutes, adulteresses and even many nuns have such knowledge as well. Whenever there is conflict between human nature's needs and the rules of society there is always a secret way out."

"You mean to say that even true believers resort to hypocrisy?"

"True believers reconcile the commands of the two principles consciously and openly without feeling guilty, simply because we do not believe in guilt. You the Catholics, on the other hand, who believe in paradise and hell, it is you who allow guilt to torment you. We, the true believers, are guided by our Perfects to the eternal and wholesome realm of the spirit without despising the material world. We simply know that the material world is subject to corruption, decomposition and death yet we can also know the exquisite and intense experiences generated in this world. It is a matter of choice, and a choice that we can make even just before our death. If we manage to be completely sincere when we make this final choice, then we have a chance for eternal life in the world of spirit."

"I do not know how a simple question about contraception evolved into a theological discussion, but since it did I can only point out to you that you are one undivided person where matter and spirit coexist and influence one another. So how can you serve one without serving the other?"

"Peire, we have been through this discussion so many times before that there is no point repeating it, particularly now that our world is falling apart and we must get to Toulouse as fast as we can."

When they arrived in Toulouse early September 1226, they learned that Avignon had just capitulated and King Louis and his crusaders were pushing on towards the city. Louis's march through Languedoc was a triumphal progress. Arnauld-Amaury, now a very old, somewhat mellowed man, went ahead of the army receiving surrenders. The King was feted at Beziers, Carcassonne and Pamiers while all opposition evaporated. Most cities and castles exchanged their immunity with money, provisions and heretics who were promptly burned in great pyres, which shone all the way from Nimes to the suburbs of Toulouse. Louis had brought his siege engines from Avignon with intentions of besieging Toulouse. Raymond and his few supporters were determined, although the general mood was downcast with an underlining element of desperation. In everybody's mind there was the terrifying and tenebrous feeling that Simon de Montfort's times were returning, only worse, with King Louis bringing down upon them a second wave of hell. The hopeful times of the past few years seemed to be coming to a horrible end and, though they were determined to fight, it was hard not to feel weary. In Louis's camp in Pamiers, however, exhilaration and triumph sounded in the air. Nicholas de Brai, the court poet, bombastically called the King "reborn Alexander" and shortly afterwards "returning Charlemagne to win back his Southern legacy." Louis himself in the short time of forty-five days had managed to set up a government of the conquered territories. Louis appointed two seneschals, one for Beaucaire and the other for Carcassonne. Beneath them a hierarchy of officials was to administer the extensive lands, which Louis had confiscated from the Faidit, and enforce his legal rights, which formed the foundation of royal power.

In Toulouse Raymond was furiously organizing his army, and the population still loyal to him, for a long siege and a valiant resistance, hoping that he would not be deserted in the end. The anxiety in Toulouse had risen to the breaking point when in the last days of October King Louis unexpectedly decided to go home, feeling ill and, perhaps, because of the approaching winter. The siege of Avignon had taken a heavy toll on his delicate health, and on the 5th of November the King suddenly died en-route, from a bowel obstruction. The news of the King's death was received with great relief and exhilaration in Toulouse. The former mood of defeatism was rapidly changing into a rekindled optimism and hope that this second wave of terror might only be a bad dream and that the happy days of the Unicorn could be sustained. In Raymond's court songs and rejoicing began in earnest. Troubadours, jongleurs, officials and other hangers on, who only moments ago had been truly scared to death, were now showing nonchalant and bold faces. Many indecent jokes were bantered around at the expense of the dead King and his family.

William Puylaurens made up a song.

> How could Alexander die
> When he was just reborn?
> How could Charlemagne pass away
> When he'd just returned?
> How could a virtuous King bloat out and burst
> When victorious was marching away?
> From excessive chastity, I would say.

Everybody cheered and laughed loudly except Raymond and a few others, including Peire and Esclamonde, who remained sober because they knew better.

The astrological prediction of the king's court of England came to pass, that Luis VIII would die, but the chaos predicted was at least partly averted because Blanche of Castile and Romano Frangipani managed the situation with an iron will.

Louis's heir was a twelve-year-old child, Louis IX, whose power was exercised in his name by the Queen Mother, Blanche of Castile, and the Legate Romano Frangipani. The achievements of a century of effective royal government were suddenly assaulted by a succession of aristocratic cabals. The government defended itself with astonishing and unforeseen success, but at a great cost. Languedoc had to be relegated temporarily to the background. A handful of officials and a military governor, the seneschal of Carcassonne, Hubert of Beaujeu, with a force of five hundred knights, represented the crown in Languedoc. Hubert was a young man of conspicuous courage and ability, but his role in the Midi was inevitably a defensive one.

Raymond VII formed an alliance with the Count of Foix and the other Pyrenean counts and took advantage of the respite to gain ground. He managed to affirm his control on the Agenais, Quercy, Rouergue and the Toulousain, but he couldn't make any progress to the East. Carcassonne, Narbonne, Beziers and the whole of Provence remained in Royal hands. For two years, a war of attrition was going on which, though successful, inflicted misery and ruin on the country and its people. The inhabitants were increasingly becoming war-weary and mutinous. Raymond VII still won many battles and at Castelsarrasin in 1228 the French were beaten badly.

It was becoming abundantly clear, though, that ultimately he would have a very hard time bringing true peace to his land and winning the war in any decisive way. The time of the Unicorn was fading and again, he was slowly but surely losing his horn. With the power of the Capetian monarchy in reserve the French could afford to lose battles, unlike Simon de Montfort who had always known that a single serious defeat might sweep his rootless dynasty away. Blanche of Castile had proved to be a ruler of first rank. An aristocratic rebellion, sedulously fostered by the English, had been suppressed with ease and an expedition to Languedoc was planned. The new Pope, Gregory IX, was directing the Cistercians to preach a crusade against the Cathar heretics in the South and at the same time he was threatening Raymond with excommunication. The new Pope had already caused untold hardship to Frederick II by excommunicating him and officially labelling him the Antichrist the year before, in 1227.

Count Raymond VII, facing the misery of war, the defection of his leading captains, a new crusade against him and the threat of excommunication, decided to sue for a negotiated peace. His negotiating party was led by the Abbot of Grandselve and included Peire Cardinal de Campagnac for his legal resourcefulness.

Esclamonde stayed in Toulouse with her Cathar brethren to reflect on her past and her future course.

The peace party arrived at the Royal Court in November 1228 with an offer of surrender from Count Raymond VII. In the majestic yet gloomy royal castle at Meaux east of Paris, Peire had the disheartening opportunity of kneeling in front of the iron queen, Blanche of Castile, and the grandiose and austere presence of Romano Frangipani.

The Abbot of Grandselve solemnly declared, "My Lord Raymond VII, the Count of Toulouse, longs with all his heart to be restored to the fold of the Church and the services of his Lord and King and begs you to show your clemency and forbearance."

The queen mother fixed each one of the embassy with her piercing eyes and said, "The House of Toulouse has been fighting against the Church and against the Royal House of Capet for far too long to beg for our forgiveness as simply as that now. Also, the House of Toulouse is known to protect heretics in its domain. We cannot forgive them for that."

"Your Grace, Count Raymond VII has repeatedly demonstrated his love and devotion for the Church by his generous donations to our holy establishments. During his rule heresy is no longer in evidence to provoke the sensibilities and the piety of good Catholics. The good government of Count Raymond VII has induced most heretics either to convert or silence themselves. Concerning your reference to military activities, I will let my colleague Peire Cardinal explain Raymond's attitude."

Romano Frangipani fixed Peire with a flare of recognition in his stare and said to him, "I think I have seen you before, in the Lateran. You were representing Count Raymond VI then, and now you are speaking for Count Raymond VII. I have also seen you in the retinue of the Emperor Frederick II. The Raymonds and Frederick are similar in two ways, their tolerance of heresy and their aversion of crusades. What have you to say about that?"

"Your Excellency, I cannot speak for the Emperor but my Liege Lords took steps to eradicate heresy in their domain by persuasion and conversion. They were not against crusades but they had the right to defend their territory against anyone who invaded it. His Holiness Innocent III recognized this right and condemned anyone who tried to dispossess them. My present Liege Lord is simply defending his territory and has never been the aggressor against royal territory. In his justified effort to defend himself he has won all battles against the invaders. Yet Count Raymond VII has shown no arrogance but, on the contrary, he declared his desire to submit honourably as a loyal vassal to the king of France and live in peace under his rule as exercised by the Queen's regency."

The Queen Mother smiled pleasantly and said, "Peire Cardinal, you argued well your Lord's case but you and your colleagues must discuss with my officials all the details of Raymond's assertion to our royal fold. However, there is one thing Raymond must agree to before we start any negotiations, the marriage of his only daughter and heir, Joan to my son, Alphonse of Poitiers. On Raymond's death his dominions will pass to their issue regardless of the rights of any male line of the house of Toulouse."

The negotiations continued in Meaux and Paris for more than three months and, finally, on April 12th 1229 a treaty was concluded. Count Raymond VII would remain, for as long as he lived, the Count of Toulouse but he was left only with the Toulousain, Northern Albigeois, Quercy, the Rouergue and the Agenais. All his eastern provinces were annexed to the French Crown including those in the Rhone Valley. The treaty commanded Raymond to restore everything that he was accused of taking from the clergy and to pay indemnities, endowments and other gifts to the Church. Also, he was obligated to seek out and burn heretics. Finally, he appeared like a beggar in front of Notre-Dame Cathedral to receive absolution from Romano Frangipani in the high presence of the young King Louis IX, the Queen Mother and Folquet, the Bishop of Toulouse. After the service, the Count was temporarily imprisoned in the Louvre while royal officials took possession of Eastern Languedoc and collected the nine-year-old Joan of Toulouse, who was the most important of all the Crown's acquisitions. Her betrothal to Alphonse of Poitiers was celebrated at Moret in June 1229.

William of Puylaurens said to Peire Cardinal, "That damn treaty and all this despicable humiliation could scarcely have been worse if Raymond had been captured in battle, and he has never lost a battle! Why are we so cursed to have to watch such infamy?"

"It is true, our Unicorn never lost a battle but in the long run he couldn't win against the relentless pressures of France and the Church. What else could he do? He has done the best he could and his tenacity has not been entirely in vain. The terms, though humiliating were certainly more favourable than those that Louis VIII would have offered him. At least he won a life tenancy to about half of his domains."

Seal of Joanna of Toulouse daughter of Raymond VII

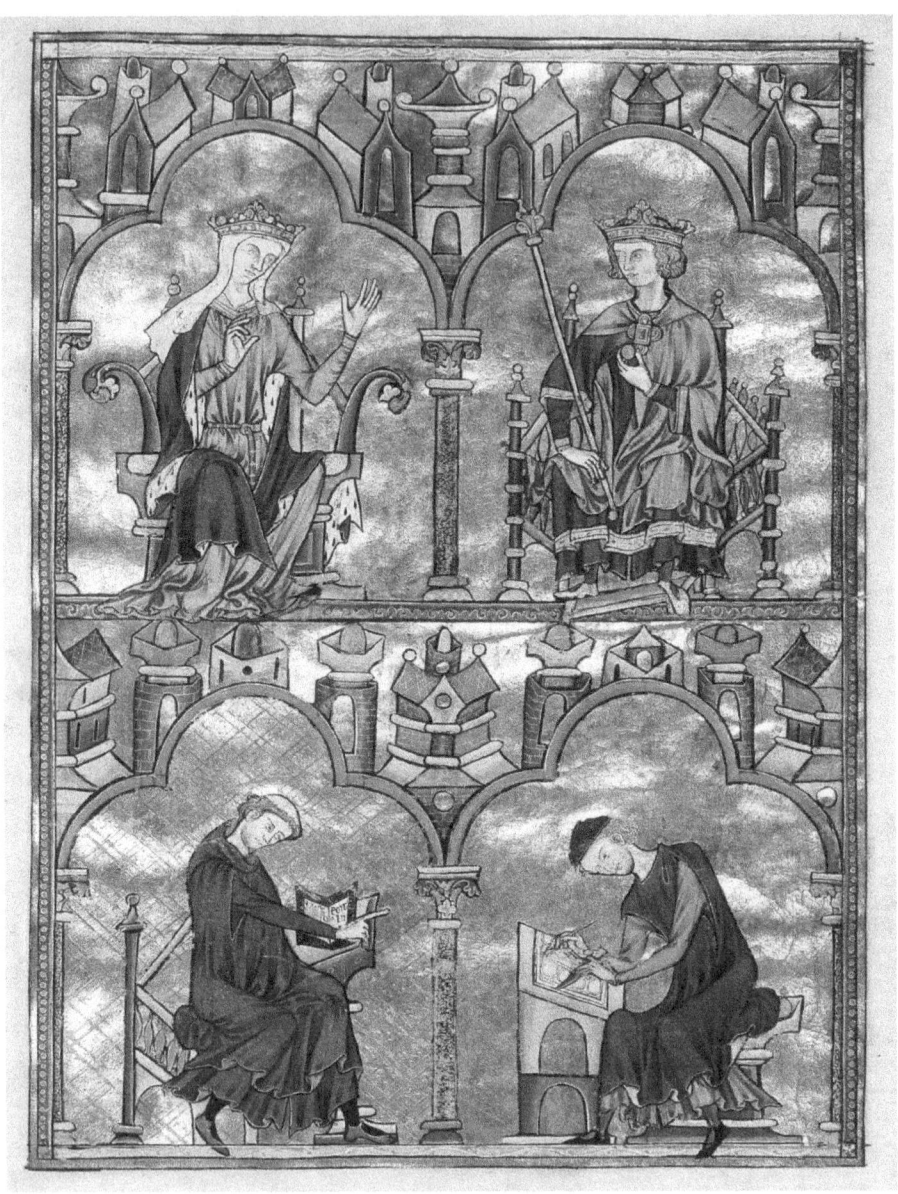

Louis IX, Blanche of Castille and Scribes
13th century Moralized Bible

CHAPTER 17

IT RAINS FOOLS

n the gloomy and solemn interior of the Dominican priory of Toulouse the stern-faced inquisitor, Arnauld Catala was interrogating Esclamonde with the assistance of a clerical secretary. Esclamonde had been suddenly apprehended a few days before in her quarters in spite of the violent protests of her husband Peire Cardinal. In a dark cell, the interrogation had been going on ever since with small intervals for sleep and some meagre food.

The inquisitor kept on relentlessly. "We know that your father was a dualist heretic. We know that you keep company with prominent heretics like Ramon de Parella, Bernard de Marty and Guilhabert de Castres. Your husband has been protecting you and for this he is as guilty as any heretic. We know that you have been committing unnatural acts of carnality compatible with your dualistic beliefs. Your friend Bieiris de Romans is under our custody for her heretic and immoral life. We learned from her that the unclean and lascivious spirit of Lilith possesses you. Bieiris confessed her crimes and she will soon face the just punishment of the cleansing fire. The same punishment is awaiting you unless you denounce other prominent heretics and reveal the hiding places of Ramon de Parella and his friends. Naturally, you must also renounce the dualist creed and return to the folds of the Church."

"I have told you again and again that I am not a practicing dualist. My father was a Perfect and he was burned at the stake for this. Ramon de Parella and the others were my father's friends but I do not know of their whereabouts. My husband is protecting me because he is my husband and not because of my supposed heresy. Bieiris de Romans is not a heretic and she has nothing to do with immoral acts. You are very wrong to have tortured her in order to secure false confessions from her. You are burning innocent people just as you are going to do with me, I am sure. I have nothing more to say to you. Take this as my final word and confession."

"Since you will not cooperate, you are to join several other heretics who will be burnt at the stake in two days' time. Your friend Bieiris will be consumed by fire also at Valence near her opulent castle. Guards take her away."

Instead of the guards, ten armed men burst in and grabbed the inquisitor and his secretary and walked them out into the city pushing them through the jeering crowds. Meanwhile, Esclamonde was whisked away to a hiding place where Peire was anxiously waiting for her. They fell in each other's arms crying while the rescuers withdrew discreetly leaving them alone.

"My dear Esclamonde, what have they done to you?"

"The point is not what they have done to me but what they were planning to do to me. For the second time, I found myself about to be burned alive. Fortunately, I was rescued again, this time by you my love. I have more terrible news to tell you though, Bieiris is in their clutches as well and they are going to burn her in Valence. She is not a heretic and not even a relaxed sympathizer. They have managed to extract a confession from her by torture. They simply need victims to burn no matter what. What are we going to do?"

"First things first, my dearest Esclamonde. We must disguise you and run away somewhere. We cannot stay here in Toulouse, one minute longer. The inquisitional guards will be after you soon enough. We must go to Verona, to our son Nascibon. That is the safest place, but to get there is not safe at all. We can find temporary shelter in Raymond's court but we cannot stay there for long. We do not want to compromise him, as the French, the clerics and the Inquisition watch him closely now.

"The new Bishop of Toulouse, Raymond Fuega, like the late Folquet is friendly to Raymond but he cannot be trusted. Everybody is afraid of the inquisition now and the inquisition answers to no one except the Pope himself. Maybe we should take a boat from Narbonne and try to find shelter with Emperor Frederick II, who still maintains his free spirit. Many of our troubadours have flocked to his court keeping the beauty of our old world alive. Of course, for being what he is he has earned the enmity of the Pope who is piling up excommunications on him, one after the other, and has now officially demonized him as the Antichrist. I do not really know, Esclamonde, where we can go to be entirely safe."

"Nowhere is entirely safe, Peire. Perhaps, we could find temporary safety in some of the places you mentioned but the Catholic Church has many very long tentacles. They stretch out from here to Jerusalem, sucking out all the vestiges of beauty and freedom they can find. Next to every baron and prince, they have placed a Bishop, an abbot and now an Inquisitor to make sure they maintain control. Even on the small island of Andros, next to Marino Dandolo, they have placed that unspeakable Bishop John. From what I hear Marino Dandolo is now in trouble too, stirred up by the Bishop of course. Next to the King of France is Romano Frangipani and next to Raymond VII is Raymond de Fuega, and so on and so forth. Our world of beauty and freedom is sinking in a cold hell of Catholic terror and conformity. My dearest husband Peire, do not trouble yourself anymore trying to find a safe haven for us. I have made up my mind to go to Montsegur and join my brethren. I do not want you to follow me there. You can save yourself and live well elsewhere, in places where I cannot go and I do not want to go myself. We can travel together to Montsegur if you want, but at the gates we must part our ways. I have left you before and we were fortunate to be together again, but this time our ways will part without return. Montsegur is a Cathar dwelling place where you do not belong and you should not try to belong, for my sake. Montsegur is a temporary shelter but, also, a place where I can be free for as long as I am allowed to live. Tell our son, Nascibon, that I have retired to a monastery, which is true in a way. Montsegur is my sanctuary."

"But why can't I come with you? Don't you love me? I want to be with you for the rest of my life."

Peire, my dear husband, I have always loved you and I still love you. As you know, I have had many lovers in my time and some of them were worth having, but you have always been at the core of my being giving me the essence of life. Some women start worshiping their lovers and end up despising them or worse, but I have always loved you the same way. You have always understood and accepted my nature and my needs even when at times you felt jealous and hurt. That is because you are endowed with a truly free spirit. Peire, you are one of the very few free men on this earth and I am proud to be your wife. I am not that free myself, because I am attached to my brethren and their beliefs. No, you cannot come with me to Montsegur because sooner or later you will suffocate there and because there is only room for my unfortunate brethren, the true believers. The Elders will not accept you unless I apply pressure on them, which I do not want to do. So, please accept my decision without protest."

No more was said and they traveled by night and slept by day escorted by the armed men who rescued them. Sometime in June of 1233 they arrived at the gates of Montsegur, situated at the top of a sheer rock rising five hundred feet out of the ground, known as the Pog. Ramon de Parella and the great lady Esclamonde de Foix received them at the gate. De Foix embraced Esclamonde saying, "We have been waiting for you and are happy to take you under our protection. Ramon de Parella will be your spiritual father as your late true father, Nicetas, had wished. We are sorry that we cannot accept anybody else from your escort to enter Montsegur, including even your husband, who is not one of us. The premises of the castle are hardly enough for the true believers who really need our protection and sanctuary."

"My Lady, my wife has already explained to me that I cannot be admitted to Montsegur. I am sure you can take care of my dear

Esclamonde much better than I could. Please allow me to embrace her one last time before we must part."

Peire embraced his wife for a long time gently sobbing, recalling all the adventures and love they had shared together. This was likely the last time they would be able to share anything together. He had a very hard time releasing her. He lingered for a while watching her as she entered the castle gate, stepping into her new life. Peire leapt onto his horse and galloped away with his escorts without looking back, tears streaming down his face.

Meanwhile, at the bottom of a deep hole dug in the basement of the Dominican Priory in Valence, slumped in a heap was the brutalized and unrecognizable body of Bieiris de Romans. For forty days, she had been interrogated by a relay of inquisitors and their secretaries and at night tortured by vicious and leering Dominicans of lower rank. Her tormentors scratched, pierced, cut, twisted, burned and removed all the sensitive parts of her flesh in order to extract confessions that she was a heretic and a pervert and that her friends and acquaintances were also heretics and perverts. The inquisitors themselves dictated all the lurid details. In fact, their manipulative questioning had forced out confessions which were completely untrue and simply the results of the agony and horrors of torture. Bieiris had resisted bravely for the first thirty days but as the torture continued getting worse she could not stand the pain endlessly burning in her body and mind. In a state of delirious sickness, she started giving them whatever they wanted by degrees. Death by fire was becoming preferable than this brutal pain and the relentless repetition of insane questions. She confessed that she was a practicing heretic and a wanton witch and a Satanist. Then she implicated other people as her partners in heresy, in witchcraft and in unnatural and depraved orgies. Exactly what her tormentors twisted imaginations created for her to confess. Esclamonde had unfortunately been one of them. Now Bieiris was waiting for her execution by fire so that there could be a cleansing of the miasma inhabiting her body and soul. She no longer cared. The torturers had stopped their horrific violence and she had become so sick, filthy and deformed that even the inhuman jailers did not care to touch her anymore. Her superb beauty had been butchered and mutilated so badly that whatever was left of her craved for the end by the inevitable cleansing fire.

One hundred broken human beings were piled up and tied on stakes on a high wooden platform together with fire logs. The mangled-up body of Bieiris had been placed among them. The resulting conflagration burned for two days before it simmered down to ashes and charred remains, which still reeked of burnt flesh and bones. The Inquisitors savoured the power of life and death given to them by the ultimate and supreme glory of an institution grown insanely evil by its belief in its own importance. Most of the spectators rejoiced in the horror show, infected by the evil insanity of their spiritual leaders. Back in the days of Simon de Montfort there were many and frequent human pyres. They had been stopped during the short period of the enlightened Unicorn but after 1230, they were begun again by the newly formed Inquisition in a more systematic and sinister way than ever before, with confessions now obtained by torture. The inquisitors had been given the power of law enforcer, prosecutor, judge and executioner all at the same time, and there was no appeal from their verdicts. Their victims were not only heretics but also their protectors and the relaxed, that is, those who were seen as even tolerating heresy.

In spite of the grave danger of being arrested, Peire Cardinal was among the spectators of the human conflagration in Valence. Under the cover of nocturnal darkness, he knelt by the ashes and cried lamenting the beauty and free spirit of his dear friend Bieiris de Romans who had perished so horribly and unjustly. He shuddered thinking that a similar fate was probably in store for his dearest Esclamonde, and quite possibly for himself if he didn't hurry away to Italy. As he was traveling south to Orange to pick up the old Roman road, the fires burning human flesh multiplied, turning the landscape into a lurid and sinister domain of living Hell. He also experienced the revolting sight of crazed mobs exhuming the remains of the dead, who supposedly used to be heretics, protectors or relaxed and throwing them into fires while equally crazed monks and clerics were chanting incantations. There were people, however, who were angered by this and were gathering against the Inquisitors and their minions for their practice of punishing the dead by exhumation and burning of the corpses. Whenever they could, they were attacking Dominican priories and slaughtering the Inquisitors inside. Yet, the majority of the people were too frightened to react. A good number of them condoned all of the Inquisitional practices as they were becoming infected by superstition. In this time of 'the King's peace', repression, fear, suspicion, depression and a general malaise pervaded the air. Countless songs and sirventes were forming in Peire's mind as a way to try and process all the pain and suffering he felt about the insane scenes around him and his recent horrific experiences. He could not sing them anywhere, though, for fear of the inquisition and the King's law enforcers.

When he crossed the Alps into Italy the situation there seemed quite the opposite from how it was at home. The general mood was optimistic and carefree, although there were still some difficulties. The Emperor, Frederick II, was still at war with the Lombard League and because of this the city-states, including Verona, were torn by civil strife. Despite this the commercial and manufacturing activities were thriving and bringing prosperity, at least to the enterprising middle and high classes. The Church, although powerful, was more scheming than oppressive and the Pope was absorbed to a large extent by his feud with the Emperor, Frederick II. Therefore, the Inquisition was, by necessity, more circumspect than heavy-handed. Also, the new monastic order of the Franciscans, with their mild and humane attitude, was becoming extremely popular. Particularly the mendicant sect called the Spirituals, who were advocating an almost anti-clerical approach to Christianity with many similarities to the Cathars. The Spirituals chose to ignore The Pope's excommunications against Frederick and all the interdicts against his dominions. They continued to minister sacraments and to grant absolutions to him and his subjects. One of the Spirituals, Arnold, even proclaimed the second coming for 1260. It was even rumoured that at this time Frederick II would confiscate the riches of Rome and redistribute them among the poor, who were considered the "only true Christians".

By the time Peire arrived in Verona to meet his son, now known as Nascibene Campagna, his mood was slowly lifting because of all of the good things he had begun to hear about from people he met on his way. All the horrible experiences he had been through, that had been haunting him, were pushed to the back of his mind as he embraced his son with genuine warmth and joy.

"Welcome back father. Where is mother?

"Your mother, unfortunately for both of us, has retired to a monastery. She had been suffering a great deal and it was her decision. I could not do anything about it, though I tried to convince her to come with me. I am so sorry, please try and forgive her absence, I know it must be very hard."

"I do not know what to think. When I was a boy she wasn't here and then, when I reached manhood, she appeared like a ghost out of the past, which was shocking at first. I learned to like her and then to love her until she vanished again into the veil beyond, never to return. I must admit, I was hoping to see her again but now you tell me she is behind the walls of a monastery, never to show her beautiful face again. She is not dead is she? Tell me the truth."

"No, she is not dead. That is the truth."

"Sadly, I feel that she is as good as dead to me now. At least you have come to see me from time to time. Do you know that you have grandchildren now? The eldest is called Peiro to honour you. My wife Cunizza is a wonderful woman and a very good mother, unlike my absentee mother and unlike my father in law Ezzelino, who can sometimes be a terribly violent man. As for me, during peacetime, I am a dignitary and a merchant of the city of Verona and during wartime I am an experienced soldier and a knight at the service of Emperor Fredrick II and of Ezzelino who still manages to be Lord of Verona. I even followed Fredrick on his crusade to the holy land and was fortunate to experience the magnificence of Jerusalem returning to

Christendom, in 1229. Now I am fighting alongside him against Milano and the other cities of the Lombard League. It seems we are winning the war."

"I am very proud of you, my son, for your successes in both peace and war. At least you are on the winning side, unlike me. As for myself, I seem to count defeats all around me. I feel deep sorrow for the loss of your mother and great pain in my heart for the miserable and tragic state of my homeland."

"I remember that you were referring to your homeland as the land of the Unicorn, a land of beauty and joy. Raymond VII used to be called the Unicorn and rightly so, for a while at least. But what happened? How did paradise become Hell again? How did the Unicorn lose his horn and become a mule? It seems, since the treaty of Meaux, that Raymond has become like a mule, sterile! It is so infuriating that his legacy has been forcibly passed down to the King of France's brother, Alphonse of Poitiers. Is all this that I hear true?"

"I see you have kept yourself well informed of the affairs of your Occitanian homeland." Peire responded. "Your comparison of my Liege Lord to a mule is hard to take but it is, unfortunately, so accurate it makes me want to laugh and cry at the same time. Is this what Frederick II is calling him? By the way, I heard that there will be a Second Coming around 1260, at which time Frederick will take Rome and will distribute all the riches of the Pope to the poor. What do you think of this nonsense?"

"Well, this is the wishful thinking of certain extremist Franciscan monks and of their beneficiary, the poor, of course." Said Nascibene thoughtfully. "As you know, the Papacy is the most powerful institution in the known World and the only thing Frederick can do is to somewhat temper its rapacity for the material and spiritual possessions of all laymen, rich and poor."

"What about all the excommunications piled against Frederick?"

"What about them? They can only affect the weak. Excommunications simply bounce off the strong armour of the powerful."

Peire, who was really enjoying this renewed connection with his son again, laughed heartily "If you were not so pragmatic, you could have been a poet like me."

For nine years, Peire divided his time between Verona with Nascibon and Palermo with Emperor Frederick II, with occasional visits to Venice. Peire was still a man wanted by the Inquisition, at least for the first couple of years of his absence, but he still managed to visit a few places back home despite all the dangers. In Verona, he had long talks with his old friend Guy de Sommerive, or Guido Sommaripa as the Italians now called him. Guido's son Leone had emigrated to Greece and had married the daughter of Guillaume de Villehardouin, the Prince of Achaia, Elizabeth, and he was valiantly fighting wars of conquest under Guillaume. Leone seemed to be successfully following his childhood dreams of creating a principality for himself and his descendants in Greece one day.

"Speaking of Greece," Guido was saying, "not long ago I met an old acquaintance of yours, Giacomo Quirini. He said he had met you in Andros, one of the Greek Archipelago islands, after the capture of Constantinople in 1204. He was a close friend of Marino Dandolo, the Lord of Andros. Do you remember these people?"

"Of course, I remember them very well. On that lovely island, my wife and I had a wonderful experience and always wanted to return one day. I have fond memories of our time there and Giacomo, Marino and his wife Feliza are a part of them. What happened to Marino? I had heard a while back that he might be in some kind of trouble."

"He is no longer in trouble. He is dead. Marino had constant problems with his meddling bishop who, in the end, helped the conniving Jeremiah Guisi overthrow him and usurp his power. Guisi imprisoned Marino and soon afterwards murdered him. It is truly sad how often these meddling priests cause so much hardship and suffering. Anyway, Marino's wife, Feliza, ran to Giacomo Quirini for protection and they ended up getting married. It seems Feliza and Giacomo had been having an affair for years even while Marino was still alive but after his unfortunate assassination they finally legalized their relationship. They now live in Venice, where I met them, and are a very sweet couple. They told me they have initiated litigations to claim Andros for themselves over the sinister sounding Guisi. Since Feliza's children are the rightful heirs this makes sense."

Peire made a point to go and visit his old friends Giacomo and Feliza in Venice where they lived in grand style in the Quirini palace. They remembered him fondly and were very happy to receive him. Feliza was still quite beautiful in her maturity in a sensuous and sultry kind of way and Peire noticed she still had eyes only for the still handsome Giacomo.

They reminisced on their common, albeit short, experiences on the island of Andros and even on the wedding feast of the late Marino Dandolo with Feliza.

Giacomo felt like confessing and explained, "Marino was an enlightened ruler who brought peace and prosperity to the island. He was loved by the schismatic Greeks and by most, though not all, of his Venetian companions. I always remained his loyal friend and supporter although I was in love with his wife and she was in love with me."

Peire interjected, "Something like Lancelot to King Arthur in Camelot it sounds. If I were not so depressed by the state of the world I could have composed a song about you two."

Giacomo laughed then continued, "The Bishop of Andros was fighting Marino every inch of the way, undermining his work and accusing him of schematic tendencies bordering on heresy. Marino was forced to imprison him but this action precipitated a reaction by the Pope, the Doge of Venice, Tiepolo and the Duke of Naxos, Sanudo. They all ended up supporting Marino's archenemy, Jeremiah Ghizi, to mount a pseudo crusade against him. They used this wretched excuse to usurp Marino's principality and eventually murder him."

Peire moaned, "It's the same story I hear over and over, again and again throughout the power domain of the Catholic Church! Whenever a secular prince intends to rule in an enlightened fashion against the repressive commands of the Church, he would invariably face excommunications, invasions, usurpation and ultimately death. The

Count of Toulouse, Emperor Frederick II and many others, including now my old friend Marino Dandolo, have faced or will face this fate. How is it possible that the war-shy clerics, without brandishing swords, can overcome the valiant knights and princes? I lament the fall of virtue under the twisted machinations of those who pretend to be holy. I am sorry to be so carried away by my indignation but tell me, my lady Feliza, how did you manage to escape from Ghizi's clutches?"

"I had help from friends of Giacomo's who took me to him by boat. After Marino's death, we got married and later I gave birth to his son Nicholas who we believe should one day become the Lord of Andros, if we win our case in the Venetian courts at least. You see, I had no children with Marino, so Nicholas is the rightful heir of Dandolo's estate."

"It is very sad for me to hear all this but I am also very happy to hear of your love and that you have each other and now a wonderful son. If you can return triumphant to that wonderful little island it would be a happy ending to a tragic tale. I truly wish you luck, my friends"

"We are going to need it because Ghizi has powerful friends everywhere and the Church is on his side, although he is nothing but a brigand and a ruffian."

"But he is their own ruffian, not any ruffian."

Peire could see that in this upside-down world the Quirinis, though their hearts were in the right place, could not win in the end. It was becoming increasingly obvious to Peire that a truly dark force was making life hellish for all those he loved and respected.

In the year 1241, Pope Gregory IX died and the news of his death brought relief and open rejoicing in the court of Frederick II. An illustrious crowd of nobles, merchants, troubadours, jongleurs, wise men, sorcerers and astrologers had gathered in Frederick's Court at Palermo to officially celebrate the demise of the Pope, in the absence of clerics of course.

Frederick addressed his guests, "If I say that I grieve for the passing of Pope Gregory IX, I would certainly be lying. He called me the

Antichrist and many other ridiculous names. He piled up so many excommunications and indictments on me and my cities that I almost lost my breath! I was even excommunicated by him when I won Jerusalem for Christendom in 1229, in spite of all the ridiculous obstacles he put in my way! Did he rejoice for this momentous event that I accomplished at his bidding? No, he sulked in a corner and he even incited rebellion against my authority. He was the main force behind the Lombard League, inciting their relentless wars against me. He was trying to frustrate all my efforts to bring peace and prosperity to my Empire. He called all my activities for spiritual freedom heresy! He called all my scientific experiments witchcraft! He called me the Antichrist because I was against him as if he were himself the Christ! So, am I supposed to mourn his death? No I cannot, because in truth, I am extremely happy that he is gone."

Frederick then looked around the room and spotted Peire Cardinal among his guests and said to him, "It is most appropriate that you are present at this important occasion, dear Peire. Gregory IX, as the Popes before him, Honorius III and Innocent III, have all worked evil miracles in order to transform your formerly happy homeland into a miserable, terrified and burnt out shell. As for the Counts of Toulouse and the peerage of that land, they have been reduced to a cringing, pathetic lot. Count Raymond VII of Toulouse who started out so valiantly is now keeping out of sight like a beaten mule in his own territory, scared of the inquisition and of the sanctimonious and arrogant French King. Now I hear that all these murdering crusaders are converging on the last stronghold of freedom, Montsegur, to extinguish its flame. We would like to hear a sirventes from a real troubadour like you, in tune with the present situations."

"Your grace, distinguished guests, I am deeply honoured that I was asked to sing a sirventes for you. However, the news about Montsegur has filled me with anxiety because a dear friend lives there and this may affect my performance. Still, I will try to do my best, as the occasion commands."

285

In a town faraway, or even here.
In a time long ago, or even now.
A dark black cloud poured down a rain
That cast a spell upon the town.

This rain of fools soaked in unaware
Till all it touched became insane.
Yet a few precious souls were found elsewhere
And staying dry sane remained.

But when the wet wild crazed fools saw
How odd the few dry souls behaved
They thrashed and burned and beat them raw
And for their flesh and blood they craved.

Now this has become the state of our land
The whole wide world turned upside down.
In this rain of fools most everyone's gone mad
In the wet fools' ignorance and greed, we drown

Freedom and virtue now appear as madness
Controlling twisted evil now hailed as sacred
Very few have escaped from this rain, alas
In blind piety, love, is twisted to hatred

In this rain of fools, the whole world's gone mad
And many around are now upset.
What's bad is now good and what's good is now bad
So be aware when they deduce you're not wet.

For a while there was silence and introspection, until a massive round of applause and laughter erupted. Frederick while laughing said, "Does that mean I am wet, as well, according to your fable? As the Antichrist I should be."

"Your grace, you have always been one of the driest people in this wet and muddy land. Your spirit is clear and good and those who call you the Antichrist have been soaked by this rain of fools. You are one of the few with a truly free spirit that has not been touched by this rain and for this reason you have been persecuted and excommunicated to death by the superstitious, the obscurantists, the self-righteous, the power hungry and in short by all those who are soaking wet."

"Apparently, my dear Peire, this rain of fools has been falling heavily everywhere on your homeland. I hear a last ray of light that's been shining at Montsegur is now surrounded by a gathering of heavy dark clouds about to be unleashed by this rain of fools again."

"Yes, that seems to be the case and so, your grace, I'm sure you will understand, I must travel again. Perchance that I may be able to offer some help to someone. It seems that I am blessed or cursed to go wherever it rains fools yet somehow remain dry."

Mass burning of heretics

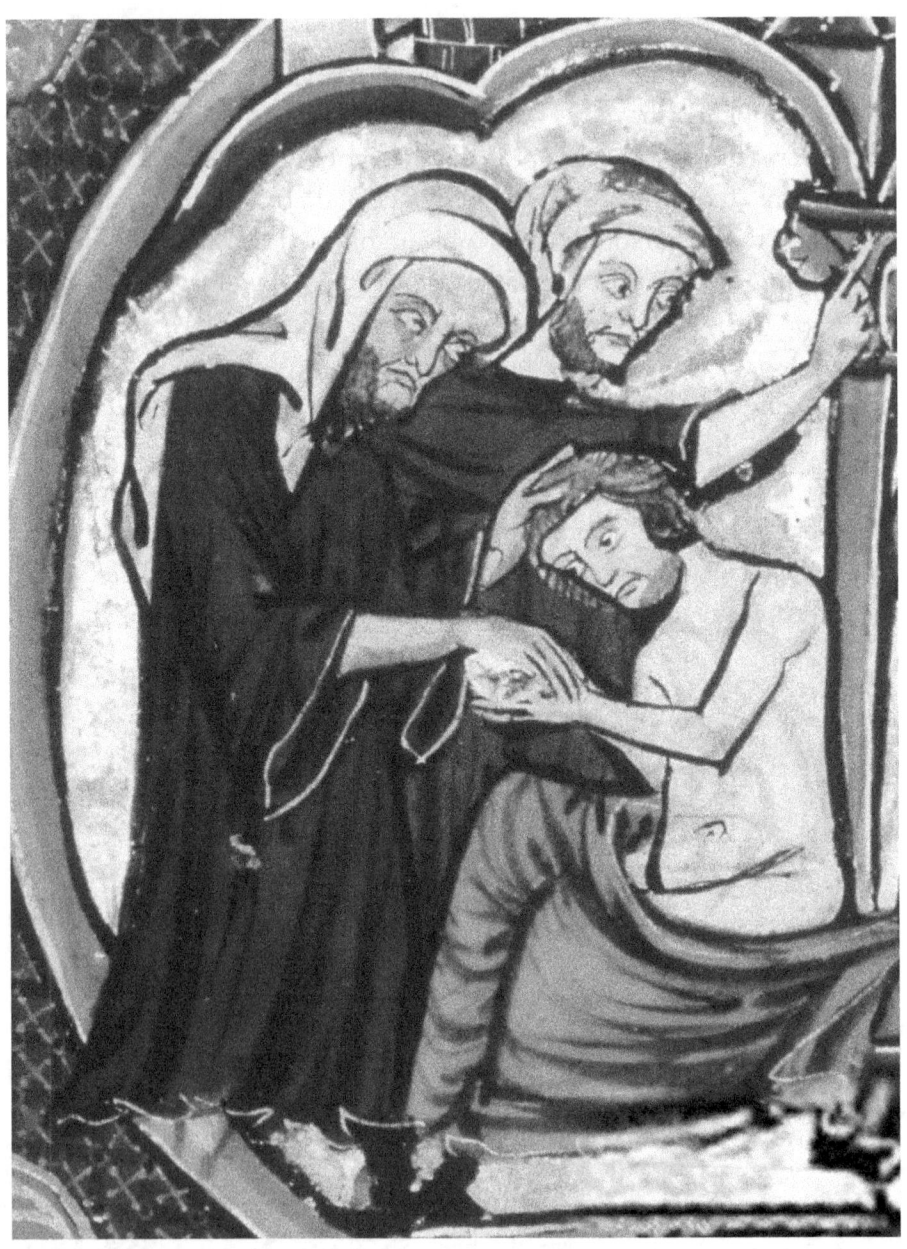

Cathar Consolamentum depiction mid 13th century

Burning of Cathars at Montsegur

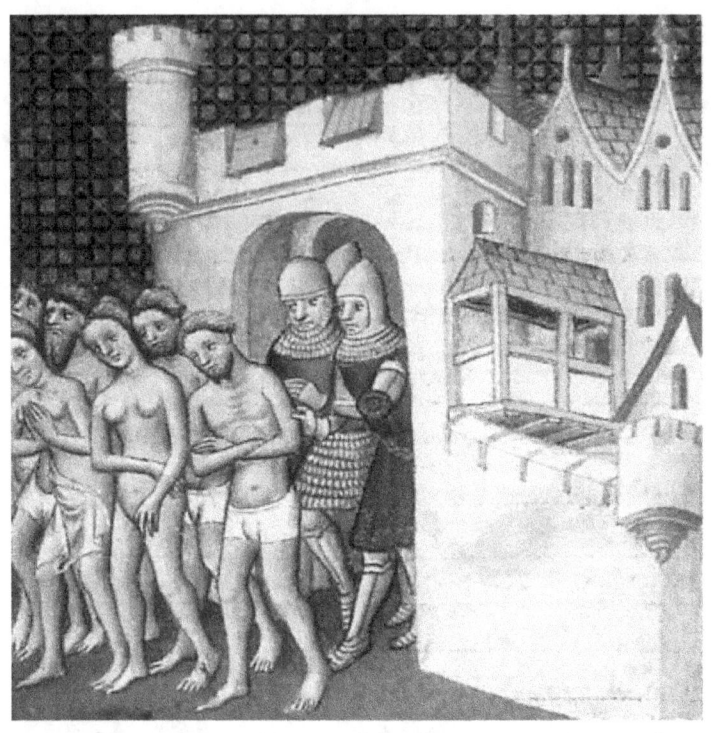

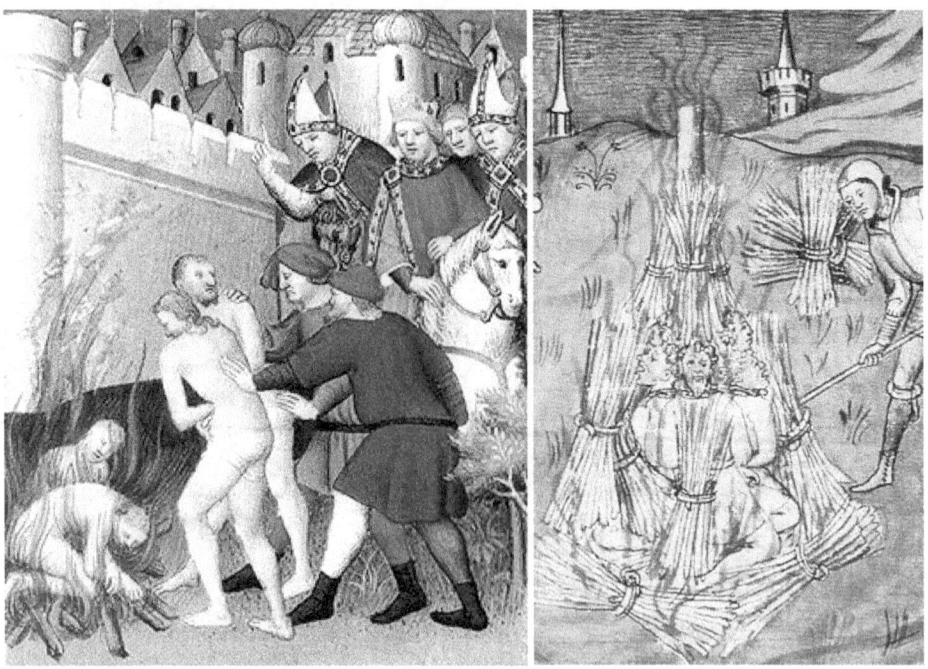

Medieval depictions of the burning of Cathars

CHAPTER 18

THE AGE OF MULES

he bulging and vertiginous mountain, known as the Pog could not be climbed except by two steep and dangerous trails leading up to the northern smaller gate and to the southern main gate of the pentagonal castle-town of Montsegur. The five external walls of the castle were strong and tall, reinforced with barbicans and seemed impregnable as they rose above the precipitous rocks crowning the Pog. Inside the walls towards the west a powerful donjon rose from the courtyard and next to it a relatively new and large cistern collected rainwater. Below the donjon and carved straight through the rock there was the great and spacious hall which served as a meeting place of the military leaders as well as for the congregation of the Perfects and of the Cathar believers. Above and below the courtyard, six hundred people had built their cramped living quarters of which four hundred were Perfects and simple believers and two hundred were knights and men at arms together with their wives and mistresses. With the close quarters and the constant comings and goings, life at Montsegur was crowded, noisy and very uncomfortable, but spirits were high and troubadour songs filled the air. Men and women with raucous, sweet and sad voices sang the savage sirventes of Guilhem Figueira, Peire Cardinal and Guilhem Montanhagol, against the Roman Church and the French Invaders, in turn. In the hearts of these men and women, passionate love burned, intensified by danger and the desire for freedom. All of these people freely and truly accepted, respected and venerated their military, religious and administrative leaders. They were prepared to fight for the common cause to live as free human beings. They used to worship

their great lady Esclamonde de Foix who knew how to teach and guide them to a good life, but she had died as a Cathar Perfect and had a 'good end'. The venerable Perfect and Cathar Bishop Guilhabert de Castres had also died recently and he also had a 'good end'. They had been fine examples for the remaining Cathars and most of them yearned for a 'good end' for themselves.

Now their Cathar Bishop was the sweet Bertrand de Marty who was increasingly administering consolamentum to those who were ready to receive it. Roman de Parella, the founder of Montsegur, was still the highest secular authority of the castle-town and his executive arm was Pierre-Roger de Mirepoix, a mature man of great valour and military skills. Prominent among them were Cobla, the beautiful wife of Parella, and his adopted daughter, Esclamonde, a passionate woman of many skills and inexhaustible energy. She was a woman to undertake difficult tasks and missions for the defence of the citadel and for the rescue and consolation of the suffering Cathars in the immediate area and beyond. She could handle the trebuchet, the mangonel and any of the other war engines and weapons. She could even deliver sermons or sing cansos and sirventes with her sweet and melodious voice. In order to be able to exercise all these skills and divine talents she had not taken the consolamentum yet, although in all respects she had all the attributes of a Perfect. She had even undertaken the 'Conveniencia' officially promising to take consolamentum at the moment when her warrior skills were no longer required for the defence of all believers and for their shrine of Montsegur. She was no other than the woman who had delivered the city of Toulouse by killing Simon de Montfort with a stone, the trobairitza wife of Peire Cardinal.

It had been ten years since Peire had reluctantly let her go. During this time, she had devoted herself to the Cathar cause without exposing him to all the mortal dangers involved. In the time since she had received spiritual instruction from Esclamonde de Foix, Guilhabert de Castres and from all the other leaders still living. She was feeling contented and focused in what she felt was a worthwhile purpose. Now the remaining leaders were gathering in the Great Hall to discuss the ways and means of their defence against an imminent attack and siege by the French troops under the Seneschal, Hugh D'Arcis. Peire Cardinal had just arrived with this news and some advice from the itinerant Court of Raymond VII. He was hoping to convince them to avoid any acts of provocation, but he had come too late. Recently, a detachment of knights from Montsegur led by Rogier de Mirepoix and Esclamonde had surprised numerous tribunals of inquisitors in the castle-town of Avignonet who were planning to hold one of their dreaded 'weeks of grace'. These weeks of grace were becoming commonplace in these dark times and allowed the inquisitors to go on a rampage rounding up and indiscriminately torturing the towns' citizens in order to extract and create confessions to fill their desire of human fuel for their cleansing fires. Unexpectedly, this time the tables had turned and the knights of Montsegur managed to kill all the inquisitors. Most Southern citizens received this act of counter-terror with wild exhilaration and a sensation of deliverance. Finally, the victims could extract some retribution from the prosecutors who had been perpetrating unspeakable acts of torture across the land. The inquisitors had been increasingly twisting and playing with the mind, body and souls of the innocent citizens to such a degree that they would beg for death. Avignonet had become a symbol of successful resistance against the Catholic Church and the hated French invaders.

However, this incident infuriated Blanche of Castile who screamed the orders; "Cut off the dragon's head at Montsegur." An army of 10,000 was mustered under Hugues de Arcis to lay a siege.

Now in the Great Hall of Montsegur, Rogier de Mirepoix was saying, "We all know that we had to strike at the sanctimonious torturers of the body and mind, the unholy inquisitors who burn our people for pleasure while pretending that they are driven by religious fervour. Our doctrine denies revenge and murder but in this case, we had to stop the disgusting practices of the inquisition and in Avignonet, to use their expression, we cleaned them out. Most importantly we managed to take from them all of their written records and their long lists of future victims. As you all know their records contain confessions obtained by torture, which incriminate many others to become future victims for more torture and burning. We broke the whole chain of terror by killing them and we are proud of it. Our comrade, Esclamonde, who once rid us of Simon de Montfort, in Avignonet decapitated the chief inquisitor Guillaume Arnauld who ten years ago was about to burn her alive. Was it revenge or a just punishment? We have always been peaceful and kind but they want to exterminate us completely just because we wish to be free. I say enough is enough! We have been forced to fight back and we will! Now, I ask our friend Peire Cardinal to share with us some of the news from the outside world."

"I am sorry to say that the news is not good at all. We all have derived great satisfaction from your expedition against the bloody Inquisitors in Avignonet where justice was dispensed. A great blow was delivered against the hideous institution of the Inquisition, but we cannot ignore the hell we have unleashed upon us as a result. The unholy alliance of the Catholic Church and the King of France is now mobilizing against Montsegur, as we speak. Raymond of Toulouse who had always been sympathetic to your cause, was beaten by Louis IX at Saintes and his ally, the King of England, was crushed at Tailleburg soon afterwards again by the King of France. The Unholy Alliance has associated Avignonet with Raymond VII and he was excommunicated yet again. Young Viscount Raymond-Roger Trencavel made a gallant attempt to recapture Carcassonne but he failed miserably and is now in the retinue of Louis IX as his admiring subject. Your other true friend Frederick II, the Emperor, is trapped between the Papal machinations and excommunications on one hand and the Mongols who are invading Germany on the other. At this point you must see that you are now very much alone. You should not entertain any illusions for outside help. The free and happy days of the Unicorn are over and, unfortunately, we have fully entered a time of darkness. I am sure Montsegur is the only place left where the memory of freedom is still very much alive. For this reason, I intend to stay with you and fight against those who continue to devastate our land and impose this suffocating tedium, this age of mules, upon us."

The people gathered in the Great Hall looked solemn although tears could be seen trailing down some of their cheeks. The elderly Ramon de Parella walked to the middle of the hall and said with a firm voice. "We are alone, that much we have guessed by ourselves. The enemy is immensely stronger than we are and yet our spirit may be stronger than theirs; we are determined to hold our Sanctuary to the end. All brethren know that after taking the consolamentum we will have a 'good end' no matter how terrible this end may look to others. Furthermore, our position is impregnable by its inaccessible nature and our strong fortifications. We have ample supplies, which can last longer than any siege could hold together. We have frequent rains, even during the summertime, that keep our large cistern full of water. We have secret ways to keep ourselves supplied ad infinitum. We are few but we believe fervently in our cause. Many of our brethren, who are ready to take the "consolamentum" like my adopted daughter Esclamonde, will not do so yet in order to fight the besiegers. If the time comes when all is lost, then they can take the consolamentum in order to experience a 'good death'. Still, I expect that we could tire the besiegers out and thereby force them to leave. If this happens, a new hope would be born in the Southern lands and, who knows, the mule may become a unicorn again."

There were more speeches that echoed these sentiments, showing the solemn determination of all the believers and their sympathizers to fight for their freedom and for the idea of freedom itself.

After the gathering of the congregation, Peire and Esclamonde spent time in private sharing their genuine feelings of love for each other. With tears in their eyes they held each other for a long, long time without a word. Then, Peire detached himself and looked at her appreciatively and said, "You are still very attractive in spite of your bloodthirsty deeds. Decapitating people, even Inquisitors, can you imagine!"

"I did not do it out of pleasure. It was Justice. Unfortunately, there will be more of that soon. I could have been a Perfect long ago, but my brethren needed my combat skills which are incompatible with being a Perfect."

"So, I see. By the way, knowing your passionate and lascivious nature, did you enjoy any carnal pleasures with some lucky partners?"

"Yes, I did occasionally but I felt good about it and it did not cause any bad feelings for anyone else. I did not burn my spiritual being over much. I can still take the consolamentum when the time comes without upsetting my relationship with Heaven. It is to be expected from a nonbeliever like you that you would be preoccupied with feelings of jealousy and sin, troubling yourself over matters of little importance. You know, Peire, I've always loved you no matter what else I did. We have been together and apart intermittently for a very, very long time. My love for you has never faded and I think you feel the same way for me. Do you?"

"Esclamonde, my love, I certainly do, although your life and your beliefs are so full of contradictions, a consequence no doubt, of the dualist premises of your creed. Although I am sympathetic to your cause, I continue to maintain that the Spirit coexists and interacts with the material world and that there is a continuous transmutation of spirit into matter and matter into spirit. This is how spirit grows and how matter is animated. After all, this is the essence of Jesus Christ and his ultimate sacrifice for humanity. But I suppose I waste my words for your brethren deny the Cross and its meaning anyway."

"Peire, you sound like a preacher. Please do not preach to me because you cannot convert me, no matter how much I love you. Since you feel and think this way, why are you joining us, knowing very well that you will suffer and may die at the end like most of us will during this final battle? Ten years ago, when I entered Montsegur, I did not want you to follow me then and persuaded Raimon de Parella not to accept you for your own good and for my peace of mind. Yet, when you declared your intentions, this time, of joining us and risking your own life I was deeply moved and glad to have you with me at this moment of mortal danger."

"If you want to know, I did it because I wanted to be with you and share your fate. My love for you is my motive and my admiration for your people who fight for their convictions and freedom has reinforced this motive. Now I am here with you and no one can change my resolution. I am also falling in love with you all over again. I find that I want to live, once more, all of our past moments of love."

They were no longer young. Peire was now 63. Still, they found the energy, the feeling and the imagination to enjoy their love passionately and tenderly. At a certain point Esclamonde remembered Bieiris, and Peire had to tell her of her terrible death at the hands of the Inquisition. She had not known and the shock was devastating. She cried inconsolably and then said with anger, "I would decapitate not one, as I did, but thousands of Inquisitors. I would line them up and chop them up piece by piece leaving their heads for last."

"Obviously, we have one more reason to kill the French and their clergy."

On May 13, 1243, the siege of Montsegur began in earnest as ten thousand seasoned French soldiers surrounded the Pog. They tried to climb it and to approach the castle by following the two trails but they were repulsed with a lot of losses. At first the French hoped to starve the defenders into surrender and expected the cisterns to dry up in the hot summer months. But attack after attack was successfully repelled. Through the summer and the autumn supplies were brought into the fortress secretly by night, carried by men along hidden footpaths unknown to the enemy. Ropes were let down from the castle walls and provisions and men were hoisted up the precipice in the darkness.

Esclamonde was in charge of the mangonels and the trebuchet with which she was raining stones and boulders on the advancing attackers scoring many direct and fatal hits. Those of the enemy who managed to approach the fortress itself were dealt with by ferocious forays of the defenders. Peire, in spite of his advanced age, took part in these forays distinguishing himself for his bravery and effectiveness.

After five months of siege the French commander, Hugues d'
Arcis, was completely discouraged, as he had achieved nothing at all.
However, in November 1243 he managed to secure a group of agile
Basque mountaineers at an exorbitant price, who were able to scale the
cliffs with ropes. They succeeded in capturing the eastern shoulder of
the Pog just below the castle and established a 'bridgehead'. On it,
Durand, Bishop of Albi, who was also a masterful military engineer and
a strategist, installed a powerful catapult. From this bridgehead, the
Basque mercenaries began to bombard the ramparts with huge stones
causing serious damage to the eastern side of the Castle. Now Rogier
de Mirepoix with the help of Esclamonde redirected their mangonels
and the trebuchet in order to counteract the monstrous French catapult
leaving other parts of the rampart more vulnerable.

Late in December a traitor, Joan Bernart, revealed to the Basques
another secret way up the sheer cliffs and one moonless night they
scaled the mountainside and captured the east bastion of the fortress
itself. All of the people in the tower were massacred and a catapulted
stone injured Esclamonde's leg while the fighting raged in the castle
and the courtyard. Durand advanced his giant stone-throwers nearer
the donjon and enormous boulders were hurled against the rugged
walls, which still held firm. By February 1244, the narrow courtyard
had become a burning inferno and the struggle to survive was intense.
Throughout this horrific time Peire remained by the side of
Esclamonde trying to heal her wound and fighting valiantly at the same
time. Her strong constitution and Peire's loving care helped her recover
somewhat and she became functional again but was now permanently
crippled.

By early March it had become obvious that they had to seek terms
of surrender, and a meeting was set up in the Great Hall to decide this
grave issue amongst themselves before they made any overture to the
French. Pierre-Roger de Mirepoix opened the subject, "Our situation is
hopeless but as long as we can still cause some damage to the French,
we should try to obtain as favourable terms as possible; we should ask

them to spare all our lives in exchange of the surrendering of the castle and our weapons."

The Cathar Bishop, Bertrand Marty, countered solemnly, "You know very well that they will never agree to spare the lives of unrepentant believers and Perfects. We must try to save the lives of the soldiers and all the others who are not believers but only sympathizers. As far as we are concerned the time has come to deliver our spirits to our God in Heaven, even by the ordeal of fire. We are grateful to you for all you have done for us but it would be unreasonable to ask you to sacrifice your lives for us if you are given a chance to save them. Now I call upon all the believers who wish it, to receive the consolamentum from me and thereby to become Perfects. Those who are not up to it are free to offer their submissions to the Catholic Church and save their lives if they can."

All the believers and a few sympathizers declared themselves ready to receive the consolamentum, including Esclamonde. Peire made a move to join them but Raimon de Parella held him back with the unyielding insistence of Esclamonde. "You have been chosen for a much more important mission for our cause than to follow the fate of the Perfects. In any case, you never intended to be a Perfect and you cannot do so now."

"What is the mission?"

Ramon de Parella took him aside where no one could hear them and said in a low voice, "As soon as we have agreed to the terms of our surrender you will be given Montsegur's treasure to take in secret to the Castle of Ussat in the High Pyrenees, where you will find the refuge of our most honourable and respected Perfects. This treasure is sacred because it serves the needs of our persecuted brethren. Our treasurer, Pierre Authier, will accompany you along with two more trusted brothers. We know that you are an honourable man and the beloved husband of our Esclamonde and that you will never betray us. In the meantime, spend all the time you still have with your wife. I assure you, this time it will be as good as all eternity."

Esclamonde was already a Perfect when she later met with Peire privately in one of the narrow cells of the donjon. An armistice had been declared waiting for the negotiations to be concluded and the old couple were taking advantage of the respite. They held hands and looked at each other with an exquisite tenderness relishing each other's presence. Peire was unbearably sad because of the finality of their approaching separation but Esclamonde glowed with the serene light of sublimated love. It was the pure essence of the deep love she had always had for him but now it had transformed into something more. They had been together, on and off, for forty-three years and had tasted most of the fruits of the earth, both good and bad. Through it all they had continued to love each other. Now, they had no more words to say, only the intense awareness of their spiritual contact and that awareness was indeed eternal.

In the French camp, there was a debate between the Inquisition and the emissaries of King Louis. The Inquisition wanted everybody in Montsegur killed by a huge fire but the King wanted to spare the lives of the repentants. Finally, the clemency of the King prevailed. Everyone in Montsegur accepted the French terms. The fortress of Montsegur was to become the property of the Pope and the King of France, but the defenders would be allowed to leave with their weapons and belongings. The lives of the heretics who repented would be spared but those who persisted in their errors were to be burned at the stake.

None of the Cathars renounced their faith and 216 of them, all Perfects, marched down the Southern trail of the Pog to deliver themselves for their final sacrifice.

On the previous evening, Peire and Pierre Authier were lowered by rope down the steep mountainside along with two other men carrying the treasure of Montsegur with orders to take it to the Castle of Ussat.

At dawn of March 16, 1244, a beacon flared from a distant mountaintop signifying that the treasure was under safekeeping. Pierre Authier and his two companions stayed in Ussat but Peire rushed back to the vicinity of Montsegur just to be near Esclamonde for her and all the other Perfects martyrdom. As he neared Montsegur he could hear a most beautiful sound. He rushed in as close as he dared and saw that a huge pile of faggots had been laid on the gently sloping meadow at the foot of the less precipitous side of the mountain to the south. Coming slowly down from the castle was the procession of all 216 Perfects headed by Bertrand Marti, Raimon de Parella and Esclamonde herself. They were singing hymns and glowing with a spiritual radiance that touched Peire to the core. As they mounted the death pyre there was a strangely peaceful presence about them all. They continued to sing hymns together even as the fires were lit and flames rose around them. Engulfed in agony they accepted completely this ordeal of pain and death as a deliverance from a world, which truly seemed to be the creation of Satan.

By the evening of March 17, 1244, nothing remained but a pile of silent smouldering ashes and the meadow became known as the Field of the Cremated. Finally, in the deep darkness of night Peire crawled to the blackened site, scooped a handful of hot ashes and secured them into a leather pouch with a tearful certainty that Esclamonde was still with him. Feverish and shivering with the still hot pouch pressed against his heart he ran, stumbled, limped and climbed, through mountain paths all night long. By dawn he found himself back at the Castle of Ussat where the kind Perfects took care of him. The treasure of Montsegur was in a safe and secret place to serve needy Cathars but Peire was sick and in a critical condition. He had succumbed to a terrible illness and was haunted by horrible recurring nightmares of people burning and the whole earth consumed by fire. Screams of agony echoed in his aching head and he felt like his own body was now on fire. He could not stop himself from feeling such intense regret and guilt that he had not been with Esclamonde to share her final ordeal. He was sick for a very long time but the kindly Perfects took good care of him and one night he had a dream that the fire was still raging in the Field of the Cremated but right in the middle of it Esclamonde, untouched by the consuming element, more beautiful than ever, was smiling at him with such intense love radiating from her eyes. With this vision, he awoke to find his fever had broken and by the end of the day he miraculously felt well again.

For the next five years Peire Cardinal accompanied Count Raymond VII of Toulouse in his travels throughout his domain and occasionally abroad in France and Italy. His function was to provide his legal and negotiating skills to his Liege Lord and occasionally to entertain his Court with his mellowed-down sirventes. He had to be very careful not to provoke the Inquisition and the Church officials who were often suspicious of him. Fortunately, when Esclamonde and the others had killed the Inquisition leaders in Avignonet they had also been astute enough to destroy all the official records of the Inquisition, which also contained damning information about him. Therefore, the Inquisition did not actually have any more evidence against him in order to persecute him with now. It was up to him not to generate any new evidence by writing anticlerical songs and tirades as he used to do. Now his sirventes were veiled with ambiguity and allegory to the point that only a select few enlightened people could truly understand the meaning of his poetry. His superb voice more than made up for his opaque verse though and he continued to be widely respected for his work.

His brother, Bertrand, had died and his nephew, who now ruled Campagnac, had accepted the authority of the Church, wholeheartedly. He even assisted the Inquisition in its search for heretics, not just Cathars, but heretics of any kind, even those who just appeared like heretics because of their open-mindedness. The Inquisition needed victims in order to justify its existence, its activities and its power, and if it could not find heretics it created heretics out of any vestiges of free thinking it could find.

Raymond VII was no longer the powerful majestic leader of twenty years ago but a kind, persevering, smart yet uninspiring figurehead who was now tethered to the Church authorities and to the King of France. Despite this terrible fall from grace he managed, still, to be loved by his subjects. The people remembered that he was once their liberator and their shining Unicorn Prince and for the past twenty years had understood and sympathized with his diminished stature. He was now their beloved mule who carried the burden of their survival and safety. In this age of mules only mules could survive.

In March of 1247, they had visited the King of France, Louis IX, in Paris to give homage. For the first time, Peire had the opportunity to observe the King and his brothers, Alphonse of Poitiers and Charles of Anjou. Louis IX was indeed majestic, handsome and benevolent. Alphonse was equally impressive but somewhat stern. By his side stood his gracious wife Joan, Raymond VII's daughter. Charles of Anjou was the youngest and yet the most arrogant of the lot. Next to them stood several Cardinals, Inquisitors and the legate of Pope Innocent IV. Behind them were arranged Dukes, Counts and Viscounts and among them the young Trencavel. They were all getting ready to follow Louis IX on a new crusade.

After the customary formalities between a vassal and his suzerain the King said, "My dear Count, your domain was infested with heresy but now I am relieved to learn that these infestations have been dealt with. Mostly by my armed forces, though, while you were standing by offering us minimal support. In the past, you allied yourself with my enemies including the King of England. I defeated you twice, but thanks to my clemency you are still in possession of your domains. Be very careful in the future, otherwise my brother and your son-in-law, Alphonse, could take over your principality. I also noticed that the famous troubadour Peire Cardinal is here with you. I was told that he has a divine voice although he has used it at times to criticize our Holy Church. Would he sing for us?"

"Your Grace, I confess that I have tried in the past to gain your respect by defending my legacy, even against you. You defeated me and now I am your loyal subject. A great number of my barons and knights will follow you in the crusade with my prompting and blessing. As for Peire, in spite of his advanced age he is my chief negotiator and yes, his voice remains divine. Let him speak and sing, if this is your pleasure."

"My dear Count, you spoke boldly and earnestly to me and I must tell you that you deserve my respect. I invite Peire Cardinal to speak and sing if he wishes."

"Your Grace, I am honoured that you are giving me the opportunity to speak my mind and sing for you. As you can see, I am now an old man who has lived in the ways of the South, good and bad. I used to think, then, that our ways were beautiful, sensational and full of inspiration. This did not mean that I was not a good Christian and that I did not respect the Catholic Church, quite the opposite in fact. My profound love for the Church was sometimes challenged and offended by those who would abuse the power entrusted to them by the Church and it was against them that some of my sirventes were addressed. Please allow me to sing one now.

> They've made themselves Inquisitors
> Judging with their whims.
> Finding fault by torture
> When there really is no sin.
>
> Though questions must be asked
> Errors must be forgiven.
> For those who have clearly strayed
> Christ's love can release them.
>
> With compassion and understanding,
> Not with burning and pain.
> May the love of our Lord Jesus Christ
> Be peacefully attained.

"Your voice touches my heart but your words play with sedition and at your age you should try to please God and his representatives on earth more."

"In this case, Your Grace, I can chant something more devotional like this one.

> True virgin, Maria.
> True life, true faith
> True truth, true path.
> True virtue, true thing
> True mother, true friend
> True love, true mercy
> Grant your true blessings
> That your heir inherit me!

"That is more like it. This is a kind of chant after my own heart and this is what you should be singing to please God, the Church and me. The old Troubadour songs ring of damnation and you must understand and accept that the time of the Troubadours is over.

They all bowed to the King in tacit agreement and submission to his will and pleasure. They headed back to their beloved South, which now had started to look and feel like the North, while the King and his army began their crusade.

Peire was thinking that naming this depressing new era the age of mules, though at first in jest, was becoming more and more appropriate. King Louis, himself the Great King of Mules, had now officially and ceremoniously inaugurated this new age in which all the beautiful expressions of love, poetry, song, inspiration and freedom were banned.

Sometime in August 1249 Count Raymond VII suddenly fell ill while visiting Millau in the area of Rouergue. All of his doctors with their medicines could not help him and his friends gathered round at his deathbed to be by his side. The emissaries of Alphonse of Poitiers were also lurking about reminding everyone with their presence that Alphonse would be taking over all of Raymond's dominions.

During a quiet moment, the dying count called Peire to approach him and asked him in a hardly audible voice, "Dear Peire, you have been with my father and with me for the last fifty years and I want to know your opinion about us. It seems to me that we achieved nothing in the end, and in reality, we worked for the aggrandizement of the Kingdom of France. Did I do anything right?"

"My Liege Lord, do not trouble yourself at this final moment. You have done the best you possibly could under extremely difficult circumstances and you survived much longer than expected. You had to deal with the most formidable adversaries, the French King and the Church, who had access and bridgeheads inside your domains. You had the choice to confront them head-on unyieldingly and perish sooner, or to do as you did and live until now. I do not know what would have been the best thing to do. I just don't know. I know for sure that in the early years you brought back a golden age to your land, and your subjects still love you for it. Your father was also a good and enlightened man but he was not as lucky as you. Please, rest in peace, have no regrets and you will have a 'good end'."

"Thank you, my good friend, for your lifetime of faithful service to both my father and me. Farewell and may we find peace at last."

Soon afterwards Raymond VII took the last rites and, comforted among his friends, slipped off to a better world. His last wish was to be buried at the Abbey of Fontevrault near his maternal grandmother, Eleanor of Aquitaine, his mother Joanne, and his admired Uncle, Richard Coeur de Lion. Raymond's coffin was placed on a barge, which sailed down the Aveyron, the Tarn and Garonne until it reached the city of Agen. There the nuns of Fontevrault gave it a temporary resting place, before taking it north to their abbey.

Raymond's funerary river journey became an unexpectedly grand event with the people of the land spontaneously gathering in unprecedented numbers lining all the river banks of the entire journey, kneeling and weeping. They wept for the death of their beloved Count. They wept for the memory of their freedom. They wept for the loss of their culture and Southern way of life. They all warmly remembered Raymond VII as their beloved Unicorn who had liberated them and given them back their free and joyful way of life, at least for a significant period of time.

The new Lord of the Midi, Alphonse de Poitiers, and his wife, Joanne of Toulouse, came only twice to Languedoc to receive the homage of their vassals and to raise money. He had also sent his agents south to find the treasure of Montsegur, which was rumoured to contain the Holy Grail, a relic of fabulous magical power. One of the things the Inquisition was ardently seeking out from its victims was the location of this treasure of Montsegur and the Holy Grail. The Inquisition, French officials and other treasure hunters, relentlessly searched out the ruins of Montsegur, and other places in its vicinity. Countless unfortunate people were tortured to death officially and unofficially for this valuable information, but in vain. This treasure hunt had become an obsession and it had given the Inquisitors an irresistible incentive in their obscene activities of torture and murder.

One of the places where Cathars were hiding out, perhaps together with their fabulous treasure, was the remote fortress of Queribus perched on the Eastern Pyrenees. An expedition was organized and Queribus was taken in 1255. All of the heretics found there were burned, yet still no treasure was found. However, the hunt for heretics and this treasure continued with unabated fervour. The Inquisition investigated Peire Cardinal several times, for heresy and for possible information regarding this treasure. It was only through his knowledge and skills of theology, canon law and argumentation that he was able to save his life and freedom each time.

After the demise of Count Raymond VII Peire found employment and patronage in the court of the Count of Rodez, who had always been friendly to the Campagnacs. He might have gone to Frederick II but the Emperor had died in 1250, one year after Raymond VII, and it seemed any possibility for freedom of expression had died with him. Like the Montsegur treasure, Enlightenment could not be found anywhere anymore.

The Count of Rodez was a kindly man who would, at times in the absence of clerics, allow some poetry and songs to be heard at his court.

Peire was now an old man in his seventies but his voice and looks were still good and certainly did not betray his age too much. He had formed around him a group of young acolytes or apprentices who were learning the art of poetry and chanting. Guiraut Riquier and Guiraut de Bornehl were the most promising ones in the group and they were showing signs of talent and inspiration, which sadly, could not find a noble and worthy audience to flourish in these dark times. Peire Cardinal and his acolytes were mostly using their talents as cantors in the Rodez Cathedral where they were greatly admired for their divine voices and their hymns to Virgin Mary, the Trinity and popular Saints.

One evening in the Court of the Count of Rodez a select group of Southern nobility had gathered to enjoy some private entertainment and to reminisce of the good old days. Guiraut de Bornehl was given permission to express his sad commentary on the times:

> Minstrels went from court to court,
> Richly attired, praising the fair.
> Today we dare not speak a word
> Honour and courtesy, no longer there.

> Now joy and love offend the great,
> So wicked have they grown.
> False piety, control and greed
> Is all we have known.

Then, Guiraut Riquier continued with his tenor voice.

> Song should express the poet's joy
> But sorrow weighs upon my heart.
> I came into this world too late
> With joy, my life is not part.

> Injustice and lies, have joined in battle
> With Justice and love, but lies have won.

Where is joy and where is song?
When there's nothing left that can be done.

Peire took the floor last to close the show with his deep and vibrant
voice.

The privilege and curse of old age
Are memories of love and carefree days.
Memories of how they were torn away
Burned at the stake when love went astray.

Memories of freedom, hope and peace
Visions of Unicorns turned into sheep.
A church corralling more souls to fleece
Visions of desolation, free spirit ceased.

The blessing and curse of becoming old
Seeing everyone believing what they are told.
Long black cassocks have twisted and sold their souls
Peddling fear and death for power and control.

The privilege and curse of old age
To see the world change from green to gray.
To have no daring, no power left to say
My tongue's been tied, I can only pray.

To learn to hate war and long for peace
Yet wishing this dangerous peace would cease.
Peace imposed, one should not bear
This shameful peace, evil chains that ensnare.

Growing old is a privilege and curse
Seeing our homeland burned into dirt.
Watching things go from bad to worse
Seeing all life upside down and reversed!

The Count of Rodez congratulated the performers and said, "Dear Peire, it is indeed the privilege and curse of old age to record past and present situations but not to be able to react to them. It is the privilege of the young to do this but our young people have been compromised and they cannot react either. The old and the young, we have accepted this shameful peace, and according to your thinking we have all become enslaved by it. This is a very hard and sad reality to accept. Though, through my long years as a count in this once free land I have to shamefully agree with you."

"My Lord, we have lived to see a devastating transition from a free world to one of terror, where freedom, even inner freedom, has become dangerous. What else can we do but accept this false peace to survive? The art of troubadours is now considered at best useless and often seditious and heretical. The wonderful feelings of true peace, freedom, sensuality and love as we used to experience them, in this day and age, are considered at best shameful, and at worst grounds for extreme torture and death. Some of us, who are advanced in age, at least we have sweet memories to fall upon. I was born a free spirit who, by an overwhelming necessity, had to eventually become enslaved, at least in outer appearances, by this false peace. Yet outer appearances eventually become real, for living under this terrible fear crushes the creative and loving spirit. Our unfortunate contemporaries do not even know any better because they do not know what true freedom is anymore, for they have never experienced it. I suppose this is what keeps me going at this advanced age. Hoping that I can share and kindle the fires of freedom and love that I have experienced in my long life with my young protégés here."

"My dear Peire, I feel for you and understand what you are saying. We are all under a brutal occupation, which is exercised by cold-hearted and cold-minded French officials and by the even colder Church authorities and its Inquisition. We have been ground down to a powder by the relentless millstones of these authorities. The occupation forces have been accumulating legal rights by a combination of luck, bullying and legal chicanery. They are encroaching on our rights to charge tolls, protect merchants, coin money, hear complaints in court, repair roads with local labour and reap all the benefits thereof. On top of that they impose exorbitant taxes and a spider web of laws and regulations forcing our nobility to cede their castles and estates to Northerners or partially demolish them or even level them to the ground! By the way, what is the situation with your homeland of Campagnac?"

"My nephews, who inherited the family estate, were forced to demolish all the fortifications of the castle and have kept only the main building. Now they are squabbling among themselves for what is left and they all have a miserable life. More or less the same thing is happening with most of the nobility and the manor holders across the South."

"What are you intending to do when you leave Rodez Peire?"

"I will spend some time in the court of King James in Aragon, where I have been invited and then, if I am still alive and well, I will go to Verona to stay with my son, Nascibon. To have lived for as long as I have with good health and with my body and mind functioning well does have a good side, for I am still strong enough to travel and create."

"It's been about 20 years since I last lived in my homeland and I was already old then." Peire was musing to himself "I was born in the year 1180 in Campagnac and now I am in Verona in the year 1280. This makes me a Centenarian, a very rare phenomenon indeed! To have lived for as long as I have is certainly a blessing because life is sweet here in Verona. The only reality I know for certain is in the here and now. Whatever is beyond life still frightens me and I would like to postpone experiencing it and to continue living here for as long as I can. Fortunately, Nascibon is still alive and well which helps me feel good about life because of the love we have for each other and his wonderful companionship. Nascibon is a well-functioning old man but still he is an old man. Although I love life I would rather go first than to stay behind completely alone. Cunizza died some time ago and my grandchildren and my great-grandchildren and their families present a confusing and blurred picture to me, which does not alleviate my loneliness. To have lived for as long as I have, is also a curse because almost all the people I used to love or simply even know have gone to the other side of earthly life, leaving me behind in a desert of loneliness. To have lived for as long as I have lived is most surely a curse because of all the brutal changes of mood, mentality and customs of the society around me, giving me a feeling of bewilderment, disorientation and uselessness. There is nobody around me anymore who could possibly understand my deepest feelings and experiences, or for me to even understand theirs, with the exception of Nascibon of course.

Sometime ago, when I was in Venice I looked for Feliza and Giacomo Querini but they had also died. I only found their son, Niccolo, who is still fighting in the Venetian Courts to be recognized as the Lord of Andros, the poor unlucky fellow. The usurper Jeremiah Ghizi had died as well but instead of Niccolo, Marco Sanudo had been appointed as the Lord of this happy fragment of my past. Strangely enough, I am still dreaming of this place because I was left with such happy memories, so long ago, with my beloved Esclamonde.

Though my friend Guy de Summerive has long since died I did learn that his son Leone is still alive and now well established in Greece. Amazing to see how that dream of Guy's finally came to pass through his son.

Constantinople now has a Greek Emperor, Michael Paleologos, who has become the mortal enemy of Charles Anjou who took over the kingdom of Southern Italy from the heirs of Frederick II. King Louis IX died in a crusade and his brother Alphonse of Poitiers died from some illness in France as well. Almost everyone I have known, both friend and enemy, is now gone. I am left to wonder why I am still here. Esclamonde is coming to me day and night to give me the kind of company I desire most. She wants to be sure that I will have a 'good end'."

One morning, in early spring of 1280, Nascibon found his father lying still on his bed smiling and clutching a leather pouch full of ashes.

THE END

Stamatis Kambanis was born in Greece and educated in Greece and Canada specializing in chemistry. He worked mainly in the chemical industry in Canada for more than thirty years where he published many scientific papers and had his innovations patented. However, his passion for history and the ancestral stories of his family's distant past inspired him to put his passions together and write historical novels. His first novel "Return to Andros" was published in Greece (2001) and the English version "Silk In The Winds" is in the process of being published. "The Troubadour" is his second historical novel.

Michael Moon is an award winning composer, lyricist and musician specializing in healing music. His pioneering music is found in healing centers, hospitals and yoga studios worldwide. He has written many songs, poems and blogs and edited a lot of music but never before has he attempted writing or editing a book.

www.thetempleofsound.com
www.michaelmoon.ca